The Spanish Bride

The Spanish Bride

A NOVEL
IN WHICH BRIGADE-MAJOR
HARRY SMITH
UNEXPECTEDLY AND
IMPULSIVELY ACQUIRES
A BRIDE...

Georgette Heyer

SOURCEBOOKS LANDMARK™
AN IMPRINT OF SOURCEBOOKS, INC.®
NAPERVILLE, ILLINOIS

Published by Sourcebooks Landmark, an imprint of Sourcebooks, Inc.
P.O. Box 4410, Naperville, Illinois 60567-4410
(630) 961-3900
Fax: (630) 961-2168
www.sourcebooks.com

Library of Congress Cataloging-in-Publication Data

Heyer, Georgette, 1902-1974.
  The Spanish bride / Georgette Heyer.
      p. cm.
  "Originally published in the United Kingdom in 1940 by William Heinemann
Ltd."--T.p. verso.
  ISBN-13: 978-1-4022-1113-3
  ISBN-10: 1-4022-1113-9
  1. Peninsular War, 1807-1814--Fiction. 2. Smith, Harry George Wakelyn, Sir,
1788-1860--Fiction. 3. Smith, Juana María de los Delores de León, 1798-1872-
-Fiction. I. Title.

PR6015.E795S63 2008
823'.912--dc22
                                        2007047982

Printed and bound in the United States of America.
            VP 10 9 8 7 6 5 4 3 2 1

To A.S. Frere

Contents

Author's Note

S INCE A COMPLETE LIST OF THE AUTHORITIES FOR A BOOK DEALING
with the Peninsular War would make tedious reading I have
published no bibliography to *The Spanish Bride*, preferring to
add a note for those of my readers who may wish to know
which were my main works of reference.

Obviously, the most important authority for Harry's and
Juana Smith's story is Harry Smith's own *Autobiography*.
Obviously again, it would have been impossible to have written
a tale of the Peninsular War without studying Napier's work, and
Sir Charles Oman's monumental *History of the Peninsular War*. I
must acknowledge, as well, my indebtedness to Sir Charles
Oman's smaller work, *Wellington's Army*; and I should like to
thank both Sir Charles Oman, and Colonel Jourdain, for their
kindness in searching for an obscure reference on my behalf.

I have not, to my knowledge, left any of the Diarists of the
Light Division unread. Of them all, I found Kincaid and George
Simmons the most useful for my particular purpose; but the
details of the rank-and-file of the 95th Rifles were culled largely
from Edward Costello's *Adventures of a Soldier*. But Rifleman
Harris was useful too; and so was Quartermaster Surtees, in spite

of his unfortunate habit of covering all too many pages with moral reflections.

Outside the Light Division, Larpent's *Journals* provided endless details. And there are grand bits to be found in Grattan's *Adventures with the Connaught Rangers;* in Sir James McGrigor's *Autobiography;* in Gleig's *Subaltern;* in Gomm's *Recollections of a Staff-Officer;* and in Tomkinson's *Diary of a Cavalry Officer.* There is a book of *Peninsular Sketches,* too, compiled by W. H. Maxwell; and all sorts of information to be gathered from the *Lives* of various commanders, not to mention the regimental histories.

And last, but certainly not least, there are the *Dispatches,* and the *Supplementary Dispatches,* of Wellington himself.

GEORGETTE HEYER

One

BADAJOS

1

THERE WAS A PLACE ON THE RIGHT BANK OF THE GUADIANA where hares ran strong. It was near a large rabbit-warren, quite a celebrated spot, which the officers of the army besieging Badajos had soon discovered. Sport had been out of the question during the first part of the siege, when the torrential rain had fallen day after day, flooding the river, sweeping away the pontoon-bridges that formed part of the communication-lines from Badajos to headquarters at Elvas, turning all the ground round the town into a clay swamp through which the blaspheming troops struggled from their sodden camp to the trenches.

Having broken ground on St Patrick's Day, the army, which boasted a large proportion of Irishmen in its ranks, was confident that this third siege of Badajos would be successful. But the drenching rain, which persisted for a week, threatened to upset all Lord Wellington's plans. From the moment of opening the first parallel, the most appalling weather had set in. Trenches became flooded; the mud in the gabions ran off in a yellow slime; and men worked in water that rose to their waists. It was harder to bear than the firing from the walls of the town, for it was disheartening work, and good infantrymen hated it. They called it grave-digging, labour for sappers, not for crack troops. There was, unfortunately, a dearth of sappers in the army. 'Ah, may the divil fly away with old Hookey! Didn't we take Rodrigo, and is ut not the time for others to ingage on a thrifle of work?' demanded Rifleman O'Brien.

On the 24th March the rain stopped, and fine weather set in. The digging of the parallels went on quickly, in spite of the difficulty of working in heavy, saturated clay, and in spite of the vicious fire from Badajos. The Portuguese gunners, bombarding the bastions of Santa Maria and La Trinidad, fell into the way of posting a man on the look-out to declare the nature of each missile that was fired from the walls. 'Bomba!' he would shout; or 'Balla!' and the gunners would duck till the shot had passed. Sometimes the look-out man would see a discharge from all arms, and, according to Johnny Kincaid, fling himself down, screaming: 'Jesús, todos, todos!'

With the better weather, thoughts turned to sport. A partridge or a hare made a welcome addition to any soup-kettle. It was Brigade-Major Harry Smith's boast that there was not an officers' mess in the 2nd brigade of the Light division which he did not keep supplied with hares. In infantry regiments, in the general way, it was only possible for Staff-officers, with a couple of good remounts, to indulge in hunting or coursing, nor was it by any means every Staff-officer who owned a string of greyhounds. But Brigade-Major Smith was sporting-mad, and wherever he went a stud of horses and a string of Spanish greyhounds went too. If he had a few hours off duty, he would come into camp from the trenches, shout for a bite of food, swallow it standing, and set off on a fresh horse, and with any friend who could be induced to forgo a much-needed rest for the sake of joining him in an arduous chase.

But however heavy the going the sport was good, hares being plentiful, and Harry's greyhounds, despised by those who obstinately upheld the superior speed and intelligence of English hounds, generally successful.

The Brigade-Major was a wiry young man, rising twenty-five, with a dark, mobile countenance, a body hardened by seven years' service in the 95th Rifles, a store of inexhaustible energy, and a degree of luck in escaping death that was almost uncanny. If he had not been such an efficient officer, he would have been damned as a harum-scarum youth, and had indeed often been sworn at for a madman by his friends, and his various Brigadiers.

His restless energy made his friends groan. 'Oh, to hell with you, Harry, can't you be still?' complained Charlie Eeles, haled from his tent to the chase. 'Oh, very well, I'll come! Who goes with us?'

'Stewart. Bustle about, man! I must be back by six o'clock at latest.'

Grumbling, cursing, Lieutenant Eeles turned out, for although he had been on duty for six hours in the trenches, and was tired and cold, it was always much more amusing to go with Harry than to stay in camp. By the time he was in the saddle, Captain the Honourable James Stewart had joined them, mounted on a blood-mare, and demanding to know what was keeping Harry.

The Light and 4th divisions being encamped on the southern side of Badajos, near the Albuera road, the three young men had not far to ride before crossing the Guadiana river. The weather, though dry, was dull, and the sky looked sullen. Badajos, crouching on rising ground in the middle of a gray plain, lay to their right, as they rode towards the river. A Castle, poised upon a hundred-foot rock, dominated the eastern side of the town, and overlooked the confluence of the

Guadiana with the smaller Rivillas river. On this side of Badajos, Sir Thomas Picton's Fighting 3rd division was encamped, and the parallels had been first cut. The French, defending the town, had built up the bridge that crossed the Rivillas near the San Roque gate, south of the Castle, and had strengthened the two weakest bastions of the town – those of San Pedro and La Trinidad – by damming the Rivillas into a broad pool, guarded by the San Roque lunette. This inundation stretched from the bastion of San Pedro to La Trinidad, its overflow seeping into cunettes dug immediately below the walls of the town. An attempt to blow up the dam had failed, on the 2nd April, and the inundation remained, blocking the approach from the first and second parallels, and covering all the ground from the walls of Badajos to the Seville road.

Beyond the inundation, an outwork, known as the Picurina fort, had been carried by a storming-party from the 3rd division, under Major-General Kempt, on the 26th March. West of La Picurina, and due south of the town, a strong out-fort, the Pardeleras, was still in French hands; and on the right bank of the river, north of the town, the San Cristobal fort, standing on a hill that overlooked the Castle, and the old Roman bridge that spanned the Guadiana, towered over all. In previous sieges, the attacks had been directed against San Cristobal, and had failed; but in this chill spring of 1812, Lord Wellington, fresh from the conquest of Ciudad Rodrigo, had marched his troops south through Portalegre and Elvas, on the Portuguese border, to invest Badajos on the south and east sides. Everyone knew that the assault was to be made on the weaker bastions of Santa Maria and La Trinidad, for these, and the curtain between them, were being relentlessly bombarded; and everyone knew that time was a more than usually important factor in these operations. Marmont, his headquarters at Valladolid, might be contained by a covering force of Spaniards to the north; but there was news that Soult, with the French army of the South, had broken up from before Cadiz, and was moving to the relief of Badajos.

The bad weather had delayed the siege-work; there had been the usual trouble over transports; and a hundred and one checks and annoyances. The Engineers' Park was stocked with cutting-tools sent up from Lisbon, but the senior Engineer, Colonel Fletcher, had had the misfortune to be wounded in the groin during the early days of the investment, and was compelled to direct the operations of his subordinates from a bed in his tent. Admiral Berkeley, in command of the squadron at Lisbon, sent, instead of the British guns he had been requested to lend to the army, twenty Russian guns which were of different calibre from the British 18-pounder, and would not take its shot; while a Portuguese artillery officer, anxious to be helpful, added to Colonel Dickson's worries by unearthing from a store in Elvas some iron and brass guns of startling antiquity.

The siege-operations were under the general command of Sir Thomas Picton, whose division divided the trench-duty with the Light and 4th divisions.

The Light division, which was composed of the 95th Rifles, the 52nd and 43rd regiments, with the 1st and 3rd Portuguese Caçadores, was at present led by Colonel Andrew Barnard, who held the command until some senior officer should be appointed to relieve him of it. He was filling the place of that great, and rather terrible little man, General Craufurd, killed in the assault on Ciudad Rodrigo. Though the Light division had not suffered as severely as had the 3rd in that assault, it had sustained several serious losses. Craufurd was dead; Vandeleur, commanding the 2nd brigade, had been badly wounded; Colonel Colborne, of the 52nd, had a ball in his shoulder which would send him home to

England; Major Napier had lost an arm; Captain Uniacke of the 95th had been killed by the explosion of a French mine at the great breach.

Death was too common an occurrence in the Peninsula for a man's friends to grieve long over his loss, nor was Brigade-Major Smith a young gentleman who indulged much in melancholy reflections; but Uniacke had been a close friend of his, and it would be a long time before he would be able to remember, without an uncomfortable tightening of the throat muscles, his last supper with Uniacke, immediately before the storm of Rodrigo. 'Harry, you'll be a Captain before morning!' Uniacke had prophesied. He had been in great spirits; he had not known that it would be his own death that would give Harry a company.

Harry had naturally volunteered for the forlorn hope, but General Craufurd had refused to let him lead it. 'You, a Major of Brigade, a senior lieutenant! No, I must give it to a younger man.'

He had given it to Gurwood, of the 52nd, no friend of Harry's: a sharp fellow, who had made the most of his own gallantry, Harry thought. However, Harry had managed to take a lively part in the main attack, seizing one Captain Duffy's company, much to that gentleman's wrath, and leading the men in a rush upon the French flank behind the line of works, and enfilading it. With his usual luck, he had only been knocked over and scorched by the explosion of the mine which had killed Uniacke, and so many others. He had lost his cocked-hat, had borrowed a catskin-forage-cap from a Sergeant of the 52nd, and had ended an eventful night by being mistaken, on account of the fur-cap and his dark uniform, for a French soldier, by a gigantic private of the 88th Connaught Rangers, who had seized him by the throat, and had then made ready to thrust his bayonet through him. Fortunately, Harry had had breath enough left to enable him to damn the man's eyes, which had quite cleared up that little misunderstanding.

2

He had got his company in February, but because it had been Uniacke's he said very little about it (which was unlike him), and received the congratulations of his friends with less than his usual vivacity.

'Harry is the luckiest devil going,' Stewart said lazily. 'Except in his horses. Where did you get that clumsy brute, Harry?'

'I bought him from poor old Vandeleur.'

'I'll sell you a real horse,' offered Stewart coaxingly.

'You won't! I've got your Tiny already.'

'Well, don't go into action on that brute,' Stewart said. 'I don't wonder Vandeleur sold him.'

'Talking of going into action,' said Eeles, 'when is it to be? Speaking for myself, I've had enough of this siege.'

'God, so have I!' Harry replied. 'The men say it's the turn of some of the other divisions to do trench-work. Damn it, did we take Rodrigo, or did I dream it?'

'I seem to remember that we did,' said Stewart. 'I must own, though, that I did catch sight of some of Picton's fellows.'

'Oh, damn Picton's fellows!' said Eeles, with all a Rifleman's cheerful contempt for the rest of the army. 'I hope his lordship leaves this business to us. Picton's lot had all the honour and glory of the Picurina affair.'

'Oh no, they didn't!' Harry retorted, his expressive eyes sparkling. 'I told off one of our working-parties to fetch the scaling-ladders from the Engineers' Park. When they brought 'em up, Kempt ordered them to be planted, and the boys of the 3rd told our fellows to stand out of the way while they went up.

That didn't suit our men's notions at all! *They* said: "Damn your eyes, do you think we Light Bobs fetch ladders for such chaps as you to climb up? Follow us!" '

His companions shouted with joy at this story, but Stewart said: 'Harry, you liar!'

'No, upon my word! It's true as death! One of the Sergeants told me – Brotherton.'

Eeles remarked that Brotherton was a good fellow, but Stewart only laughed. Harry was still defending the story when they reached the vicinity of the rabbit-warren, for his energy led him into vehement argument as easily as it led him into impetuous action. A hare, getting up suddenly, put an end to the discussion; sport drove sieges and assaults temporarily out of mind. An unusually strong hare was presently found; Harry, always agog to demonstrate the speed of his dogs, gave her twenty yards law before hallooing the hounds out of the slips. She twice gave them the go-by, and although the dogs fetched round a dozen times, she kept on working her way towards the warren.

'By God, I'll have to head her off!' exclaimed Harry, seeing to-morrow's dinner escaping from his clutches.

'No, don't!' said Eeles, intent only upon the sport. 'Damn it, you can't do that!'

'Oh, can't I, by thunder!' Harry flung over his shoulder.

'You fool, 'ware rabbit-holes!' shouted Stewart, seeing Harry clap spurs to his horse's flanks, and career away at a gallop in the direction of the warren.

Harry, however, was off in his headlong way, trusting to his horse, his whole attention concentrated on the hare. Irish Paddy put a hoof in a rabbit-hole, and came down heavily, and rolled over Harry.

Stewart was up with him in a flash, and had leaped out of the saddle, all thought of the hare forgotten. 'Oh you fool, you damned fool!' he said, on his knees beside Harry's inanimate body.

'Is he dead?' Eeles asked anxiously.

'No – yes – I don't know!' replied Stewart, ripping open Harry's tight green jacket. 'No, I can feel his heart beating! Harry! Come on, old fellow, wake up! Open your eyes, now!'

It was soon seen that such adjurations were of no avail. When they raised him, Harry's head lolled alarmingly; and although Eeles, who boasted a rough knowledge of surgery, pronounced that no bones were broken, no amount of coaxing, of chafing of hands, of slapping of cheeks, produced any sign of returning consciousness.

'It's no use: we shall have to bleed him,' said Stewart.

'Try some brandy!' urged Eeles, pulling a flask out of his pocket.

The brandy ran out of the corners of Harry's mouth. 'Oh, Harry, why *will* you be such a careless devil?' Eeles said distractedly. 'It all comes of trying to head the hare! Damned unsportsmanlike! I told him not to!'

'Never mind talking! You hold him, while I bleed him!' said Stewart.

Eeles made a knee for Harry's slight, wiry frame, while Stewart pulled his jacket off. A whip-thong made a serviceable tourniquet about one limp arm, and Stewart had just opened a blunt-looking pocket-knife, and had made a slight incision with it in the flesh, when Harry's head, which was resting on Eeles's shoulder, moved, and Eeles, eyeing Stewart's preparations with some misgiving, cried: 'Stop! Wait a minute, he's coming round!'

A drop or two of blood welled up from the scratch on Harry's arm; his eyes opened, blurred and dazed for a few instants, but regaining brightness and clarity in surprisingly little time. They blinked up into Stewart's anxious face, travelled to the knife in his hand, and widened. The next instant, Harry had leaped to his feet, rather shaky still, but in full possession of his faculties. 'Keep off, you villain!' he exclaimed, swaying on his feet. 'What the devil – ?' He became aware of the thong bound round his upper arm, and plucked at it, weakly laughing. 'God save me from my friends! Why, you old murderer! Oh, look! If I'm not bleeding to death! Where's Moro?'

In the agitation of the moment, his friends had forgotten both hare and hounds, but at this enquiry they looked round involuntarily, to find that the sagacious hound, Moro, had killed the hare without any assistance from his master. Relief made them scold, but Harry, dabbing at the scratch on his arm with his handkerchief, was quite unrepentant, and merely abused the clumsiness of his horse.

Paddy, having picked himself up, was quietly grazing a few yards away. While agreeing that he was the clumsiest brute alive, Stewart told Harry that he deserved to be dead. But Harry was making much of Moro, and paid no attention to him. It was evident that he had sustained no serious injury, for though dizzy at first, he soon declared himself to be well enough to mount, and ride back to camp.

'What made you buy a stupid brute like this?' demanded Stewart, leading Paddy up to him. 'What's wrong with Tiny? He'd not let you down like that!'

'Strained a tendon,' replied Harry, hoisting himself into the saddle.

Stewart cast his eyes up to heaven. 'Ridden him to death, I suppose!'

'Will you stop scolding?' retaliated Harry. 'There's no harm done, I tell you! What's the time? Oh, by God, I shall be late! Come on, Charlie!'

'The luckiest devil in the whole army!' said Stewart.

3

His fall seemed to have no ill-effect upon Harry; he was, in fact, not a penny the worse for it; and the hare which Moro had caught made an excellent soup. Stewart prophesied an aching head and bruised bones next day, but he was wrong. A little thing like a tumble from his horse could not hurt an old campaigner, boasted Harry, looking absurdly young as he said it.

The remark did not even make Stewart smile. Harry was a very old campaigner. At the age of nineteen, he had been at Monte Video; six months later he was with General Whitelocke on his ill-fated expedition to Buenos Ayres. He had been to Sweden with Sir John Moore; he had been at Corunna; at the Combat of the Coa, where he had got a ball lodged in his ankle-joint, and had had to be sent to Lisbon to recover from it. Not that he did recover from it at Lisbon. Oh dear, no! None of your Belemites was young Mr Smith, malingering in hospital while there was fighting going on somewhere in the interior. As soon as he could put his foot to the ground, nothing would do for him but to rejoin his regiment. He found it at Arruda.

'You are a mad fool of a boy, coming here with a ball in your leg! Can you dance?' demanded his Colonel.

'No, I can hardly walk but with my toe turned out,' had responded Harry coolly.

'Well! Can you be my A.D.C.?'

'Yes, I can ride and eat,' had said Harry, grinning to conceal the excruciating pain in his ankle.

And ridden he had until he had gone back to Lisbon with his Colonel, and had had the ball cut out of his tendon.

As soon as he could walk, he had rejoined his regiment, in time to take part in the skirmish at Redinha. ('Ah, now you can walk a little, you leave me!' said Colonel Beckwith. 'Go, and be damned to you; but I love you for it!')

Since Redinha, he had been in upwards of half-a-dozen sharp skirmishes, and three major actions: Sabugal, Fuentes de Oñoro, and the assault of Ciudad Rodrigo. He had emerged from all these affairs without a scratch. When half the army was down with the deadly Alemtejo fever, Brigade-Major Smith was enjoying some capital hunting on the Spanish border. Anguish? Devil a bit! He had never felt better in his life.

When his duties took him up to the trenches outside Badajos, he was often covered with mud from the bursting of shells in the soft ground, but no splinter, no charge of grape, lodged itself in his spare frame. Shot-proof and fever-proof, that was Harry Smith: a roaring boy, the broth of a boy! said Private O'Brien, admiring his Brigade-Major's flow of bad language when the explosion of a shell knocked him off his feet. A damned good duty-officer, said Colonel Barnard; crazy as a coot! complained Harry's exasperated friends.

Nothing was going to keep Harry from making one of the storming party that would presently assail the breaches in the walls of Badajos. By April 6th there were three of these: one in the bastion of Santa Maria; one in the bastion of La Trinidad, farther to the west; and the last in the curtain-wall between the two. The main attack was to be launched at these points, and the troops chosen to carry it out were the Light and the 4th divisions. That was just as it should be, but there were some gloomy spirits who thought old Hookey was wasting his time with all this bombardment of the walls. George Simmons, rather a serious young man, said that the way General Phillipon's men were repairing the breaches was going to make them more formidable than any unbroken bastion. The French evidently meant to defend the town pretty desperately, for the British Engineers reported on the morning of the 6th that every sort of obstacle was being piled behind the breaches. The guns would batter away at them while the daylight lasted, and that would prevent much work being done to repair the gaps; but when the hour for the assault was changed from half-past seven in the evening to ten o'clock, the Engineers looked a little grave. With the inevitable slackening of gun-fire, as darkness fell, the French would get to work again, and they could work to some purpose, those grenadiers. It looked like being a bloody business, however well planned it might be.

It was not only well, but very extensively planned. Though the Light and the 4th divisions were expected to carry the town by storming the breaches, no less than five secondary attacks were to be made. The trench-guards were to try to rush the San Roque lunette; old Picton was to make an attempt to take the Castle by escalade (a very forlorn hope, this: not at all likely to succeed); Power's brigade of Portuguese was going to threaten the bridge-head beyond the Guadiana, on the opposite side of the town to the damaged bastions; the Portuguese troops belonging to Leith's 5th division were to make a false attack on the strong Pardeleras fort; and – a last-minute decision, this – the rest of Leith's division was to brave the mines which had been laid outside the eastern walls of the town, and try to force the river-bastion of San Vincente.

These five secondary attacks, timed to begin simultaneously with the main attack, were not expected to succeed, but to distract the defenders' attention from the breaches.

The approach to these, from the camping grounds of the Light and 4th divisions, lay between the Rivillas river, with its spreading inundation, on the right, and a quarry cut in rising ground to the left. It was preconcerted that the 4th division was to keep nearest to the water, and, upon reaching the ditch dug round Badajos, to swerve to the right, and to assail the breaches in the curtain-wall, and in La Trinidad. The Light division was to strike westwards, to attack the breach in the flank of the Santa Maria bastion. Each division was to provide an advance of five hundred men, accompanied by several parties carrying haybags and ladders. These were to facilitate not only the storming of the breaches, but the descent into the ditch, which was reported to be as much as fourteen feet deep.

There was no lack of volunteers for the forlorn hope: the only difficulty lay in selecting from the eager crowd of warriors clamouring each one to be the first to assail the walls, the fittest persons for the task. The British army, hating the trench-work it had been forced to do, irked by the fire from Badajos, and depressed by the soggy condition of the ground, desired nothing better than to come to grips with the enemy. Nor had the army any objection to coming to grips with the Spanish residents, held within the walls. Since Talavera, when the Spanish General Cuesta had abandoned the British wounded left in his charge to the French (who, if the truth were but known, had treated them with far more consideration than their Spanish allies had done), Lord Wellington's soldiers had added loathing to the contempt they already felt for the Spanish. If Badajos fell at the end of this third siege, the inhabitants need not look for mercy at the hands of its conquerors. Not only had Lord Wellington's men a grudge against the Spaniards, but they were further incensed by the knowledge that the inhabitants of Badajos had yielded very tamely to the French. If a besieged city surrendered at discretion, it might look for clemency; God help it if it resisted to the end! for then, by all the rules of war, it belonged to the victors to sack and pillage as they chose.

The officers knew what kind of temper the men were in. 'They'll regret it, if they hold out,' said Cadoux, in his soft, finicking way, admiring a ring on his finger, anxiously smoothing a

crease from his smart green pelisse. He flickered a glance, a whim-
sical, mocking glance, under his long lashes at Brigade-Major
Smith. 'I'm afraid it will be a very bloody business,' he sighed: 'Do
you think I should wear my new coat, Smith? It would be dreadful if it got spoiled. Isn't it a damned bore, this horrid assault?'

Harry could not bear Daniel Cadoux. There was just the suggestion of a lisp in Cadoux's speech. Harry said that he assumed
it. He said that Cadoux, with his dandified dress, and his pretty
jewellery, made him feel sick. He could not imagine why
Cadoux had ever joined the army, much less the Rifles; or how
it was that he could induce his men to follow him. 'One of the
Go-ons,' said Harry contemptuously.

'What's that?' enquired a very young subaltern, quite a
Johnny Raw.

'That, my boy,' said Harry, 'you'll very soon discover for yourself.' Relenting, he added: 'The men say there are only two kinds
of officers: the Go-ons, and the *Come*-ons!'

'Oh!' said the very young subaltern, digesting it, and reflecting that there was no need to ask to which category the energetic, fiery young man before him belonged.

No need at all: Harry Smith, dining with some of his friends
a few hours before the attack on the night of the 6th April, was
in tearing spirits, his eyes keen and sparkling as they always were
when there was dangerous work to be done. 'Come on!' would
shout Brigade-Major Smith presently. 'Come on, you devils!'

4

A double ration of grog was served out to the men before the
attack, but it would not have appeared, to a casual observer, necessary to hearten the troops with rum. All was bustle and high spirits in the camp, old warriors giving a last look to their rifles, and

Josh Hetherington enlivening the occasion with a ventriloquial display as popular as it was scandalous. 'Man-killer' Palmer was adjuring Tom Crawley, sober for once, to kill a Frenchman for himself: a Peninsular catchword that would never grow stale; while Burke, who had volunteered for more forlorn hopes than anyone else, was alternately boasting of his past exploits, and exchanging good-natured abuse with a friend from the 52nd regiment.

The army was not in Lord Wellington's confidence, nor had his extensive plans for the capture of Badajos been communicated to the men, but in their usual inexplicable fashion they knew all about those plans, just as they had known a full day before most of their officers the date of the attack.

'Queer, ain't it?' remarked Jack Molloy, refilling his glass from Harry's bottle of wine. 'Never known 'em wrong yet. I wish I knew where they get their information.'

'Oh, orderlies and bâtmen!' said Kincaid, who had just lounged in as though he had nothing to do and had not that instant returned from a perilous reconnaissance journey with his Colonel almost to the very edge of the glacis above the ditch outside Badajos. 'They pick up the news, and pass it on. Hallo, Young Varmint! Where did you spring from?'

Mr William Havelock, of the 43rd regiment, who was the gentleman addressed, made room on Harry's portmanteau for Kincaid to sit down beside him. There was very little space in the tent, and what there was seemed to be full of legs. Kincaid picked his way over three pairs of these, accepted a cigarillo from his host, and lit it at the candle that was stuck into the neck of a bottle on the table.

'Well, and how is our acting Adjutant?' enquired Stewart. 'Dined, Johnny?'

'If he hasn't, he can't dine here,' said Harry. 'He can't even have any port, because – oh yes, he can! I've got a mug somewhere!

Stretch out a hand and feel in that case behind you, Young
Varmint! A beautiful mug from Lisbon – yes, that's it.'

'Port? You haven't got any port?' said Kincaid, hope battling
with suspicion in his face. 'Don't think to fob me off with any
Portuguese stuff! I've been dining with the Colonel.'

'Exalted, aren't you?' said Molloy. 'Don't waste the port on
him, Harry!'

'By God, it is port!' exclaimed Kincaid. 'Where the devil did
you get it, Harry? Old Cameron gave me black strap!'

'Elvas,' replied Harry. 'The Beau himself hasn't any better.'

'The Turk!' said Kincaid, raising the Lisbon mug in a toast to
the army's most famous sutler. 'I thought you must have got it
by wicked plunder.'

'He probably did,' said Molloy. 'You haven't got any money,
have you, Harry? Not real *money?*'

No, Harry had no money, but he had borrowed three dollars from the Quartermaster, after the fashion of all hard-
pressed officers who had several months' pay owing to them.
But the two skinny fowls which had formed the major part of
the dinner had been almost certainly dishonestly come by,
since they had been provided by his servant, who was an experienced campaigner.

'That man of yours will be hanged one of these days,'
prophesied Stewart. 'What's the news, and where have you
been, Johnny?'

'No news, except that Leith's fellows are going to try the
river bastion.'

'We know *that*! Talk of forlorn hopes! The men say if the
Light Bobs and the Enthusiastics can't take the town, there are
no troops that can. I suppose the hour's been changed to suit the
Pioneers. I thought all the ground in front of the river bastion
was mined?'

'Captain Stewart will now move a vote of censure on his lordship's plans,' said Molloy, looking round for somewhere to throw the butt of his cigar. 'Unless I can stub this out on Young Varmint's boots, I shall have to get up and go.'

'Well, go, then,' said Havelock. 'I'll have you know these boots of mine are the only ones left to me. Besides, there'll be more room with you gone. Oh, by God, will there, though! Here's George!'

The officer peeping into the tent was a somewhat stout young man, with a serious face that matched a certain sobriety of out-look. He had entered the army in the expectation of being enabled to assist in the support of his numerous brothers, a prospect that might well have appalled a less earnest man, and did indeed prevent Mr George Simmons from sharing his friends' light-hearted spirits. He was a little prone to moralize, but he was a good officer, and a faithful friend, and the company assembled in Harry's tent greeted him with affectionate ribaldry.

'No, I mustn't stay,' he said, shaking his head. 'I just heard you fellows funning, and I thought I would look in on you. I've been talking to one of Beresford's Staff. Would you believe it? – one of Beresford's A.D.C.s had the abominable bad taste to remark at table just now that he wondered how many of those present would be alive tomorrow! You can imagine what a look the Marshal gave him!'

His shocked countenance made Harry's guests laugh, but Harry said quickly: 'Damned young fool! Who was it?'

'No, it wouldn't be right to tell you. I daresay he is sorry now. It's very strange, the inconsiderate things a man's tongue will betray him into saying.'

'Not yours, George, not yours!' said Kincaid, getting up.

'Well, I do hope it does not, for such observations as *that* are bound to produce some gloomy reflections,' said Simmons.

5

Dusk, and the consequent slackening of gun-fire in the distance, soon made Harry's guests glance at their watches, and bethink them of their duties. The party began to disperse, the host being the first to leave. If the story told by George Simmons had produced gloomy reflections in the minds of his auditors, not one of them gave any outward sign of an inward discomposure. They wished one another luck; they cracked a parting joke or two; and very close friends exchanged hand-shakes that perhaps expressed something more than the light words they spoke.

The night was dark, but quite dry, though the sky was heavily clouded. The Light and 4th divisions had to march down the ravine that lay to the east of the Pardeleras hill, and as they approached the trenches the air grew vaporous with the unhealthy river-exhalations. The storming-parties, conducted by the Engineers, trod softly, all talking being hushed in the ranks, since it was vital to the success of Lord Wellington's plans that every one of the five attacks should be launched simultaneously. Even the trench-guards were unusually quiet; there was nothing to be heard from the trenches but a low murmuring noise. It was difficult marching, when no one could see more than a couple of paces ahead, but Badajos could be located by the little bobbing lights that moved along the ramparts. Someone whispered that Lord Wellington had taken up a position on the top of the quarry, from where he could observe the progress of the main attack, but it was too dark for even the most eagerly straining eyes to pick out his well-known figure in the surrounding murk. The men liked, however, to know that he was watching their exploits. It put them on their mettle, and gave them an added confidence, for though he was a cold, often a harsh, commander, he was one who knew his business, a man one could put one's trust in.

The river-mist was cold, and grew thicker as the storming parties crept up the slope of the glacis. From the ramparts, the sound of an isolated voice, loud in the stillness, drifted to the besiegers' ears. It was only the usual warning, *Sentinel, gardezvous!* that was quite familiar to troops who had all done trench-duty outside the walls, but in the darkness and the quiet it sounded unaccustomed, rather fateful.

Colonel Cameron, and Johnny Kincaid, his Adjutant, having reconnoitred the ground by daylight, the services of the Engineers were not much needed to conduct the storming-parties to their positions. The men stole up the glacis, through the haze, and lay down as soon as they got into line, the muzzles of their rifles projecting beyond the edge of the ditch, ready to open fire. The clouds were parting overhead, permitting a little faint moonlight to illumine the scene. The Light troops, staring up at the walls of Badajos, which seemed to rise sheer out of the river-fog, could see the heads of the Frenchmen lining the ramparts. A sharp *qui vive?* from one of the sentries was followed by the report of a musket, and the noise of drums beating to arms. Colonel Cameron, commanding the four companies of the 95th Rifles which were already extended along the counterscarp to draw the enemy's fire, stole up to Barnard. 'My men are ready now: shall I begin?'

Barnard was giving some low-voiced instructions. He had his watch in his hand, and a wary eye upon the men of the ladderparties, who were gently lowering the ladders into the ditch, between the palisades. No fear that Barnard would strike before the hour. 'No, certainly not!' he said under his breath.

The storming-parties were still creeping up the long slope to the edge of the glacis, when in the distance, to the east, the sky was suddenly lit by a flaming carcass, shot into the air. This was followed almost immediately by the roar of cannon-fire, mingled with the sharp crack of musketry. The time was a quarter-to-ten only, a circumstance that made Barnard curse softly. It was evident that the approach of Picton's escalading parties must have been seen from the Castle, since it was unthinkable that Picton could have wantonly opened the attack before the appointed hour. While the last of the storming-parties of the Light and 4th divisions were stealing up the glacis, the darkness away to the right was lit by lurid bursts of flame; and the cannon-fire momently increased, until it seemed to the men crouching above the ditch that every gun in Badajos must be trained on to the very forlorn hope assailing the precipitous Castle-hill. What accident had occurred to discover the 3rd division's stealthy advance to the French could only be a matter for conjecture, but that Picton, finding that his movements had been seen, had launched his attack a quarter-of-an-hour before time, was soon apparent.

O'Hare, commanding the 95th storming-party, was fretting to give the word to advance, but was too old a hand to betray his impatience to the men watching him so eagerly. Barnard was as cool as if upon a field-day; but Cameron, waiting beside him, could scarcely contain himself. His party, he was convinced, had been seen by the French on the ramparts, who were now silently watching them. He expected his men to be under fire at any moment, and could not bear to keep them inactive until it should please the enemy to open on them. But Barnard was watching the stealthy ladder-parties. Once he sent Harry Smith to hurry a party that was a little behind the others, but he gave his orders in a quiet unagitated voice, and seemed not to be paying any heed to the gunfire and the rockets on the eastern side of the town.

The last ladder was in place as suddenly, deep and melodious, and quite audible through the noise of the cannons, the Cathedral clock within the town began to strike the hour.

'Now, Cameron!' called Barnard.

6

The volley from the British troops was answered by the crash of such a fire as even the most hardened soldiers had never before experienced. A flame, darting upward, disclosed to the besiegers the horrors that lay before them. The storming-parties were some of them swarming down the ladders, and some, too impatient to await their turns, leaping down on to the hay-bags dropped into the ditch to break their fall. There, fourteen feet below the lip of the glacis, every imaginable obstacle, from broken boats to overturned wheelbarrows, had been cast to impede the progress of the attackers. All amongst them, wicked little lights burnt and spluttered. George Simmons, trying to stamp out one of these was jerked away by a friend. 'Leave it, man! leave it! There's a live shell connected with it!'

The roar of an explosion drowned the words; somebody screamed, high and shrill above the uproar, a fire-ball was thrown from the ramparts, casting a red light on the scene. Men were pouring down the ladders into the inferno of bursting shells in the ditch; within a few minutes the ground was further encumbered by scores of dead and dying men; and the most horrible stench of burning flesh began to be mingled with the acrid smell of the gunpowder. Every kind of missile seemed to rain down upon the stormers. The air was thick with splinters, and loud with the roar of bursting shells, and the peculiar muffled sound of muskets fired downwards into the ditch. The Engineers, whose duty it was to lead the storming-parties, were shot down to a man. The troops, choked by the smoke, scorched by the flames, not knowing, without their guides, where to go, charged ahead to the one breach they could see, only to fall back before defences more dreadful than they had ever encountered.

The breach was covered from behind by a breastwork; the slope leading up to it was strewn with crowsfeet, and with beams, studded with nails, that were hung from the edge of the breach. The men struggled up, fast diminishing in number as man after man was shot down by the steady fire maintained by the defenders behind the breastwork. But when the obstacles on the slope had been passed, the breach was found to be guarded by a hideous chevaux-de-frise of sword-blades stuck at all angles into heavy timbers that were chained to the ground. Those behind tried to thrust their foremost comrades forward; someone flung himself down on to the sword-blades in a lunatic endeavour to make of his own writhing body a bridge for the men behind him. It was in vain. While his brains were beaten out by the butts of French muskets, the storming-party was hurled back in confusion, into the indescribable hell below. Powder-barrels, rolling down upon them, exploded with deadly effect; from the breastwork the exultant French were shouting mockery and abuse, while they poured in their volleys.

The trench was crowded not only with the dead and the wounded, but with the troops which still poured down into it. Harry Smith, unscathed, was hurled against someone by the bursting of a shell, and found it to be an acquaintance from the 4th division. He shouted above the din: 'What the devil are you doing here?' for it had been decided that the 4th division was to wheel to the right, to attack the breach in the Trinidad bastion.

'We couldn't do it! The trench is flooded!' screamed the man in his ear. 'Half of us were drowned! There's a cunette, full of water!'

'My God, then the divisions are mingled!' gasped Harry, realizing now why the ditch was so packed with struggling redcoats.

He was thrust on to the foot of a ladder. Here, on the dead ground, a man lay crumpled up, with his hands pressed to his chest. The leaping flames in the ditch showed Harry a face he knew. It was livid, but the eyes were still intelligent.

'Smith! Help me up the ladder! I'm done for!'

'Colonel Macleod! Oh no, dear fellow!' Harry cried, flinging an arm round him.

'I am, I tell you! Be quick!'

Half-supporting, half-carrying him, Harry got him up the ladder. He was groaning, but managed to say: 'The 4th are mingled with ours!'

'I know it! It's that cursed inundation! There, my poor friend, God be with you! I must go back!'

He left the wounded man, and swarmed once more down the ladder. The 4th division, finding the trench below the Trinidad bastion impassable, had instinctively swerved to the left, and were almost inextricably mixed with the men of the Light division. The most appalling confusion reigned; a lane of fire now separated the attackers from La Trinidad; little parties of troops, rallying round isolated officers, again and again charged up the slope of the breach, only to fall back before the ghastly chevaux-de-frise at the top. Mistaking an unfinished ravelin for the breach in the curtain wall, a heroic band charged up it, only to find a waste of earthworks lying still between them and the wall of the town.

Harry fought his way to where Barnard, by superhuman endeavour, was separating his own division from the 4th. The

Light fell back to the ladders, overwhelmed by a fire no troops could withstand. Harry, almost swept off his feet, saw the face of little Frere of the 43rd regiment, ghastly in the glare of the fire-balls. They were forced on together to the ladders.

'Let's throw them down! The fellows shan't get out!' shouted Harry.

A wild-eyed tattered private behind him heard, and roared: 'Damn your eyes, if you do, we'll bayonet you!'

Harry's sash was loose, and got caught in the ladder. An angry growl, and the gleam of the threatened bayonet set him insanely laughing. He tore his sash free, and went on up the ladder, thrust forward by the irresistible surge of men behind him.

At the top, the surviving officers were re-forming their men, who, indeed, wished only for a breathing-space before plunging again into the ditch below. A brigade of Portuguese of the 4th division came up at the double, and went down into the ditch with an intrepidity that put renewed courage into the Light division.

Again and again the troops struggled through the reeking ditch to the slope of the breach, and up it to the defences at the top. 'Why don't you come into Badajos?' mocked the French.

More than two hours passed in this dreadful slaughter. The dead lay thick by the breach, and were trodden underfoot amongst the burning débris in the ditch. Between the attacks, which were launched now by dwindling bands of soldiers rally-ing round any officer who still survived, and could still lead his men, the troops stood immobile, enduring doggedly the fire from the ramparts. There was no thought of retreat; a sullen fury possessed the men; the horrors of the assault, which at first had shocked, now aroused only the most primitive instincts in even the mildest breasts. Humanity seemed to have deserted the eyes that glared up under the leathern peaks of shakos to the ramparts; the fire-balls and the rockets fitfully illumined faces that were rendered unrecognizable not so much by the smoke that had blackened them as by the rage that wiped out every other emotion, and transformed good-humoured countenances into strange masks of animal hatred.

When the hail of missiles drove the besiegers to the ladders, they went up them only to re-form, and come on again. The main columns of the two divisions had been pouring reinforcements into the ditch for over an hour; Harry Smith, scorched, filthy with mud and blood, but untouched either by musketry or shell-fire, thought that he and little Frere must be the only two officers of the original storming-party who were not dead or wounded. Of his own regiment, officer after officer had fallen, some dead, some mortally wounded, some able to drag themselves out of the ditch to the rear. At midnight, a Staff-officer had galloped up to Barnard with Lord Wellington's orders for the Light division to draw off, but neither Barnard nor the men who followed him would give way. Again they attacked, and again they were driven back, always in diminishing numbers. A little before daylight, when the exhausted troops had drawn back beyond the glacis, Lord Fitzroy Somerset, Wellington's Military Secretary, rode up, and encountering Harry, called out: 'Smith, where's Barnard?'

'I don't know,' Harry answered. 'He's alive, that's all I can tell you. By God, this is a hellish night's work!'

'I know, I know, everything has miscarried! Picton was too soon, and Leith was late. You are the only troops that kept to the right time.'

'Well,' said Harry, dog-weary, but still game, 'what did you expect? We are *The* Division, aren't we?'

Lord Fitzroy, a Guardsman, smiled, but only said: 'His lordship desires the Light and 4th divisions to storm once again.'

'The devil!' Harry said. 'Why, man, we've had enough! We're all knocked to pieces!'

'I daresay,' Fitzroy answered in his quiet way, 'but you must try again.'

'If we couldn't succeed with two whole, fresh divisions, we're likely to make a poor show of it now!' Harry snapped back, letting his quick temper ride him for a moment. It was soon over; before Fitzroy could speak, he had smiled, and added: 'But, by Jupiter, we will try again, and with all our might! Yet one of our fellows was sent off not five minutes ago to inform his lordship we can make no progress.'

Fitzroy said nothing; officer after officer had come up to Lord Wellington, where he stood above the quarry, watching the waste and the failure of his main attack, always with the same report to make: that the divisions were suffering terrible losses; that there were not officers enough left to lead the men; that the rope-parties could not drag away the chevaux-de-frise of sword-blades, or the stormers penetrate beyond it.

When he received the last report of failure at the breaches, his lordship was standing with two only of his aides-de-camp: Lord March, and the young Prince of Orange. March was holding a flaming torch which cast its glare on to his lordship's haggard face. It looked ghastly, the jaw a little fallen, yet the expression was as firm as ever. His lordship, aware of someone standing behind him, turned, and laid a hand on the man's arm. 'Go at once to Picton, and tell him he must try if he cannot succeed on the Castle!' he said quickly.

There was a moment's hesitation; the gentleman addressed said with a strong Scotch accent: 'My lord, I have not my horse, but I will walk as fast as I can, and I think I can find the way. I know part of the road is swampy.'

Lord March shifted the torch; its glow showed Wellington the face of Dr James McGrigor, Chief of the Medical Staff. He removed his hand. 'No, no, I beg your pardon! I thought it was De Lancey.'

'My lord, I am ready to go.'

'No. It is not your business to be running errands.'

A little commotion was heard; someone was urgently calling: 'Where is Lord Wellington?'

'Here! here!' shouted the group round his lordship.

A mounted Staff-officer pushed up to them through the surrounding gloom. 'My lord, the Castle is your own!'

The grim jaw seemed to shorten. Wellington shot a question at the officer, who answered exultantly: 'My lord, Sir Thomas Picton, and, I believe, the whole division are in possession!'

'Good God, is it possible?' exclaimed the Prince of Orange.

'Go back to Sir Thomas, and desire him to push down into the town!' said Wellington. 'The Light and 4th must assail the breaches once again. You, sir, get back to your division, and desire Colonel Barnard to make another attempt. Inform him that General Picton is in, and will go to his assistance through the town. Send for my horse, March, and for yours and the Prince's too!'

The officer from the Light division saluted and wheeled his horse; as he rode off, he was joined by a Quartermaster of the 95th regiment, who had been standing all the time quite close to Wellington. Together they made their way back to where the Light division, withdrawn from the glacis, were lying beside their arms, officers and men together, in bitter silence.

The news that the 3rd division had taken the Castle was received with sullen disbelief. It was some minutes before Quartermaster Surtees could convince the soldiers of the famous Light division that the 3rd had succeeded where they had failed. To men who had tried so long and so unavailingly to fight their way past impregnable breaches, it seemed impossible that any troops could have entered Badajos. But a bugle-call, sounding within the town, corroborated the incredible tidings. Receiving the order to re-form, and assail the breach again, the men, who had staggered exhausted down the glacis a short time before, leaped to their feet again with their weariness and their hurts forgotten, got into formation, and went forward with a will. They trod over their own dead, and mounted the breach, under a slackened fire. There was now very little resistance from the defenders; sounds of fierce fighting within the walls could be heard; the weakened Light and 4th divisions passed the breach almost unopposed, and established themselves upon the deserted ramparts.

'By the living God, we're in!' gasped Charlie Eeles, tattered, blood-stained, and reeling with fatigue.

7

It was soon discovered that the abandoning by the French of the breaches had been caused, not, as was at first supposed, by the advance of the 3rd division from the captured Castle, but by General Walker's brigade of the 5th division. This scarcely-regarded force, whose assault upon the river-bastion of San Vincente had been planned, like an afterthought, at the last minute, had been an hour late in launching its attack, a mischance due to a mistake made by the officer detailed to bring up the scaling-ladders from the Park. But at midnight, after some very fierce fighting, the brigade had won the San Vincente bastion, and proceeding along the wall, had soon carried the San José as well. Penetrating to the next bastion, they had met with such a spirited resistance that they were swept back to the San Vincente, and seemed even in danger of being repulsed from the town. But a reserve force, left at the San Vincente, soon set matters to rights, and the brigade swept forward, the French, whose numbers were considerably depleted by the calling up of more and yet more reinforcements to repulse the attacks on the breaches, retreating before them. The western bastions fell, one after another; and while a part of the brigade occupied these, the rest went down into the town, and made their way through the deserted streets to where they could hear the pandemonium that raged at the breaches.

It was strange, after the racket and thunder of the struggle on the wall, to find the town so silent. Every fighting man seemed to have been drawn to the ramparts, or to the Castle, where Picton, finding every gate blocked but one small postern, was battling his way out of the fortress. The battle-noises could be heard, but seemed distant, no longer distinct, but merged into a kind of roar. No one was encountered in the streets, but lights glowed under door-sills, and between the chinks of shutters, and whispering sounds could be heard in the houses, so that the men who passed down the streets knew that they were being watched by unseen eyes.

They took the main defending-force in the rear. As the survivors of the Light and 4th divisions reached the top of the breach, the French, after a short, flurried skirmish with the 5th division, were throwing down their arms; while General Phillipon, with a few of his Staff-officers, was escaping to the protection of the San Cristobal fort, beyond Guadiana.

Only a little isolated fighting took place after this. Lord Wellington, entering the town through the Santa Maria breach, from which the chevaux-de-frise of sword-blades had at last been dragged, passed between great mounds of red and green coats, and was saluted by ghastly figures that could manage still, in spite of their wounds, to drag themselves clear of the encumbering dead, and raise themselves on their elbows to give a faint cheer for his lordship. Wellington saluted stiffly, but the dawn-light showed the tears glinting on his cheeks.

The first battalion of the Light division was detailed for picket-duty in the town. Harry Smith, bruised in every limb, limping from a contusion on one thigh, his uniform cut to ribbons, came upon Kincaid, posting a picket, and hailed him in a cracked, hoarse voice. 'Alive, Johnny?'

'Oh, untouched!' said Kincaid, whom nothing could shake from his lazy unconcern. 'You look as though you had had enough. Hurt?'

'Devil a bit!' said Harry. He had worn his voice out with cheering on his men; a little tremor shook it. 'But O'Hare – poor Croudace – Charlie Gray – M'Leod – God, what a night! I tell you, Johnny, the men are ripe for murder.'

'Well, if it stops at murder I shall be surprised,' said Kincaid coolly. 'Cameron has our lot well in hand, but he'll let 'em fall out to amuse themselves presently.'

'Yes! and the whole division will go to the devil!' said Harry, with a kind of weary violence.

By ten o'clock in the morning, the garrison of Badajos was marched off under strong guard to Elvas, and the British troops were told to fall out. Lord Wellington had lost, he said, the flower of his army in the assault upon the town. The French had ignored the long-established rule of surrendering a town once practicable breaches had been made in its walls, just as they had done at Ciudad Rodrigo. '*I should have thought myself justified in putting both garrisons to the sword,*' wrote Wellington to Lord Liverpool; '*and if I had done so at the first it is probable that I should have saved 5,000 men at the second.*' So it was not to be supposed that his lordship had ever the least intention of denying his soldiers their immemorial right to sack a town that had resisted to the end.

The men swore that every Spaniard in Badajos was an Afrancesado, which was the term used for anyone in sympathy with the French. When the terrors of the night were done, and the French garrison made prisoners, and the order to fall out was given, men who had fought through the dark hours like demigods, rushed into the town like hyenas. By noon all semblance of order had disappeared; Badajos was a hell of misrule in which the horrors of the breaches were being fast surpassed.

Those who had censured the excesses committed by the troops after the fall of Ciudad Rodrigo were smitten to silence by the atrocities seen on all sides in Badajos. Murder, rapine, and rape were the orders of the day, and no efforts of the officers could quell the unleashed brutality of men who had shot their way into the wine-shops, and tapped the barrels in the streets.

Harry was amongst those who tried at first to curb the disorder. That he was not shot down by one of the privates of the 88th regiment was due not to any prudence on his own part, but to the intervention of a reeling Rifleman who recognized his Brigade-Major, and called for a cheer for him.

A dishevelled woman was embracing Harry's knees; one or two soldiers fired their pieces in honour of the Brigade-Major; an individual, sitting astride a wine-barrel, and dressed in a priest's cassock, a woman's skirt, and a shako bearing the number-plate of the 95th regiment, drank a toast to him. The Brigade-Major swore at him, and was dragged off by one of his friends, before the humour of the men had had time to change.

'It's no good, Harry, it's no good, and there's work to be done at the breaches!' Charles Beckwith said urgently. 'None of us can stop this bloody sack! For God's sake, let's get out of the town!'

They were unable to get out, however, before drinking a cup from the barrel in the street. The motley creature astride it had a musket in his hand, and swore to shoot any man who refused to drink with him. Harry saw a nun being dragged, almost senseless, down the street, by a couple of redcoats, and tore himself out of Beckwith's hold to go to the rescue. The demented woman, still clinging to his knees, detained him for long enough to allow the nun's captors to drag her round the corner, and out of sight, and in so doing probably saved Harry's life, since the two soldiers were mad-drunk, and already quarrelling with one another over their prize.

As the day wore on, the carnage in the town grew worse. Though the inhabitants locked their doors, and shuttered their windows, the soldiers burst into the houses. The graceful, outward-curving iron bars to ground-floor windows were wrenched out of their sockets; locks were blown in by musketry-fire; doors were torn off their hinges; traders were either flung out of their shops into the streets, or, if they resisted, spitted on bayonets, while the troops installed themselves behind the counters, and carried on a roaring trade between themselves, until the inevitable quarrel broke out, and all ended in naked steel, or the hasty discharge of a musket. No religious house was safe from the mob of savages that marauded through the town; nuns were as easy to get as prostitutes, and could be as well enjoyed, whether in the open market-place, or in the pillaged Churches, or in the reeking taprooms. From every house and shop soldiers issued, staggering under their loads of plunder. Nothing came amiss to men too drunk with wine and fighting to discriminate between the valuable and the worthless. A man would cherish a wicker bird-cage as jealously as a golden chalice from the Cathedral; and fight as bitterly for the possession of a copper cooking-pot as for the necklace torn from some woman's neck. Many of them, who had entered the town in singed and rent uniforms, were to be seen lurching about in the oddest of costumes: female dress, priestly vestments, or the grandeur of a hidalgo's wardrobe.

The camp-followers, women of almost every nationality, who had been amongst the first to enter the town at daybreak, were like a swarm of vultures. Indifferent to everything but plunder, they stripped the dead on the ramparts, rifled the pockets of men too badly wounded to do more than moan their ceaseless appeals for water, and even trod over the mounds of slain and wounded in their haste to get into the town. Once in, they drank as freely as their protectors, and showed an even more horrible rapacity. About two hundred of them took part in the sack; they were to be seen in all the streets, questing harpies who did not scruple to drag girls out of hiding-places for the soldiers to make merry with, while they, business-like even in drink, possessed themselves of the trinkets, and even the torn dresses of their victims.

Here and there, in the midst of this scene of unbridled license, an officer's cocked-hat was occasionally to be seen, its owner trying to escort parties of terrified women to safety. Sometimes he would succeed, quite a number of the men still retaining a hazy respect for their superiors, and responding to the voice of authority. But there was very little the officers could do when their men faced them with a red, brutish glow in their eyes, and swore they would shoot any man down who stood in their way. Most of them retired to the camp, outside the town, or busied themselves with collecting as many of their men as seemed the least drunk, kicking or dowsing them into comparative sobriety, and forcing them to carry away the wounded from the breaches and the bastions.

A brilliant day had succeeded the clouded night; the sun beat down upon the old walls, and the plaster-coated houses; and from the ditch where the dead lay in heap upon heap, a faint, growing stench of putrefaction began to rise like an unhealthy miasma.

Quartermaster Surtees had got a party of decent men to-gether, and had been at work dragging the wounded out from under the dead ever since dawn. Harry was there too, of course, with his brother Brigade-Major, Charles Beckwith; old Dr Burke, whom every man in the Light division loved, was there, heartening the worst cases by his loud, cheerful bullying, all the time the tears were pouring down his cheeks. Stretcher-parties, some sober, some too drunk to carry their burdens without stumbling over inequalities in the ground, were employed in carrying the wounded men to the rear. Some of these died before they reached the camp; some, their hurts roughly bound up in the ditch, were tipped off the stretchers by the clumsiness of the bearers, and started bleeding copiously again.

Now that the sunlight disclosed the results of the night's struggle at the breaches, men who had borne their part in it looked on the scene with horrified eyes. The carnage was more frightful even than they had known, the dead so numerous that they looked like wooden soldiers spilled out of a child's toy-chest – those of them who had not been stripped naked, and left in strange, sprawling attitudes to fester in the ditch.

George Simmons found Major O'Hare thus, upon the breach, shot through the chest by musket-balls that had torn great gashes in his flesh. He had volunteered to lead the storming-party, and had been almost the first to fall. He lay beside Sergeant Fleming, who had always been with him. They were both dead, and George, composing their twisted limbs, and drawing down the lids over their dreadfully glaring eyes, could not help shed-ding a few tears. 'A Lieutenant-Colonel or cold meat in a few hours!' O'Hare had said last night, shaking George's hand before he went off to lead the advance.

Well, he was cold meat, like Stokes, and Crampton, and Balvaird, and McDermid, like the hundreds of rank-and-file who lay piled up at the foot of the breach, in a fantastic, incredible mound. George brushed away the tear-drops, reflecting with the detachment of those who had fought in many engagements and had learned to look upon the loss in battle of friends as passing griefs, sharp yet soon over, that it was a bad soldier who mourned the dead overlong, as bad a soldier as the man who dwelt on the chances of his own death. A friend was killed, and one wept over him; but soon one would find another friend, not dead but miraculously alive, and a spring of gladness would make one forget the first sorrow.

Such a spring George felt when he saw Harry presently. His honest face grew lighter, its dejection vanished in a beaming smile. He grasped Harry's hand, ejaculating: 'Thank God! You're safe! Well done, old fellow!'

'If only we had carried it!' Harry said, casting a fierce, hungry look upwards at the breach.

'Never mind, they're all saying it was our attacks that made it possible for Leith's and Picton's fellows to break in. And Johnny's safe too, and dear old Charlie Beckwith! Oh, but, Harry, though there's no denying we are *The* Division, it makes one's heart swell, indeed it does, to think of those noble fellows of Picton's scaling the Castle-hill as they did! And the Pioneers, too, winning the river-bastion, with everyone ready to swear they must fail!'

'Yes!' Harry said, kindling with ready enthusiasm. 'Noble fellows, all of them, and the bloodiest, most glorious action, George! By God, I would fight every one of our battles again, but not this one!'

'Oh, no, not this one again!' George agreed, with a shudder.

'I hate sieges!' Harry said, viciously jerking the knot of his sash. 'The men behave like heroes, brave, drunken blackguards that they are! and then they go straight to the devil, as they're doing now!'

'Very true,' George said. 'It is melancholy, and upon more counts than one.'

'It plays the dickens with the brigade!' snapped Harry.

8

When the living had been disentangled from the dead, and carried to the camp; and fatigue-parties of Portuguese had begun to dig great pits to receive the hundreds of the slain, there was nothing for even the keenest duty-officer to do but to visit wounded friends, or kick his heels in camp until it should please his men to reel out of Badajos, sick, probably, from excess of wine; richer, certainly, by the value of the goods they had plundered; sullen, some of them, from the knowledge of beastliness committed while they were mad with battle-fury and the wicked magic of unlimited liquor, elated, others, and bragging of unspeakable deeds; demoralized, all of them: heart-rending objects to officers whose business was their welfare, and whose pride, their efficiency; and who cared for them, in a queer, rough way, even when they cursed them for a set of black-hearted, gutterborn scoundrels. It would take time to shoot, and flog, and bully the divisions into shape again; and the best men were dead, and their bodies heaved one on top of the other into deep, stinking pits. New draughts would arrive presently from England: regular Johnny Raws, landing at Lisbon, and working their way goggle-eyed through Portugal to join the army, under a subaltern as raw as themselves, who would thus early in his career be given a painful chance to prove his worth. If there was stuff in him, he would get his draught to its destination intact, with most of its baggage, and without leaving a trail of pillaged farmsteads in its wake; if he lacked confidence in himself, or was found to have a strain of weakness in him, he would bring only the more

tractable of his men to the division, and have a shameful tale to
tell his Colonel of desertions on the road.

'And if we get all the new draughts it will take months licking them into shape!' said Harry, fretting at forced inaction, and
so in a brittle temper, snapping at every ill. 'And the old hands
sunk to the level of gutter-sweepings after this filthy, bloody,
damnable sack!'

'Don't be downhearted, Harry: we shall be on the march
again before the week's out, if all I hear is true,' said Kincaid,
who had lounged over to Harry's tent to talk over the assault
with him. Nothing like a few hard marches to pull the men
together. You should look on the lighter side of things.'

Harry acknowledged the bantering note with one of his
quick smiles, but shook his head. 'Damned little lighter side to
this affair!'

'Oh, isn't there, by God! You should have been with me in the
small hours, when I was posting the pickets in the streets. A man
of ours brought a prisoner up to me. Said he was the Governor,
and plainly thought he would get a big reward for taking him.'

'I thought Phillipon escaped to the San Cristobal?'

'He may have, for anything I know. My fine fellow − by Jove,
he was a fine fellow, too! quite the dandy, and with enough gold
lace for a hussar! − well, he made no bones about admitting to
me that he wasn't the Governor, but had told poor Allen he was
to ensure protection. He told *me* he was the Colonel of one of
the regiments − I forget which − and that all his surviving officers were waiting in his quarters hard-by, to surrender themselves to any English officer who would be so obliging as to go
to them. Ah well! I'm a Scot myself, but I went.'

'Ambush!' said Harry, his eyes beginning to dance.

'Devil a bit! I took two or three men with me, and there, sure
enough, were these precious French officers − fifteen or more

of 'em – all assembled in the Colonel's quarters, and not one of
'em able to understand why the town was lost, or how the devil
I got in. I didn't choose to tell 'em that. I said I'd entered at the
breach, which was true enough; though how we any of us got
in, when you consider the way the Johnny Crapauds hurled us
back like so many recruits, was a thing that was puzzling me as
much as it was puzzling them. I never saw a set of fellows so
dejected! All except the Major, a big, jolly-looking Dutchman,
with medals enough on his breast to have furnished the window
of a tolerable toy-shop. He was a good fellow: cracked as many
jokes as corks out of wine-bottles. Damme if I remember the
jokes, but the wine was excellent.'

'You villain, Johnny, do you tell me you stood there and drank
with them?' Harry demanded.

'Stood! We sat round the table, to a dish of cold meat, and
drank each other's healths! After supper, off went my Colonel to
secure his valuables. He was so grateful to me for allowing it that
he told me he had a couple of good horses in the stable, which,
as he wouldn't be permitted to keep 'em, he recommended me
to take. So, as a horse is the only prize we poor devils of officers
can consider strictly legal, I had one of 'em saddled. And a handsome black beauty she is, my boy. Three hundred guineas at
Tatt's: not a penny less!'

Harry, always on the look-out for a good horse, was loudly
envious of so much good-fortune, and proposed that he should
instantly go with Kincaid to his quarters to inspect the animal.
They were on the point of strolling off together when Kincaid
saw two ladies coming towards them from the direction of the
city. 'Hallo, what's this?' he said, detaining Harry.

Harry bestowed no more than a cursory glance on the
approaching women. 'What should it be but a couple of camp-
followers? Come on, man! *You* don't need a woman to-day!'

'No, but wait!' Kincaid said. 'They're ladies. Look at their mantillas!'

By this time the two veiled figures, the smaller and slighter of the pair supported by the arm of the other, had come within earshot. Harry, a little impatient, favoured them with another look, more searching this time. He decided that Kincaid was right. Ladies they were, if quiet elegance of dress was anything to go by. He stood still, waiting beside Kincaid to see what they could want in the British camp.

The taller woman led her shrinking companion straight up to the two officers, and put back her mantilla with one thin hand. A handsome, careworn face was disclosed. The lady was no longer in the first blush of youth, but her features were fine, her eyes dark and liquid, and her bearing that of a princess. She addressed the two officers in Spanish, speaking in a voice that retained its natural dignity in spite of evident agitation. 'Señores, you are English. I implore your aid!'

'Anything in our power, señora!' Kincaid replied promptly.

A look of relief spread over the strained face. 'You speak Spanish!'

'Tolerably well, señora, but not as well as my friend here, I believe.'

The lady's eyes turned towards Harry, slight and wiry, and a little fidgety beside his tall friend. He bowed, but he knew that there was nothing any officer could do to help a Spaniard from Badajos, and wished that Kincaid would make an end.

The lady seemed to feel his impatience, and addressed herself again to Kincaid. 'Señor, you must wonder at my coming into your camp thus unattended. I am of the family of Los Dolores de León. If you doubt me, let me but be brought to Colonel Campbell, or Lord Fitzroy Somerset, for they know me well!'

Her tongue tripped a little over the names, but Kincaid nodded his understanding. She continued anxiously: 'We are of the true hidalgo blood, señor. Lord Fitzroy would know. After the battle of Talavera, he and Colonel Campbell were billeted in my house. You recall?'

'Yes, I recall. We made Badajos our General Headquarters.'

'It is so. I know well Lord Wellington. But then, alas, we were of consequence, señor! rich, respected! All that is gone. This war! You understand, it was from the olive groves that we had our fortune. But the accursed French have ravaged all, all!'

Her eyes flashed, her bosom heaved. Kincaid intervened, saying, with a questioning lift of his brows at Harry: 'Yes, indeed I understand! But you must not stand here, señora. Will you not come into the tent? Harry, you've got two chairs!'

The lady murmured her thanks; Brigade-Major Smith, casting an extremely speaking glance upon his friend, did the honours of his tent, setting two camp-chairs for his unwanted guests. The smaller figure, who had not yet put back the mantilla from her face, seemed to be half-unconscious, for she hung heavily on her companion's arm, and when put gently into her chair, sank down as though exhausted, and gave no other sign of life than the shudders which from time to time shook her frame. These convulsive rigors had the effect of riveting Harry's attention upon her. His keen eyes were unable to pierce the veil that hid her face from him, but he saw that her hands, which were tightly clasped in her lap, were small and smooth, the hands of a young girl. He could fancy that from behind the mantilla her eyes, perhaps as large and as fine as her companion's, were watching him. His interest was aroused; he waited for her to put back her veil, attending only with half an ear to what the elder lady was telling Kincaid.

The lady's agitation made her lose some of the calm which seemed, from her periodic attempts to recapture it, almost a part of her nature. She recounted her story disjointedly, dwelling upon irrelevancies, and several times assuring Kincaid that she was nobly born, and that such an excursion as this, into the English camp, could never have been undertaken by her except under the stress of direst need.

She was married, she said, to a Spanish officer, fighting in a distant part of the kingdom, but whether he lived, or was dead, she knew not. Until yesterday, she and her young sister were living in quiet and affluence in one of the best houses in Badajos. A gesture indicated the figure at her side.

'To-day, señor, we know not where to lay our heads, where to get a change of raiment, or even a morsel of food! My house is a wreck, all our furniture broken or carried off, ourselves exposed to insult and brutality – ah, if you do not believe me, look at my ears, how they are torn by those wretches wrenching the rings out of them!'

She pointed to her neck, which was blood-stained. Kincaid spoke soothingly to her; his easy sympathy had the effect of calming her. She pressed her handkerchief to her lips, and tried to speak more quietly. 'For myself, I care not! I have friends who will assist me to go to my husband. I am no longer young; I do not fear! But for this child, this poor little sister who has but just come to me from the convent where she has been educated, I am in despair, and know not what to do! Señor, do you know, have you seen the ruin that is desolating the city? There is no security there, there is only rapine and slaughter! I cannot take her with me, perhaps into worse danger! There was only one thing that I could do. Indelicate it must seem to you, yet oh, señor, in your national character I have such faith that I believe my appeal will not be made in vain, nor my confidence abused! We have come to throw ourselves upon the protection of any English officer whose generosity will afford it us!'

'Señora, upon my word of honour as a gentleman, you have nothing to fear in this camp,' Kincaid said. 'Every protection –'

She brushed his words aside, as though impatient of them. 'I need nothing. There are those who will assist me to find my husband. It is for my sister, who is so young, that I implore your kindness!'

She had been clasping the girl in her arms as she spoke, but she released her now, and murmuring some fondness, put back the mantilla from her face.

The sweetest little face Kincaid had ever seen was thus revealed. It was woefully pale, and of a fairness of skin more English than Spanish. The eyes, under rather strongly marked brows, were large, dilated a little with lingering terror, but of a soft brilliance which dazzled Kincaid into thinking that he beheld a beauty. But she was not strictly beautiful. Her little nose was not classic; her mouth was too large, and with a full underlip rather firmly supporting the upper, in a way which gave a great deal of character to the face, and some impression of stubbornness. This was borne out by a decided chin, rounded, to be sure, but no weakling's chin, as Kincaid saw at a glance.

He felt his heart melt within him; his ready tongue faltered; he could think of nothing to say, and looked helplessly towards Harry.

Then he was startled, for Harry was not looking at him, but at the girl, still leaning against her sister's shoulder. Kincaid saw to his amazement that he was perfectly white under his tan, with a queer, set look in his face, that made him seem suddenly much older, almost a stranger.

The girl looked back at him. The fright was fading from her eyes; the glimmer of a smile crept into them, just a hint of mischief in it.

'What is your name?' Harry said. Kincaid did not know that voice; it did not sound like Harry's.

'Juana,' the girl answered, like a sigh.

'Juana!' Harry repeated it, lingering a little over its gentle syllables. 'How old are you?' he asked, softly, as though by the lowering of his voice he sought to exclude her sister, and Kincaid.

'I am now more than fourteen, señor,' she said.

'Fourteen!'

Kincaid reflected that southern girls ripened quickly. He had supposed Juana to be seventeen; she had the figure of a girl verging on womanhood. He wished that it was on him that her gaze rested so steadfastly, but he saw that Harry filled her vision. His inches and his charm had never stood him in less stead. She was not aware of him.

Harry was looking at the trickle of blood upon her neck. Kincaid saw his lower lip quiver. He put out one of his thin, strong hands. It shook slightly as he touched Juana's little torn ear. 'They hurt you – *querida!*'

The endearment slipped unconsciously from his tongue. She replied simply: 'Yes. It is nothing, however.'

'God damn them!' Harry said, in English, and under his breath. 'God damn their souls to hell!'

She sat up, disengaging herself from the sister's embrace. The fright had quite disappeared; a delicate colour had come into her cheeks; her mouth began to lilt at the corners. It gave her an enchanting look but it was decidedly mischievous: not a doubt of that, thought Kincaid, silently adoring the pretty creature.

'Please, I do not understand English,' Juana said.

'I will teach you,' Harry answered, in a lover's voice, smiling down into her eyes. 'Will you let me take care of you, *mi pobrecita?*'

She nodded trustfully.

'*Toda mi vida!*' he said, as though recording a vow.

Good God, where is this leading us? thought Kincaid, catching the low-spoken words. All my life indeed! Harry, take care!

Juana seemed to think the promise quite natural. She gave back Harry's smile with such a beaming look in her own dark eyes that Kincaid was not surprised to see Harry lift her hand to his lips.

'I do not know your name, señor?' Juana suggested hopefully.

'Harry Smith,' he replied, holding her hand between both of his.

She repeated it hesitantly. 'Harry?' she said, trilling it, and shaking her head at her own pronunciation.

'Enrique,' he translated.

That pleased her; her whole face quickened with sudden laughter. 'I like it better so!'

'Señor!' the sister intervened. 'May I count upon your protection for this fatherless child?'

Harry replied, without taking his eyes from Juana's face: 'She stays with me. You need have no fear. I will arrange everything.'

Kincaid, aghast, thought it time to call a halt. He touched Harry's arm, saying in English: 'Harry, what the devil are you about? She can't stay with you! A child – a lady!'

'She's not a child. Oh, in years – !'

'But, you crazy fool, you can't keep her with you! A gently-born girl, reared in a convent, thrown upon your generosity –'

'Yes, I can.'

'Harry, will you listen to reason? This won't do! She's of the true hidalgo class! What can you do with such a girl? She's not –'

'Do with her? I'm going to marry her!' replied Brigade-Major Smith.

Two

'A TREASURE INVALUABLE'

1

MARRY HER HE DID. HE WOULD LISTEN TO NO ARGUMENT; he snapped his fingers at every impediment. The same ardent spirit which sent him headlong into the thickest part of any battle drove him headlong into marriage. To look at Juana was to love her, said Kincaid, adding, years later, with his twisted, rueful smile: 'And I did love her, but I never told my love, and in the meantime another and more impudent fellow stepped in and won her.'

But Juana did not think Harry impudent. A kindred spirit in her had leaped to meet his. Kincaid, offering protection to her sister, had scarcely made an impression upon her; half-fainting, his pleasant voice had had no power to rouse her from her state of terror. If he was good to look at, she did not know it. Sunk in the chair he had set for her, shrinking within the shelter of her sister's arm, she had become aware of Harry, intently watching her. Though he had not been able to see her face through the mesh of her mantilla, she had seen his, deeply tanned, with a close-gripped mouth, a masterful, aquiline nose, and bright almond-shaped eyes tremendously alive under their rather heavy lids. He was fined down to bone and muscle; the line of his jaw stood out sharply; there were clefts running from his nose to the up-tilting corners of his mouth. His hands seemed all sinew; his slight frame a small, tough thing, compact of energy. Not a handsome man, Harry Smith: he would improve with age, like his Commander-in-chief; not a big man, nor one to use many graces in his dealings with his fellow-men; but a vivid, vital creature, instinct with a force, far removed from mere charm, which was a strong magnetism: the quality which made him, in spite of his impetuosity, his quick temper, and his flaming impatience, a born leader of men. There was something fierce about Harry, the look of a hawk in his eyes: a similar spirit in Juana, the daughter of a long line of hidalgos, responded to it. They were made for each other, and were simple and direct enough, both of them, Kincaid reflected, to know it at a glance.

After his first astonishment, he refrained from expostulation. Harry, held for those initial moments in a trance of wonder, awoke soon to a fit of whirlwind energy. Arrangements had to be made for the marriage, for the sister's safe conduct through the lines, for Juana's comfort, for both ladies' lodging for the night. He might have escorted them to Elvas, but he would not let this treasure he had found out of his sight. She and her sister must be accommodated in his tent; he sent his bâtman, Joe Kitchen, providentially returned in a moderately sober condition from Badajos, to beg, borrow, or steal a mattress for his love. He wrested a pillow from Stewart, a blanket from Jack Molloy, and would not stay to listen to arguments against his hasty, ruinous marriage.

The sister, blinking at Juana's amazing lover, demurred at his autocratic decree that they should take possession of his tent. Having seen the British troops in Badajos, she placed small dependence on the protection of canvas walls. 'Shall we be safe? Will not the soldiers break in?' she asked nervously.

Harry stared at her in astonishment. 'Break in?' he repeated, even his swift brain finding it hard to assimilate the enormity of her suggestion. 'The men break into an officer's tent? By God, they will not!'

She seemed to be doubtful; to set her mind at rest, he called up his private groom, a stolidly respectable person who inspired even a nervous Spanish lady with confidence, and laid on him strict orders to keep his guests' privacy inviolate.

'Yessir,' said English West woodenly, betraying no surprise. He took a look at the elder lady, and decided that there was nothing in it; he looked at Juana, all her alarms now ended, sitting on the edge of Harry's bed, like an inquisitive robin, and encountered a shy smile that reminded him of an urchin detected in crime. He was visibly shaken, and retired with his head in a whirl.

Despairing of getting Harry to listen to reason, James Stewart, seeing in the marriage the ruin of his friend's career, suggested desperately that it was not fair to pitchfork so young a girl into matrimony. Speaking to her in halting Spanish (for he could never achieve any fluency in a foreign tongue), he tried to ask her what her real wishes were, at the same time assuring her of protection in the camp.

She caught at his meaning, and smiled happily. 'Please, I will marry Enrique,' she said.

She was quite sure, neither bashful nor coquettish. Life in the tail of an army held no terrors for her. She liked soldiers, she told Jack Molloy sunnily. Her own brother had been a soldier. Dead now, of course: killed by the French. Jack, seizing the opportunity afforded by Harry's temporary absence, tried hard to paint for the little Spanish lady a true picture of the privations and the dangers ahead of her if she became Harry's wife. She listened to him politely, encouraging his stumbling Spanish, occasionally supplying him with an elusive word, but she did not seem to be in the least impressed by what he said. When he described the discomforts of travelling in the rear of the army, all amongst the cumbrous baggage-train, and surrounded by camp-followers, perhaps not setting eyes on Harry for days together, she looked wise, and said with considerable decision that she thought better, perhaps, not to travel in the rear of the army.

'Much better!' Molloy assured her. 'You see, you did not entirely realize, señorita, what such a life would mean to a delicate female.'

'It is very true. Besides, if I could not see my Enrique for days together I should not like it,' said Juana.

'How should you, indeed? And for him, consider the anxiety of being separated from you, not knowing how you fared, and unable to go to you!'

'Yes, that is so,' she agreed. 'It is a very good thing that you have told me all this, for I am quite ignorant, though not, I think, stupid. I shall not go to the rear. It is not at all what I wish. I shall stay beside Enrique.'

She seemed to think that she had discovered the obvious solution to any possible difficulty in the way of her marriage. Molloy felt rather helpless. He tried to tell her that what she suggested was quite unheard-of, but faltered under her candid, trustful look of enquiry, and muttered: 'Oh, the devil!'

'The worst of it is that she's such a dear little soul – really, an angelic creature, Charlie! – that it makes it hellish hard to tell her the brutal truth,' he told Eeles later. 'Dash it, there she sits, not a bit shy, and with no more knowledge of what's ahead of her than a baby!'

'Well, why couldn't you tell her?' demanded Eeles irritably. 'That's what you went to do, isn't it?'

'I did try. But she's got a way of looking at one that makes it impossible for a man to go on. She says she shall stay beside Harry.'

'Then poor Harry's lost!' said Eeles. 'He, who used to be the example of a duty-officer! Damn it, he must listen to reason!'

'Well, he won't. He's quite mad, and is gone off to find a decent woman to be the girl's servant.'

'Barnard must speak to him, then!'

'No use. By what Kincaid tells me, the girl's family is well-known to his lordship. Lord Fitzroy stayed with them after Talavera. Harry means to lay the whole story before Lord Wellington.'

'Good God, if he does, he'll ruin himself with Wellington!'

'So I warned him, but he will have it that his lordship has only to see his precious Juana to be won over. And when you come to think of it,' Molloy added, reflecting on his lordship's predilection for the fair sex, 'he's probably right.'

2

His lordship, happily for Brigade-Major Smith, was in high good-humour. He remembered the family of Los Dolores de León perfectly, and although he privately thought the careworn woman before him shockingly aged, he was delighted to meet an old acquaintance again. As for Juana, there was never any need to doubt that she would captivate his lordship. He said he had known her when she was a child (it was not quite three years since his lordship's stay at Badajos, but possibly Juana had grown to womanhood since then, thought Colonel De Burgh, his lordship's interested A.D.C.); he did not suppose that she remembered him, but he claimed the privilege of a very old friend, for all that, and kissed her cheek, and called her his Juanita.

Nothing could have passed off more smoothly. The victor of Badajos was not the Wellington whose blistering tongue caused quite senior officers to come away from an interview with him chalk-white and stuttering, and with knees trembling so much that they could scarcely walk. The Wellington who stood exchanging reminiscences with Juana's sister was a cheerful, rather loud-voiced gentleman, very plainly but neatly dressed in a blue coat, and biscuit-coloured pantaloons; a gentleman whose frequent laugh showed him to be in excellent spirits, and who was no more unapproachable now that he was a peer than he had been when he was merely Sir Arthur Wellesley. A most unaffected creature, Viscount Wellington of Talavera (but they would make him an Earl after his brilliant successes at Ciudad Rodrigo and Badajos); none of the airs of your consciously great man about him. He could be a little stiff sometimes, to be sure; and he had a way of looking down his high-boned nose which made strong men shake in their shoes; but if nothing had occurred to make him irritable he was excellent company: very easy and natural, no airs and graces at all, in fact; and hugely enjoying a good joke.

Brigade-Major Smith's lightning courtship made him laugh. If he disapproved of a promising young officer's tying himself up in matrimony, he did not say so. The baggage-train of the army was already clogged and hampered by wives and camp-followers; it is possible that his lordship, a realist, thought that one more would make little difference to an already existing nuisance. He said that Smith was a damned lucky young fellow; and at the end of twenty minutes' bantering conversation with Juana, announced that he would give the bride away himself. It was evident that he had taken a great fancy to the sparkling little creature: quite fatherly, of course, or perhaps avuncular. A shocking flirt, his lordship, but not the man to poach on a junior officer's preserves.

He seemed genuinely distressed to hear of the sister's predicament, but the elder's condemnation of the sack of Badajos merely drew from him a cool: 'War is always a terrible business, señora. The town ought not to have held out against us once the breaches were practicable.' He turned to Juana, adding in a softer voice: 'But Smith will take care of you, my dear. Report him to me if he doesn't!'

He quite saw the need for Smith to marry Juana. 'One of the best families,' he told him. 'Fallen on hard times, have they? Ah – h'm! You'll have to get a priest. Probably devilish strict.'

But Harry had already arranged that. The priest attached to the 88th Connaught Rangers had been engaged to perform the ceremony. Harry and Juana were going to have a drumhead wedding.

'Very well,' said his lordship. 'But you'd better get it done quickly. We shall break up from camp in a day or two.'

It was done two days later, in spite of the protests of Harry's friends. Everyone of them took the gloomiest view of his future. They said he was a fool, before they had been presented to Juana; and after that, they said that from now on he would be sure to neglect his duty.

'You're wrong, you're entirely wrong!' Harry answered, very bright-eyed these days, walking as though on springs. 'I'll stick to my duty. Why, how the devil can I support a wife if I don't get preferment? You'll see!'

But he was careful to explain it all to Juana. Sitting with his arm round her waist on the eve of their wedding-day, he told her what his duties were, how they would keep him often from her side, yet how impossible it would be for him to shirk the least part of them.

She flamed suddenly, chest swelling, eyes flashing. 'Do you think that I would *permit* you to neglect your duty?' she demanded. 'You are abominable! a villain! *I* am a de León!'

'Oho!' said Harry, amused by this glimpse of his love's fiery temper. 'Little *guerrera*!'

'Oh!' To be called a virago made her speechless. She would have boxed his ears had he not caught her hand, and held it. 'It is *not* true!'

'No, no! *Una niña buena!*' he assured her, laughing at her.

'*No!* I am not any longer a child, and you shall not mock at me. And I have *not* got a very bad temper. Not at all. *Absolutamente no!* I am – I am – '

'*Dulce como la miel,*' he suggested.

She regarded him suspiciously, saw the betraying quiver of a muscle at the corner of his mouth, and burst into a little crow of laughter. 'Yes! Yes! *Sweeter* than honey when people are polite to me!'

He jerked her roughly into his arms, crushing the breath out of her. '*Enamorada! amanta!*' he said huskily, covering her face with kisses.

She whispered: 'Love me! Love me always!'

'*Mientras viva!* As long as life!' he answered.

She nestled against his breast. 'And I too, Enrique. *Con toda mi alma, bien amado!*'

Seeing him swept off his feet by this tempestuous passion, Harry's friends accepted defeat, yet accounted him lost. There was very little for even the keenest duty-officer to do while the British troops continued to ravage Badajos, so that Harry's vow not to neglect the least part of his work could not at once be put to the test. The inward glow in his narrowed eyes, a certain tautness of muscle, that consuming look of hunger he had, did not promise well for the brigade, thought his anxious friends. But they attended his wedding, putting good faces on the disaster; and even poor Johnston, that superb Rifleman, lying in his tent with a shattered arm, roused himself from his agony to send Harry a message of good luck.

There were tragic gaps in the ranks of Harry's friends, but still they mustered a good many, gathered about the upturned drum in the camp of the Connaught Rangers, those brave, drunken blackguards of old Picton's. Overhead, a wind-tossed sky showed patches of blue between billows of white cloud. A strong sunlight beat down upon the deserted tents; the wind fluttered the priest's stole, and the mantilla cast over Juana's head. There was an unaccustomed silence in the camp, but from the walled town faint shots sounded from time to time, and the subdued murmur of tumult, hushed by distance. The troops inside Badajos were shooting at the pigeons that wheeled and circled round the Cathedral tower; the muted noise of an army let loose to enjoy itself made Juana's sister shiver, and glance fearfully across the Rivillas stream to the bastioned walls.

But, after all, there were two ways of looking at the sack of Badajos. 'Well!' said Paddy Aisy, brewing a strong potion of spiced wine in one of the camp-kettles, 'now id's all past and gone, and wasn't it the divil's own dthroll business, the taking that same place; and wasn't Long-Nose a quare lad to shtrive to get into it, seeing how it was definded? But what else could he do, afther all? Didn't he recave ordhers to do it; and didn't he say to us all, "Boys," says he, "id's myself that's sorry to throuble yees upon this dirty arrand; but we must do it, for all that; and if yees can get into it, by hook or by crook, be the powers, id'll be the making of yees all – and of me too!" and didn't he spake the thruth? "Sure," says he, "did I ever tell yees a lie, or spake a word to yees that wasn't as thrue as the Gospil? and if yees folly my directions, there's nothing can bate yees?" And sure,' added Paddy, refreshing himself from the contents of his kettle, 'afther we got in, was he like the rest, sthriving to put us out before we divarted ourselves? Not he, faith! It was he that spoke to the boys dacently. "Well, boys," says he, when he met myself and a few more aising a house of a thrifle, "Well, boys," says he (for he knew the button), "God bless the work! id's myself that's proud to think how complately yees tuk the concate out of the Frinch 88th, in the Castel last night!"'

Not very like his lordship's laconic style, perhaps; yet certainly his lordship was turning a blind eye and a deaf ear to the atrocities being committed within the walls of the town. The only thing that had made his lordship angry was being nearly shot down by a *feu-de-joie*, fired enthusiastically in his honour by a mob of drunken privates, when he rode through Badajos. Paddy Aisy's sentiments were very much his lordship's own, however crudely expressed. After the sack had lasted for eighteen hours, his lordship had issued a cool General Order. '*It is now full time that the plunder of Badajos should cease,*' he wrote, accepting war as it was, no affair of ancient chivalry, but a bloody, desperate business. '*An officer, and six steady non-commissioned officers will be sent from each regiment, British and Portuguese, of the 3rd, 4th, 5th, and Light Divisions into the town at 5.0 a.m. tomorrow morning, to bring away any men still straggling there.*'

But on the 8th April, when his lordship stood at the drumhead with Juana on his gallant arm, his orders had not been obeyed, for no officer, and no six non-commissioned officers, however steady, could hope to control the activities of any regiment at present rioting in the streets, or wenching in the white-washed houses of Badajos.

Yet his lordship seemed quite unperturbed, whispering his nonsense into Juana's ear. His lordship did not love his men, but without effort he understood them. Presently he would send a strong force into Badajos, and erect a gallows there, but not until his wild, heroic troops had glutted themselves with conquest. Had his lordship cared, after the bloody combat at Ciudad Rodrigo, when he had met the men of the 95th Rifles clad in every imaginable costume, excepting only the dress of a Rifleman? Not a bit! They had had their swords stuck full of hams, tongues, and loaves of bread; they were weighed down by their plunder; but when they had set up a cheer for his lordship, he had acknowledged it in his usual stiff way, and had asked the officer of the leading company, quite casually, what regiment it was? And when he was told that he beheld some of his crack troops, he had given a neigh of laughter, and had ridden on.

No, his lordship was not worrying over the conduct of troops who had cracked the hardest nut of all his Peninsular campaigns. Truth to tell, his lordship had very little sympathy to spare for his Spanish allies. He had suffered too much at their hands.

His lordship was all attention to Juana and her sister, all joviality towards Harry Smith, whom he knew to be one of his promising young officers. He had found time, in the midst of his worries, to arrange for the elder lady to be set on her way through the British lines. You would not have thought, seeing his lordship clapping Harry upon the back, cutting a jest, giving that laugh of his that was like the neighing of a horse, that Soult was on the march, that the Spanish garrison he had left at Ciudad Rodrigo was proving itself utterly incapable, that his own troops were out of hand, and most of them roaring drunk, that he must break camp, and march as soon as possible.

Such preoccupations, shelved for the moment in his lordship's mind, were yet present in Harry's brain, when he received Juana's little hand in his. No moment, surely, could have been more inauspicious for an officer in Lord Wellington's army to take a wife to himself. The month was April, the summer lay ahead: charming for a civilian, of course; but for a soldier summer meant campaigning. No cosy, happy-go-lucky winter quarters for Harry's child-wife, with balls, and amateur theatricals, or trips to Lisbon to break the monotony of a domestic existence. Lord Wellington kept his plans to himself, but everyone knew that in a very short time now he would launch his

summer campaign, driving a wedge into Spain, making Marshal Marmont, who had succeeded to Masséna's uneasy command and was reported to be a conceited fellow, look as silly
as every other French general who had come against him.

'Blur-an-ouns, boys, ain't he the man to stand by? Don't he
take the rough and the smooth with us, and ain't he afther kicking the French before him, just as we'd kick an old football?'

No one doubted that that was just how his lordship would
serve the French. He might have political opponents in England
who declared his victories to be exaggerated, too hardly won;
but the men who fought under his Generalship had a serene
faith in him which only defeat could shake. For his lordship had
never lost a battle. Roliça, Vimiero, Talavera, the Coa, Bussaco,
Sabugal, Fuentes de Oñoro, El Bodon: the long list of his Peninsular victories stretched over three years – difficult, hampered
years, when lack of money, the incompetence of some of his
Generals, scepticism at home, jealousies in Spain, machinations
in Portugal, all combined to build up obstacles that would have
driven a lesser man to suicide or insanity. They made his lordship querulous (awful, his temper was, some days), but they
never made him lose heart.

Harry, as much as his friends, had tried to warn Juana of what
lay before her. He spoke Spanish like a native, so she could have
no excuse for misunderstanding him. Jack Molloy thought that
words conveyed little to a girl whose life had been bounded by
convent walls; he thought she listened to Harry, yet, through her
inexperience, formed no mental picture of the hardships and
the alarms lying in wait for a lady travelling with Wellington's
army. She insisted that she would enjoy the life very much. No
qualms shook her; she knew no virginal shrinking; when she
and Harry were pronounced man and wife, she looked up at
him trustingly, her eyes quite unshadowed. Johnny Kincaid saw

that look, and his smile was more twisted than ever, but he was the first to step forward and wish the bride good luck.

3

No honeymoon for this bride; no driving away in a chaise-and-four, with the wedding-guests waving farewell, and corded trunks full of bride-clothes piled high on the roof. One small portmanteau contained the few necessaries which had been procured for Juana at Elvas, and one small tent was her first home. She and Harry walked to it by moonlight through the silent camp, when they rose from the wedding feast which the officers of Harry's regiment had given in their honour. Juana leaned lightly on Harry's arm, and felt it trembling. When they reached his tent, he would have trimmed the lamp which hung there, but Juana said no, that was her work. She stood on tiptoe to do it, absorbed in this first wifely duty. He watched her, wondering at her, amused by the little serious air she had. The lamplight filled the tent; Juana took off her cloak, and folded it, and laid it neatly away; and began to move about the constricted space, setting small disorders to rights, as though she had kept house all her life. She found a sock of Harry's, with a great hole worn in the heel. She lifted her eyes to Harry's face, laughed at him, and said: 'Oh, how bad! I think you need a wife very much indeed, mi Enrique! When we go to Elvas, I will buy needles and wool, and there shall be no more holes.'

To see her with his sock in her hand made his heart swell; he said unsteadily: 'Can you darn such holes as that, *alma mia*?'

'Of course! I can do everything!'

He smiled. 'Ride?'

'I can learn,' she replied with dignity. 'It will not be at all difficult, for already twice I have ridden upon a donkey.'

That made him laugh. The desire to take her in his arms was beginning to master him; he controlled it for a little while yet, afraid of frightening her, himself strangely moved and diffident. His voice was rather strained, unnaturally light. 'Bravo! And these great journeys?'

'Once I went to visit my grandmother; and once we went, all of us, to Olivença, to escape the siege of Badajos. Not this siege. And I rode on a donkey.'

'Now you must learn to ride a horse.'

'Naturally. A donkey is stupid and slow, besides being not at all English.'

'Do you wish to become English, *hija*?'

'Yes, for I am your wife. Do you not wish it, Enrique?'

'I love my Spanish wife.'

She shook her head, frowning, but pleased. 'What did they call me, your friends?'

'Mrs Harry Smith.'

She tried to repeat it, but stumbled over it, and gave a trill of laughter. 'I am too Spanish!'

He moved a pace towards her, and removing the sock from her hand, tossed it aside, and gathered both her hands in his, holding them against his chest. She looked up at him, not timidly, but suddenly submissive. Staring down into her eyes, he read a girl's hero-worship there. For the first time in his heedless life, he was afraid. His sinewy clasp on her hands tightened unconsciously; his face, in the lamplight, looked a little haggard.

She said wonderingly: 'How strongly your heart beats!'

'Yes. It beats for you.'

She drew his hands away from his chest to lay them on her own slight breast. 'And mine for you,' she said simply.

He felt the flutter of her heart under his palms; he put his arms round her, but gently, and held her so, his cheek against her hair.

'What are you thinking of, mi Enrique?'

'Praying to God you may not regret this!'

'Why?'

'I am – I am a frippery, careless fellow, not worthy of you!' he said, as though the words were wrung from him. 'I'm selfish, and bad-tempered – '

'Ah, ah!' A gurgle of laughter escaped her. 'I, too, *amigo!*'

'No, listen, *mi queridissima muger!* I swear I will try to be worthy of you, but they'll tell you – Stewart, Molloy, Beckwith, Charlie Eeles, all my dearest friends! – that I'm thoughtless, conceited, not fit to be your husband, and O God, it's true, and I know it!

'*Mi esposo!*'

'Yes! And what a husband!' he said. 'Forgive me, forgive me! I should not have done it!'

'But how is this? Do you not love me?'

'*Con toda mi alma!* With all my soul!'

'It is enough! Think! I am only a silly girl: I know nothing, merely that I love you. I have all to learn: my sister told me I should make you a sad wife. Mi Enrique, I too will try.'

He thrust her away from him, holding her so, at arm's length, while his eyes stabbed hers. 'No regrets? You're not afraid? Even though your sister has gone, and you are left amongst a foreign people, to a life that's hard, and bitter for a woman?'

'But this is folly!' she said. 'How should I be afraid? Will you not take care of me, *mi esposo?*'

'Till death!' he said in a shaking voice, and at last released that iron hold he had kept over himself, and seized her in a cruel embrace, crushing her mouth under his.

Her body yielded adorably; one arm was pinned to his side, but the other she flung up round his neck, to hold him closer.

He lifted her, and strode forward with her, checking under the lamp she had trimmed, and putting up a hand to turn it down. The little flame flickered blue, and went out.

4

Harry had got a woman belonging to a man in the 52nd regiment to wait upon his bride. She was a rough, stalwart creature, but decent. If she knew little of an abigail's work, she knew well how to guard a girl from the crudities of camp life. When Harry's friends saw big Jenny Bates, standing belligerently at the entrance to his tent, they laughed, and asked him whether his soul were still his own. But Jenny, a gorgon to any interloper, knew her place, and seemed to respect the thin flame-like creature who possessed her mistress. She was gruff, and dour, and no man could greatly impress her. If Harry turned his tent upside-down in a storm of impatience, all for the sake of a handkerchief, which would finally be discovered in his own pocket, Jenny would stand over him with arms akimbo, a grim smile on her lips, ready to set things to rights when he should have done. If he cursed her, she took it in indulgent silence; if he praised her, she would very likely snort. But if he gave her an order for Juana's well-being, she would obey it to the letter. Her knowledge of Spanish was elementary, yet she always seemed to understand her mistress. She watched over Juana, rather like a sour-tempered yet faithful mastiff. In her spare moments she pursued a never-ending feud with West, Harry's groom, who was as devoted to Harry as she was to Harry's wife. Joe Kitchen, his bâtman, she despised. He was a creature of no account, easily bullied. She did not hold with Harry's greyhounds, but tolerated them, not because they were the pride of Harry's heart, but because Juana loved and fondled them.

A fine establishment, young Harry Smith's: just the thing, mocked his friends, for an officer employed on active service! It consisted of a wife, her maid, a groom, a bâtman, a stud of horses, a string of five greyhounds, a Portuguese boy in charge of a cavalcade of goats, and a sprinkling of villainous-looking persons whom Harry always managed to collect, wherever he went, to act as guides through a strange country. Did any officer desire to find the way to some inaccessible village? Ask Harry Smith for one of his cut-throat guides!

Harry, the very morning after his marriage, paraded his stud, and finally chose from it a big Portuguese horse of sluggish disposition to be his wife's first mount. Captain Ross's Chestnut Troop, of the Royal Horse Artillery, was attached to the Light division, and Captain Parker, temporarily in command, owing to Ross's having been wounded during the siege, was beset by Harry, quite early, with an urgent demand that someone, anyone, should immediately convert one of his saddles into a lady's saddle. Harry had the saddle over his arm, and Parker, though he might groan, knew him too well to expostulate. By nightfall Juana had a passable saddle, and next morning was taking her first lesson. It was her intrepidity, perched upon the back of Harry's great brute of a horse, that won English West's heart. 'She's a rare one, the missus!' he said, chuckling over her gritted-teeth endeavours to master this difficult art of riding.

Juana cared nothing for the grins of the soldiers who watched her, nothing for her aching limbs, or bruises. All she thought of was to be rid of the obnoxious leading-rein, which Harry insisted on. He had to be very firm with her, so firm, in fact, that they found themselves, almost before they knew it, right in the middle of their first quarrel. Both being hot-tempered, the quarrel rose quickly to an alarming pitch.

'*Espadachín! Tirano odioso!*' Juana spat at Harry, transformed from a loving, eager child into a raging fury.

'*Estupida!*' Harry tossed back at her. 'Why, you obstinate little devil, if ever I saw such a shrew!'

A torrent of swift Spanish invective drowned his words. He laughed, and Juana, wrenching at the riding-switch he had given her, struck at him. Harry caught the switch, twisted it out of her hold, and grasped her by the shoulders, and shook her till she caught her breath on an angry sob.

'Now, listen, you!' Harry said, in the voice his men knew well. 'You will do as I bid you! Is it understood?'

'No!'

'Then you'll ride on a pack-mule, with the baggage,' said Harry coolly, releasing her. 'I'll procure one.'

'You dare not!'

'Wait and see!' said Harry, over his shoulder.

Tears sprang to her eyes; Harry whistled carelessly between his teeth, a snatch of one of the songs of the moment. Juana stamped her foot. '*Insensato!* I hate you!'

'It is seen!' said Harry, flinging up his hand to show the weal her switch had raised across his palm.

There was an awful silence. 'I did not do that!' Juana said chokingly. 'No! No!'

'*Sí!*'

She flushed scarlet; the tears chased one another down her cheeks; she turned away, hanging her head. 'I am sorry! *Indeed*, I am sorry!'

Two strides brought Harry to her side. 'It's nothing, *hija*, nothing at all! I was only teasing you!'

She nursed his hand against her wet cheek. 'I am horrible and wicked! I am ashamed! Yet I do not wish to have my bridle held. *Please*, Enrique?'

'No, you little varmint, no!' Harry said, pinching her nose. 'Not till you can ride well enough to satisfy me.'

'When we go on the march?'

'I promise nothing.'

'*Ay de mí!*' sighed Juana, temporarily accepting defeat.

Harry would not let her stir beyond his quarters without himself or West's being in attendance on her. Happily, her strict upbringing led her to yield without protest to this decree. The camp, ever since their marriage-day, fairly seethed with activity. Country people from miles round drifted in to buy the plunder which the soldiers, lurching out of Badajos, brought with them for sale.

'Damme, the camp looks like a lousy fair-ground!' exploded Charlie Beckwith, glaring at a knot of bargainers vociferously besieging a gentleman in a French grenadier's coat, and a Rifleman's green-tufted shako, who was offering to the highest bidder a roll of cloth, and a picture in a gilt frame. A soldier, who looked as though the sack of Badajos had exhausted him more than the siege, stood owlishly at gaze. 'Get to your quarters, you drunken swine!' rasped Beckwith. 'I'll tell you what, Harry: you'll do well to keep that wife of yours under guard! I never saw the men in such a state!'

'Damn all sieges!' said Harry heartily. 'Juana's safe enough. Thank God, we're to shake the dust of this hellish place off our feet at once!'

But before he could collect all his men from the ravaged city, Lord Wellington was forced to march a regiment of Portuguese into the market-place, and to erect three grim gallows there. He hanged one or two men, and the rest took timely warning, for they knew his lordship's temper, and slunk back to camp. There, the officers wrought with them to such purpose that on April 11th, five days after the storm of Badajos, the Light division was able to break camp, and march north to Campo Mayor.

They left behind them scores of smouldering bonfires, for every man, before he marched, was ordered to open up his kit-bag, and to disgorge any plunder he had hidden there. Every illicit possession that could be burnt was flung on to the fires, but most of the soldiers had contrived to sell what they had brought out of the town, and cherished in place of useless treasures a few precious coins.

It was a division sated with excesses that marched away from Badajos. Some men returned cheerfully to the normal routine of army life; some grumbled; and some were dangerously sulky. 'Give us but a week on the march, and the Sweeps will be themselves again!' said Jack Molloy, casting a fierce, affectionate glance over his ragged company.

5

They had a fortnight. They marched out of Spain into the deadly Alemtejo province of Portugal. They did not linger there. 'Once in Alemtejo, never out of it again,' ran the proverb. For six days, until they reached Castello Branco, they marched every day, always northward. They went by way of Campo Mayor, Arronches (where Juana, wrapped in Harry's boat-cloak, bivouacked in a wood, sleeping soundly on the ground by the embers of a camp-fire), and Portalegre, somewhat battered, but still one of the best of the Portuguese border towns. They crossed the Tagus by Villa Velha, a ruined village built on the side of a ravine, and reached Castello Branco on April 16th, there to halt for a day, to rest the men, and to give the supplies time to come up.

If Harry had doubted Juana's ability to keep up with the division, or to bear with equanimity the fatigue of long marches, and the discomfort of primitive lodgings, his doubts were very soon put to rest. She was a born campaigner. She rode her Portuguese horse in the rear of the column, with West, when Harry went ahead, and never a murmur of complaint was heard to pass her lips. Unused to riding, she was, during those first days, so stiff and cramped when she was lifted down from her saddle that sometimes her legs would not bear her, and she would have fallen had no arm been there to support her. But there was always an arm: if not Harry's, West's, or, very soon, the arm of any officer or private who was at hand. She had a genius for making friends, and this quality in her, coupled with the romantic circumstances of her marriage (the story of which was, in a very short time, known to everyone in the division), made her an interesting figure. The men's imaginations were fired before ever they saw her; when they became familiar with her friendly smile, and saw how her gallant, erect little figure never sagged in the saddle, they took her to their hearts, and were even pleased when she rode with the column, a thing not generally popular with infantry regiments.

Nothing could quench Juana's spirits. The weather was inclement, but if it rained she buttoned up the frieze cloak Harry had procured for her, and laughed at the mud which spattered her from head to foot. If her teeth chattered with cold, she clenched them, and twisted her bridle round her hand that it might not slip from her benumbed fingers. A lodging in a half-ruined cottage, flea-ridden and filthy, drew from her no ladylike shudders or fits of the vapours, but only a pungent and unflattering comparison of the Portuguese nation with the Spanish. She and Jenny Bates would immediately set to work to make their quarters habitable, and by the time Harry came to join her he would find a temporary home, no mere billet.

She had promised Harry that never would she grudge the hours he must spend away from her, and she kept her promise to the letter. 'Are you sure you have done all your duty?' she would ask him, holding herself aloof. Then he would open his arms to her, and she would run into them, with no reproaches for neglect on a hard march, and no complaints of weariness, or the discomfort of their quarters.

She began to give Harry scraps of information about the men in his brigade. 'George Green has eight children,' she would say. 'Five of them are boys, but he says they shall not join the army.' Or, 'Willie Dean gets boils in Alemtejo, and he has one now on his neck, which is why he holds his head so. But I have given him some ointment to put on it, and he says already it is better.'

How did she come by this knowledge? Harry never knew. Apparently she had no difficulty in understanding the men's rough Spanish, or West must have translated their odd confidences to her. Harry was afraid she might meet with insult, but soon realized that for all her friendliness she knew how to command respect. Ladies who travelled in the wake of the army (and there were many of them), attended by abigails, nurses, squalling infants, and a waggon-load of comforts, were the subjects of much lewd ribaldry; but Brigade-Major Smith's wife, sharing the roughest bivouac with her husband, laughing at hardships, greeting the most insignificant private as courteously as she greeted the Brigadier, was a lady quite out of the common run.

'And a lady she is, and don't nobody forget it!' said Man-killer Palmer, re-nicknamed, since Badajos, the Bombproof Man.

'Ho!' drawled Tom Crawley, sprawling by the camp-fire. 'Nobody hadn't better, considering the cut of our Brigade-Major's jib.'

'They got me to reckon with if they do,' said the Bombproof Man, rolling a belligerent eye around the group. '*She* don't hold her wipe to her nose because of the ungenteel smell of them horrid, rough soldiers! "Is your poor wife the better of her ague?" she says to me, as though I might be old Hooknose himself.'

'And since when will you have been owning a wife?' enquired a black-browed Scot politely.

'It's Pepita she was talking of, ye cattle-thieving fool! Would you have me soil the ears of the likes of her (and she no more than a baby!) with explaining the true state of affairs? If you don't know the way to treat a lady, there's others as does, and will learn ye!'

'Och, spare yersel' the trouble, ye miserable little Southron! I've naught against the bairn. She's bonny enough,' replied the Scot peaceably.

If the men regarded Juana with affectionate respect, the officers, from Barnard down to the latest joined Ensign, adored her. She was a sister to most of them, treating them as though she had known them all her life, yet with an instinctive discretion that gave evil tongues no food for slander. Though Juana, adopting the whole brigade, visited sick friends, darned holes in feckless lieutenants' socks, sewed on buttons, and had always some kind of a meal prepared for anyone who chanced to visit her quarters at dinner-time, never, from first to last, did the least whisper of scandal attach to her name.

'A treasure invaluable!' Harry boasted, and even those who had most earnestly warned him against marriage agreed with him. His friends, lamenting the change that must take place in their relations with him, early discovered that Mrs Harry Smith was not one of those brides who made it their business to wean their husbands from old friends. No need to do the dandy on Juana's account; no need to doubt one's welcome in Harry's quarters; no fear of boring Juana with the inevitable army-talk. You need not turn your baggage upside-down in the search for a respectable shirt if you were going to call on the Smiths nor need you wait for an invitation to dine with them, and then spend a dull evening chatting of insipidities. You could stroll off to their quarters just as you were, and you would very likely find Juana cooking a savoury stew, and be told to come in, and set the table for her. You could lounge as you pleased, and fill the room with cigar-smoke: Juana had no objection. Ten to one, she would have the coat off your back to mend a torn lining, or tighten a button, while you sat talking to Harry.

Major-General Vandeleur, rejoining the brigade on April 15th, and taking up his old command of it, was thunderstruck to discover that his efficient young dare-devil of a Brigade-Major had acquired a wife in his absence. He was inclined to be wrathful, but his gallant heart was not proof against the appeal of so youthful and pretty a creature. No one was in the least surprised to see the subjugation of old Vandeleur, for he was, said his men, the kindest man alive. He was very fatherly with Juana, and saw not the smallest reason why his marriage should interfere with Harry's continuing to share his General's quarters whenever there was a shortage of accommodation, or circumstances made it desirable for the General to have his Brigade-Major within call. A sociable old fellow, Vandeleur: not one of your stiff-necked, ceremonious Brigadiers. 'What have you got for us today, Juana?' he would say, as he took his seat at the dinner-table, Harry on one hand, his A.D.C. on the other, and Juana opposite to him. 'By Jove, you make us so comfortable we shall be spoilt, m'dear. Eh, Harry?'

By the time the Light division reached Ituera, and went into cantonments on the Agueda, Mrs Harry Smith was the divisional pet. 'Really remarkable!' murmured Harry's bête noire, Daniel Cadoux. 'What *did* she see in Smith?'

Kincaid knew that her unclouded instinct had recognized a kindred spirit in Harry. For himself, had she chosen him instead of his volatile friend, he would have adored and protected her, he thought, his life long. There would have been no hard marches for Mrs John Kincaid; no dirty quarters in ruined Portuguese villages; no bivouacs in streaming woods, with the howling of wolves for an uneasy lullaby. He would have guarded her from every danger or discomfort, would have sent her home to England rather than have let her face the hardships of campaigning. But Harry, not consciously wise, knew her better. Kincaid felt his heart ache for her weariness after long days in the saddle; Harry never weakened her by showing his sympathy. When he came to her with his duty done, he was her lover; but at all other times he was her commanding officer, treating her much as he treated his young brother, Tom, who had taken command of his company whilst he himself continued to be employed on the Staff.

6

If Harry showed no sympathy, there were others who did. If the ground were muddy, half a dozen officers would spring up, all anxious to emulate the chivalry of Sir Walter Raleigh; if Juana expressed a desire, it would be a point of honour for her friends to fulfil it. Harry was at first inclined to be jealous, and the Smiths' quarters were more than once enlivened by the reverberations of a royal quarrel. Juana's hot temper was swift to match Harry's; she could storm as well as he could, hurling insults as well as more tangible missiles at his head; but every quarrel ended soon or late in reluctant laughter, and no two hotheads could have been quicker to forgive.

By the time the Light division had reached the Agueda, Juana knew very nearly as much about the brigade as Harry. She did not appear to miss her own relations, or to regret, for the most fleeting minute, her precipitate marriage. If she had a preoccupation, it was with her progress in the art of horsemanship.

The leading-rein had been early dispensed with, but Harry, for all his carelessness, would not permit her to ride any other of his horses than the placid Portuguese animal he had originally allotted to her. Juana wanted to ride the little Spanish horse, Tiny, which Stewart had given him.

'When you can ride as well as you can dance and sing, you shall,' Harry promised her.

Dancing was very popular with the officers of Wellington's army. Whenever opportunity served, some regiment or other would be bound to arrange an impromptu ball, often held in a rickety barn with a defective roof, and a most uneven floor. Nothing pleased Brigade-Major Smith more than to see his Juana the undoubted belle of such functions. She danced beautifully, whether in the formal dances of her own country, or in the waltzes and the country-measures favoured by the English. There was never any dearth of females to grace the balls given by the English officers, but Mrs Harry Smith never lacked a partner. There might be half a dozen more lovely women present, but the crowd round Juana was always so thick that Harry had very often to fight his way through it to claim her hand.

'*My* dance, I think!' would say Harry, measuring his rivals with a gleam in his eye which meant business.

But there was no need for that jealous sparkle: Juana would melt into his arms, transparently happy to be wrested by him from other claimants.

'Do you love me, little devil?' Harry would say fiercely into her ear, as they circled round the hall.

The pressure of her hand answered him, the glow in her eyes. '*Mi esposo!*' Juana would breathe, on an adoring sigh.

'Don't you forget it!' said Harry, his arm like steel round her waist. 'These admirers of yours!'

'You do not like that I should dance with those others?'

His arm tightened; her fingers whitened under the grip of his. 'Never think it! Of course I do! I deserve to have my ears boxed!'

'But not here,' she said seriously.

Tom Smith thought that Harry ought to teach his wife to speak English, but Harry never did. Harry spoke Spanish like a native, and saw not the slightest need to plague Juana with lessons in his own tongue. A little English she picked up, some of it from the soldiers, which made Harry laugh, when she reproduced it; French she spoke fluently, so if she encountered anyone who could not converse in Spanish (which was seldom), she was quite ready to turn to French, and chatter away to the visitor as easily as you pleased.

'Well, but when you take her home to Whittlesey?' Tom said dubiously.

'That's a long way off,' replied Harry. 'Time enough!'

'Yes, but if she can't make my father and mother understand her, it will be doubly hard for her.'

'Doubly hard? What do you mean?' demanded Harry.

'Well, for them, too!' said Tom, persevering. 'I mean, she's a foreigner, and it is bound to seem odd to them – I mean, it *will* be difficult, Harry!'

'Nonsense!' Harry said impatiently. 'They will love her the instant they clap eyes on her!'

'I'm sure I hope they may,' said Tom, trying to picture the scene, and not quite succeeding. 'You have written to tell them, haven't you?'

'That comes well from you! Of course I have! Why, what a fellow you think me!'

'No, I don't, only you *are* a careless devil, and you can't deny it will come as rather a shock to the old people. Alice, too!'

'Oh, Alice be hanged!' said Harry, recklessly disposing of his favourite sister.

'You can *say* that, but you know very well it won't do.'

'I'm not afraid of Alice!' declared Harry.

'No, not while she's in England and you are in Portugal!' responded Tom, with a grin.

'Nonsense!' was all Harry would say.

Tom did not care to pursue the matter. He was only five years younger than Harry, but there was quite a considerable difference between Brother Harry, a mere member of a large family, and Captain Smith, Tom's superior officer.

So Juana was not troubled with English lessons, but concentrated her energies instead on the arts of horsemanship and housewifery. A provident little lady, Mrs Harry Smith: she hoarded the money Harry handed over to her; chaffered in the market (Harry said) like any Portuguese matron; darned socks which another woman would have pronounced beyond repair; and was very saving over such precious commodities as lamp oil and candles.

The army remained in cantonments for nearly six weeks, while supplies were collected, and clothing renewed, troops rested, and Lord Wellington's plans for the summer campaign completed.

Lord Wellington's original plan had been to strike at Soult, had Soult lingered in Estremadura. But Soult, harassed by the incalculable movements of the Spanish General Ballasteros about Cadiz, retired, after the fall of Badajos, into Andalusia, whither Lord Wellington was far too cautious to follow him. His lordship, furthermore, had received disquieting intelligence from Don Carlos de España, skirmishing to the north, that Ciudad Rodrigo, though perfectly tenable, had most unfortunately only sufficient provisions to withstand a twenty-day siege.

'This damned policy of *mañana*!' snapped his lordship, preparing to march northward, to force Marmont to retreat.

Marshal Marmont, commanding the French Army of Portugal, had received express orders from his Emperor not to attempt the relief of Badajos, and had been occupied for some weeks in raiding Beira Baixa, while General Brennier block-aded Ciudad Rodrigo.

His lordship left a Portuguese force in Badajos, entrusted the task of containing Drouet to General Sir Rowland Hill, and himself marched north with the main body of his army. Marmont, in Sabugal on April 8th, in Castello Branco on April 12th, executing a raid on Guarda two days later, retreated before his lordship, not because of the Allied army's advance, of which he had no intelligence, but because he could not find, in all that ravaged countryside, sufficient provender for even a third of his army. By the time he was aware of Wellington's proximity, he had reached Fuente Guinaldo, on the wrong side of the Agueda. Rains had swollen the river, and held the Marshal at Fuente Guinaldo until the 21st April. But by the 23rd April he had got his army across, not without difficulty, by the fords near Ciudad Rodrigo, and had begun to retreat upon Salamanca.

So his lordship abandoned the pursuit for the time being; his army went into its winter cantonments; and Juana Smith learned to waltz.

7

Early in May, Major-General Baron Charles Alten, of the King's German Legion, was appointed to the command of the Light division. He was forty-eight years old, a hard-bitten warrior with a dark hatchet-face, stern, bright eyes, and a strong German accent. Rather an odd choice of General for *The* Division? Not at all: no Englishman had anything but the most profound respect for the King's German Legion. As for Baron Alten, he was just the kind of leader the Light Bobs liked: a General who knew his work; never, even under the most trying circumstances, lost an atom of his cool presence of mind; was calm in action; and did not irritate those under his command with unnecessary orders, or the teasing habits of many an English General. It was by no means an easy task to command the Light division to the Light division's satisfaction; it was a very hard task indeed to fill the place of General Craufurd.

'The fellow who commands us will have to be a damned good fellow,' said Charlie Beckwith. 'None of your old women, thank you!'

'And no marches and counter-marches for God alone knows what reason!'

'And no damned reviews and inspections!'

'Must understand outpost duty!'

'Mustn't be one of these cats on hot bricks who won't go into action unless they're pushed!'

'Take heart!' said Harry Smith, entering in the middle of this discussion. 'The news is out. It's old Alten.'

'Alten?' There was a pause. 'Well, I don't know,' said Eeles cautiously. 'They say he's a good fellow. Won't worry us, will he?'

'Devil a bit!' said Kincaid. 'He's a gentleman, is old Alten. If we can't have dear Barnard, I'd as soon have the Baron as any other I can call to mind. Except Erskine, of course,' he added, dulcetly.

'Oh, my God! Sabugal!' groaned Beckwith.

'Well, nothing like *that* will happen under Alten,' said Harry, 'even if he isn't a Craufurd.'

But it was not everyone who desired Alten to be a Craufurd. Craufurd had made the Light division the superb fighting unit that it was, but he had been no easy man to serve under. A less irascible General, thought some of his officers, would be a relief.

General Alten was neither irascible nor fussy. He noticed as little as Lord Wellington himself irregularities of dress, and made not the slightest attempt to correct the slouch which the Light Bobs found so much less tiring than a correct military carriage. They were not at all the sort of troops a general would wish to review in Hyde Park, but old Alten did not care a jot for that. They did everything in the easiest way possible; though they might not march smartly, they could march far; and though their uniforms might be patched with strange colours, and their shakos shapeless through being exposed to much rain, their pieces were always in perfect order, with never a speck of rust in the well-oiled barrels.

'H'm! They look remarkably well, and in good fighting order,' said Wellington, when he reviewed them near El Bodon, late in May.

'I dink so, my lord,' replied Alten, observing his motley division with calm satisfaction.

Three

⌁

SALAMANCA

1

IT WAS JUNE BEFORE THE REGIMENT LEFT ITS CANTONMENTS. THE pits and the wheel-ruts in the roads, which had been full of slime, with films of brown ice crackling into splinters under the army's patched boots, were by this time baked hard by the sun and wind. Summer-marching could be quite as uncomfortable as winter-marching. You could wrench your ankle horribly in those deep ruts, and although no bitter wind-driven sleet came to make your very bones shudder, a blistering sun beat down, excoriating your skin, making the veins in your throat swell until you felt that they must surely burst the tight high collar hooked round your neck. Stained, faded uniforms were darker-stained by sweat; packs dragged from aching shoulders; and Brown Bess became an intolerable burden, her long barrel oven-hot to the touch. But the country north of Ciudad Rodrigo, through which the army marched on its way to Salamanca, brought a faint, not unpleasant nostalgia to many Englishmen in the long dusty columns. If you could shut out from your senses the sight and the rank scent of the gum-cistus, you might fancy yourself in Wiltshire, by Salisbury. 'Though you wouldn't be choked by this filthy dust on Salisbury Plain,' said Harry, wiping his smarting, red-rimmed eyes.

Harry was looking ill, but his complaint was not the prevalent fever. Nothing so romantic! Brigade-Major Smith, riding
close-lipped with his column, was suffering from boils. He had
one on the inside of his knee which made riding an agony, and
shortened his temper. It was a damned sight worse than any
fever, but too prosaic to arouse sympathy, except in one tender
breast. Harry, like his friends, made game of his boils, but the little creature he had married anointed his legs with strange
unguents, brewed awful potions for him to swallow, and
watched him anxiously with big, questioning eyes. A Spaniard,
none of the ills which Englishmen suffered in her country
attacked Juana. When the hot weather crept upon them, her skin
darkened to a golden tan, but never showed the raw red patches
that made life a minor hell for many an Englishman. She rode
through the scorch of the midday sun, her eyes, under the shade
of her hat, narrowed against the glare certainly, but bright and
clear. None of your fine ladies, Juana, reclining against the
squabs of a travelling-carriage, fan in one hand, hartshorn in the
other. Just as she never pressed a scented handkerchief to her
nose to shut out the reek of dirty humanity, so she never denied
the comfort of her body to Harry, though he came to her
grimed with dust: as rank, he said, as any private. Her slight
breasts were the pillow for his head after long marches. 'Are you
tired?' he would whisper, rousing her from the sleep of exhaustion. 'No, not tired, mi Enrique,' she would reply, all her body
responsive to the touch of his thin, nervous hands.

Indeed, although her limbs sometimes ached with fatigue, in
these first months of marriage her spirit was never tired. All the
routine of an army on the march, wearisome with the monotony of accustomed toil to the men about her, was astonishingly
new to Juana. To a convent-bred girl, there was romance in the
sight of the long, plodding columns; excitement in the clatter

and jingle of a squadron of light cavalry as it went by at the trot; and warm interest in the interminable baggage-train, cluttered up with camp-followers, spring-carts, waggons overloaded with stores and ammunition, and very often foundering in deep ditches, or losing wheels over the abominable surface of the roads. English eyes might find the string of gaily caparisoned mules in charge of native muleteers in velvet breeches and bright, flaring sashes more interesting, and think the appearance on the road of a company of guerrilleros worthy of noting down in a diary; but these had little power to hold Juana's attention. A scarlet jacket with its buttons tarnished almost black; a shako, beaten out of shape by successive rain-storms; the swirl and flurry of a silver-laced Hussar's pelisse; the black-japanned helmet of an artilleryman; the piled arms at alarm-posts; even the ordered spread of little Portuguese tents in camp: these were the humdrum sights which delighted her. 'A little world that moves,' she said, struggling for words to express the thought in her mind.

Harry smiled, but with a crease between his brows. 'Commissariat's late,' he murmured. 'As usual!'

'There are always the goats,' she suggested helpfully.

There were indeed the goats: you could smell them half a mile away, and some strayed kid was for ever getting entangled with guy-ropes, or scrambling up from the ground under your horse's nose. Everyone collected goats, the more the better, since, ten to one, goat's was the only milk you would be able to get in a land ravaged by the French. A swarm of little Portuguese boys, as noisy and as quarrelsome as monkeys, tended the animals. They drove them along the dusty roads in the rear of the army, little squabbling savages, half-naked under the sun.

It was not until the 16th June, when the army was within five miles of Salamanca, that any sign was seen of the enemy's presence. Mounting the low hills near the city, the advance guard encountered a small force of scouting Frenchmen, and drove them back after a slight skirmish.

They learned that Marmont had withdrawn from Salamanca, leaving garrisons in the three forts; and on the 17th June they passed the Tormes by way of deep fords.

Watching the infantry struggle across, up to their shoulders in the water, Juana looked a little doubtful. Someone slipped and disappeared from view. He was hauled up again, and reached the farther bank safely, but it was not a very comforting sight. A little sick feeling gripped the pit of Juana's stomach; she had thought the heat intense, but discovered suddenly that she was rather cold. She was standing by her horse, awaiting Harry's pleasure. He had ridden off somewhere, she didn't know where, and she was left with only West to look after her.

Kincaid came up to her, leading his mare. 'Juana!'

She turned, and as she looked up at him he saw how pale she was under the shade of her hat. The would-be jauntiness of her smile hurt him; he took her hand, saying softly: 'Don't be afraid! It is quite safe.'

'There ought to be a bridge,' said Juana in a scolding voice. 'My habit will be quite spoiled!'

'Let me carry you across,' he said. 'The mare will take us both easily.'

Harry came riding up: 'Hallo, Johnny! Up with you, Juana! I'm ready to take you over.'

Frowning a little, Kincaid said under his breath: 'Take her up before you, man!'

Harry's keen, quick eyes flashed a searching look at his wife's face. 'Nonsense!' he said. 'Mount, *alma mia*! I must get across.'

His tone whipped up her courage. She nodded to Kincaid to give her a leg-up. Perched high on the back of the big

Portuguese horse, she looked Harry in the eye. 'I am ready, and, in fact, quite tired of waiting for you, but I think it is right that you should know that I cannot swim.'

'Swim! Who's going to swim?' said Harry, removing the curb-rein from her grasp, and taking it in his own hand. 'Sit tight, now, my little love, and be a brave girl!'

'I see nothing to be afraid of,' she responded haughtily.

'Then don't shut your eyes. You must learn to ford rivers without me to lead you. I may not always be at hand.'

'I should be happy to learn, but I do not know how I may when you take my bridle away, without even asking me if I desire you to lead me, which, I assure you, I do not. *Absolutamente no!*'

'*Tirano!*' supplied Harry, forcing her reluctant mount into the river.

'*Espadachin!*' snapped Juana.

Kincaid, following on their heels, caught the echoes of a lively interchange of personalities. The river was crossed without any other mishap than the soaking of the skirts of Juana's habit. Upon the opposite bank, she retrieved her rein from Harry, informing him that she desired him never again to lead her across a ford. 'For you do it very badly, let me tell you; and by myself I should do very much better. Moreover, if you think that I am afraid of going through rivers, you are quite mistaken, and a great fool – *insensato!* – for I am not afraid of anything. But *nothing!*'

Harry gripped her hand for an instant. 'My sweet, I love you! Did you know? I'm off now. Don't sit about in that wet skirt!'

2

Lord Wellington rode into Salamanca that day, Marshal Marmont having retired to Fuente el Sauco, on the Toro road.

Salamanca lost no time in hanging out flags and decorations; and, upon the appearance of the English General and his Staff, went mad with excitement. His lordship had quite a difficult journey through the wide streets, for what with flowers being flung at him, and making his indignant horse shy, and hysterical women all but dragging him out of the saddle in their enthusiasm, it looked at one time as though he never would succeed in pushing through to his headquarters. He took it all very well – he had a surprisingly happy way with foreigners – and reserved his acid comments for the ears of his Staff.

The French occupation of the three forts did not in the least interfere with the English in the town. The task of reducing them was given to Clinton's 6th division; his lordship made Salamanca his headquarters; and everyone who could contrive to snatch a few hours' leave sought recreation there. It was a lovely, golden city, with broad streets and wide squares, a gracious Cathedral, and some very fine colleges. The shops seemed particularly good to men who had known nothing better than the sutlers' booths for months past; and if only everyone's pay had not been in arrears, an orgy of spending would have been indulged in.

Women were plentiful. A number of men acquired temporary mistresses, and were to be seen strolling under the colonnades in the Plaza Mayor with dark-eyed beauties on their arms. Several of Harry's friends were thus fortunate, notably Kincaid, whose tall person had found favour with a brunette with very white teeth, and a pair of entrancing dimples. Juana said that she did not think his Dolores a ladylike person, but she did not in the least blame Kincaid for taking her. She had lived amongst soldiers for two months, and she already understood that women, next to the Commissariat, were most necessary to the army's comfort. Only Harry was not permitted to cast an eye in the direction of the ladies of Salamanca. For the life of him, he could not resist flirting with a pretty female. He explained to Juana that there was nothing in it. She threatened to kill him with his own sword, and had to be fended off with a camp-chair. When he caught her in his arms, she boxed his ears, not in the least the trusting child who adored him, but like the jealous little vixen he called her. Only when, all cajolery failing, he shrugged, and said: 'I hate shrews. I'm off to find better company,' did her rage fall from her, leaving her defenceless, gazing at him with mute lips, and imploring eyes. He could never withstand that look. However angry he might be, and she very often made him blazingly angry, he melted before it, and held open his arms to her. '*Hija, hija*, only teasing!'

Trembling in his close embrace, she said passionately: 'You love me! Say it! Swear it!'

'Oh, my sweet!' Harry said huskily. He kissed her again and again. 'Little devil! Little vixen!'

'Do I plague you, mi Enrique?'

'Yes, and yes! Dear plague!'

'I am ashamed. But you smiled at her. You did! I saw you. Did you think her pretty?'

'No,' lied Harry.

Her delightful gurgle of laughter broke from her. 'Oh, it is not true! For she was pretty! Prettier than I am. I will be good.'

She was entranced by Salamanca. She had never seen a larger town than Badajos, and spent hours gazing into shop windows. Her purchases were few, since Harry's pockets were lamentably to let. Once she said wistfully that she wished they had some money. It touched him on the raw, and because he wanted to buy things for her and could not, he was angry, and said in an unkind voice: 'What do you want money for?'

'You need new shirts,' she said, sighing.

His mouth quivered; she saw it, and directed an enquiring gaze up at him. 'Juana,' he said, and stopped short.

'But what is it, mi Enrique?'

'Nothing. I don't need new shirts. When we reach Madrid – '

'Madrid!' exclaimed Juana. 'Are we going to Madrid?'

'By Jupiter, we are! Only wait till we settle accounts with Marmont!'

'It does not seem to me as though there is going to be a battle at all,' said Juana.

This opinion was shared by others, for Lord Wellington, numerically superior to Marmont, seemed oddly loth to engage with him. While Clinton besieged the Salamanca forts, the rest of the army remained inactive on the heights of Christoval, five miles to the north of the city. Twice an engagement seemed to be certain; on each occasion it ended in nothing but a little skirmishing, although for two days Marmont held his army in an exposed position on the plain before the Allied position. Many outspoken gentlemen said that his lordship, in pursuing so much caution, was making a mistake for which he would pay dearly; and even his admirers wondered at his making no attempt to prevent Marmont's retreat to the Douro. Don Julian Sanchez's guerrilleros so infested the roads that nearly every French dispatch was intercepted; and everyone knew with what difficulties the Marshal was having to contend. Everyone knew, too, that for the first time in the Peninsula Wellington had more cavalry at his disposal than the enemy. But what very few men knew was how little Wellington could afford to run the risk of a defeat. Impervious to the feelings of his officers, his lordship adhered to the cautious path of his choosing.

'One of these fine days we shall be forced to fight,' said Jack Molloy. 'You mark my words!'

'Fight?' said Eeles. 'Where do you get these notions from? We're not here to fight, my boy!'

'If anyone mentions the word *manoeuvre*, I shall vomit,' said William Havelock, in a soft voice.

'Speaking for myself,' offered Cadoux, 'I'm quite happy. I should hate to get my new coat cut up in a horrid, messy battle.'

'Don't worry! You won't!' said Harry.

Cadoux's languid gaze drifted to his face; he smiled. 'Oh, do you think I shan't?' he asked. 'I wonder if you know? I should like to stay here for months. It suits me.'

'My dear fellow! Now don't play the fool!' begged George Simmons, intervening to prevent an explosion from Harry. 'Depend upon it, we shall be on the move soon enough.'

'Too soon,' murmured Cadoux. 'This insufferable heat, George! One will be bound to sweat. The army's no place for a gentleman. I can't think why I joined.'

'Nor anyone else,' said Harry, getting up abruptly. 'Coming, Jack?'

He walked away with his hand in Molloy's arm. Cadoux watched him go, smiling. George Simmons said: 'You should not, you know. It is very stupid. Besides, we ought to stick together, don't you think?'

'Oh, you Sweeps!' said young Havelock gently, a scarlet coat amongst green ones. 'You insufferable Sweeps!'

3

It was not until the 28th June that the Light division at last broke camp. The Salamanca forts had fallen on the previous day, after a protracted siege, and the same evening Marmont began to retreat towards the Douro.

'Didn't I say we should soon be on the march?' demanded

George Simmons, very hot and dusty, but jubilant. 'Now we'll show the Johnny Petits!'

He expressed the feelings of the whole army; but Lord Wellington had reason to be less sanguine. Only he knew how insecure was his position in Spain. Not all his victories had sufficed to silence powerful enemies at home. He had no illusions: a defeat would in all probability mean his recall. His successes at Ciudad Rodrigo and at Badajos were all very well in their way, but had been costly, and had had no effect upon the main French armies. He wanted a victory, a big victory, but he was not going to run any risks to win it. To make matters more difficult, General Picton, who had been slightly wounded at Badajos, had had to relinquish his command of the Fighting division, and was in hospital at Salamanca. A grim old dog, Picton: foul-mouthed as any trooper, but one of his lordship's best and most trusted Generals for all that. His lordship handed over the Fighting division to his brother-in-law, Ned Pakenham, perhaps the only man who could have taken the command of it to Picton's satisfaction. Graham would be the next General to leave his lordship: a more serious business, that, for Graham, no soldier by profession, could be trusted to manoeuvre on his own. He was suffering, however, from some sort of eye-trouble, and would have to go home.

These preoccupations, which made his lordship curter even than usual, did not weigh much with the rest of the army. Heat and thirst excluded other considerations from nearly every mind, for the plain that lay between Salamanca and the Douro was parched and treeless, so that the columns marched in clouds of reddish dust which got into men's throats, and under their eyelids, and sifted into their clothes to rasp against their sticky bodies. One or two unwise souls, feeling themselves unable to bear the weight of their shakos, which seemed to tighten about their heads like iron bands, discarded them, and suffered all the tortures of sunstroke in consequence. Hardened campaigners, knowing that the first drink out of a water-flask made the craving for water only more insistent, refrained from broaching their flasks for as long as possible; but young soldiers could scarcely be restrained from draining theirs within the first few hours of the march.

It was thought that the Guards suffered most on long, scorching marches, and the Light Bobs least. The Gentlemen's Sons, trained to a smartness of step and bearing that made them the admiration of all beholders, could never bring themselves to adopt the famous slouch which carried the Light Bobs unbeautifully over such incredible distances.

But even the Light Bobs found the march towards the Douro more than ordinarily wearing. There seemed to be no water to be had for mile upon sweltering mile. The heat-haze danced and wavered before eyeballs that felt red-hot between dust-inflamed lids. Occasionally a soldier would lurch out of the column, and sink down exhausted on the road; and once a man went suddenly mad, and began to scream abuse in a crackled, maniacal voice. They said it was the sight of a bleached skeleton which had turned his brain, but the bones were after all only horse bones, and a common enough sight in all conscience. It was more probably thirst: when they overpowered him, it was seen that his tongue was blackened and swollen.

Brigade-Major Smith, harassed by boils, very busy now that the army was on the march, was anxious for his Juana, but whenever he came riding down the length of the column in search of her, dreading to find her wilting under the merciless sun, he found her sitting erect in her saddle, as gay as you please, staunchly disclaiming any extraordinary fatigue. Was she tired? Was she thirsty? Would she ride on one of the spring-waggons in the rear? *Madre de Dios, de ninguna manera!* George Simmons had told her all about those spring-waggons. She thanked her Enrique, but she desired nothing, and ailed nothing. '*Nada me duele*,' she said always, when solicitous friends thought her pale, or flagging.

'By Jove, m'dear, you're the best soldier in the army!' said old Vandeleur, patting her shoulder. 'An example to us all, eh, Harry?'

It took the army five days to reach the Douro, where they found the French encamped upon the opposite bank. The Light division occupied the ground about Rueda, a blessed spot, abounding in wine-cellars which were huge caves hewn out of the rocks, so full of wine-casks that even the depredations of a thirsty army seemed to make little diminution in the store of liquor.

It was very pleasant at Rueda, with nothing to do but to watch the French across the river, to drink oneself into a stupor in the vaults, or to bathe in the Douro, exchanging good-humoured abuse with the enemy, similarly disporting themselves. 'Coming across, Johnny Petit?' would sing out a British private, wallowing in the cool water.

'When we choose, *sacré bauftake*!' the answer would flash back. 'You will run then, be sure!'

'Come across, and see what we'll give you!'

'In good time! Wait till we come to take back Salamanca!'

'You take back Salamanca? That's a good one!'

'But tell us, *sacrées pommes de terre*, why do you not come across to *us*?'

'We will when we've finished up the wine on this side!'

This retort served well enough to bring the interchange to an end, but it is doubtful whether any of the Englishmen cooling themselves in the river knew the real reason for their inactivity. 'Our orficers,' said a stout individual, inspecting a blister on his heel, 'are too bloody-well took up with dancing, that's why.' He

added, thoughtfully, a groundless libel on the morals of his commanders, which was an instant success with his audience.

The fact was that Lord Wellington, confronting the enemy
across the Douro, considered the locality and the season quite
unsuitable for an offensive action. The French held the bridge at
Tordesillas, and the various fords were still too deep to permit
of his crossing by them. If the Spanish Army of Galicia could
bring the siege of Astorga to a close, and come up to threaten
Marmont's rear, the consequent diversion would place him in a
more favourable position, but he had learned not to rely too
much upon his Spanish allies.

The Light and 4th divisions, forming the right wing of the
army before Rueda and La Seca, found nothing to complain of
during their fortnight's sojourn there. Rueda was a charming
little town, its female population much above the average, its
light, sharp, white wines most palatable. Dancing was certainly
the order of the day, and as only half of each division was
obliged to bivouac before the towns each night, as a precaution-
ary measure, there were always plenty of officers off duty to
partner the ladies of Rueda to impromptu balls.

4

Kincaid had fallen in love with the sexton's daughter. He said he
had seen her baking a loaf of bread in her father's house, and had
promptly lost his heart to her.

'But I do not find that she is beautiful,' objected Juana.

'But the loaf was excellent,' explained Kincaid.

She shook her head. 'You love too easily, I think. I do not forget that one in Salamanca.'

'But what is the use of a beauty in Salamanca when I am in
Rueda?' said Kincaid reasonably.

'True,' she replied. 'But a sexton's daughter! Shall you take her to the dance to-night?'

'Oh, surely! Do you go?'

'No, because Enrique will be on duty, visiting pickets. Enrique says that the French are repairing the bridge at Toro, and we shall soon move to our left.'

'Yes,' said Kincaid, yawning. 'They tell me the rest of the army's on the move already.' He glanced up as Harry came into the room. 'Hallo! What's the news?'

'Nothing much. We shall get our marching-orders soon, I suppose. Marmont means to cross the river, from the looks of it.'

'Why can't the fellow leave us in peace? What's he about? Trying to turn our left and break through to Salamanca? I wish him joy of it! I take it we shan't be disturbed for a while yet? How far off is Toro? Twenty miles? Twenty-five? I shall take Pepita to the dance to-night.'

The dance was held, but was destined to be interrupted by the sound of trumpets calling to arms. This martial noise brought the scraping of fiddles to an abrupt stop.

'Ten to one, it's a false alarm,' grumbled Eeles, reluctantly releasing his partner. 'That will make the third we've had. All the same, we shall have to go, my dear.'

'But don't you go!' said Kincaid, squeezing the sexton's daughter's waist. 'Make yourselves at home, and we'll be back presently!'

This light-hearted promise was never fulfilled. Upon assembling by torch and lantern-light at the alarm-posts, the officers discovered that Rueda and La Seca were to be evacuated immediately. The little town seethed with sudden activity, men flying to their billets to snatch together their belongings, and the companies steadily forming and marching off into the darkness.

Juana was in bed when the warning trumpets sounded. She had heard them before, and knew what they meant, so that by the time Jenny Bates came to thump on her door she was already dressed, and hurriedly packing her clothes and Harry's in their portmanteaux. She did not know where Harry was, but he had drummed such precise instructions into her head as to what she must do in such an eventuality as this that she did not waste West's time or patience by refusing to stir until Harry's return (which he had been half afraid of), but sent down a message to him that she would be ready to start within ten minutes. He had her horse, and a spare horse of Harry's, waiting in the cobbled street; and Harry's bâtman, Joe Kitchen, was ready to lead the mule which carried the baggage.

No one seemed to have the least idea of where they were going, but there were naturally plenty of pessimists who thought the whole business a hum, and in all probability due to the command's being temporarily in Stapleton Cotton's hands. If Old Hookey had not gone to watch the Frog-eaters at Toro, it would never have happened, said one disgruntled gentleman, who had his own reasons for resenting the sudden call to arms. It was just like Cotton, he added unfairly, to go off at a tangent in the middle of the night for God alone knew what reason.

West made Juana stay with the baggage-train, which was being covered by Anson's horse. At first she wondered how the columns could find their way through the darkness, but after a time her eyes grew accustomed to the gloom, and she announced buoyantly that night-marching was preferable to day-marching. Her anxiety on Harry's behalf was presently relieved by a brief sight of him. He came in search of her, greeting her with a quick-voiced: 'Juana? You're all right?'

'Yes, oh yes! And, *sobre todo*, you are safe, mi Enrique!' she answered joyfully.

'Of course I'm safe, *hija*! I can't stop, though. Keep at the head of the baggage-train. West will look after you. I must go. You know how it is, *alma mia*!'

'*Sí, sí! Adelante!* But where are we going, *amigo*?'

'Ten miles to our rear: to Castrejon. The French are over the river at Tordesillas.'

'But that is quite close!' cried Juana.

'Don't worry! We're safe enough.' He put his hand over hers for a moment, grasping it strongly, and with one more adjuration to her to keep up with the column, shot off again into the darkness.

She was perfectly satisfied. Had Lord Wellington himself appeared to inform her that the two divisions were in imminent danger of being cut off from the rest of the army, she would have paid very little heed: Harry had said that they were quite safe.

The truth was that Marshal Marmont had succeeded in foxing his English adversary. Having completed the repairs to the bridge at Toro, he had sent Bonnet's and Foy's divisions across the river. Wellington, from the outset jealous of his left wing, began to concentrate his army on the Toro road, only to discover that the wily Marshal had suddenly reversed his marching orders. Bonnet and Foy, re-crossing the Douro, formed, instead of the van, the rearguard, and the entire French force counter-marched on Tordesillas.

Cotton, whose last orders had been to halt the two divisions under his command at Castrejon, reached that village on the 17th June, and drew up his small force into position. The news brought in by the patrols was disquieting. The French were pouring over the Douro at Tordesillas, and by nightfall the bulk of Marmont's army had reached Nava Del Rey, a bare ten miles north of Castrejon.

Castrejon was situated on the Trabancos river, a small tributary of the Douro, in the middle of bare, rather down-like country.

The two divisions lay by their arms all night, by the smouldering camp-fires, with the distant croak of frogs, and the intermittent fidgeting of the picketed horses disturbing the night-silence.

A little after sunrise on the morning of the 18th June, a cannonade began. Cotton's outposts were driven in, and he at once formed his cavalry in front of the two infantry divisions, which were separated one from the other by a wide ravine. A hill, beyond the Trabancos, hid the French army from view, but parties of horsemen could be seen through the wreaths of the ground-fog which lay over the river-valley. Harry found time to send Juana to the rear, for the situation had begun to look a little dangerous, no word of support having as yet come from Lord Wellington. Cotton was cautiously advancing his cavalry into the fog, but although nothing could be seen by the waiting infantry, a sharp outburst of musketry-fire soon gave them to understand that Anson's horse had encountered more than cavalry in the valley. A regiment of foot passed through Castrejon at the double, moving up to support Anson, as the cannonade intensified.

The river-mist began to curl upwards, forming a kind of dome that was shot with iridescent colours by the rising sun. Through the heavier, smoke-laden vapour below, the figures of horsemen seemed to flit restlessly in mazy convolutions. The flashes of muskets flickered incessantly; and as the mist lifted higher the head of land beyond the stream became apparent, and was seen to be thickly covered with French troops.

'Queer sight,' remarked James Stewart, in his pleasant disinterested drawl. 'Really remarkable!' He glanced at Harry, who had paused for a moment beside him. 'I should hate to make a rash pronouncement, but it would appear that we are in a rather tight hole.'

'I wonder how long we can hold our ground?' said Harry.

He sounded worried. Stewart, remembering a younger Harry who would have revelled in such a situation as this, realized that when a Staff-officer, in addition to his other cares, had a young wife depending upon him, it was apt to take the edge off his natural enjoyment of tight corners. He said gently: 'I hope Juana isn't frightened?'

'Not she!' The harassed look vanished in a grin. 'She thinks it a huge adventure to be waiting with her horse ready saddled for a quick retreat.'

Stewart smiled. 'What a child it is! Is there any word come in yet from the Peer?'

'None that I've heard of. If we're cut off – ' Harry stopped, and gave a shrug. 'Well, I suppose we shall start retreating soon.'

'To tell you the truth, I wonder we didn't start an hour ago,' said Stewart. 'I suppose Cotton don't like to act without orders.'

Whatever the reason, Cotton seemed bent on holding his ground for as long as he was able. A cavalry General, his handling of the one brigade at his disposal was skilful enough to keep the French in temporary check; but by seven o'clock, the infantry, who had been standing to their arms since daybreak, were conscious of a restive desire to have Lord Wellington amongst them again.

5

Kincaid, who had been sent on picket the previous evening, and was still unrelieved, had found himself, at an early hour, in a position of some discomfort. When the cannonade began, a quantity of round-shot peppered the ground over which his picket was posted. He remarked coolly that the Frogs seemed to have chosen the picket as their pitching-place, and cast an experienced eye around him to discover the nearest cover. A broad ditch, about a hundred yards distant, offered the only obstacle to an enemy advance. He noted its position in case of a future need, and turned to find his Sergeant at his elbow. A splutter of dust, kicked up by a charge of shot falling quite close to them, freely bespattered them both. 'Don't seem to be firing blanks, do they, Sergeant?' said Kincaid.

The Sergeant grinned. 'No, sir. What will we do, sir?'

'Oh, just watch the plain!' Kincaid replied. 'Seems to be a little trouble going on behind that hill.'

The Sergeant, who thought, from the confused uproar, that there must be a good deal of trouble going on, grinned more broadly, but said: 'Yes, sir. As you say, sir!'

The picket remained in position, keeping a look-out over the plain. The rising ground to the left hid the operations of the cavalry from sight, but in a short while such a violent commotion arose from behind the hill that Kincaid lost no time in removing his picket to a position behind the ditch he had previously noted. He had barely executed this movement when (as he afterwards described it) Lord Wellington with his Staff, and a cloud of French and English dragoons and horse-artillery intermixed, came over the hill at full cry, over the very ground he had that instant quitted.

A picket of the 43rd regiment having formed on his right, Kincaid was forced, for fear of shooting them instead of the enemy, to remain inactive. He was so astonished, he said, by the spectacle of Lord Wellington and Marshal Beresford hacking their way through the mêlée with their drawn swords, that he doubted whether he could have collected his wits sufficiently to give the order to fire.

'And how they came there, I know no more than my old mare!' Kincaid told Harry, much later. 'Old Hookey, and Beresford, and the two guns, and all the beautiful Staff, took refuge behind my picket. Old Hookey didn't look more than half-pleased, I can tell you. But it was a pleasure to hear Alten swearing. I wish I understood German.'

'I don't wonder the Peer wasn't pleased!' said Harry. 'He was bringing up two cavalry brigades to reinforce us, and rode ahead of them to the left of our skirmishing line, where the 11th and 12th Light dragoons were supporting Ross's guns. Just as he arrived, a French squadron broke in from the flank, straight for the guns. The 12th couldn't stand against them, and began to retire. From what I heard, some fellows on Beresford's Staff tried to stop 'em, shouting out: "Threes about!" That's where the trouble started, because the 11th, who were coming up in support, heard it, and thought the order was meant for them. So they went about, and down came the French, right on top of all the headquarters Staff! Luckily the 11th soon saw that there must have been a mistake, and faced about, and drove the French off.'

'My God, to think I missed seeing all that!' said Kincaid, with heart-felt regret.

'Damn it, you can't have everything!' objected Eeles. 'You saw old Douro laying about him, which is more than we did!'

'All very well!' said Harry. 'But a pretty mess we should be in now if he had been killed!'

'I suppose you think we've had a nice sort of a day, with that long-nosed beggar hounding us on one of his cursed forced marches?' said Eeles, with awful sarcasm. 'I've got a blister on my heel the size of a crown.'

'The French are in a worse case than we are.'

'Well, isn't that a comfort!' said Eeles. 'I hope I die before morning, that's all.'

The two divisions had indeed passed a trying day. Lord Wellington, having brought reinforcements of cavalry to them in person, had immediately taken over from Cotton the direction of the retreat, and had lost no time in setting the divisions in motion. They had marched in two columns, with the Guarena river as their immediate, and Salamanca as their ultimate goal. Covered by cavalry, they retired in two columns, and had not covered any appreciable distance before they had sighted two French columns, marching in the same direction, for presumably the same goals. For eight miles, the rival forces paralleled each other, engaging for the entire distance in a desultory dog-fight, as wearing to men's nerves as any pitched battle. The undulating country lying between the Trabancos and the Guarena was rich with vast fields of ripening corn, intersected by dry water-courses. The corn was yellowing fast, and presented the appearance of a shimmering golden sea. A shot from one of the French guns set a field alight, and the fire spread with hungry rapidity. The roar and crackle of the flames, the cloud of heavy black smoke that rose to hang lazily on the air drew a bitter exclamation from a sweating Rifleman. 'Jesus! Ain't it hot enough without them bleeding Frogs lighting camp-fires?'

The 4th division, forming the column nearest to the French line of march, suffered most from the intermittent artillery-fire, and it was not long before the men, fretted by the casualties in their column, began to hope that the rival commanders would decide to call a halt to the march, and form battle-fronts. It was thought that the cavalry were having the best of it; and one Light division man, watching a slight skirmish, loudly expressed his desire to be exchanged into a cavalry regiment. He complained of blisters on his feet, but a prosaically-minded friend replied scornfully: 'Yus, and if you was on 'orseback you'd 'ave boils on your arse, so for Christ's sake shut your blurry bone-box!'

At the end of the long day's march, when the columns, reinforced since Torrecilla de la Orden by the 5th division, drew near to the Guarena river, the pace of both armies quickened. The firing almost ceased as the dog-weary troops strove to be the first to reach the river. The Light division began to gain on the French column, and even the candidate for a cavalry regiment forgot his grievances in a determination to gain the rising ground beyond the river before the enemy could occupy it. 'By Gob, we'll do it!' he said, rather breathless, but happy for the first time that day. 'Regular Talavera march, this 'ere!'

'Christ, I'm dry!' croaked a recruit, passing the tip of a swelling tongue between his cracked lips.

But although every man amongst them was parched with thirst, the Light division did not halt by the river, but drank as they marched through the shallow ford, scooping up the tepid, muddied water in their hands or their shakos. Some of the recruits were inclined to grumble at the inhumanity of officers who would not permit them even a few minutes' respite, but they got no sympathy from the veterans. 'You stop here swilling your guts, and you'll be put to bed with a shovel!' said a Rifleman grimly.

The truth of this pronouncement was demonstrated a little later, when the 5th division, reaching the stream, halted there. The French guns, hurried into position on the hills above, at once opened fire, providing the Johnny Raws, said Tom Crawley, watching the flurry and carnage in the river, with an excellent object lesson. 'That'll learn the Pioneers,' he remarked dispassionately. 'If you start in to take liberties with them Frogs, my lad, you'll find yourself in a peck of trouble, and don't you forget it!'

Lord Wellington was not allowed to occupy his ground quite without opposition, but after a somewhat costly attempt to dislodge him, Marmont called in his skirmishing parties, and allowed his exhausted troops, who had covered a distance of eighty miles in two days, to bivouac for the night.

'And if anyone can tell me what the devil all this manoeuvring has been about, I shall be grateful!' said Eeles.

'Marmont's too clever by half,' said Charlie Beckwith, who was feeding a camp-fire with bundles of stubble. 'He gained a day's march on us when he crossed the Douro, too, not to mention turning our whole position. He could have got to Salamanca, if he hadn't been so anxious to show us how prettily he can manoeuvre.'

'Damn his eyes!' said Eeles, tenderly inspecting his afflicted heel.

'Well, he's gained nothing by it but the devil of a lot of casualties,' said Beckwith.

'Yes, he has,' said Harry, grinning. 'He's gained George's canteen!'

Beckwith looked up. 'Oh no, has he really? Careless fellow, George! Always dropping your things about!'

'It's all very well for you to start funning,' said Simmons, receiving this baseless accusation with his usual good-humour. 'It's no joke for me, though, for I've lost my mule as well. A fine young mule, too. He got a kick from a stallion on the march, and my fellow had to cut him loose. Broken thigh-bone. The worst is, I had a variety of comforts packed up with my canteen, which I shan't easily be able to replace. It's a sad grievance, I can tell you.'

'Never mind, George, you shall have supper with us,' Harry said. 'We've got a chicken.'

Eeles, who had been smearing tallow on his heel, rolled over on to his elbow, and called out: 'Juana! Oh, Juana! Mrs Smith! *Queridissima amiga!* Will you invite me to supper with you?'

Juana came out of Harry's tent, and walked over to the fire. '*Qué fastidio!* No, because there will not be enough food.'

'Where did you manage to pick up a fowl, Juana?' Beckwith asked, folding his greatcoat to make a seat for her.

'Joe Kitchen stole it,' she replied.

Harry laughed, holding her in the crook of his arm. 'I'll swear you told him to!'

'Well, I thought we should need it,' she explained, leaning gratefully against his shoulder.

'Tired, *bija?*' he said.

'*Muy cansada*,' she admitted, sleepily smiling. 'When must we march again?'

'That's easily answered,' said Eeles. 'At dawn, just when you're dropping into your second sleep.'

'Señor Kincaid,' remarked Juana inconsequently, 'says that dawn is when one can see a gray horse a mile away.'

'Well, let's hope to God there isn't any cavalry in our front,' said Eeles.

6

When the dawn came, however, all was quiet in the French lines. The sky was overcast, and a hot wind blew steadily. Particles of dust seemed to penetrate even into the most tightly closed receptacles. Jack Molloy swore that there was some even in the egg his bâtman boiled for his breakfast.

In spite of the heat, the fatigue of the previous day, and the depressing effect of finding friends missing from the ranks, the spirits of the men were good. Not many of them understood the purpose of their gruelling march, but they could all see that they were facing the French, and placed in a strong position which they could defend all day, if need be.

'*They* won't attack us!' said an old hand. 'They're eating their breakfasts, that's what they're doing. Bacon, and eggs, and hunks of beef, what they plundered off the poor, blurry Spaniards. What we ought to 'ave 'ad, if we wasn't bleeding little gentlemen.'

'That's right,' agreed a disreputable individual, who was frying slices of pork on the end of his priming-rod. 'Cruel it is, the way them Johnny Petits plunder the country. All they left for us was one scrawny porker. Where's the Commissary?'

'Lorst, *as* usual!'

'Well, damme, boys, if he don't show his front, we must either find a potato-field, or 'ave a killing-day!' said a stout Rifleman cheerfully.

As the morning wore on, without any other sign of activity in the French lines than the movements of various reconnoitring parties, it became apparent that Marshal Marmont, having neatly turned Wellington's flank on the 16th July, and, during the two succeeding days, superbly manoeuvred the French army over eighty miles of sun-burnt country, had decided to give his stoical infantry a rest. The entire army remained stationary all day, and moved off in the cool of the evening, in a southerly direction.

'Oh, damn it! I believe they're as chary of coming to grips as we are!' said Young Varmint despairingly. 'All this watching and prowling reminds me of nothing so much as the start of a cat-fight!'

It really began to seem as though the caution of the opposing Generals would result in nothing but a stalemate, for the weary marches continued for two more days, in much the same fashion, the armies sometimes within half-musket shot of each other, sometimes out of sight, but never engaging in any more serious hostilities than artillery-fire, and some cavalry skirmishing. Once, when the rival columns were seen to be converging on the same village, a general engagement seemed to be inevitable, but Wellington, to the wrath of the major part of his army, refused battle by avoiding the village.

By the time the Allied army reached the Tormes, a number of sick and wounded men were missing from the ranks, and the baggage-train, shepherded by a Portuguese brigade of cavalry, had begun to straggle. Nothing had been seen of the French for some hours, but when the camp-fires were presently lit, it was observed that some of the French divisions were bivouacking within striking distance of the fords of Huerta.

Early on the following morning, Wellington withdrew his army to its old position on the heights of San Christoval, above the more northerly fords of Aldea Lengua, and Santa Marta.

'In fact,' Eeles said, 'we might as well have stayed here the whole time, and never have gone to Rueda at all. Then I shouldn't have had the worst blister in the army.'

As Lord Wellington seemed to have decided to allow Marshal Marmont to pass the Tormes unopposed, Charlie Eeles was able to nurse his heel all day. The Allied army remained in position on the heights until sundown, while the French troops slowly crossed the river by the fords of Huerta, marched up the valley on the farther side, and encamped at the edge of a forest barely six miles from Salamanca.

Juana seized the opportunity to wash and iron two of Harry's shirts. He found her propping her iron up on a stubble-fire, which she had ordered Joe Kitchen to build for her. She looked hot, with her dark ringlets clinging damply to her forehead, and beads of sweat on the bridge of her nose. Harry took the iron away from her, and gave it to Kitchen. 'No, my little love,' he said, leading her away. 'Not so!'

'But Kitchen does not iron at all well, *amigo*! I assure you —'

'And I assure you I won't have it. I gave you orders to rest, you little varmint!'

'Indeed, I am not tired! *De ningún modo!*'

'*Tanto mejor!*' He drew her into the shade of a tree, and sat down on the ground, pulling her down beside him. He was looking tired, finer-drawn than he had been at the start of the campaign, with the lines running from his nose to the corners of his mouth deeper-cut, giving his thin face a sterner expression.

Juana said: '*En efecto*, it is you who are tired, mi Enrique!'

'Very. It's these cursed boils.' He stretched himself out on the ground, with his head pillowed in her lap. 'Comfort your boy,' he murmured, his eyes smiling up at her under their weighted lids.

She let her fingers stray over his hair. They trembled a little; a rush of tenderness welled up in her. She stammered: 'Do you think I am a bad wife?'

'I don't know. I never had another.'

'I tease you with my bad temper!'

'*Sí!*' Harry's eyelids were drooping.

'I meant to be so good!' she said distressfully.

His eyes opened again. 'What's all this?'

'I am afraid you will be killed in the battle.'

'Juana, you goose!'

She bent over him, gently pressing her hands against his hollow cheeks. 'I have only you. If you die, I must also. Do you see?'

He reached up a hand to clasp one of her wrists. 'Who's talking of dying? Not I, I give you my word! They'll tell you in the regiment that I bear a charmed life.'

'*Al contrario*, they say you are a reckless one.'

'Be damned to 'em! I'll take good care of my skin, I promise you. If anything does happen to me, Tom will look after you, and see that you are sent to England. I've told him what to do: you've no need to worry your head. Aren't I a provident husband?'

'No, no, you are a fool, a fool! Do you think I will live with-out you? *Jamás!* I have made up my mind to die also. It will be quite easy.'

'The devil it will! Now, what am I to do with you?'

'You can do nothing. Only, I thought I would tell you.'

'*Muchas gracias!*'

She traced with one finger the line of his cheek-bone. 'It will be better so, don't you think?'

'I think it will be better still if I take precious good care not to be killed, my wife.'

'Oh, yes! Much better!' she agreed, brightening. 'But it does not seem to me that there will be any battle. When do we march?'

'This evening.'

'Well, I think it is going to rain,' she said.

'God forbid! I know what your Spanish storms are like.' He looked up at the sky. 'All the same, I believe you're right. We're in for a regular Tam o'Shanter's night. Good! That means we shall be engaged to-morrow. It always rains before the Peer's battles.'

As the afternoon wore on, the sky grew steadily more sullen, some very black clouds rolling up from the west. In the last half-hour of daylight, the landscape looked leaden. As the Light divi-sion, bringing up the rear of the army, began to descend the slope of the Aldea Lengua mountain to the river, the fast-gathering darkness closed down on them, and some heavy drops of rain fell.

'Here it comes!' said Kincaid.

'Damn! I wish I had sent you across with the Pioneers!' Harry said, fastening his boat-cloak round Juana's neck.

'Oh, *vamos!* I am not afraid of rain,' Juana answered gaily. 'And I would not leave the brigade, I assure you!'

A sudden gust of wind nearly carried her hat away; by the time the ford at the foot of the hill was reached, the rain was

falling in torrents, and the river was already swollen. The flicker
of lightning, and some threatening growls of thunder, rolling
round the hilltops, frightened Juana's horse. She could feel him
trembling under her, and was obliged to force him into the
river. The water, swirling and foaming round his legs, made him
snort and jib badly, backing away. The more she tried to urge
him forward, the more obstinate he became, carrying her in his
terror into the deeper water beyond the ford, and there becoming too frightened to move. West, who was leading Harry's spare
horse, could do very little to help her, beyond shouting advice,
and trying to induce her horse to follow his lead. He was beginning to be seriously alarmed, for there were quicksands in the
river, when Harry came splashing through the torrent on Old
Chap, and, seizing the Portuguese horse's bridle above the bit,
fairly dragged him to the opposite bank. They had scarcely
scrambled up it when a deafening clap of thunder so startled the
horses that even Old Chap flung up his head, while the
Portuguese stood stock-still, shaking, Juana said, in every limb.

'Why the devil didn't you wait for me?' Harry said wrathfully. 'You might have been drowned, you little fool!'

He could barely distinguish her face in the darkness, but her
voice was brimful of mischief. 'You said I must learn to ford
rivers by myself! *Muy bien!*'

'I'd like to wring your neck! Do you know what a fright you
gave me?'

'It is all the fault of this stupid, cowardly horse. I won't ride
him any more. I will have Tiny instead.'

'We'll talk about that later. Go on, and get under cover, if you
can find any!'

He was obliged to leave her, for he had his duties to attend to,
and it was not until an hour or two later that he found her again.
Meanwhile, undaunted by the rain which beat remorselessly on

her head and shoulders, Juana joined Kincaid, whose brigade was already across the river. He seemed to be in some kind of trouble. He said in a shaken voice: 'My God, I thought I was blind!'

'Why? What has happened to you?'

'Nothing, my dear. That terrific flash so dazzled me I thought I had been struck. I tell you, I couldn't see a thing, not even the lanterns, for a full ten minutes! Never had such a scare in my life! By Jove, though, what a sight it is!'

The storm, by this time, was at its height. The lightning, which was almost continuous, luridly lit up the whole scene, casting into sharp relief the background of towering hills and woods, and seeming actually to flicker on the points of the long column of bayonets still moving steadily down the mountainside to the river at its foot. The Light division, keeping close order, passed the river without losing its formation, but a jagged fork of fire, falling amongst some of Le Marchant's dragoons, already bivouacking on the low ground near Santa Marta, killed several men and beasts, and frightened the picketed horses so much that hundreds of them broke loose from the ropes and galloped off into the surrounding gloom, squealing with panic. The noise of their pounding hooves, as they careered wildly round, the shriller note of their squealing, mingled with the roar and clatter of the thunder, created such an infernal pandemonium that Kincaid was quite astonished to find Juana apparently unperturbed by all the commotion, but laughing, with the raindrops splashing off the sodden brim of her hat, and running down her neck.

'My poor dear, you ought to be under cover!'

'Yes, but I like this better. The rain does not hurt me, and I must stay with the brigade.'

'Where's Harry? Gone off with the Q.M.C. to find quarters for Vandeleur?'

'He did not tell me, but certainly that is what he must be doing. Enrique *never* neglects his duty.'

'Only his wife?' said Kincaid quizzically.

'You know better! *A decir verdad*, he is very angry with me, because this stupid horse would not cross the river. I am going to ride Tiny in future.'

'Are you, by Jove! Does Harry know?'

'Yes, for I have told him,' replied Juana firmly.

7

Vandeleur's headquarters for that night were fixed in a cottage, which, though very small and poor, had the advantage of possessing a barn in which the horses, and Harry's greyhounds, could be sheltered from the storm. There was only one room in the cottage besides the kitchen, but Vandeleur would not hear of the Smiths camping out in their little tent. Himself suffering from rheumatism, which had attacked the shoulder that had been wounded at the storming of Ciudad Rodrigo, he could not bring himself to believe that the drenching rain had not given Juana as much as a cold in the head. He wanted to make her drink the glass of brandy and hot water which his A.D.C. brewed for him, and when she made a face over the first sip, and choked, and would not take any more, he shook his head, prophesying an inflammation of the lungs for her. 'And as for you, Harry, you'll report yourself sick, and let's have no more nonsense about it!' he said.

'Not I, sir!'

'You damned fool of a boy, you can scarcely ride! You're no use to me with fifteen boils, so don't flatter yourself you can't be spared!'

'Only eleven, General,' pleaded Harry.

'Preposterous!' said Vandeleur testily.

Over the stew which was prepared for their dinner, Juana announced that she had given West orders to put her saddle on Tiny's back on the following morning.

'West takes his orders from me,' said Harry.

'*Seguramente!* I said that it was your order.'

'That's an attack on your flank, Harry,' said Vandeleur. 'Have at him, m'dear! Roll him up, horse, foot, and guns!'

'General Vandeleur,' said Juana, without the flicker of an eyelid, 'wishes to see me on Tiny.'

'Quite right! Can't bear to see you on that clumsy brute of a Portuguese.'

'Have it your own way,' said Harry. 'But don't blame me if you can't handle Tiny. He's not an easy horse to ride.'

But Juana showed next morning that she was perfectly able to manage the little Spanish horse. He had been Mameluke-trained, and she made him caracole in front of the troops, showing off like the child she was.

'You ought to be ashamed of yourself!' Harry said, but without much conviction. Quite as much as she did, he enjoyed the applause the troops accorded her. To Charlie Beckwith, he said: 'I do believe there isn't one of those rascals that wouldn't lay down his life to defend her. Awful blackguards some of 'em are, too.'

Since there did not seem, at first, to be any prospect of an engagement, he allowed her to remain with the brigade through-out the morning. The Light division, which formed the left wing of the army, was stationed behind a hill, as a reserve force. Nothing much could be seen of the enemy from this, or any other position, Lord Wellington having followed his usual disconcerting custom of drawing up his force on the reverse slopes of the hills that fronted the French. With Salamanca only four miles to the rear, it seemed unbelievable that no engagement would be fought, but the news that the entire baggage-train had been sent off at dawn towards Ciudad Rodrigo came as an unpleasant surprise to men who had been fretting for days to stop marching, and fight. No one knew exactly what his lordship's intentions were, but plenty of critics remembered that he had the reputation of being a good commander chiefly in defence.

The army was drawn up in an advantageous position (trust his lordship for that!) along a three-mile front. The country was well wooded, and undulating, and was marked by two steep hills, called the Arapiles, one of which, the Northern, or Lesser Arapile, was occupied by Allied troops. The Greater Arapile, larger but not as steep, was some six hundred yards in advance of the position. Beyond it, on the southern side of the valley, Marmont had his divisions drawn up on the edge of a thick forest.

The storm of the previous evening had given place to a brilliant day, with a cloudless sky, and a hot sun swiftly drying the ground which had been so drenched a few hours before. The men lay by their arms, grumbling and smoking, and trying to protect themselves from the glare by such means as came most readily to hand. Except for some changes in the disposition of the divisions, the morning was spent in almost complete inaction. Outposts and vedettes reported the French to be similarly undecided, which was felt to be some comfort; but at noon, when it was rumoured that a plan of retreat was being drafted, feelings began to run high.

Harry, who, as Brigade-Major, was in a position to know rather more about the movements of the various divisions than his friends, saw no reason to banish his wife to the rear until after two in the afternoon. Except that Pakenham, in command of Picton's division, had been ordered up from the north side of the Tormes to a position in the right rear of the front, near the Ciudad Rodrigo road, no movement of any importance had

taken place. Lord Wellington, who with his Staff, Marshal
Beresford, and the Spanish Commissar, General Alava, had established his headquarters in a farmhouse, somewhere towards the
right of the line, was reported at two o'clock, by one of his
aides-de-camp, to be sitting down to a belated lunch of hunks
of cold meat clapped between slices of bread. It was at this
moment that Marshal Marmont began to extend his left.

Maucune's division was the first to move. Just before two
o'clock, it was observed to march towards the centre of the narrow plateau, which extended for three miles to the west of the
French position. A smooth slope to the north led up to the
Allied line, but since this was cleverly masked, the French had
no very exact knowledge of either its formation or its strength.
They marched to the centre of the plateau, until the road leading from Salamanca to Alba de Tormes was reached, and here,
before the village of Arapiles, which was held by Leith's division,
they halted, and began to deploy. Their voltigeurs were sent out
to work down the slope to the village, and the thunder of
artillery-fire broke out. Someone, returning from headquarters,
said that a Staff-officer had ridden off to the farm, where
Wellington sat in the yard, eating his lunch at a deal table, and
had announced that the French were extending. 'The devil they
are!' had said his lordship, stuffing the rest of his sandwich into
his mouth, and striding off to a place of vantage. 'Give me the
glass quickly!'

Lord Fitzroy Somerset handed it to him, and for a few
moments his lordship observed the French movement in
silence. Presently he lowered the glass, and said in a brisk tone:
'Come! I think this will do at last!'

'Did he?' Harry cried. 'By Jupiter, then we're going to fight!'

'Yes, and that Spanish fellow – what's-his-name? – Alava! –
kept on saying: "*Mais que fait-il? Que fait Marmont là-bas?*" and

old Hookey gave one of his laughs, and said (for I heard him): "*Mon cher Alava, Marmont est perdu!*"'

'Oh, famous!' Harry said. 'But I must get my wife out of this at once.'

But West had already taken Juana to the rear, telling her woodenly that Master's orders had been explicit. She was in a rage with him, because she wanted to stay with the brigade, and watch her first battle, and she thought that if Harry were wounded he would like to have his wife at hand to attend to him. West said, No, it was the last thing Master would like, a statement which made Juana so cross that she sulked all the way to Las Torres, a village situated about a mile behind the Allied right.

However, the reserve was stationed at Las Torres: a force consisting of a Portuguese brigade, España's Spanish contingent, and Anson's, Le Marchant's, and Arentschildt's cavalry, and the throng of troopers with their sleek mounts made Juana feel much more cheerful. She liked the warm smell of horseflesh, the jingle of accoutrements, and the splendour of scarlet uniforms, glittering helmets, and swirling plumes, and she very soon stopped sulking, and began to look about her in the hope of perceiving an acquaintance. In the crowd of horses and lounging troopers it was hardly surprising that she did not recognize anyone, but upon entering Las Torres she had the excitement of seeing Lord Wellington himself ride past at a full gallop. There was no mistaking that low-cocked hat, and bony profile, but to see his lordship going hell-for-leather, and unattended, was something quite out of the ordinary way. His Staff rode past in pursuit of him a few moments later, going hard, but clean outpaced. Juana, who had dismounted in the village, and found herself standing beside an officer of the 3rd dragoons, asked him in the friendliest fashion if he knew where his lordship was bound for. He said, in halting

Spanish, that he had no certain knowledge, but supposed he must be going to order Pakenham up.

It was not until much later that they heard Wellington had ridden up to his brother-in-law, not entrusting to anyone the order he had for him.

'Edward,' had said his lordship in his cool, imperative way, 'move on with the 3rd, take the heights in your front, and drive everything before you!'

It soon became known, of course, that the 3rd was moving up to the front, but as the division had two miles of rough ground to cross, it was a long time before anything more was heard of its doings. The artillery-fire continued; scraps of news filtered through to the rear; and her new acquaintance in the 3rd dragoons was able presently to assure Juana that the Light division was not engaged, being placed on the extreme left of the line, containing Foy's and Ferey's divisions in their front.

These tidings were clearly excellent, and Juana, her mind relieved of its chief anxiety, began to enjoy herself. Her henchwoman had gone off with the baggage-train, but West remained in close attendance on her, so that she did not miss rough Jenny at all, but, on the contrary, was rather glad that she had only one person to watch over her.

After a time, a number of wounded began to trickle towards the rear, but from what they said it did not seem as though the two armies had as yet come to grips. They were all suffering from gunshot wounds, and the only news seemed to be that the French army was still extending along the plateau, Thomières's division having followed Maucune's, and the whole force now presenting a dangerously elongated appearance. Nobody knew quite what was happening, though it was obvious that Marmont's object was to cut Wellington off from Ciudad Rodrigo. Maucune's division was still before the village of Arapiles, and there was some hand-to-hand fighting going on, but only between advance-guards. Thomières, one officer with a grape-shot wound in his chest said, had passed Maucune, and was forging westward along the plateau, leaving a very unsoldierly gap between the two divisions. In fact, the opinion held by most of the men who had been in a position to observe the French movement, was that it was a slovenly manoeuvre, such as would never have been initiated by the English commander.

8

Juana, who had taken up temporary quarters in a *posada* in the centre of the village, was joined there presently by a lady who came into the yard with a soldier-servant, and desired the landlord to bring her a glass of lemonade. After looking at Juana for a few moments, she went over to her, and asked if she too had a husband in the army. She was a good many years older than Juana, an Englishwoman with a deeply tanned and weather-beaten skin, and careworn lines at the corners of her eyes.

West, who had just come out of the shed where he had tethered the horses, touched his hat, and explained that his mistress spoke no English. The lady repeated her question in Spanish, and when Juana answered, Yes, she was married to an English officer, she said wonderingly: 'I had not thought it possible! You are so young, my dear.'

'Oh no!' Juana assured her. 'I shall very soon be fifteen. I have been married since three months already.'

The lady smiled. 'My dear! And your husband? What is his regiment?'

'He is a Rifleman,' said Juana. 'Also he is a Brigade-Major, which is a position of great responsibility, you understand.'

'Indeed, yes,' agreed the lady, a twinkle in her eyes. 'Do you know, I think I have heard of you? Were you not married after Badajos?'

'Yes, I am Mrs Harry Smith,' said Juana. 'And you, señora?'

'I am Mrs Dalbiac. My husband is Colonel of the 4th dragoons. These are very anxious times for us poor wives, are they not?'

'Yes, but also they are very exciting,' Juana pointed out.

'Ah, when you have followed the army for as long as I have, you will not care for the excitement!' sighed Mrs Dalbiac.

Juana did not think this was very probable, but being too polite to say so, she asked Mrs Dalbiac instead if she would like to see her horse, Tiny. Mrs Dalbiac seemed to think that Tiny was rather a mettlesome mount for a lady, but Juana explained how stupid the Portuguese horse had been in crossing the river, and how frightened he was of the storm, and Mrs Dalbiac said, but with that look of wonder in her eye, that certainly nothing could be worse than a cowardly horse. She asked Juana questions about her family, and seemed greatly moved by Juana's graphic account of the circumstances leading up to her marriage. She shuddered at the description of the sack of Badajos, and evidently pitied Juana very much for being an orphan, and having lost all means of getting into touch with her sister. Juana, although she was not above drawing, in moments of stress, the most heartrending picture of her orphaned condition, for Harry's benefit, was not really in the least concerned with her sister's disappearance from her life, and found this conversation rather tedious. However, Mrs Dalbiac, having drunk her lemonade, went away presently to rejoin her husband, promising to return in a little while.

The distant noise of gun-fire, now that Juana had leisure to notice it, seemed to have considerably increased. She judged,

from the position of the sun, that the afternoon was already
fairly advanced. There did not seem to be anything much to do,
and she was beginning to be a little bored, when the blare of trumpets sounding the advance whipped up her waning interest. West
came running into the yard to tell her that the cavalry had been
ordered up, and that the news was flying round that Pakenham,
supported by D'Urban's Portuguese cavalry brigade, had brought
the Fighting division beautifully up the hill, away to the right, and
had fallen upon the leading column of Thomières's division with
such impetuous fury that Thomières's entire column, caught all
unawares, was nearly annihilated. Staff-officers, sent to order up the
cavalry reserve, told of the utmost confusion in the French van.
Half Thomières's force had fallen, an Eagle had been captured, and
the victorious Fighting division was even now continuing its
charge along the plateau towards the centre of the line. The
ground, one officer said, was covered with dead and wounded,
and the broken remnants of the French column were flying
before the Allied advance. Nothing more superb than this
charge had ever been seen, and now let who dared say that Lord
Wellington's genius lay solely in defence!

Juana was naturally very much excited by this news, and ran
out to see the cavalry move off. They looked so splendid that
she had to clap her hands, and wave to them. After they had
gone, and the clatter and jingle had dwindled to a distant
thud, and then faded quite away, the village seemed very quiet
and deserted. Even West began to be rather restive, for
although the Light division was still being held in reserve,
there was no knowing when it would be called into action,
and Harry perhaps have need of the spare horse he was leading. After a short period of indecision, he yielded to Juana's
entreaties to move a little nearer to the front, and went off to
bring out the horses.

As they rode towards the rear of the Light division, the noise of the battle grew steadily louder. The nature of the ground prevented their seeing anything of the encounter on the plateau, but the din was appalling: worse, Juana thought, than the horrid noise made on the night of Badajos. A groom, leading up a remount, said that Leith's and Cole's divisions had come into action at five o'clock, and that their encounter with the French centre was a bloody business, in the course of which Leith had been so badly wounded that he had been obliged to leave the field. But Le Marchant's brigade of dragoons, coming up the hill, passed in the interval between Leith's and Pakenham's divisions, and reached the crest of the plateau just as Maucune was beginning to fall back. A most impressive sight that seemed to have been: a thousand sabres advancing in two lines, and charging down at the gallop upon Maucune's flank. Right through the French column they crashed, and on, led by Le Marchant himself, fighting like any trooper, until they met the leading regiment of Brennier's supporting division. They lost their formation, of course, and there were scores of empty saddles, but no infantry, taken thus by surprise, could hope to stand against their charge. But the pity of it was that Le Marchant had fallen, and there was no getting the brigade into order again.

'Racing one against t'other to be the first in amongst the Frenchies, that's what it looked like,' the groom told West. 'Clean crazy, sabring right and left, and the whole ground fair covered with dead! I never saw anything to equal it! One minute the French was there, all drawn up in battle-order, thousands of 'em! – and the next, by God, if they wasn't scattered all over the place, and them dragoons sweeping up the remains!'

He was unable to give West any news of the Light division, his master being in Clinton's division, but he thought they had not been engaged. There was a very sanguinary affair going on by the Southern Arapile, that rocky knoll in advance of the Allied line. Pack's Portuguese had been trying to gain possession of it, but there was no scaling it under the withering fire of the French on the summit.

By the time Juana and West arrived at their objective, which was some way behind the Light division, amongst the ammunition-carts, the remounts, the doctors, and all other persons belonging to the division who had no immediate business in the front line, a rumour that Marmont had been killed was quickly spreading. This seemed too good to be true, but amongst the French losses, which were enormous, anything, it was thought hopefully, was possible.

The incessant and sometimes deafening gun-fire, the sight of wounded men making their way to the rear, and the various tales she heard of the fierce nature of the battle, awoke all Juana's fears again, and it was not until she found herself beside old Dr Burke, in the rear of the Light division, and was assured by him of the division's complete inaction, that her mind could be at all at rest. She hoped for a sight of Harry, but almost immediately after her arrival the division was ordered to advance in pursuit of the retreating army.

The French retreat to the Tormes, covered by Ferey's and Foy's unbroken troops, closely resembled a rout. Hundreds of soldiers were escaping into the protection of the thick woods on the southern side of the plateau; the plateau itself was strewn with dead men and horses; smoke still hung heavily where the artillery-fire had been hottest; and a litter of discarded accou-trements gave an air of confusion to the whole scene.

Juana heard someone on the Quartermaster-General's Staff say that the remnant of the French army, which was making for the fords across the river, would be caught by the Spanish troops left at Alba.

The sun was sinking, and the chill night wind made Juana glad of her big cloak. West pitched her little tent on the battle-field, in the middle of some green wheat. He cut sheaves of it to make a bed for her, since he thought there was little chance of her being able to rejoin the brigade that night. He had a pair of lanterns with him, and by the light of these Juana ate a supper of sandwiches, washed down with some of the wine of Rueda. When she lay down presently on her bed of wheat, she had to hold her horse. The moon rose and lit the field with a cold silver light, but it could no more prevent Juana's dropping asleep than the confused noises of the army bivouacking for the night, or the crackle and glow of the camp-fires. She had spent an exhausting day; she was not yet fifteen; and not even the thought of Mrs Dalbiac, whom she had seen again, riding towards the scene of Le Marchant's magnificent charge, and looking strangely haggard, had the power to keep her awake. Mrs Dalbiac had seemed scarcely to recognize her; she had said over and over again: 'I must find my husband. You must let me find my husband!' All Juana's warm young heart had gone out to her; she could picture herself in just such distress, searching for Harry's body amongst the slain; but there was nothing she could do to help Mrs Dalbiac; and meanwhile Harry was safe, and West was unwrapping some thick sandwiches, and she was very hungry.

The bed of wheat, though it scratched her cheek a little, was wonderfully comfortable. She curled herself up with Harry's boat-cloak spread over her, and dropped into a deep dreamless sleep, which lasted until a persistent tugging at the wheat roused her. She opened drowsy eyes upon a moon like a silver plate, and found Tiny's soft muzzle close to her ear. Another tug made her realize what was happening. She sat up, waking West by breaking into peals of laughter. 'Oh, oh, Tiny has eaten all my lovely bed!'

Four

❧

MADRID

1

JUANA WAS IN HARRY'S ARMS AGAIN BY NOON ON THE FOLLOWING day. Like the rest of the army, he was torn between jubilation and extreme irritation, this last being occasioned by the miscarriage of the pursuit of the broken French army through the night. The mob of fugitives crowding through the forest to the river should never have been allowed to get away, and indeed Marmont's entire force must have been shattered beyond hope of re-forming had not the Spanish General, Carlos de España, taken it upon himself on the morning of the battle to withdraw the force he had been ordered to leave at Alba, to guard the fords across the Tormes. He thought, of course, that he was doing quite the right thing, and when a tentative feeler, thrown out by him, disclosed the fact that Lord Wellington most decidedly desired the Spanish troops to remain at Alba, he had not cared to confess that they had already been withdrawn. It was one thing to act on one's own initiative, but quite another, when it came to the point, to tell his lordship one had done so. In fact, it proved to be quite impossible, as anyone having the slightest knowledge of his lordship's character must surely realize. So the French rout streamed across the Tormes all through the night, without encountering any opposition; and the pursuing force, instead of finding them attempting the fords of Huerta, discovered that they had retreated by way of Alba de Tormes instead.

The Light division was continuing the pursuit, but Harry was not going with the brigade. Old Dr Burke had cursed him for a feckless madman, and had told him to take himself, and his boils, and his wife off to Salamanca, on sick-leave. This command having been endorsed by General Vandeleur, there was nothing for Harry to do but to hand over his duties to Brother Tom, dispatch his bâtman to disentangle his hounds and his portmanteau from the baggage-train, snatch Juana up in his arms, singing out: 'We're going to have a honeymoon, *alma mia de mi corazón!*' and ride off with her to Salamanca.

That they had no money did not worry either of them. If the worst came to the worst, they could live on their rations. '*A buen hambre no hay pan duro!*' said Juana gaily.

Salamanca was crowded with sick and wounded, but the Smiths found themselves a billet in the house of a tender-hearted lady who mothered Juana, supplemented the surgeon's treatment for Harry's boils with remedies of her own, and eked out the army rations with coffee, and other such luxuries. Juana, detecting at the outset the maternal gleam in the lady's eye, pandered to her shamelessly; accepted all the ointments and drenches she produced for Harry; and wheedled fresh eggs and pats of butter out of her by describing in the most harrowing style the awful privations of life in the British army. If that failed, a highly coloured account of her own adventures at Badajos could always be relied upon to conjure a few cakes or a freshly baked loaf out of the good lady. Harry swore that during the fortnight they spent at Salamanca Juana ruthlessly slew all her family in the siege of Badajos.

'I never knew you had so many aunts and uncles and cousins!' he declared.

'Well, I haven't,' said Juana.

'Oh, you little varmint, how can you say so? There was your uncle Tomás, who was shot by the French; and your uncle Juan, who died of starvation; and your heroic cousin, María, who flung herself on a soldier's bayonet rather than lose her precious virginity – very difficult thing to do, that: she must have jumped out of the window on to the bayonet, I think and your sainted aunt from the convent, who –'

'*Basta!*' said Juana. 'You know very well I have no aunt in any convent, and as for my uncle Tomás, he died before I was born, and of *course* you could throw yourself on a bayonet, if it was pointed at you, *estupido!*'

'Speaking for myself, I never point bayonets at girls I mean to rape,' said Harry.

'*Pechero! malvado!*' Juana cried, pummelling him, but bubbling over with laughter.

Harry grabbed at her wrists. 'Peace, vixen! Now, speak the truth! Did you ever have a cousin María, or an Uncle Juan?'

'Yes, certainly I have both, but they live a long way from Badajos, and I do not think I shall ever see them again, so what does it matter if I tell a few little lies about them?'

'Little lies!' scoffed Harry. 'You're an unprincipled female, *hija.*' He let go her wrists, but held one of her hands lightly in his. 'Tell me, *mi pobrecita*, do you miss them, that family of yours?'

'Not very much,' confessed Juana. 'Only when I think that I have now no one but you, and then perhaps I do, a little.'

'You don't regret our marriage?'

'Only when you are unkind to me, and unfaithful,' said Juana mournfully.

'What?' Harry gasped. 'When have I ever been unfaithful to you?'

'You looked at the landlady's niece in a very unfaithful way,' said Juana, gloomily shaking her head.

'I've a good mind to wring your neck!'

'No, don't. Tell me how we can buy a pair of socks, for that you must have.'

'I'll be hanged if I know! I must see if I can borrow a *crusado novo* from someone.'

'A *crusado novo*! It is not enough!'

'It's all I'm likely to get.'

The luck, however, was with him, for he fell in with General Cole's A.D.C., who, upon hearing of the straits to which he was reduced, promptly lent him a dollar from the forty which had been doled out to him for the support of his General and his Staff. He thought that since Cole was in hospital, together with the other General-officers who had been wounded in the battle, he would scarcely miss it.

The possession of a whole dollar made the Smiths feel so wealthy that they at once discussed the most enjoyable ways of laying it out. These included such alternative entertainments as tickets for the theatre, or a dinner in the best part of the town but no thought of replenishing their meagre wardrobes or their bare larder ever entered either of their heads. Juana did indeed, for conscience's sake, insist on buying a pair of socks for Harry, but the rest of the money was spent in a way which George Simmons, Harry said, would undoubtedly condemn as frivolous.

They visited George's young brother, Joseph, who was lying in hospital with a bad attack of fever. He was an engaging youth, who had enlisted as a volunteer, and for whom George was busy getting a commission in his own regiment, so that he could keep him under his eye, and attend to his education. 'Only I don't know but what I wouldn't rather be with Maud,' confided the lad, referring to his other brother, a

young gentleman of a very different kidney, who graced the
34th Foot, and was at present in Estremadura, under General
Hill. 'Except that I rather badly need some money,' he added,
'and one can depend on old George, though he does jaw a
fellow so!'

'We ought to have saved some of our money to give to poor
Joe!' Juana said remorsefully.

But they had not saved any, so it was no use worrying about
that. Harry said he thanked God he had never set out to be a
model elder brother, because if ever he did as much for Tom as
George did for Maud, and Joe (and for the apparently unending
line of younger brothers and sisters at home), ruin would stare
him in the face.

They spent fourteen blissfully happy days in Salamanca, and
left the city at the end of that time to join the army, which was
marching on Madrid. Harry still had his boils, though they were
not quite as painful as they had been, but he was not going to
miss the army's entry into Madrid for any consideration what-
soever. Did Juana feel that she could do some hard riding to
catch up with the division? Of course she could! She desired
above all things to see Madrid: *adelante*!

So off they went, dogs, horses, pack-mules, and groom, with
not a penny to fly with, but in the best of spirits. The sun
scorched them; the dust-laden wind rasped their skins and
parched their throats; they had to sell Harry's watch in Valladolid
to provide themselves with ready money; but they over-took
the division as it was about to cross the Sierra de Guadarrama,
and were welcomed with open arms.

'Harry, you old ruffian!'

'Juana, my only love!'

'Oh, how good it is to be back again!' Juana cried, running
from one to the other of her friends, and embracing them all

impartially. 'Johnny! Jack! Dear Charlie Beckwith! Oh, I am so happy to see you all!'

2

The Smiths had rejoined the division in time to share its first sight of the spires of Madrid, which were seen from the top of the Guadarrama Pass, rising out of the heat-haze far below.

There was a good deal of excitement at this first view of what had come to figure in most men's minds as the Promised City. The soldiers broke from the ranks to run forward, when the cry of: 'Madrid! Madrid!' was heard; and if there were those who thought that the plain of New Castile, which seemed to be such a long way below them, looked flat and singularly unattractive, there were many more who, though extremely footsore, felt themselves filled with renewed energy at the dim view of the capital's spires.

The Light division camped that night in the park of the Escurial, and while the more serious-minded persons went off to look at the palace, others engaged in an impromptu boar-hunt. In the end, they had the best of it, for the palace was discovered to be an unbeautiful edifice, wholly stripped of the pictures and statues which had once adorned it.

When the weary columns, plodding across the interminable plain, came within five miles of Madrid, they encountered the vanguard of a host of Madrileños, who were streaming out of the city to welcome them. From then onward, the march became a triumphal procession, and the thirst the soldiers were suffering from was quenched with wine, grapes, lemonade, all of which were pressed upon them by an excited populace, who hailed them as deliverers, and even flung down palms on the causeway for them to tread on. The road was choked with civilians, women as well as men, and no one seemed to have come empty-handed. The grinning soldiers had sweetmeats popped into their mouths by pretty girls, or sprigs of laurel stuck in their shakos; and several persons of consequence had actually hired porters to carry wine-jars out for the refreshment of the troops.

'Oh, by God!' laughed Harry, catching a rose tossed to him. 'We shall take the whole division into Madrid as drunk as wheel-barrows!'

'It's all very well, you fellows, but it's very embarrassing, upon my word it is!' said George Simmons, mopping his heated face. 'Two of those girls pretty nearly pulled me out of the saddle just now!'

'They wanted to kiss you!' Harry told him.

'Well, I know that, but it's not seemly. Besides, one doesn't want to be kissed by such forward hussies!'

'Who doesn't?' demanded Beckwith. 'Where are they? Why doesn't someone pull me out of my saddle?'

'Charlie, now do be serious! Really, I am astonished! I thought Spanish ladies were so strictly reared, but just look at them! For they *are* ladies, quite a number of them. You can tell by their mantillas.'

The scene outside the mud walls of the city was as nothing, however, to the welcome which was being prepared for the troops within them. Lord Wellington rode in at the head of the army, and several of the regimental bands, catching the spirit of the populace, struck up *See the Conquering Hero Comes*. Compared with the wild enthusiasm of the Madrileños, the entry into Salamanca two months before was a colourless affair. Not Talavera, not Bussaco, had been victories in any way approaching the magnitude of Salamanca. Never before had the French had to evacuate the capital, but this time not only had Marmont's force suffered a crushing defeat, but King Joseph had had to withdraw from Madrid in a belated attempt to bring reinforcements to his lieutenant, leaving only a garrison in the fort of the Retiro. The Madrileños, therefore, greeted Lord Wellington as their liberator, and a very awkward time he had of it, forcing his slow way through the decorated streets to his headquarters. Shawls, veils, and flowers were strewn on the cobbles for his horse to tread on; rose-petals showered down on him from every balcony; women clung to his stirrups, and actually kissed his knees; and on more than one occasion he was nearly unseated. Behind him his devoted troops marched in, dusty, shabby some of them, and all of them footsore, but every one on the broad grin, and a great many of them with laughing beauties already attached to them.

'As good as ever went endways!' That was the opinion the British soldiers held of Spanish women.

The army was quartered in and around Madrid, the Light division being placed at Getafe, a small town situated a few miles south of the city, on a rather dreary plateau. The Smiths found a comfortable billet there, but they, like everyone else, spent all their leisure hours in Madrid. Harry had managed to get some of the pay which was owing to him, and nothing would do for him but to deck Juana in the finest raiment his purse could afford. Strolling with her on his arm along the Prado in the cool of the evening, he declared that not one of the fair Castilians Madrid had to show could compare with his little Estremenha.

As for Juana, she was so much enchanted by Madrid that it remained for ever in her mind the touchstone by which she judged all other cities.

It was a strange place, abominably placed in the dullest kind of country, quite bleak and treeless, menaced by the grand chain of the Guadarrama mountains, which in winter rained down storms from their snowy summits, and in summer cut off from the plain the cooling north-west winds. In all Spain, no greater heat was to be found than that shimmering day-long over the capital. A mean little river watered Madrid; mud walls surrounded it, with, beyond them, fields of tilth stretching away in unbroken monotony to the foot of the sierra. Inside the walls, wealth and poverty lived side by side in startling contrast. Nowhere could be found such broad, clean streets of fine houses, but behind them lurked twisted alleys lined with filthy hovels. Beggars were scarcely ever seen, but in the poorer parts of the town people died like flies of starvation and night after night emaciated corpses were thrown out of the houses, to be collected and carted away in the morning on hand-barrows.

It did not take the army long to discover this shocking state of affairs. The 3rd division started soup-kitchens, and the other divisions quickly followed the example. Pay was months in arrear; no new clothing could be got to replace worn, patched uniforms; officers sold their watches, their silver spoons, and sometimes even their horses; the men lived on their rations; but everyone somehow or other managed to contribute towards alleviating the distress of the city.

But although famine reigned in the background, the festivities planned for the entertainment of the British were on the most lavish scale. No one heard the moaning in the mean streets when the guitars and the mandolines played waltzes and fandangos for British soldiers and their Castilian partners to dance to. The hovels showed blank, dark windows at night, because their inmates had no money to buy as much as a tallow-dip; but on the Puerta del Sol, and the Prado, all down the Calle Mayor, huge wax candles were set out in scores on every balcony, their little tongues of flame burning straight upward in the hot, still air, so brilliantly lighting the town that it seemed like noon at midnight.

The shops displayed the most attractive wares; the cafés set out their little tables on either side of the Prado; guitar-players sang to any party of officers who looked as though they might be good for a peseta or two; the ladies of the town paraded in their best silk petticoats, and smartest satin bodices, flirting their fans, setting the long fringes on their skirts swinging with the provocative play of their hips; lemonade-sellers, in sleeveless waistcoats and white kilts, went up and down, doing a roaring trade under the avenues of trees; the gayest mats were hung out as sunblinds, creating a strange medley of bright hues in streets where the houses were already stained every colour of the rainbow.

Two days after his entry into the town, a grand ball was given in Lord Wellington's honour. Everyone who could beg or steal a ticket attended it. Harry took Juana, dressed in the height of the Spanish fashion, and looking enchantingly pretty, with a high comb in her hair, and a black mantilla draped over it. Kincaid was there, too, in great spirits, because he had sold his baggage-horse, which (he said) ate as much and more than it could carry on its back, and was consequently so thin that he could hang his hat on its hindquarters. But it was a fine, big animal, and he had got a mule and five dollars in exchange for it, so that he was now able, according to Charlie Beckwith, to support a mistress in the first style of affluence.

Lord Wellington, always a splendid man for a party, was very affable, not to say jovial. His hawk-eye picked Juana out surprisingly quickly, and he carried her off on his arm to introduce her to several of the most notable people present. 'My little *guerrière*,' he called her; and nothing would do but he must see her perform a Spanish dance. So one of her countrymen led her on to the floor, while Harry stood by, as proud as a peacock, said his friends. His lordship told Harry, with his loud whoop of a laugh, that he was a lucky young dog. Nothing, in fact, in his lordship's demeanour would have led even the keenest-eyed observer to suspect that he was preoccupied with matters far removed from balls, and congratulatory addresses. The truth was that his brilliant victory over the Army of Portugal at Salamanca, though it might win for him the thanks of Parliament, the long-postponed appointment as Generalissimo of the Spanish armies, an English marquisate, a Portuguese marquisate, a grant from Parliament, and as much flattery as any man could desire, had waved no magical wand over his most pressing difficulties. His army was so much reduced by sickness that the field hospitals at Salamanca and Ciudad Rodrigo were filled to overflowing, and some of his battalions could muster no more than three hundred bayonets in line; the war-chest was so diminished that he could neither pay the hale troops, nor support the sick men in the rear; two of his most competent generals, Graham and Picton, had been invalided; Beresford, Cotton, Leith and Cole, all wounded at Salamanca, were in hospital; the Spanish officials with whom he was obliged to deal seemed to have been chosen for their inefficiency ('an impediment to all business,' he called one of them); he had to leave Clinton's division to contain what remained of Marmont's army on the Douro; and he was quite uncertain of what Soult's movements in Andalusia would be.

But no trace of these cares was allowed to appear in his lordship's public manner; indeed, very few people knew that such cares existed. To most of the light-hearted gentry making merry at the ball, the Allied army's prospects seemed to be rosier than ever before. They had shattered Marmont's force ('Forty thousand men beaten in forty minutes,' someone said); Marmont himself, at first reported slain, was badly wounded; two of his Generals had been killed; the French losses were anything from ten to fifteen thousand men, two Eagles, and twenty guns; and here was the Allied army, actually quartered in King Joseph's capital! Never had there been more excuse for dancing!

3

There was every facility for dancing. Those who could not obtain tickets for the state balls could go any night of the week to the Principe, and enjoy themselves at the public balls held there. Nor was dancing all that Madrid had to offer its visitors. There were theatres; and concerts; plenty of sport to be had in the Grand Park, which abounded with game; public executions in the Plaza Mayor, if you had a fancy to witness a garrotting; and bull-fights in the Plaza de los Toros, shut for years, but opened again in honour of the British army. Business in Madrid on a bull-day was at a standstill. From ten o'clock in the morning onwards, crowds besieged the gates of the bull-ring, struggling and fighting for the best places, and apparently quite content, having won them, to sit for hours in all the heat and glare of the August sunshine, waiting for the show to begin, with nothing to do but to drink lemonade, and eat sticky sweetmeats fast melting into glutinous masses on the vendors' trays.

The English liked some part of the bull-fights, but very few cared to see the slaughter of broken-down horses which formed an apparently essential feature of the spectacle; and all of them were agreed that it was no sight for women. Harry would not take Juana, which made her cross, until she heard that Kincaid had seen his erstwhile baggage-horse driven into the ring, and then she was glad, and quarrelled with Kincaid for laughing about it.

The garrison of the Retiro surrendered within a few days, and Lord Wellington, having given a superlatively grand ball at the end of August, left Madrid, with the 1st, 5th, and 7th divisions, some Portuguese troops, and two brigades of heavy cavalry, to reinforce Clinton. He left the 4th division at Escurial, and the 3rd and Light divisions in and around Madrid. He had learned, late in the month, that Soult had at last begun to evacuate Andalusia, raising the siege of Cadiz, which had been dragging on for a little matter of three years. General Hill, commanding the containing force in Estremadura, wrote that Drouet's troops in his front had vanished, presumably having marched off to join Soult, who was concentrating at Granada. Since King Joseph, with the Army of the Centre, and the most immense train of baggage and refugees ever seen, was marching slowly eastward to Valencia, to effect a junction with Suchet, there could be no possibility of Soult's continuing to maintain himself in Andalusia. He, too, would in all probability march eastward. That would take him many weeks, and a warm welcome he would receive from King Joseph (if ever he got into touch with that much-harrassed monarch), for he had been behaving in the most intransigent fashion, quarrelling with him in dispatch after dispatch, giving him quite erroneous information, and even refusing to obey his positive orders.

Lord Wellington, deciding that no immediate danger threatened Madrid, left the city on the last day of the month, instructing Hill, as soon as he could be assured of Soult's departure for the east, to march on the capital, and to take over the command of the troops left there. When he should have settled accounts with the French Army of Portugal, which was lifting up its head again, under Clausel, his lordship meant to return to Madrid, to confront the combined forces of Joseph, Suchet, and Soult.

Meanwhile, the divisions left at Madrid continued to amuse themselves as well as they were able. Lack of money was, as always, the chief bar to enjoyment, but there were ways, if one was an old campaigner, of getting over this difficulty. One enterprising gentleman, instead of indulging in a little honest plunder, or some legitimate pilfering, took under his protection a singularly ill-favoured widow who owned, in addition to a large wart on her nose, quite a tidy little nest-egg. But such shifts as these were not much approved of in the ranks. 'You'd marry a midden for muck, you would!' a frank-spoken friend told the complacent bridegroom.

The officers, most of them deep in the toils of money-lenders, contrived to go on indulging in all the usual amusements offered by a capital city. The Smiths, neither being handicapped by an imperfect knowledge of the language, made a number of friends, and began to lead, Harry said, quite a respectable and domestic existence.

'If by respectable you mean that you've scraped up an acquaintance with a probably disreputable priest,' drawled James Stewart, 'and if by domestic you mean that your scoundrelly servant always manages to steal a hen or a sucking-pig for your dinner –'

'*Ingrato!*' cried Juana. 'You ate it! And as for Don Pedro, he is a very good man, very well educated, very intelligent, and not at all disreputable. Enrique likes him!'

'Your precious Enrique likes him because he's a good shot, and as mad on sport as he is himself. Don't tell me he cares a fig for his intelligence, because I'll swear he doesn't know anything about it!'

'If you were not so stupid that you cannot speak Spanish, and only very bad French, you would know that Enrique has very interesting talks, very clever talks, with the Vicar,' said Juana, bristling in defence of Harry.

But Stewart only laughed, and shook his head, and nothing would make him admit the domestic nature of the Smith's life. He said that the only sign of domesticity he had ever been able to perceive was Juana throwing cooking-pots at Harry's head, a statement which made Juana quite speechless with indignation, but drew a shout of laughter from Harry.

'But it is not true!' stammered Juana. 'Enrique! Tell him!'

'It's no use, *queridissima*: he knows you for the wiry, violent, ill-tempered little devil that you are!'

'I am not! Oh, I am not!'

'Who boxed my ears for spilling ink on the table? Who sulked for five hours because I wouldn't take her to a bull-fight? Who –'

'If you say one word more – but *one, comprende!* – I will run away, and never come back!' Juana said, with very bright eyes, and very red cheeks.

She spoke in her own tongue, and he answered her in the same. 'I'm not afraid of that. You're a loving, always-faithful little varmint, *hija.*'

Her expression softened; she whispered: 'I do love you. Yes, and I hate you, too!'

4

When Sir Rowland Hill's force arrived in Madrid, George Simmons saw his brother Maud again, a doubtful pleasure, since Maud, an improvident young gentleman, was a great trial to his elder brother. Poor George had been obliged to slide away from his merrymaking friends, for he had received very distressing tidings from Joe, still sick in Salamanca, and had sent him his last gold piece stuck under the seal of his letter. Very unfortunately, he had just been sitting for his likeness, which he had had taken for his sister Ann, so that he found himself, after sending off the gold coin to Joe, all to pieces.

Others were in much the same predicament, but by hook or by crook most men contrived, by the sale of still more of their belongings, to keep their pockets sufficiently lined to enable them at least to amuse themselves on the Prado each evening.

The divisions left to guard Madrid remained there until the end of October. The news that came from the north was not good, and it soon became apparent that Lord Wellington was not going to return with the rest of the army to Madrid after all. A whisper of retreat began to circulate through the ranks. His lordship, besieging Burgos with an insufficient battering-train, was making no headway; and, meanwhile, the forces of King Joseph, Suchet, and Soult had effected a junction, and were marching on the capital. The autumn rains, which Wellington had counted upon to make the passage of the Tagus an awkward business, were late in falling upon New Castile; the Tagus, General Hill thought, was still perfectly practicable. There was a good deal of coming and going between his headquarters and Wellington's throughout October, and on the 23rd of the month, the Light division received unexpected orders to be at the alarm-posts at six o'clock in the evening.

'Where's Harry? Where are we off to? What's the meaning of it?' asked more than one of Harry's friends, finding time to call at his quarters.

Juana only knew that the brigade was being moved to Alcala de Henares, north-east of Madrid. George Simmons said that Alcala was the birthplace of Cervantes; but Jack Molloy, who had made arrangements to attend a ball at the Calle de Banos, said that that made it no better.

Nobody wanted to leave the immediate neighbourhood of Madrid, but it was thought, on arrival there, that Alcala was a very good sort of a town, very clean, and with an air of antiquity lacking in the capital. But why the division had been moved few people knew.

The truth was that Hill was in an uncomfortable position, with the army of King Joseph closing in on Madrid, the Tagus perfectly fordable, and General Ballasteros, who should have joined forces with him, nowhere to be seen. In point of fact, Ballasteros, instead of keeping Soult occupied, had got himself arrested by the Cortes, at Granada, as the result of seizing the moment of Wellington's being made Generalissimo of the Spanish Armies, to publish a manifesto, violently objecting to the appointment; and to attempt a coup d'état with the purpose of making himself supreme ruler of Spain.

The brigade spent four days in Alcala. On the 27th October, just, complained Kincaid, as everyone was beginning to feel at home, orders came for the division to move towards the right, to Arganda.

'Here we go round the mulberry bush!' said Jack Molloy. 'We shall find ourselves back at Getafe before we know where we are.'

'Don't raise your hopes too high,' recommended Captain Leach. 'This looks to me like forming a battle-front. Well, I'm glad old Daddy Hill means to make a push to defend Madrid.'

The division marched south, crossing the Henares, and reaching Arganda at dusk. Arganda was found to be quite a small place, but no one cared a penny for that, since it was famous for the excellence of its wines. Upon being told to fall out, the men made haste to put the reputation of the town to the test; and Vandeleur, who was in temporary command of the whole division, General Alten's headquarters still being fixed at Alcala, procured several bottles of something very special, and proceeded to make a night of it.

By ten o'clock, the division had reached a state of brief, riotous happiness. An orderly arrived at the Smiths' quarters with an urgent message from Vandeleur for Harry to go at once to headquarters; and Harry, who had been sitting before a snug fire, with Juana on his knee, cursed, and said: 'What in thunder does the old man want now, I wonder?'

He went off to the house he had taken for the General. Vandeleur was seated at a table with an impressive array of dead men before him. When Harry walked in, he hailed him in a loud, cheerful voice. 'Hallo, is that you, Harry? That's right! Go and order the assembly to sound, my boy.'

'Order the assembly to sound?' gasped Harry. 'What, now, sir?'

'That's what I said, isn't it? Just heard from Alten. Whole division's got to countermarch on Alcala.' He waved a hand in a lordly fashion. 'Sound the assembly!'

'But, good God, sir, we can't march now! The men are all top-heavy!' expostulated Harry.

'Drunken sots!' said Vandeleur, with a magnificent disregard for his own condition.

Harry glanced at the A.D.C., but that gentleman was smiling vacantly at nothing in particular, so that it was plain there was no help to be got from him. Harry turned his attention to Vandeleur again, saying persuasively: 'Listen, General: it's as black as pitch outside, and the brigade's in no case to march. Wait a few hours, till the men have had a chance to get sober!'

'Damme, sir, do I command the brigade, or do you?' demanded Vandeleur, crashing a fist on to the table, and making all the empty bottles jump.

'You do, more's the pity!' retorted Harry, no respecter of persons.

'I'll tell you what!' declared Vandeleur. 'You're an impudent young dog, sir! That's what you are! Good mind to have you broke. Go and order the assembly!'

'You'll regret it if I do. Now, sir, only be reasonable! The brigade won't get back to Alcala any the sooner for reeling off now as drunk as wheelbarrows! Give me till a couple of hours before dawn, and I'll engage to have 'em all in fit marching-order!'

But the good General had imbibed enough of the wine of Arganda to make him obstinate. He would listen to no argument, so there was nothing for Harry to do but to go off to order the assembly to sound. The trumpets blared through the town, and out of every house men came tumbling, buckling on sword-belts, hooking jackets together, falling down steps, and into gutters, and rollicking up to the alarm posts in varying stages of inebriety. Such a noise of good-humoured riot was never before heard in Arganda; and staid citizens, who had gone to bed hours before, hung out of their windows in their nightcaps to see what was happening; while those officers who were capable of any sustained effort tried to get the division into some sort of soldierly shape.

'If any one thing is more particularly damned than another, it's a march of this kind!' said Kincaid, in a rage. 'What's it for? Whose orders?'

'Comes of having Hill in command. Old Hookey would never have played us such a trick,' said Eeles. 'Damn his eyes, I've got the worst jag I've had in months!'

'Come on, boys!' Private Hetherington sang out from the ranks, his shako over one eye. 'Who's for going rabbit-hunting with a dead ferret?'

'Blur-an'-ouns, what did we come 'ere for if we was to turn cat-in-pan before we've 'ad time to play off our dust?'

'Making *panadas* for the devil, that's what we're doing! 'Oo sent us 'ere?'

'Sure, an' who would ut be but Farmer Hill, an' he as wise as Waltham's calf that ran nine miles to suck a bull?'

Cursing, stumbling over the cobbles, the division moved off into the darkness. The roads were rough, the way little known, and long before Alcala was reached Vandeleur was repenting of his obstinacy. 'Where the devil are we?' he asked testily, when a halt was called to discover which of two roads led to Alcala.

'Lord, I don't know, sir!' said Harry cheerfully.

'Where are those guides of yours?'

'Plundering the baggage-train for anything I know. Shall I give the order to bivouac, sir?'

'Damn it, no, we'll push on! I wish I hadn't started this march, but I did, and we'll finish it. Get on, Harry, get on! Find those fellows of yours, and tell 'em I'll have the hide off their backs if they don't discover the right road!'

'I've sent out a scouting-party, sir.'

Vandeleur grunted. 'Very well. The devil's in it I was a little bosky to-night. But the trouble with you, Harry, is that you think you command the brigade!'

Harry grinned. 'I got in the way of it with General Drummond, sir. "Have you any orders for the pickets, sir?" I asked him, the first day I met him. "Pray, Mr Smith, are you my Brigade-Major?" says he. "I believe so, sir." – "Then, let me tell you," says he, "it's your duty to post the pickets, and mine to have a damned good dinner for you every day!" so that's how we went on: he cooked the dinner, and I commanded the brigade.'

5

The leading column of the division reached Alcala at dawn, and the men bivouacked in the streets. An air of unrest brooded over the town; no one at Alten's headquarters seemed to have any very precise information, but the sudden countermarch from Arganda so plainly pointed to a retreat, that Harry, in despair of getting any money from the war-chest, sold the Irish horse which he had bought before Badajos from his General. He got a fine big Andalusian in exchange for Paddy, and three Spanish doubloons as well, which he handed over in triumph to Juana.

The 30th October saw the division bivouacking in a suburb of Madrid, by the Segovia Gate. There was by this time no question of any part of the army's remaining in the capital. Nothing was talked of but a long retreat to the frontier. Wellington had failed in four costly attempts on Burgos, and Staff-officers from his headquarters reported that there was a great deal of sickness amongst his men. He was withdrawing across the Douro, and had sent orders to Hill to evacuate Madrid, and to retreat, not by way of the valley of the Tagus, but across the Guadarrama Pass to Areveto.

No sooner had the news of the impending retreat broken upon the unfortunate Madrileños than scenes of the most painful distress harrowed the feelings of men already bitterly disappointed at this end to their brilliant campaign. A moan of despair went up from the town; the soldiers were implored not to leave Madrid to the mercy of the French; weeping women clung round the knees of embarrassed officers; and when it was realized that no entreaties could avail against the positive orders of the Commander-in-chief, the feelings of the mob veered suddenly, and the British became, overnight, objects of Spanish hatred. There were one or two ugly incidents, and some rioting; and the baggage-train of the army was swollen with refugees who preferred to undertake the ardours of marching with the army than to remain in Madrid to be punished by the French for the welcome they had extended to Lord Wellington.

The division remained outside Madrid for a few hours only, but for long enough to allow Juana to discover an irreparable loss. She had lost the three Spanish doubloons.

Such a scene as Harry entered upon when he had joined Juana at the bivouac! His wife was in tears, Jenny Bates was storming at Joe Kitchen, and Joe was stubbornly defending himself against a charge of gross carelessness.

'Jupiter! What's all this?' Harry had demanded.

Three people had told him, but he only attended to one of them. 'Oh, mi Enrique, our money has gone!'

'Good God, is that all?' said Harry. 'I thought you had broken your leg at least!'

He drove Jenny and Joe Kitchen away, but he could not console his vivacious wife, who, from having been in the gayest spirits, was plunged in the deepest misery.

'I put them in your portmanteau, between your shirts! Oh, what a fool I was! I thought they would be so safe! Oh, do not speak to me! I am so ashamed!'

'Cheer up, *hija*! We can always live on our rations.'

'It was all the money you had, and I have lost it!' wept Juana, pushing him away.

'Why, you little goose, what do you think I care for that?' said Harry, laughing at her. 'Kiss me, and forget the money!'

But it was many hours before she could be persuaded to stop blaming herself, and she might indeed have continued to brood over her folly indefinitely had not a diversion offered, in the person of their clerical acquaintance, the Vicar of Vicalbaro, who presented himself at the bivouac, and, drawing Harry aside, begged to be taken under his wing.

'Why, what's this, Padre?' Harry said. 'You don't mean to march with us?'

'I do, if you will let me join you,' replied Don Pedro earnestly. 'The fact is that I have in the past made myself so obnoxious to the French, that I dare not stay in my parish. I have come to crave your protection, *amigo*.'

Harry could not help laughing at him. 'It's yours, for what it's worth. But what do you think I can do for you?'

'You can take me with you,' said Don Pedro. 'I have brought a bundle with me. You know what a hatred I bear the French! No, really, my dear friend, I am afraid to stay in Vicalbaro! You have no idea what things I have said about them!'

'Oh, haven't I, by Jove! But are you sure you know what campaigning means? It will be no joke, I assure you. Here we are, almost into November, with the rainy season upon us, and the devil of a march before us! No snug evenings round a comfortable hearth, you know: the only fires we're likely to see will be camp ones. Ten to one, we'll be fighting a rear-guard action all the way, into the bargain.'

Don Pedro struck an attitude. 'I am young and healthy, like yourselves. What you suffer, I can! My only fear is that I may inconvenience you, and my young countrywoman, your wife.'

'Is that all?' said Harry. He lifted his voice: 'Juana! Ohé, Juana!'

Juana came running. 'You have found the money!' she cried eagerly.

'No, nothing of the sort! But see whom we have here, *hija*! The poor Padre fears for his life to stay near Madrid. Shall we take him along with us?'

The thought of Don Pedro's sharing all the hardships of winter campaigning with them instantly woke Juana's sense of fun. She said: 'Oh, my dear Padre, how would you do without your comfortable chair, and your books, and all your pictures, and furnishings?'

'It is a sacrifice!' sighed Don Pedro, shaking his head. 'But I am in great dread of the French! I have very bad nights, quite sleepless, I assure you!'

'That is bad,' Juana said. 'But if you come with us you will have much worse ones, I think. For I must tell you, that there will be very little to eat, and if you are not clever at stealing pigs and hens there will be nothing!'

Don Pedro looked quite horrified. 'But señora, you would not expect me to steal!' he said. 'Consider my habit! I – I really do not think I should!'

'You will starve, then,' Juana replied, solemn as a judge. 'Then you must know that we shall have to swim across the rivers – all the rivers – and bivouac in the rain, and also Enrique is very severe upon the march.'

'I do not regard any of those hardships,' said the Padre unhappily, 'but only that I should incommode you.'

'She's quizzing you, Padre: don't pay any heed to her! What do you say, *hija*? Shall we take him along with us?'

'Why, I think we should indeed, for perhaps the French would be unkind to him if we left him behind!'

'Señora!' The Padre seized her hand to kiss it. 'You are all goodness! What shall I do? Must I have a pony? Should I buy a mule also?'

Juana thought that his one small bundle, which contained, he said, a few shirts, could be carried on a pony, but told him to be sure and buy a warm cloak. Leaving his untidy package in the Smiths' tent, he darted off, sped on his way by teasing adjurations from Juana not to be gone long, or he would find on his return that the division had vanished. He came back presently, dragging a reluctant pony, and draped in such a voluminous cloak that Juana was thrown into a fit of giggling. Charlie Eeles happened to be outside the Smiths' tent when he arrived, and he naturally lost no time in spreading the news of the addition to Harry's household through the division, where it was greeted with uproarious ribaldry. 'Harry Smith will do now he has a father confessor!' declared his friends.

6

It was distressing, marching away from Madrid, and everyone was glad, since there was no help for the retreat, when the columns drew out of reach of the capital. They were accompanied for miles by crowds of weeping Madrileños, who saw in the Allied army's withdrawal the ruin of all their hopes.

'Yes, yes, all very sad, but it's their own fault!' Vandeleur said testily. 'They're a lazy, vain, improvident people! What can be done for them?'

It soon became evident that the retreat was going to be arduous. The rainy season had set in, and their long rest in Madrid had not done much to improve the condition of the troops. There was a good deal of sickness; everyone was wearing patched and threadbare clothing; and some of the regiments early showed that they were badly out of hand. The 4th division fell into trouble almost at once, and was obliged to return a list of three hundred missing. After a long, wet march, the Enthusiastics had indulged in an orgy of drinking, at Valdemoro, and no efforts of their officers could round up men quite incapable of marching. They had to be left behind, and the temper of the division was as frayed as its raiment.

It poured with rain on the very first day of the march. Shooting-pains attacked General Vandeleur's old wound; by the time his brigade arrived at Aravaca, to find every cottage in the village occupied by Hill's headquarters Staff, he was in a real Irish temper. In he stalked, to the first decent dwelling-place he found, startling an officer who was toasting himself before a bright fire. 'Who are you, sir?' barked the General, shaking the raindrops from his cocked-hat.

'Captain Brown, of the Royal Waggon Train, attached to

General Hill. And this house,' added the officer, a little impudent, 'is given me for my quarters.'

The General fixed him with a fulminating eye. 'I, sir,' he said, 'am General Vandeleur, and I am damned glad to see you in my quarters for *five minutes!*'

They measured one another. 'Yes, sir,' said Captain Brown meekly, and began to pack up his traps.

There was no space for anyone but the General in the tiny cottage, but Harry had found a room, no more than six feet square, into which he packed his wife, the Padre, and all his greyhounds, which by now numbered thirteen. The Padre, astonished at such congestion, thought at first that he would prefer to inhabit Juana's small tent, which had been pitched on the wet ground; but after spending an uncomfortable quarter of an hour in it, he changed his mind.

The division reached the foot of the Guadarrama Pass next day, in fitful sunshine, and there was roast pork for supper, since the troops went pig-sticking, upon being dismissed in bivouac. The weather improved; the sun grew brighter; and when Harry came in from his duties next morning, he found Juana in her tent, as neat, he said, as a new pin, with all the soaked garments she had worn on the previous day hung out on a line to dry. She had a very good breakfast waiting for him, and Harry said that the least he could do was to furbish up his person.

'Shave, perhaps?' said Juana, teasing him, for he had a boy's smoothness of cheek and chin.

'No, not yet,' grinned Harry. 'But I'll wear a clean shirt in your honour, *alma mia.*'

To find a clean shirt in his portmanteau was easy, to find a dry one very difficult. In his usual haphazard fashion, Harry tossed all his belongings over in the search. 'Eureka!' he said at last, shaking out a shirt untouched by the prevalent damp.

Juana gave a scream, for out of the folds tumbled three gold doubloons. 'Enrique, Enrique, the money!' she cried, pouncing on the coins as they rolled over the ground. 'We are rich, we are rich!'

The Padre entered the tent to find his protectors performing a spirited fandango amongst the litter cast out of Harry's portmanteau. Any fears he might have entertained for their sanity were set at rest by their telling him the whole wonderful story. He at once took charge of the precious money, promising them an endless supply of bread, and chocolate, and eggs, and sausages.

'Oh yes, you take it!' Juana said, giving the doubloons into his hand. 'You understand, Enrique, don't you, that the poor people will always let a friar buy their eggs, even when they won't sell to us?'

Yes, Harry understood that; Harry thought they could not do better than to make the Padre their treasurer; and for his part, the Padre said that the money, carefully handled, would last them all until they reached the frontier.

By the end of November, the whole of Hill's force was over the Guadarrama Pass, with nothing seen of the enemy in their rear. The Light division was at Villa Castin, and Kincaid, riding into the town at dusk, after posting guards and pickets, fell into an adventure which nearly ended his career. He was in a royal rage over it, but a providentially good dinner restored his temper. He had found a mad bull charging round the market-place, tossing any unfortunate who came in his way. Not in the least wishing to become a victim, Kincaid had opened the door of a house immediately behind him, and had retreated into it, driving his horse before him. 'However, there arose such an uproar within that I began to wish myself once more on the outside on any terms,' he said, when food and drink had mellowed him. 'The house happened to be occupied by English,

Portuguese, and German bullock-drivers, who had been seated at dinner when my horse upset the table, lights, and everything on it. The only thing I could make out amid their confounded curses was that they had come to the determination of putting the cause of the row to death. But as I begged to differ from them on that point I took the liberty of knocking one or two of them down, and finally succeeded in extricating my horse, and groping my way back to camp. Anyone seen anything of the enemy? I haven't!'

No, no one had seen as much as an advance-guard. Hill could afford to draw breath again, and even, two days later, to allow his troops a brief respite. Dysentery had broken out amongst the men; and rheumatism was playing havoc with old wounds. The rain fell steadily from a sky like a gray pall; the returns of the sick began to assume alarming proportions; and a messenger from Lord Wellington's headquarters arrived, plastered in mud, with orders for Hill to march, not to Arevalo, as had been arranged, but to Alba de Tormes, by way of Peñeranda. Lord Wellington, his force ravaged by sickness, was falling back on Salamanca.

'Failed at Burgos, has he?' said Young Varmint. 'That's what comes of not taking his best troops with him. How do we get to Peñeranda?'

They got to Peñeranda painfully, by shocking roads. The spring-waggons foundered in troughs of thick slime, and the yokes of half-starved bullocks, straining and slipping under the lashes of their drivers, could scarcely drag them out again; wheels came off, and boxes of ammunition spilled all over the sodden ground; Ross had to make causeways of broken planks and stray flints to get his guns over stretches of the road which looked as though they had been subjected to heavy gun-fire; the long-suffering infantry splashed its way through standing ponds of yellow water, or ploughed through sticky mud which gave up their feet with a sucking sound, and caked their boots till they weighed three times their weight.

'I wept when I was born, and every day shows why!' said a Rifleman, hunching his shoulders under the driving rain. He became aware that the man on his left was stumbling, bent almost double, and said roughly: 'Here, you! Don't halt before you're lame. This ain't nothing yet!'

'I'm burnt to the socket!' gasped his companion. 'I'd liefer die by the road than go on! I got to fall out!'

'Call yourself a Sweep! You'd ought to have been with Moore, you had! Blur-an'-ouns, what do you think *you* know, you bloody Johnny Raw, whining for a drop o' rain? When *we* fell out on the road to Corunna it warn't till the dead lice was dropping from us! Catch hold o' my arm, and shut your bone-box!'

By the 8th November, the Tormes was reached, and crossed, at Alba. 'Damme if we ain't back where we started from!' said Private Grindle disgustedly. 'The further we go, the further behind, and me with corns like pumpkins on all me ten toes!'

'Corns!' ejaculated Tom Plunket. 'What about my new jacket? Hell and the devil confound it, it's spoiled entirely, and me well-known to be the smartest man in the regiment!'

'Don't fret, boys!' said Sergeant Ballard. 'We're off to join the Peer!'

'Glory be to God!' sang out Plunket, tossing his shako in the air. 'Now we'll see some sport! Ah, if that long-nosed beggar had taken *us* with him to Burgos there'd have been a different tale to tell!'

'Where are we going, Sergeant?'

'Salamanca, by what I can make out.'

'God love us, are you bamming us, Sergeant? Salamanca, by Jiminy! We'll be feeding like freeholders again!'

But when the British entered Salamanca, they found that the fickle temper of the townspeople had changed. A retreating army seemed to rouse in their breasts a sort of pack-savagery; men who had welcomed the troops with hysterical fervour five months before now seized every opportunity that offered to do individual soldiers all the mischief they could. Reports of murders, of hand-to-hand fighting in the streets, showered upon his lordship's headquarters; it was said that even the young Prince of Orange had narrowly escaped having a bayonet stuck through his slender person by one of the civil guards.

The grumblers in the Light division found the troops from Burgos in such bad shape that they began to think they themselves had not suffered so very much after all. The divisions from the north had had a gruelling time of it in the trenches before Burgos, and had been harassed on their retreat by the French; they were dog-weary, and sullen with a sense of frustration; and a dangerous spirit of discontent had undermined their discipline. The Staff was being cursed for inefficiency; commissariat-carts had been delayed, and sometimes lost; and a trail of rapine in their wake bore witness to the deterioration of the men. The cavalry was in still worse case, horses looking like scarecrows, and some regiments scarcely able to muster half their correct number of sabres. There was neither money in men's pockets, nor full rations in their bellies, but in this country of vineyards there was always wine to be seized. The army was indulging in its besetting sin, with fatal consequences.

Once on the plateau, the cold became intense. There was a brief respite from the incessant rain, but the wind that cut knife-like across the sierra jarred every bone in a man's body, and brought on attacks of ague that set teeth chattering till the very roots ached.

Wellington had taken up his old position behind the Arapiles, but Soult, warier than Marmont, showed little disposition to attack him in force. To the disgruntled British soldiers it seemed as though nothing had been gained. It was not very cheerful on the old battlefield, with a French force hovering, ninety thousand strong, in the vicinity; the bitter wind thinning the blood in one's veins; and one's horse setting horribly well-preserved skulls rolling with every step he took on 'Pakenham's Hill.'

7

The rain began to fall again on the 15th November. All the stores, and the sick men in Salamanca, were being evacuated to Ciudad Rodrigo. Whatever were King Joseph's wishes in the matter, Marshal Soult, for all his superiority of numbers, was not going to attack Lord Wellington on ground of his lordship's choosing. At two in the afternoon, orders to march reached the various divisions, and they moved off in two lines to the west, in torrents of rain, the Light division forming the rearguard of the centre column.

Juana had bought worsted stockings and mits in Salamanca for herself and Harry. The Padre told Harry that she was the oddest mixture of elderly wisdom and youthful carelessness. You never knew, he said, when you went to look for her, whether you would find a provident housewife, or a little girl escaped from the schoolroom. He was quite astonished at the liberty Harry allowed her. To come upon her, as he often did, visiting the tent of a sick friend, or moving quite freely about the camp, all amongst the troops, shocked his sense of propriety. 'Don't worry!' Harry said. 'She has more good sense in her little finger than you'll meet with in anyone. I never interfere with her.'

Harry, indeed, had very little time for interference with his wife's activities. While the division marched as rearguard, his duties were never-ending. It was an anxious time for Staff-officers; lack of sleep was beginning to make Harry's eyes red-rimmed, and more heavy-lidded than ever.

The army had an uncomfortable time of it on their first day's march, for the rain fell in torrents, and quagmires on the roads made progress a heavy labour. The Zurgain river, a trickling stream when last seen, had become a raging cauldron of fast waters, and rose to the men's shoulders as they waded through its fords. There was no halting until after dusk, when the division bivouacked in a dripping wood. Men began to draw comparisons between this retreat and that of Sir John Moore upon Corunna, but when Harry heard them, he laughed. Nothing they could ever suffer again could compare with that hell of snow and ice through which the troops had struggled, by long, forced marches, fighting every yard of the way, with boots worn through and clothing in rags, and ice congealing on their unshaven beards. 'Corunna!' Harry exclaimed scornfully. 'Why, you chicken-hearted crew, we covered thirty-seven miles in one day alone then! The men were starving, too!'

'Starving, did you say?' drawled James Stewart, looming up out of the surrounding gloom. 'Well, so are we now. We've lost the Commissariat.'

'You fellows on the Q.M. staff ought to be shot!' Harry said wrathfully. 'What's happened to it?'

'Gone to Rodrigo by the northern route.'

'It's not true!'

'Oh yes, it is!' said Stewart. 'Now, don't blame me! Go and curse the Q.M.G., if you want to curse anyone. His ears should be burning already.'

Although the army had had plenty of opportunity of judging and condemning Colonel Gordon's inefficiency, no one could be brought to believe at first that the story was true. But no food was forthcoming for the hungry troops, who groped for acorns on the saturated ground, and chewed them sullenly round camp-fires which fizzled damply, and gave out more smoke than heat. No one enjoyed much sleep during the night, for only the side of a man's body which was turned to the fire was warm, and the sticks, collected to make dry mattresses, sank into the mud under the body's weight. Firing was heard in the small hours, and there was an alarm of an enemy attack, which made the men struggle up, groaning for the cramp in their limbs. Nothing could be seen beyond the light of the fitfully burning fires, and it was discovered later that the firing had been caused by some men of the 3rd division's discovering a herd of tame pigs in the patch of forest where they lay. The rest of the army, disturbed from its uneasy slumber, denied any share of the fresh-killed pork, was angry with Picton's 'black-hearted scoundrels'; and few men had any sympathy for the hangings that took place in the morning.

The army marched at dawn, cold, and hungry, and brittle-tempered.

'Come on, my lads!' Harry said. 'We'll show 'em what *The Division* can do!'

'Bellies ain't filled with fair words,' somebody growled.

'Fair words! God damn your eyes, you'll get no fair words from me, you gin-swizzling, cribbage-faced, cow-hearted Belem-ranger!' Harry retorted.

He raised a laugh. The grumbler was elbowed into the background, and informed that he had chosen the wrong officer to try that game on. 'You silly gudgeon, what do you want to sauce 'im for? 'E'd swear the devil out of 'ell, 'e would! 'E's a bruising lad, our Brigade-Major. Damned if we hadn't ought to give 'im a cheer!'

The idea took well; a ragged cheer was raised, which Harry acknowledged by a grin, and a recommendation to the unshaven scarecrows confronting him to save their breath for the march.

Except that the men were hungrier, there was nothing to distinguish the day's march from the previous one. Along the route, the Light division met stragglers from the main body of the army, slinking off in search of plunder, or dead from exhaustion at the side of the road. It was all very depressing, and although the sight of bleached skeletons of horses was too ordinary to attract any attention, no one much liked to see the stiffening carcases of horses which had failed on the march, and had been dispatched by a merciful musket-shot; or to hear the faint lowing of oxen driven off the road to die miserably in the sodden fields. A little very bad beef, cut from the still-warm bodies of some of the draught-animals, was served out during the usual noon halt. It was rather nasty, and there was no time to cook it properly. A few of the men, kindling fires, toasted slices on the ends of their ramrods, but most of them stuffed the raw chunks into their canteens, where the meat soon turned the little bread they carried with them into a kind of bloody paste. One of Arentschildt's troopers was seen making his portion into a sandwich, and sharing it with his mount. That made the Englishmen laugh, but there was no denying that the soldiers of the King's German Legion took much more care of their horses than any British trooper. They would none of them think of eating a morsel before their horses had been fed, and they most of them trained the animals to eat the same food as they ate themselves.

The rumour that the supply-train had gone off by the Ledesma road was confirmed during the halt. That meant there would be no more rations issued until the army reached

Rodrigo. The Staff was bitterly cursed, as much by the officers as by the men; quarrels began to break out over trivialities; and even the sunniest-tempered soldiers marched in sulky silence.

The bivouac that night was quite comfortless. It was almost impossible to kindle fires with the green wood, which was all that could be found; and the iron kettles hung over the damply smoking sticks took so long to boil that the men fell uneasily asleep as they waited for them.

The French were hovering close in the rear, but they did not show themselves until the following day, when they began to press the rear-guard rather sharply. Through another of the Quartermaster-General's errors, the cavalry that should have covered the Light division had marched off at dawn, ahead of the infantry, with the inevitable result that the column was a good deal harassed by skirmishing parties of French horse-men. Some of these troops actually penetrated the interval between the Light division and the 7th, and plundered the greater part of the 7th's baggage; while a party of three light dragoons had the incredible good fortune to snap up General Paget, just arrived from England as second-in-command of the army. He had been riding, with only his Spanish servant, to hasten the progress of the 7th division, and, being short-sighted as well as one-armed, he had been taken prisoner with almost ridiculous ease. The news raised perhaps the only laugh indulged in by the disgruntled troops that day.

8

The centre column, of which the Light division formed the rear-guard, had orders to encamp on the farther side of the Huebra, but when the rest of the column, jumping down the steep bank into the swollen river, had struggled safely across, a considerable body of French infantry appeared behind the squadrons of dragoons who had been bickering with the Light division all day. This changed the complexion of things rather seriously, and Harry lost no time in sending Juana forward, with strict orders to stay with the 52nd regiment, who were to move into bivouac while the Riflemen held the bed of the river.

Knowing that Harry would remain with the Riflemen, Juana showed him a white face, pathetically small under the big, dripping hat-brim. Words seemed to be strangled in her throat; she wanted to cling to him, to hold him fast; but of course she knew she must not do that. She managed to say, 'Take care of yourself!'

He nodded, and patted her cheek. 'Of course I will. Cheer up, *hija*! I'll be with you presently!'

He wheeled his horse, and rode off in a spatter of mud. Juana found the Padre nervously begging her to make haste, and said grandly: 'Do not be afraid! We shall be quite safe with the 52nd. How surprised they will be to see me, all our friends in the regiment!'

The Padre seemed to think this remark irrelevant, but the prospect of surprising her friends made Juana feel more cheerful; and she rode on at a smart pace, coming up with the regiment just as it was about to ford the river.

She had the satisfaction of encountering two of Harry's friends, Major Rowan on the Quartermaster-General's staff, and Captain Mein; and although neither of them betrayed much surprise at her having joined the regiment, both greeted her with real, if hurried, kindness.

'Hallo, Juanita! Did Harry send you on?' Rowan said. 'That's right! we'll take care of you. Stick close to the column, there's a good girl: wish I could take you under my wing, but you know how it is!'

'Of course I know, and I don't want to be under your wing!' said Juana. 'Go and attend to your duties! I have West, and I have also Don Pedro.'

'*What* a good duty-officer you'd make, Mrs Smith!' grinned Rowan.

Billy Mein teased her about a splash of mud on her cheek; he asked her, too, *sotto voce*, where in thunder Harry's confessor had found his enormous cloak, which made her giggle. But he could not remain with her for more than a few minutes, because he had his company to attend to.

With the French infantry pressing the rear, there was no time to be lost in crossing the Huebra. At this season of the year, it was a wild-looking river, swirling beneath such steep banks that the soldiers, instead of climbing down, jumped into the fast waters. The Padre, watching with a good deal of misgiving, said: 'But how shall *we* cross?'

West, always close to his mistress, smiled rather grimly, for he did not much like the Padre. Juana said: 'I'll show you!' and rode Tiny straight for the bank.

'Lord ha' mercy!' ejaculated West. 'Missus, missus, wait!'

He had been attaching various small goods and chattels firmly to the saddle of Harry's spare horse, which he was leading, and before he could do more than scramble into his saddle again, Tiny, pausing for an instant on the bank, had leaped into the river. Without paying the least heed to the unfortunate Padre, West went after Juana, led-horse and all. By the time he had forced both horses into the river, Tiny was half-way across, swimming strongly, with Juana still in the saddle, though drenched to the skin. She reached the farther bank safely, and a dozen eager hands were ready to seize Tiny's bridle, and haul him out of the river.

'Juana, you *bad* child!' cried little Digby. 'Whatever would Harry say?'

'*Bien hecho!*' Juana replied, sparkling with laughter.

'I suppose he would,' Digby admitted. 'But what's to be done now? You're soaked, and here's the regiment ordered to move downstream to watch the San Muñoz ford!'

'Oh, do not concern yourself! I will come too, because Enrique said I was to stay with you, and so I shall. Only where is the poor Padre?'

The Padre, bravely emulating Juana's dashing exploit, had made his pony jump into the river, but had got into serious difficulties. The pony, scarcely up to his weight, was carried away by the current. Juana could not help laughing to see Don Pedro swept downstream, with his huge cloak blown out like a sail behind him, but it soon ceased to be a laughing matter. Unable either to make headway against the current, or to continue swimming with the Padre on his back, the pony was drowned, and only his preposterous cloak, which kept him afloat, saved the Padre from suffering a like fate.

'Oh, Bob, pull him out!' begged Juana, trying hard not to laugh.

'Can't the fellow swim?' asked Digby. 'What in the world possessed you two crazy people to saddle yourselves with him? Look, some of our men have got hold of him! Here, you, West! Look after your mistress, will you? I must get on.'

'*Adios!* Tell Billy Mein I have no longer any mud on my face!' said Juana.

The Padre, dragged out of the river farther downstream, was looking a good deal shaken when Juana and West rode up to him. Juana had wrung some of the wet out of her habit, but the Padre stood shivering on the bank in a large puddle. Water dripped from the brim of his sombrero, from the hem of his cloak, and even from the tip of his nose. When Juana said how sorry she was for his misfortune, he answered between chattering teeth that he had not dreamt that the retreat would be like this. He asked West if he could mount the spare horse, but West replied woodenly: 'Never lend master's other fighting horse; not to nobody.'

'But you must lend it to me!' said the Padre indignantly. 'How shall I do without a horse? Do you wish me to fall into the hands of the French, you wretched fellow?'

'We shan't march far,' replied West. 'The river bothered us, and it will stop the French. Our Riflemen don't mean to let those fellows over. The walk will warm you.'

'Señora!' exclaimed the Padre, trembling as much from wrath as from cold. 'Do you hear? Will you permit this outrage?'

Juana looked doubtful. 'But, you see, it is my husband's spare horse, and if Old Chap were hit he would instantly require it. Only, since he is on the other side of the river – Could he have the horse, West? Just for this once?'

'Can't lend master's horse, missus,' said West obstinately.

'Well, then, I am so very sorry, but I am afraid you will have to walk,' said Juana, tempering the words with one of her persuasive smiles. 'And please, could you start to walk now, because if we do not remain with the 52nd my husband will not know where to find us!'

'But Señor Smith assured me we should bivouac immediately! Where are we going? Why do the soldiers march downstream?'

'Oh, I don't know,' said Juana cheerfully. 'It is always like that in the army, which is what makes it so exciting.'

The Padre did not look as though he cared for such excitement, but he squeezed some of the water out of his cloak, and began to plod along beside Juana's horse.

The ford of San Muñoz was not far down the river, and when they reached it they at once saw why the regiment had been ordered there. The French were trying to force a crossing.

It proved to be impassable, but almost before she was aware Juana found herself in the middle of a hail of shot. A shell plunged feet deep in the mud quite close to her, making Tiny shy so violently that she was nearly unseated, and something, whether a musket-ball, or a fragment of grape-shot she knew not, whistled over her head. She dismounted in a hurry, but just as West was shouting at her above all the commotion to come with him out of range, a private was struck, and fell almost at her feet. Down she plumped on her knees to see what she could do for him. It so happened that he was not very badly wounded, and she was able to make a bandage for him, and to help him to the rear. Then Captain Dawson was killed, and quite a number of men wounded, and there was no time to think about the danger she was in, for she had naturally to help the wounded men. It was horrible seeing Captain Dawson killed; she thought she was going to be sick, and so very sensibly turned her eyes away from his body, and began to tie the Padre's handkerchief round the brow of a boy who was bleeding from a gash in his forehead caused by a flying frag-ment of case-shot. Major Rowan caught sight of her, and exclaimed: 'Good God, you here? Get to the rear, you foolish child, get to the rear!'

But since he had no time to spare in enforcing his com-mand, Juana stayed where she was. Captain Dawson's body had been carried away; no one else seemed to have been killed; and the French fire was already slackening. The rain was coming down in sheets, but as she was already soaked to the skin with river-water, that, she said, did not signify in the least.

It was a draggled little wife whom Harry found half an hour later, seated beside the Padre on the ground, and hug-ging her knees. Harry had been sent to recall the 52nd, and

was thunderstruck to discover that Juana had been in the thick
of the skirmish. 'My darling!' he cried, flinging himself out of
the saddle. '*Queridissima!* Oh, *mi pobrecita*, how wet you are!'

'Enrique!' Juana squeaked joyfully. 'Oh, how glad I am to see
you safe!'

'I?' he said. 'I'm safe enough, but you, dearest? What the dickens have you been about?'

'Oh, I have had such adventures! I made Tiny swim across the
river, and the poor Padre's pony was drowned, but not him, and
we have had a battle!'

He was holding her by the shoulders, and gave her a little loving shake. 'You varmint, Juana! Come, I must get you to the
bivouac quickly! *What* a drowned rat of a wife!'

He tossed her up into her saddle, and put the bridle into her
cold hand. The Padre said: 'But how shall I go? I do not think I
can walk, and I have certainly caught a chill.'

'Oh, take my spare horse!' Harry said over his shoulder.

9

The bivouac was the worst imaginable, but Harry found that
some of the Portuguese in the brigade had built up a large fire,
and bought it from them for a dollar. The pack-mules had all
been sent on, so there was nothing to eat but acorns, no tent to
shelter Juana from the drenching rain, and no change of clothes
for her. She assured Harry that she was not at all hungry, and not
very cold either, but her face looked pinched and white, while
as for the Padre, he might, Harry said, have been drawn for the
Knight of the Woeful Countenance. The saddles were placed in
a circle round the fire; wet steamed out of Juana's clothes, but as
fast as the fire drew out the moisture from them, the rain soaked
them again. Kincaid, who was acting Brigade-Major to the 1st

brigade, saw Harry for a few moments, and told him that acorns were quite palatable if roasted: rather like chestnuts; so West collected a hat-full, and they held them over the fire in the lid of somebody's canteen. Juana, munching resolutely, said they tasted very peculiar, and she was glad she was not a pig.

'Nasty?' Harry asked.

'Oh no, not nasty! Just strange.'

'My poor sweet!' Harry said, peeling another, and popping it into her mouth.

'Why? I am enjoying myself very much, I assure you.'

'Oh, Juana, how I love you!' he said unsteadily.

'Good! I love you too.'

She fell asleep presently, with her cheek on her hand, one side of her pleasantly warm, the other cold and muddy. The Padre, his damp cloak drawn right over him, slept too, and snored cavernously. Harry sat up, feeding the fire, but he had had no rest for three days, and try as he would he could not keep awake.

Juana awoke in the small hours, roused by cold. She struggled up on her elbow, still half-asleep, and in the grip of a shuddering fit of ague. Harry was lying sound asleep between her and the fire. Juana burst into tears and shook him.

He woke with a start. 'Juana? What is it, my heart?'

'You are horrible, and thoughtless, and cruel, and stupid!' sobbed Juana through chattering teeth. 'Why must you lie just there, *espadachín*? I hate you!'

'Oh, my sweet, I'm so sorry!' Harry said remorsefully. 'I must have fallen between you and the fire. Don't cry, *queridissima*! I didn't mean to do it.'

He gathered her into his arms. She stopped crying at once, and rubbed her eyes. 'Oh, how foolish!' she said, snuggling close up against him. 'I was asleep! And now I have waked you up, when you must have been nice and warm! I am very sorry, Enrique.'

'Darling, darling!' Harry said, kissing the damp curls that were tickling his chin.

'No: bad wife!' murmured Juana, drifting back into sleep.

The rain ceased a little before daybreak. The Light division had expected to march at dawn, but were held up by the 1st division, which they were to follow, and which made no movement. Harry was able to find a mule for the Padre, and Juana managed to dry her clothes, and to seek out George Simmons, who was seriously alarmed by his brother Joe's condition.

The river began to fall almost at once, and it was expected that the French would effect a crossing before noon. General Alten, who saw no profit in any brush with the enemy at this juncture, sent off more than one messenger to Sir William Stewart, who had been in command of the 1st division since Paget's capture by the French.

'What the devil ails the old man?' Barnard demanded.

'I dink he is mad,' said Alten calmly.

Time went on, the sun broke through the clouds; and still the 1st division did not move. Suddenly a Guards officer appeared, picking his way daintily on a blood horse.

'Oh, Christ! The Honourable Arthur!' said Charlie Beckwith.

'My dear Beckwith!' said Arthur Upton, perceiving him and riding up close. 'You could not inform me where I could get a *paysano*? The 1st division can't move: we have no guide.'

'Oh, damn, is that it?' exclaimed Beckwith. 'We'll do anything to get you out of the way! Come to Harry Smith! *He* has a *paysano*, I know. Harry, Harry! Where the devil are you, man? Here, the 1st want a guide! Trot out your cut-throats!'

Harry, as usual, had three or four natives of the district under guard, and was able to hand one over to the Honourable Arthur, who went delicately away again, drawling his thanks.

The Light division had formed a battle-front, but it was presently ascertained that instead of forcing a crossing of the Huebra the French were dismissed, and were all engaged in drying their clothes.

The division marched at last, in cold but dry weather. As Harry was seeing the last of the rear-guard off, he heard himself hailed, though faintly, and looking round, saw a Rifleman lying under a tree with his leg bound up. He recognized the man, and rode up to him. 'O'Donnell! Why, my poor fellow, this won't do!'

'Don't leave me here, Mr Smith!' O'Donnell said imploringly.

'Are you badly hurt?'

'It's me leg, sir. Got me thigh fractured yesterday by a cannon-ball. Don't leave me, sir! Please, don't!'

Harry hesitated. There was no provision for wounded men in the column. The casualties had to be left behind, where it was hoped that they would presently be picked up by the enemy. The French treated their prisoners perfectly well, of course. It was no use being sentimental about it; you could not help every wounded or sick man who came in your way. But Harry knew this man for as gallant a Rifleman as ever breathed. He said in his quick way: 'There's only one way I know of helping you, and I believe it won't do. Could you ride on a gun-tumbril?'

'Oh yes, sir, I can ride!' O'Donnell said gratefully. 'Only don't leave me!'

'Wait, then. I'll see what can be done,' Harry said, and galloped off to where Ross was riding ahead with his six-pounders.

You damned fool!' Ross said, when the matter was explained to him. 'Very well, you can take one of my guns back. And I think you're crazy, Smith, d'you hear me?'

'And I think you're the best of good fellows!' Harry said, reining back to allow the gun to be detached from the troop.

When they hoisted the wounded man on to the tumbril, it was plain that the slightest movement caused him great agony. He almost lost consciousness, but by an effort of will managed to cling to his senses, and to thank the gunner for so cheerfully giving up his seat. 'I shall do now,' he said, but they could only just catch the words, so faintly were they spoken. The gunner said that he was welcome, but he thought privately that Brigade-Major Smith was wasting his time, and the Rifleman would never last out half a day's march. As a matter of fact, O'Donnell died two hours later, but the gunner, resuming his seat then, said that perhaps he would have chosen that rather than have been taken prisoner.

Nothing more was seen of the French, who were finding it impossible to subsist any longer upon an already ravaged countryside. The day was marked by frosts, and by horrid sights encountered all along the line of march. The horses and the oxen seemed to be dying like flies; and the sick men who fell out of the column, to be shepherded on later by the cavalry in the rear, were growing steadily more numerous. A diversion was created by Sir William Stewart, a nice old gentleman, quite incapable of obeying an order (said Lord Wellington), who prevailed upon the commanders of the 5th and 7th divisions to join him in deserting the prescribed line of march to follow a route of his own choosing. Both these commanders were newcomers, and it was not until they found Sir William's route blocked by the Army of Galicia, which had been ordered to follow it, that they realized how unwise they had been to listen to him. All three divisions were finally discovered by Lord Wellington himself, who had set out to look for them, waiting in the mud until the Spaniards in front of them should have moved on. 'You see, gentlemen, I know my own business best,' said his lordship, in withering accents.

The weather grew colder and colder, but on the following day, the 19th November, the army came in sight of Ciudad Rodrigo. 'Thank God, I shall be able to cut the boots off my feet at last!' said Kincaid.

Five

◆

WINTER QUARTERS

1

B Y THE END OF THE MONTH, THE ARMY WAS IN ITS WINTER quarters with Hill's 2nd division placed as far south as Coria, in Estremadura; and Cole's 5th division as far north as Lamego, on the Douro. Lord Wellington's headquarters were fixed at Frenada, a dirty little town only seventeen miles distant from Ciudad Rodrigo; and the Light division, with Victor Alten's brigade of German horse, was posted, like a screen, in various villages on the Agueda, in Spanish territory. This was a cold, rather comfortless situation, but the Light Bobs knew the locality so well that it was quite like home to them. The villagers gave them a warm welcome, enquiring after many men by name, and seeming really glad to see them again. The 2nd brigade had its headquarters at Fuentes de Oñoro, a village which was still looking somewhat battered as a result of the battle which had raged round it eighteen months before. Vandeleur occupied the local Padre's house, but Harry found a lodging at the other end of the village, in the cottage of a widower. There was some tolerable stabling near to this billet: an important consideration for a young gentleman owning six riding-horses and thirteen greyhounds.

Everyone felt more cheerful when the retreat was at an end, but the sickness in the army was appalling. The hospitals were crammed with cases of dysentery and ague; and nearly every man was found to be suffering from an unpleasant form of frost-bite. George Simmons, who had been obliged to mount Joe on his own horse during the retreat, had his legs covered with bad patches. He had worn out the soles of his boots, trudging beside a sick brother, and his feet were in a sad way. He made far less fuss about his ailments than many who were not nearly as seri-ously affected; indeed, he seemed to worry far more about Joe's dysentery. Poor Joe had been so ill on the march that had it not been for George's care of him he must either have died or have fallen into the hands of the French. Joe was one of Juana's pro-tégés, and he used to lie and watch the door to see her come in, her cheeks and her curls wind-whipped, a basket on her arm containing delicacies she had cooked for him, and always a laugh in her roguish eyes. A visit from Juana, Harry's sick friends said, did one more good than all the bark-wine the doctors made them swallow.

Harry had many sick friends, and Juana spent her time cook-ing for them, and riding to the various villages where they were quartered. Charlie Eeles was down with dysentery; John Bell of the 43rd regiment; Jack Molloy; and any number of others. Harry, of course, was as well as ever he had been in his life, and sporting-mad. While Juana and the Padre cooked, he went out coursing every day. James Stewart had a pack of harriers, and asked Harry to act as his whipper-in; there were Harry's own greyhounds; and, when these forms of sport began to pall, there was fox-hunting to be had with Lord Wellington's pack. If you had a fancy for shooting, you could go with Jonathan Leach, and stand up to your middle in icy water, waiting for wild-duck; or try for woodcock anywhere in the vicinity of the Agueda; or practise your marksmanship on the white-headed vultures which seemed to hover day-long above Gallegos. It was a mistake, of course, to shoot this scavenger of the skies, but somehow the sight of these rather horrible birds tugging the putrid flesh from the carcases of the horses which lined the route of the army's late march made the men feel an irrational anger.

Wolf-hunts were popular amongst the rank-and-file. The country was infested with wolves; they used to slink after a marching army, hidden by the never-ending gumcistus, but howling incessantly at night, and always waiting for the chance of finding a wounded man on the road, or a shot horse.

There were five thousand men missing when the army went into winter quarters, and an overwhelming number of those still present were suffering from one form of sickness or another. Everyone thought that the hardships of the retreat had been aggravated by the inefficiency of the Commissariat, and the Staff generally, so that the Memorandum issued for the consumption of officers by Lord Wellington sent a storm of indignation through the army. His lordship, in the worst temper imaginable, had condemned every one of the regiments under his command on the strength of the excesses of a few which had come under his own eye. *A Memorandum to officers commanding Divisions and Brigades*, the document was headed, but there was not an officer in the army who had not a copy to read. The Light division officers, proudly showing a return of only ninety-six men missing out of five battalions, looked in vain for some acknowledgment of their devotion to duty. All they found was a bitter reference to *the habitual inattention of officers of the regiments to their duties.*

'My God!' Charlie Beckwith said, when Kincaid read this aloud.

'Wait, that's not all!' said Kincaid. 'You'll be glad to know that the army *has suffered no privation which but trifling attention on the part of the officers could not have prevented!*'

'That's one for the Commissary-General's Staff,' interrupted little Digby. 'Quite true, too!'

'Not at all! *It must be obvious to every officer that from the moment the troops commenced their retreat from the neighbourhood of Burgos on the one hand, and of Madrid on the other, the officers lost all control over their men.*'

'Ha!' said Young Varmint. 'Someone told him about the Enthusiastics getting drunk at Valdemoro. Go on, Johnny! Any more tributes?'

'Oh, the devil, this is too bad!' George Simmons exclaimed, reading the Memorandum over Kincaid's shoulder. 'Just listen, you fellows! – *I have frequently observed and lamented in the late campaign the facility and celerity with which the French cooked in comparison with our army.*'

'He has, has he?' snorted Leach. 'Well, if we could boil those damned kettles of ours on anything less than half a church door, we'd cook with facility and celerity too!'

'Wrong!' said Kincaid. '*The cause of this disadvantage is the same with that of every other – want of attention of the officers to the orders of the army and the conduct of the men.* Now we know, don't we?'

'God, I think I'll sell out!' said Digby disgustedly.

'My oath! I'm glad I'm not on the headquarters Staff!' said James Stewart, taking the Memorandum out of Kincaid's hand, and glancing through it. 'I suppose the truth is that that pig-sticking affair annoyed him. He's a bad-tempered devil.'

'Daresay the lot he took to Burgos did misbehave themselves,' said Leach. 'That ought to be a lesson to him in future.'

'What the hell does he mean by *irregularities and outrages were committed with impunity?*' demanded Digby, in his turn seizing the document.

'Horrid scenes at Torquemada,' said Beckwith. 'I heard about that.'

'Damn it, *we* had nothing to do with it!'

'Much his precious lordship cares for that! Blast him, why should we worry? If he thinks he can find a finer set of fellows than our men, let him go and look for 'em! Who's coming out after snipe?'

2

It would be a long time before the army could forgive its Commander for his sweeping condemnation, but meanwhile there was much to be done to make the various quarters habitable, and to ensure suitable recreation for the winter. Most of the cottages which were requisitioned for billets consisted of two rooms built on a mud-floor, the outer of which housed not only the owner of the property, but any livestock he might possess as well. Fires were kindled in the middle of the floors, and the smoke was allowed to drift towards a hole in the roof, so that the first task on being allotted quarters was to build a chimney. The second was to cover up broken windows, to keep out the cold; and the third to ride to Almeida in search of crockery, and all other domestic comforts. There were sutlers to be found in Frenada, but the prices charged at headquarters were beyond the means of most officers' purses. Six shillings for a loaf of white bread was what you would have to pay, if you were green enough to do your shopping there; and twenty-two shillings for one pound of good tea; while long-forage for your horse would not cost a penny less than four shillings for one small bundle.

The officers of the Light division, who were famous for their dramatic talent, lost no time in looking about them for a suitable playhouse. They found it in a disused chapel in Gallegos. They soon had it fitted up, and gave some excellent performances, which were attended by everyone, including Lord Wellington, who was quartered near enough to make a ride to Gallegos feasible. The Bishop of Ciudad Rodrigo, when he heard of it, laid a solemn curse on the enterprise, according to Kincaid, but nobody cared a penny for that.

The rank-and-file, meanwhile, were settling down with that peculiar facility of the most insular people in the world to make themselves at home in any quarter of the globe. A great many of the camp-followers, widowed during the retreat, were finding new husbands. This was usual; indeed, it was inevitable, since there were no means provided for their return to England. Generally, there was no lack of suitors for them, since a capable woman who could be relied upon to get into camp ahead of her man and have a strong hot cup of tea waiting for him, when he arrived cold and tired and hungry, made all the difference to a soldier's comfort. Most of them could be relied on, too, in spite of anything the exasperated Provost Marshal could do. Even when he had their donkeys shot under them, in a vain attempt to discourage them from choking the line of march, they struggled on afoot, carrying their chattels on their backs, calling down curses on his head, and impeding the army's progress just as much as ever. The stoutest-hearted amongst them could never be induced to travel in the rear. 'Sure,' said Mrs Skiddy, 'if we went in the rear the French, bad luck to them, would pick me up, me and my donkey, and then Dan Skiddy would be lost entirely widout me!' Most of them had had three or four different husbands since they landed in Portugal, and although there were some men who thought the advantages of possessing a woman to sleep with one, and to cook for one, were outweighed by the certainty of having a dead man's head thrown in one's dish every time the creature was out of temper, there were usually half-a-dozen candidates for the widow's hand by the time the first shovelful of earth had been thrown on top of her deceased mate. They were a rough set, always fighting, even more addicted to plunder than the soldiers themselves, and every bit as hardy.

Juana's henchwoman was no exception to the rule, and several times presented herself at the Smiths' billet with a scratched face, or a black eye; but Harry thought that her fighting qualities would be of more practical use to Juana than any of the accomplishments of a real lady's maid.

The Smiths had made their winter-quarters so snug that the Padre decided to remain with them until the spring. After his adventure at San Muñoz, it had seemed probable that he would leave them as soon as he could. He was for a time extremely disgruntled, and moralized a good deal over the selfishness of soldiers. 'When you told me at Madrid what were the hardships of a soldier's life in retreat, I considered I had a very correct idea,' he told Harry. 'I see now I had no conception whatever. Everyone acts for himself alone! *There* you see a poor, knocked-up soldier sitting in the mud, unable to move; *there* come grooms with led horses. No one asks the sick man to ride; no one sympathizes with the other's feelings – in short, everyone appears to struggle against difficulties for himself alone.'

'On river-banks, Padre?' Harry said, with a grin.

'It appears to me extraordinary and un-Christian,' said Don Pedro coldly.

But when he saw how cleverly Juana had contrived comforts in the little cottage in Fuentes de Oñoro, he thought that after all he would stay with the Smiths through the winter-months.

Both Juana and Harry had begun to find him rather tiresome, but it turned out that he was a splendid cook, so the arrangement, irksome at times, had its compensations.

Various messes had been formed amongst the officers, and with a little ingenuity, and plenty of wine procured from Lamego, it was surprising how jolly and comfortable even a barn with half the roof swept off by a cannon-ball could be. Charcoal braziers kept one warm; a little boarding and a great deal of baize excluded the worst draughts; and a good mess-president saw to it that there was always plenty of pork in the larder, however little beef he was able to procure. The local pork was very sweet and rich; there was mullet in the Agueda; and dried Newfoundland ling to be bought from the sutlers; and those who knew the district said that there would be good trout-fishing in the spring.

As soon as any mess had fitted up its room tolerably well, the next thing to be done was to send out invitations for a bolero meeting. These were held throughout the winter, and very amusing they were. All the local ladies came to them, dressed in their brown stuff bodices, and with their petticoats stuck all over with patches of red cloth. They taught the English officers how to dance the fandango, how to manipulate the castanets, and the correct height of the elbow in the bolero; and the officers taught them the way to romp through Sir Roger de Coverley. There was always plenty of hot punch; and the meetings were apt to become rather rowdy towards midnight; but the only real objection to them was the reek of garlic which the ladies brought with them.

Juana, as much a foreigner in León as any Englishman, learned one of the country measures to dance at the wedding of her landlord. He was marrying for the second time, but the festivities stretched over three days, and were conducted on a scale of great magnificence. If you went to a wedding in this part of the country, you took your present with you, and gave it to the bride during one of the dances. She held a knife in her hand, with an apple on top of it, and provided your gift was of suitable size, you cut a slice out of the apple and stuffed your offering into the gap. Juana begged a doubloon from Harry to give to the bride. It was thought to be a very handsome present, and everyone said that in spite of being an Estremenha Juana had very proper notions, and was the kind of girl anyone would be glad to welcome to his house.

3

By Christmas, everybody, except those who still filled the hospitals to overflowing, had settled down into the usual winter routine. The weather was very cold, sometimes wet, sometimes snowy, occasionally foggy, but provided one got plenty of exercise this was not much of a hardship. While Staff-officers followed his lordship's hounds, others, not so well provided with mounts, took shot-guns out, and tramped for miles after woodcock, or went coursing with Harry on plains that teemed with hares. The rank-and-file went rabbiting with ferrets and a native pack of mongrels and harriers. They enjoyed far better sport than his lordship did, for they never came home empty-handed, while it was well known that his lordship's hounds had only killed one fox that season, and that by mobbing. Foxes used to head for the banks of the Coa, and go to ground in holes in the rocks, but as his lordship hunted more for exercise than for sport, that never seemed to worry him.

Headquarters amusements were voted very tame by the gay Light Bobs. To begin with, Frenada was a flea-ridden village, with dung between all the cobble-stones, and refuse from the cottages cast out into the street. Most of the houses were in a state of decay, and not even his lordship's headquarters were weather-tight. His secretaries, having stopped the rickety windows, were obliged to work by candlelight all day, and even then their fingers were often numbed by the cold. Most of the houses were of the pattern common to the district: white-washed dwellings with stables beneath. There was only one lady at head-quarters that winter, Mrs Scovell, who gave evening loo-parties from time to time. His lordship kept open house, of course, and a very good table besides (he would pay as much as eight shillings for a hare); but it was only the great men who were invited to his dinners. There were rather too many great men at Frenada for comfort, thought the rest of the army. The Leg of Mutton, and the Cauliflower, the only decent inns in the place, always teemed with Staff-officers, some of them very good sort of men, but too many of them conceited young sprigs, doing the dandy in velvet-forage caps with gold tassels, gray-braided coats and fancy waistcoats of every colour of the rainbow. Several of these 'Counts', as the army called the dandies, were his lordship's aides-de-camp, and by no means conciliating in their manner towards regimental officers. Of course, if you had the luck to run into Lord March, or Ulysses de Burgh, or Fitzroy Somerset, you would carry away with you the kindest memories of old Douro's family; but it was quite a puzzle to know how his lordship had come to choose some of the other young suckers to be his aides-de-camp.

Then there were the servants: a shocking set of idle good-for-nothings, swarming all over the town, loud-voiced in the sutlers' shops, drunk in the *posadas*, overbearing with the villagers. If you wanted to get a few plates from the tinman, you had actually to force your way through a clamorous crowd of bâtmen at his door: and if you tried to buy some writing-paper at the sutler's, it was all Lombard Street to an eggshell some Staff-officer's pert private servant would snap up the last quire of English cream-laid from under your very nose, leaving you to pay an extortionate price for the thin, cross-grained folio made in the country.

But if you wanted to hear the latest news, or to see an English newspaper before it was months old, you did your shopping at Frenada rather than at Almeida. You picked up the latest songs there, too: there were two much in vogue that winter, and it was odd if you spent an hour in Frenada without hearing either *Ah, quel plaisir d'être soldat*, or *Ahé, Marmont*, hummed in the streets. Very good tunes they were: it was said that old Douro was particularly fond of *Ahé, Marmont*, and often called for it at his parties.

Old Douro left Frenada in December, and went off to Cadiz for six weeks. Small blame to him! said his troops, spreading scandalous stories of his supposed activities there. The wonder was that any man, with the power of choosing his ground, should have selected Frenada for his headquarters. What was left of you, after the fleas and the bugs had eaten their fill, was blown away by the bitter winds that swept through the streets; and there was not a woman in the place worth looking at. Good luck to his lordship, the old dog! with the pick of the southern beauties at Cadiz to share his bed!

Although Frenada might be an unappetizing town, the country round it was extremely picturesque, particularly in the vicinity of the Coa, a wild river running between masses of weathered rocks, through grand ravines, and bordered by stunted trees, and the ruins of once fortified villages. Rather reminiscent of Mrs Radclyffe's tales, some thought, with far too many wolves for comfort. It was not at all the kind of country you could fancy settling in. All very well for lovers of the romantic, but a plain man would prefer a more placid and a richer countryside. One of the greatest difficulties was to get sufficient fodder for your horses. All the mules had to be sent miles away for forage; and barley (if you could get it) was shockingly dear. Staff-officers at Frenada said that his lordship talked quite openly of wintering in the district next year; and when it was pointed out to him that the army had eaten up nearly all the available bullocks, he replied with his neigh of a laugh: 'Well, then, we must now set about eating all the sheep, and when they are gone, I suppose we must go.'

4

By the New Year, all the sierras were white with snow, and the weather had become extremely inclement. The soldiers had formed a Trigger Club at Espeja, but the Riflemen had had to give up playing their favourite game of Nine Holes: it was really too cold, and the ground too rough to make it worth while. There was still much sickness, but many had managed to escape from the hospitals and rejoin their regiments. Most of the convalescents suffered from intermittent agues, which made their teeth chatter like castanets. Joe Simmons, proudly wearing a pair of Rifle wings, was still far from well, but George, who had begun his career by studying medicine, was taking great care of him, and hoped to have him in good fighting trim when the spring came. Meanwhile, he was keeping his nose to the grindstone. Joe was made to study for five hours a day. He grumbled a little, but as his second brother, Maud, was out of reach, there was no one to encourage him to revolt, and he submitted with a good grace. George was able to tell his parents that he had grown quite two inches, and was learning to apply.

Some Spaniards had been recruited for the Light division, and

those responsible for the task reported that they were being tolerably well licked into shape. They were rather like the
Portuguese in one respect: if they were commanded by their
own officers they would be just as likely to retreat in disorder as
to advance; but if you put good English officers amongst them
they did very well. In time, they might become as reliable as the
Portuguese Caçadores Marshal Beresford had made into such
splendid troops.

There were other innovations, notably the exchange of the
great iron kettles for lighter and smaller tin ones. Apparently, his
lordship, having had time to recover from the rage which had
governed him when he had written his *Memorandum to officers
commanding Divisions and Brigades*, had realized how much the
unwieldly nature of his soldiers' kettles was to blame for their
dilatoriness in cooking their meals. The new kettles were hailed
with acclaim, and so too were the shakos for officers' wear, in
place of the cocked-hats which had made them targets for every
French sharpshooter.

It was thought that no advance into Spain could be expected
until May, since the horses would need at least a month's green
feed before they would be fit for another campaign. Remounts
were being sent out from England, of course, and fresh troops to
replace the depleted second battalions, which had gone home to
the depôts.

Meanwhile, life went on much as usual in the army. A number of men acquired Spanish or Portuguese mistresses, so that
the horde of camp-followers was becoming oddly polyglot.
They quarrelled even more violently than the Irish women, and
could not be trusted to refrain from using knives as weapons
when they were angry, but the stews which they cooked in their
earthenware *penellas* made it worth while putting up with their
murderous tendencies.

All Spanish women were expert in the management of the *penella*, which stood day in, day out, at the side of the fire, and was turned from time to time. Juana, taking lessons from the Padre, learned to make a stew the very smell of which set one's mouth watering. But when Billy Mein, riding over to dine with the Smiths, asked her what she put in the pot to give it such a flavour, she never seemed to know, but answered vaguely: '*Oh, un poco de aceyte y una cabeza de ajos!*' But since her stews all tasted different, no one believed this, and 'a little oil and a clove of garlic' became a standing-joke, the stock-answer to any culinary question.

Billy Mein was often to be found in the Smiths' quarters. He used to ride into Fuentes de Oñoro to drink grog made of bad rum with Harry. Major Rowan was a frequent visitor, too, bringing news of the regiment's Colonel, who had been invalided to England after the taking of Ciudad Rodrigo. The men of the 52nd would not be happy until Colonel Colborne was in command of them again, for there was no officer who more thoroughly understood outpost work, none more beloved. 'Oh, for Colborne!' they groaned, whenever anything went amiss. But he had had his shoulder so badly shattered in the assault on Rodrigo that it was doubtful whether he ever would return to the Peninsula.

At the end of January, the troops had the satisfaction of knowing that Beau Douro was amongst them again. The sight of his well-known figure had always a most cheering effect upon the army. It was hoped his lordship had enjoyed himself, junketing about Cadiz: he looked very well, and seemed to be in excellent spirits, so no doubt he meant to give King Joseph some hard knocks in the coming campaign.

Early in February, much to their disgust, the Smiths had to leave their billet in Fuentes de Oñoro, to go with General

Vandeleur to Fuente Guinaldo. Brigade headquarters had been moved there, to make room for the Spanish headquarters in Fuentes de Oñoro. No one appreciated the change, for it was much colder at Guinaldo, besides being twenty-four miles distant from Frenada. The Smiths would have taken the Padre with them, but he had made up his mind to go back to Vicalbaro. Perhaps he was tired of cooking. At Guinaldo, Vandeleur was busy with Courts Martial. He had made the acquaintance of the new Judge-Advocate, a civilian, but a very pleasant fellow, who came over from Frenada on a handsome black horse, and seemed to be astonished at the army's way of life. Since he happened to be spending the night in Vandeleur's quarters, he accompanied him to a masked ball given by the officers of the Light division. All the belles of Guinaldo were present, some dressed as English officers: an indelicate frolic which rather shocked Mr Larpent: and all of them remarkably free and easy with the gay Light Bobs. Indeed, one plump, seductive creature was the cause of a minor disturbance, for she cuddled into the arms of Vandeleur's wiry young Brigade-Major, in a convenient alcove, and cooed gently to him, with her cheek against the frogs on his jacket. The Brigade-Major's eyes gleamed laughter between the slits of his mask; he did not seem to be unresponsive to his partner's advances, judging from the way his arm encircled her waist; but while Mr Larpent idly watched him, a little stormy creature descended upon the Brigade-Major in a sudden flurry of fringed petticoats, and dealt him a ringing box on the ear.

The Brigade-Major jumped up, shaking off the plump lady, and looking as though he would very much like to return the slap. His assailant addressed him in a torrent of low-voiced Spanish, which Mr Larpent was unable to understand; he shot out a rapid answer in the same tongue, and just as Mr Larpent, quite scandalized, moved forward to intervene, a very tall man in Rifle green strolled up, and swept the little dark creature into a waltz that was just starting.

Mr Larpent found General Vandeleur chuckling at his elbow. 'By Jove, that young devil of mine has married a tartar!' said the General. 'Dear little soul, isn't she?'

Mr Larpent was unable to agree with him. Juana, waltzing with Kincaid, still flushed and raging, did not look in the least like a dear little soul.

'*Malvada!*' Kincaid scolded softly. 'What do you think you deserve for making scenes in public?'

'I don't care! I wish I had hit him harder!'

'He'd have murdered you! Now, you know you are behaving disgracefully! English ladies don't box their husbands' ears – at least, not at masquerades!'

'I am not English! I do not want to be English! He is faithless – *no se inquieta por nada!*'

'You little devil, he'll care for being made a fool of in public fast enough! Besides, you know he doesn't mean anything by just flirting a little.'

'He is dancing with her!' Juana said in a shaking voice.

'Of course he is! I would myself, if my wife came and slapped my face for putting an arm round a pretty girl's waist!'

'You are as horrible as he is, and I am going home – *instantáneamente!*'

'No, no, you can't do that! Everyone will laugh at you if you do!'

Juana informed him between gritted teeth that the whole army was at liberty to laugh at her. He led her off the floor at the end of the dance, and was still persuasively arguing with her when the band struck up the next waltz. Juana said: 'Either you will take me home now, or I go by myself!' and suddenly saw Harry, his mask discarded, descending upon her.

'You'll dance this with me!' Harry said, grasping her hand, and pulling her roughly into his arms.

'I won't!' Juana said, but in rather a frightened voice.

He paid no attention, but began to waltz with her. He held her in an arm that felt like steel, and his grip on her hand crushed all her fingers together. He said in a molten under-voice: 'What the hades did you mean by slapping my face? Answer me!'

'You know very well, and if you don't let me go I will do it again!' whispered Juana.

He looked down at her for an instant, his face rather white, and his eyes bright with anger. 'You had better not, *mi muchacha!*'

Juana thought that perhaps she had better not. She said: 'Then *you* had better not flirt with that – that *ramera!*'

'I'll flirt with whom I damned well please! And don't let me hear that word on your tongue again! How dare you use such language?'

'If I knew a worse word, I would say it! I shall say anything I like!'

'You're a vulgar, stupid, jealous, ill-conditioned brat!'

'And you are a libertine!'

Harry gave a sudden crack of scornful laughter. 'It would serve you right if I was! If you ever dare to make a fool of me in public again, I'll leave you! *Comprende?*'

Her steps faltered; she replied with difficulty: 'You would like to be rid of me, I daresay.'

'Very much, when you serve me a trick like that!'

The music stopped. Juana wrenched her hand out of his, and walked away to where Kincaid was lounging against the wall. He straightened himself, and said: 'You know, Juana, you and Harry are the best dancers in the room!'

'I am going home,' said Juana, in a stifled voice.

'Very well,' Kincaid said, catching the glint of a tear on her cheek. 'I'll take you, then.'

There was a light crust of snow in the cobbled street, and the night air was very cold. Juana pulled the hood of her camlet cloak over her head, and walked beside her tall escort in silence. At the door of her lodging, he said: '*Mi querida amiga,* cheer up! If Harry has a regular pepper-pot of a temper, so have you, you know!'

'Yes,' said Juana. 'I know.'

She said good night, and went into the house. The fire had sunk very low in the room she and Harry slept in, and a biting draught whistled under the rickety door. Juana put some charcoal into the brazier with shaking hands, shed all her finery, turned down the lamp, and crept shivering into bed. Half-an-hour later, sobs still catching her breath, she heard the outer door open, and shut with a crash. She shrank under the blankets, pulling them over her head, and clenched her teeth on her damp handkerchief in an effort to suppress her convulsive sobs. Harry's quick step sounded; he came into the room. 'Juana!' he said sharply.

She lay mouse-still. He turned up the lamp again, saw the pathetic mound under the blankets, and went up to the bed, and relentlessly pulled the clothes from over his wife's head. 'Don't pretend you're asleep!' he said wrathfully. 'If this doesn't beat all! First you slap my face, then you –' He broke off, his anger suddenly evaporating at the sight of Juana's wet eyelashes, and shivering limbs. 'Oh, you wicked, precious, little varmint!' he exclaimed, gathering her into his arms. 'Don't cry, don't cry, my poor baby! It was all my fault!'

'Oh no! Oh no!'

'You silly, naughty child, you're ice-cold! Do you want to catch your death, bad one?'

'I don't c-care, for you w-wish to be rid of me!'

'Never!'

'You said you did!'

'No, no, I didn't say that!'

'But you did, and I wish very much to die!' wept Juana.

'If I said it, it was a black lie! *Mi queridissima muger!*'

'Oh, mi Enrique, I am so very, very sorry!' Juana said, flinging her arms round his neck. 'It was bad of me to hit you, and vulgar, and – and ill-conditioned, and I expect she was not that thing which you have forbidden me to say! And perhaps you were not flirting with her after all, and it was only my wicked jealousy!'

'Alas, alas!' Harry said, kissing first one eyelid and then the other, 'I was, and she was, and I deserve to have both my ears boxed!'

'Oh, *malvado!*' Juana said, her tears turning to laughter. 'Shameless one!'

'Libertine!' grinned Harry. 'Oh, Juana, you absurd infant, what should I do without you?'

5

They were never going to quarrel again, not even when the ladies of Guinaldo tied ribbons to Harry's coat, and blew him kisses in the street. Luckily the Green-jackets were not as popular as the officers of the 52nd, now quartered in the town, and so much caressed by the natives that it was a wonder their heads were not turned.

Reinforcements of cavalry, arriving from England, provoked some admiration and a good deal of ribaldry from the shabby, weather-beaten Peninsular veterans. 'As fair and beautiful as lilies!' mocked Captain Leach, encountering a squadron of Life Guards in all their unsoiled magnificence.

Cadoux shook his head, murmuring wistfully: 'If I could afford it, I think I should exchange into a cavalry regiment. Really, you would be hard put to it to find smarter uniforms! I do what I can, of course, but one is terribly hampered.'

'Oh no, don't leave us!' begged Jack Molloy. 'You couldn't indulge your taste in fancy waistcoats if you joined the Life Guards!'

'True, very true!' Cadoux said, the lurking smile, which Harry could never be brought to see, narrowing his sleepy eyes. 'I have such a pretty new one for the party, too.'

'Oh, are you going to it?' asked Molloy. 'No one sent *me* an invitation.'

Yes, Cadoux, obtaining his invitation through God knew what underground channels, said his brother-officers, was certainly going to the party. He had not been able to get himself asked to the dinner, however.

The party was being given by Lord Wellington, in Ciudad Rodrigo, on the occasion of the investiture of General Lowry Cole with the Order of the Bath. It was to consist of a select dinner, followed by a ball and supper. Never having given one of his grand parties at Rodrigo, of which battered city he had been made Duque, his lordship was anxious to do the thing in style. All the headquarters plate was requisitioned; waggon-loads of glass were sent from Almeida, twenty-five miles away; and as soon as Colonel Colin Campbell, who managed his lordship's household, reported that there was no possibility of getting a banquet prepared in Rodrigo, arrangements were made to carry a half-cooked dinner there on carts and mule-back from Frenada. Colin Campbell swore, and said in his rough way that he could not imagine what could possess a sane man to go to such trouble for the sake of a dinner-party. But his lordship liked parties, and he could not see that to carry every dish seventeen miles would be the least trouble in the world. Depend upon it, the headquarters cooks would make nothing of it.

Harry, happening to accompany his Brigadier to Frenada on business, had the good fortune to come under his lordship's notice. His lordship liked young Smith, who never applied for leave, nor went sick when he was most needed, and he remembered that he was married to a charming representative of one of the best families in Estremadura. He told him that he must be sure to bring his little *guerrière* to the ball, and promised him an invitation.

Harry thought that twenty miles was too far to take his wife, but Juana speedily undeceived him.

'You will be too tired to dance,' Harry said.

'I am never too tired to dance,' replied Juana simply.

So the Smiths were going to the party, too, and Harry rode all the way to Almeida, no little journey from Guinaldo, to buy the most handsome Braganza shawl there for his Juana to wear.

Cadoux drawled that he would make it his business to dance with Juana, to annoy Harry.

'I doubt whether it will,' said Kincaid. 'Why annoy him, in any case?'

'But he annoys me,' said Cadoux plaintively. 'There's no getting away from him. Wherever you go, there's Smith: a skinny little devil, making enough noise for two of his size, never still, never thinking anyone can do anything but himself, and always so damned sure that there's nothing he couldn't do, if he did but wish to.'

Kincaid laughed, but said: 'Oh, Harry brags atrociously! We all know that! But he's a damned good Staff-officer, Dan. If you had served under some of the real bad 'uns I've met in my career, you'd thank God for a Harry Smith! You never see him tired —'

'I find that very annoying,' murmured Cadoux. 'When every man in the brigade is dropping with fatigue, it isn't decent, it isn't seemly, to be full of energy.'

Kincaid smiled, but shook his head. 'All very well, but you wouldn't get the men to agree with you. They know that no matter what may have occupied the day or night, or what elementary war may be raging, Smith will never be found off his horse until he's seen every man in the brigade under cover.'

'He damns them up hill and down dale,' Cadoux complained.

But the men did not care a button for any of the fearful expletives their Brigade-Major was in the habit, in moments of stress, of flinging at their heads. In battle, there was no oath beyond the range of his vocabulary, but any officer who shared the hottest shell-fire with them, and wore himself down to bone and muscle in their interests, was welcome to call them individually and collectively the foulest names he could lay his tongue to.

It was hardly to be expected that he and soft-spoken, dandified Cadoux would ever agree, but men who liked both tried several times to point out the good points of one to the other. George Simmons said that the silly enmity was mostly Cadoux's fault, because he never let slip an opportunity to irritate Harry's quick, intolerant temper.

But when Cadoux waltzed with Juana at Lord Wellington's ball, Harry paid very little heed. He was sorry for Juana's having to stand up with such a frippery fellow, and merely shrugged his incomprehension when she said she found Cadoux quite a pleasant companion.

The ball was a great success, and everyone but Colin Campbell, and the Spanish General O'Lalor, who was responsible for its management, enjoyed it hugely. The best house left standing in the town had been taken for it, and the depredations of the siege were covered up by some very fine hangings of yellow damasked satin, which had been brought away from the Palace of St Ildefonso, and hidden in Rodrigo to save them from the French. General O'Lalor discovered these, and they were hung up tent-like in the ballroom, providing at once an air of magnificence and a certain degree of protection from the cold air which came into the room through a large hole knocked out of the roof by a cannon-ball. The supper-rooms were hung with crimson satin and gold, and looked very well too. Claret, champagne, and Lamego, which was like the best port, had been brought from Frenada in spring-waggons; the dinner, over which the agitated cooks tore their hair, did not seem to have suffered from having been partially prepared seventeen miles away; and the headquarters plate was enough to provide each guest with one change of silver during the meal. A blaspheming mob of bâtmen staggered about behind the scenes with immense cauldrons of hot water, and washed all the spoons and forks with feverish haste between courses; and the band of the 52nd regiment arrived after dinner to play the latest dance-tunes for the company.

It was rather chilly in the ballroom, and there was one dangerous hole in the floor; but dancing soon warmed one, and as for the hole, a mat laid over it, and a man posted to see that no one plunged a leg in it, made it of no particular consequence.

Lord Wellington, who had been hard at work in Frenada until half-past three in the afternoon, rode over to Rodrigo in excellent time for the dinner, and appeared at it, dressed in all his orders. He was quite the life and soul of the party. He danced himself, several times, quizzed his Staff, flirted with all the prettiest ladies, stayed to supper, and rode back by moon-light to Frenada, with every intention of being in his office again by midday. Of his family, only Colonel Gordon could be got to go back with him. Everyone else had procured a lodg-ing in the town, so that the party did not break up until five

in the morning. It got a little rough after his lordship's departure, and Harry took Juana away to their quarters. When he
had seen her safely into bed, however, he went back to the
ball, and was in time to assist in teaching the excited Spanish
guests to shout hip, hip, hip, hurrah in place of their *vivas*. The
toasts were becoming incessant, the most popular being 'The
next campaign', and 'Death to all Frenchmen!' It presently
seemed good to the other members of his lordship's personal
Staff to chair the young Prince of Orange, for no particular
reason except that he was a nice lad, and they liked him. The
idea took, and the next person to be carried on high round the
room was General Vandeleur. There, however, the chairing
stopped, for the General's bearers were distinctly foxed, and
they let him fall.

Harry rejoined his Juana when daylight was shining through
the shutters, and tumbled into bed beside her with a rueful
groan which woke her. She sat up, saw his head buried in the
pillow, and demanded: 'Why, what is the matter? Are you ill?'

'No, I'm drunk,' said Harry in a thickened voice.

Juana gave a gurgle. 'Horrid creature!' she said, nestling down
again, and pulling his head on to her shoulder. 'Go to sleep,
then: you will have a very bad headache presently.'

He put a heavy arm across her body. 'You're a wife in a thousand, m'darling,' he said sleepily.

6

By April, four of the invalided Generals had returned to the
Peninsula; and Murray, to the army's profound relief, was back
in his old position of Quartermaster-General. The cavalry's elegant commander, Stapleton Cotton, was still in England, plaguing the life out of Lord Bathurst, said the irreverent

head-quarters Staff, to get him a peerage; but no one doubted that he would rejoin the army in time for the coming campaign. Whether he came back with or without a peerage, he would be bound, thought his officers, to bring a waggon-load of smart new uniforms, for he was a great Count, and was said to be worth, when fully accoutred, man and horse, not a penny less than five hundred pounds.

With the return of General Picton to his division, Pakenham was appointed to command the 6th division during General Clinton's continued absence. He was felt to have done very well by the Fighting 3rd, and the men were sorry to see him go. On the other hand, they were accustomed to old Picton, and they liked him, roughness and all; and when he arrived amongst them, looking as disreputable as ever in a travesty of a uniform and a large beaver hat, they surprised themselves and him by raising a cheer for him.

Nothing was now talked of in the army but the prospect of a move. The news of Napoleon's Russian debâcle had reached the Peninsula; and Wellington, who had written the year before, '*I shudder when I reflect upon the enormity of the task which I have undertaken*'; and in November had thought the prospects of a successful campaign extremely bleak, was talking now, in the best of spirits, of putting himself in fortune's way as soon as possible. But he was not going to entrust the Spanish forces under him with any separate or important task. In fact, he meant to employ as few Spanish regiments on the campaign as he dared. 'I have never known the Spaniards do anything, much less do anything well,' said his lordship acidly.

At the beginning of the winter, the three French armies confronting the Allies were cantoned over an enormous stretch of country, Soult, with the Army of the South, occupying Toledo, Avila, and a part of La Mancha; and the Army of Portugal forming a triangle between Palencia and Valladolid, with Zamora as its apex. Between these two armies, King Joseph's Army of the Centre was spread; but in March, news of considerable troop movements was brought to Wellington's headquarters by guerrilleros and Intelligence-officers. King Joseph had got rid of Soult at last, who went off in February to assist his Emperor in forming a new Army of Germany. He took all his Andalusian plunder with him, including a complete gallery of Murillos; and Joseph began to draw in the Army of the South, till it lay between Madrid and the Douro.

The French had passed an uncomfortable winter, worried by guerrilleros, who attacked them rather in the manner of tiresome wasps; and by native insurrections. In the north, in Navarre and Santander, a horribly dangerous part of the country, the insurrections had been serious enough to cause them a great deal of trouble, for not only was the guerrilla chief Longa a real fighter, but the British Admiral, Sir Home Popham, was pouring munitions and stores into the country for his support. Clausel was sent north to overcome this menace, and his departure laid open the plains of León to the Allied advance. When King Joseph removed his headquarters to Valladolid, Suchet, much harried by the English force on the Mediterranean, lost touch with him. It was no wonder that Lord Wellington was in good spirits. Some of his battalions were greatly under strength, of course, but between British and Portuguese he expected to march with over sixty thousand bayonets, and eight thousand sabres. Counting the artillery, the Engineers, his new mounted Staff Corps, and all other departments of the army, he could put a force of eighty-one thousand men in the field, and most of them tried troops, too.

In May, the news that the headquarters servants were busy packing up his lordship's claret put the army on tiptoe with expectation. Eight showy gray stallions were brought up from Lisbon to Frenada, to draw his lordship's travelling carriage. They were a present to him from the Prince Regent, and the first time they were harnessed to the carriage one of them got astride the pole, another reared up, and fell over backwards, and the whole eight behaved as though they had never been in harness before. It was the loudly expressed opinion of his lordship's sweating grooms that his six old mules would do the work very much better, but after a good deal of training, the grays began to go quite well, and would certainly make a fine show on his lordship's progress through Spain.

On the 17th May his lordship reviewed the Light division on the plain of Espeja, and seemed pleased with their appearance. The men had got new equipment, and although there was still a good deal of sickness thinning the ranks, the two lines drawn up for inspection made an impressive sight. The Light division, with three brigades of cavalry, was going to form the centre column of the march, and if anything had been needed (said critics from other divisions) to puff them up any further in their own conceit, it was supplied by the knowledge that with them would go Lord Wellington himself.

Nothing definite was known about the date of the army's breaking up from its winter quarters. Marching-orders were daily expected, but did not arrive. It was rumoured that the pontoon train was late in coming up. Meanwhile, old Douro had a bad cold, and the soldiers kicked their heels, cursed the Engineers, and fished for trout and roach in the teeming rivers.

His lordship's good spirits had infected his army. There was no longer any talk of recapturing Madrid. Everyone realized that his lordship was setting out on a much larger enterprise, and meant to chase the French over the Pyrenees. He would do it, too, swore his troops. 'Come back next winter? Not us! We'll be in Paris by then!' said one optimist, light-heartedly packing up his greatcoat to be put in store. 'Damme, what with not 'avin' to lug our coats along with us like we always 'ave, and what with them new tents, to say nothing of changing them bastards of iron kettles for these 'ere tin ones, I don't see as anything can stop us.'

'Look high and fall in a cow-turd!' retorted a prosaically-minded friend. 'Likely we'll freeze to death without our coats!'

7

'All ready for the march? When do we rompé for it?' Harry's friends enquired, trying to worm a little information out of him.

But Harry had never been less ready for a march. He was in the devil's own temper, too, snapping at everyone. Harry had had six capital horses when the brigade moved to Guinaldo, but winter quarters to his stud, he admitted ruefully, was no holiday. He had killed the Andalusian he had bought at Alcala, swimming him through two rivers in the course of a very severe run when out with Stewart's harriers; and of the remaining five only two were fit for work. 'If I were to fall backwards I should break my nose!' Harry said savagely. 'No one had ever such fiendish ill-luck!'

'I told you you were far too bruising a rider,' said Stewart, from behind a cloud of cigar-smoke. 'What's the matter with Old Chap?'

'Picked up a nail in one hind foot. Won't be fit to ride for months!'

'Careless fellow! I shan't give you any more horses,' Stewart said, quizzing him.

But Harry flung away in a rage with the whole universe. His predicament was certainly bad enough to try the most even temper, and the condition of his stud was not all his own fault. An English mare, quite a reliable mount, had thrown out a ring-bone; and Tiny, now Juana's property, had pulled down the heavy bullock-manger in the stable, and seriously damaged his off fore-hoof. That left the Smiths with two horses between them, one a good charger, the other a thoroughbred mare, very showy, but inclined to be clumsy.

'I suppose you think I'm going to mount you?' said Vandeleur, trying to look severe.

'Well, if you don't, sir, I don't know how I shall manage,' replied Harry coolly.

'Damn your impudence!' said Vandeleur. 'A pretty state for a Major of Brigade to be in! Well, well, I daresay I can let you have one of my horses now and then.'

Marching-orders, when they came at last, came without previous warning, at midnight on the 20th May. By dawn the whole division was assembled at the village of San Felices el Chico, and the scene resembled nothing so much as a social rout-party. Friends, whose respective quarters had lain too far apart to permit of their visiting each other, met with laughter, and back-slapping. Old jokes were remembered, and many questions asked. If a man had a fresh mule, it was remarked on; while all the most insignificant persons, such as Portuguese goat-herds, or someone's sloe-eyed mistress, were enquired after.

The army was marching in three main columns, with Giron's Galician force coming down from the north to join the six divisions under Graham, which were to cross the Douro in Portugal, heading for Braganza. These formed the left wing of the army. Hill, with three divisions, was on the right, marching towards the Tormes.

The Light division, with their old friends, Arentschildt's German Hussars, passed Ciudad Rodrigo on the 22nd May, and camped on the Yeltes River. Everyone was in fine fettle; the new tents, one to twenty men, turned bivouacs into the most luxurious camps: a great improvement on a looped blanket stuck up on sticks, said the troops.

They were marching over ground which they had last seen under leaden November skies, but nearly everyone agreed that you would never recognize it. Remembering the bogs, the submerged stumps of trees against which they had stubbed their blistered feet, the sleet, and the biting winds, the men looked about them as though they could scarcely believe their eyes. A blue sky, a warm sun, fields of green grass, were things they had never associated with this stretch of country. At San Muñoz, the contrast seemed particularly marked. The river across which Juana had swum her horse had dwindled to a placid stream, its fords no more than knee-deep.

They halted there for a day. Jonathan Leach took his subalterns to fish for dace, and fried them afterwards in a shallow pan. Some of the men fished too, but most of them lazed on the river-bank, recalling the flurried skirmish of six months before, and contrasting their dreadful diet of acorns with their present well-filled canteens.

The Life Guards and the Blues joined the column that day, big fellows on glossy horses, all in the pink of condition. The tanned, weather-beaten veterans privately thought them a fine-looking lot, but they naturally concealed their admiration, and roasted the newcomers. 'Wait for a little duty and starvation, and then talk!' they shouted at the resplendent troopers. 'You've done nothing but come up the best time of the year in the grass season!'

'Gawd love me, if ever I see such a cursed set of green 'uns!' remarked a Rifleman, lying on his stomach, with his head propped in his hands.

'Keep your tongue within your teeth, laddie. Raw leather will stretch,' said a bony Scot.

'It'll need to. Someone told them blurry 'Yde Park soldiers the enemy was in the neighbour'ood, and now whenever they see a *burro* in their front they think they've come up with Johnny Crapaud's rear-guard.'

The Household Cavalry, painfully conscious of their greenness, did indeed seem to expect to find a Frenchman behind every bush. They were all very zealous, but they would get over that, said the cynics. They spent a good deal of time cleaning their accoutrements, and they would get over that too.

'But my dear fellow, *really*, my dear fellow, is it necessary for your men to look so – so damned out-at-elbow?' one of their officers asked Kincaid. 'Now, don't think I'm criticizing! One knows what splendid troops you have, but upon my word, when I first saw them slouching along I – really, I was shocked!'

Kincaid, who was entertaining the officer to dinner in his tent, refilled his glass, and said: 'My poor greenhorn, when *my* men saw your lot, all so pink and pretty and polished, they said "much bran, little meal." I don't, of course. I'm sure you'll all be capital soldiers when you've cut your milk-teeth.'

'Oh, come! That's too bad!' protested his guest, blushing and laughing. 'Naturally, one hasn't come out to Spain to teach you fellows your business, but one can't help thinking – it *does* strike one that you're damned careless! Not what I should call on the alert, don't you know?'

'What the hades have we got to be alert about?' enquired Kincaid, surprised.

'Well, with the enemy in the neighbourhood –'

'Someone's been gulling you!'

'No, indeed! Why, we actually captured some of their horses this morning! That's what I mean. You don't seem to –'

'Captured some of their horses?' Kincaid interrupted. 'What are you talking about? *I've* heard nothing of any enemy in our front!'

'You might not, but –'

'The hell I might not! I'm field-officer of the day!' The Corporal of the guard came into the tent at that moment, with the orderly-book. Kincaid held out his hand for it, saying: 'Go on: tell me more about these mythical horses of yours.'

'Mythical! You can come and see them for yourself if you don't believe me!'

Kincaid raised his eyes from the orderly-book. They held a look of awe; there was the faintest quiver in his voice. 'Were they – could they have been – light dragoon horses?' he asked.

'Yes, certainly they could! What the devil's the matter?'

Kincaid had burst into a shout of laughter. 'Done, brown as a berry!' he gasped. 'You'll never live this down, never! It's all here, in the orderly-book. Reward offered for the detection of the thieves, too! Damme, if I don't claim it!'

'Reward?' stammered his guest. 'Thieves? You don't mean – they weren't some of *ours*?'

'But they were!' Kincaid assured him. 'Turned out to graze – and you nobbled 'em!'

8

By the 7th June, the division had come in sight of Palencia, the enemy always retiring before them. At Salamanca, the rear-guard left in the town had been pursued and rather mauled by light cavalry; and on the 2nd June, on the road to Toro, the 10th Hussars had made a brilliant charge, taking two hundred prisoners.

The Douro was crossed by means of planks, and flying bridges, several arches of the bridge at Toro having been destroyed. Once across the river, the army entered upon a sunburnt, parched country, almost treeless, and badly watered. The water in the few small streams tasted brackish; the heat of the sun was terrific; men began to recall the sweltering marches before Salamanca. The Household Cavalry lost their fresh complexions, suffered agonies from blistered skins, passing through all the stages of bright red to the final leathery brown. White dust powdered their shining boots, and sweat darkened their uniforms.

'Bite on the bridle, bite on the bridle!' the old soldiers told them, when they groaned under the unaccustomed heat. 'You don't know what heat is yet!'

Rain fell, enough to make the chalky ground slimy. On a greasy bank, the mare Juana was riding slipped and came down, falling on her. The mare scrambled up unhurt, but Juana, after making an attempt to rise, gave a whimper, and clenched her teeth on her underlip.

'Are you hurt, missus?' West asked anxiously. 'The clumsy creature! I knew we'd have a set-out like this!'

Rather white about the mouth, Juana said faintly: 'My foot. I've hurt my foot. I don't think I can stand on it.'

Fortunately, she had been riding with the column, and in a very few minutes Harry was beside her, and a young subaltern had been sent galloping to the rear to find one of the surgeons.

It was evident that she was in much pain, although she said it was not very bad. Harry made her swallow some brandy from a flask he carried, and George Simmons, gently handling the hurt foot, said that the boot must be got off it, as it was already swelling. This was an agonizing business, and Juana, held tightly in Harry's arms, turned her face into his shoulder, and bit on the rough cloth of his jacket. Old Vandeleur, riding up in the middle of all this, in great concern, sent his orderly flying off to hurry the surgeon, told George to be careful what he was about, damned all stupid horses, and wished he had some hartshorn.

'She'll do, sir: don't worry!' Harry said. 'Keep quite still, *hija*! What's the damage, George?'

'I can't tell that. I hope it may not be found to be serious. The thing is, how to carry her to Palencia?'

Juana unclenched her teeth, and turned her head. 'I can ride,' she said, in a ghost of a voice.

'Ride? Nonsense, my poor child! Preposterous!' said Vandeleur. 'Where the devil's that damned surgeon? We must have up one of the spring-waggons at once.'

'I won't go in a spring-waggon. I am better already. See, it is true, I am quite better! Please put me on my horse again!'

'Good girl!' Harry said. 'She'll suffer less on horseback than in one of those waggons, General. Here, George, take my sash, and bind her foot up with it. Listen, *alma mia*, we're close to Palencia: you won't have to bear it for long. George will take care of you, and bring you safely into the town.'

'Oh yes!' Juana said, pulling herself out of his arms. 'You must go! You have your duty to attend to, and indeed I don't need you! You will see what a good soldier I can be!'

'Best soldier in the whole division, my dear!' Vandeleur said. 'Now, we'll all take the greatest care of you, never fear! When I see that damned sawbones I'll – Get on with you, Harry, get on! And mind you procure a decent lodging for the poor child!'

Harry kissed Juana, put her into George's arms, and rode off. Dr Burke came trotting up on his rat-tailed gray a few moments later, and after feeling and probing the swollen foot, an operation which made the tears roll down Juana's cheeks, relieved everyone by announcing that there was not much damage done, only one small bone broken.

However, by the time the walls of Palencia were reached, George was obliged to walk beside Juana's horse, holding her in the saddle, and even Dr Burke, who was a very cheerful person, was beginning to be worried to know how to get his patient under a roof before she swooned right away.

The division camped outside the walls, only the Staff entering the town. An excited crowd of townspeople thronged out to welcome the troops, waving handkerchiefs and shouting *viva los colorados!* Harry met the cortège escorting his wife just outside the gate, thrusting his impatient way through the mob. He had procured a respectable lodging on the main street, and no time was lost on conveying Juana to it. Once she was laid on her bed, Dr Burke was able to attend more particularly to her foot. It was very much inflamed, and he did not think she would be able to ride for quite a week, a pronouncement which made her cry, and deepened the harassed lines on Harry's face. When the doctor had gone, he knelt beside the bed, petting and soothing Juana, promising that West should bring her after the division as soon as she could put her foot in the stirrup.

He managed to hide his own anxiety from her, but he was at his wits' end to know what to do. 'I daren't leave her here!' he told Kincaid, one of the many who came to enquire after Juana. 'You know what these people are! They shout *viva los Ingleses*, but they're such cursed bigots they'd do nothing to help a true Catholic married to a heretic!'

It was Juana who solved the difficulty. The mere thought of being separated from Harry made her forget the pain in her foot, and rouse herself from her state of self-pity. She stopped crying, drank the tea Harry brewed for her, and said in a determined voice: 'Now I am much better – *muy agradable!* – and I will tell you what we must do. I do not stay in this place, which I think is dirty. That is certain. Get me a mule, or a *burro*, mi Enrique, and put a Spanish saddle for a lady on it. My foot will rest on the footboard, and go I will!'

'My poor girl, do you think you could bear it?' Harry said worriedly. 'You will be so jolted!'

'*Eso no es de consecuencia!*'

'I ought to be shot for even thinking of such a thing! Juanita, are you sure you can bear it?'

'Yes, yes, I tell you! Only find me a good mule!'

As soon as Juana's resolve was known, dozens of volunteers presented themselves at the Smiths' billet with offers of service. The division, luckily, was not to march until late on the following afternoon, and the morning was spent by the officers of the brigade in scouring the town for a well-cushioned saddle, and trying the paces of every available mule, to find a very easy one. Juana sat at the window of her lodging, watching the stream of cavalry, artillery, infantry, and baggage pass through the narrow main street. Kincaid looked in to see how she did, and made her laugh by describing the town to her in the most unflattering terms. The front of every house was supported on pillars, which made them look, said Kincaid, like so many worn-out bachelors on crutches.

By the time the brigade was set in motion, Juana's mule was ready for her, and it only remained to carry her down, and set her on its back. She stoutly denied feeling any pain, but received a great deal of sympathy from everyone but Harry. One or two tender-hearted officers were quite indignant with him for the bracing tone he took, but Harry, whose heart ached for every wince Juana gave, never let her see how much he pitied her. Her gallant spirit responded to the ruthless demands he made upon it; she was not in the least resentful, but sat up straight in her cushioned lady's saddle, desperately trying to live up to his expectations.

She bore the march well, following the column with the doctors and the baggage-waggons. When she arrived at the village where the brigade headquarters were established, there was no chance for Harry to lift her down from the mule's back. Laughing, he found himself elbowed out of the way, while an eager guard of honour turned her dismounting into quite a ceremony. The doctor commanded; cloaks were spread on the ground for her reception; half-a-dozen officers claimed the privilege of lifting her down, and there was such a confused babble of advice and instruction, with sharp adjurations to 'Take care, now!' or to 'Mind the leg!' that the villagers gathered round to stare in surprise at such doings.

She was riding the mare again before the week was out, very lame, but determined no longer to plod along in the rear, with only the doctor for company. 'My place is with the column,' she said, with the sauciest tilt of her chin; and when she joined them again, the soldiers cheered her, and Harry had to rap out the sharpest of commands to prevent her putting the mare through all her paces. Juana was always obedient on the march. She saluted, and said: 'Yes, sir!' in such an exact mimicry of Harry's subalterns that a roar of laughter went up, and Harry shook his fist at her.

As the column wound northward, they left behind them the sterile plains, and entered upon a countryside rich with already yellowing corn, and thick vineyards. There were no dykes or hedges to separate one man's land from another's, and the corn stretched in an unbroken shimmering sea as far as the eye could reach.

The chief difficulty to be overcome was the scarcity of wood for firing. There were hardly any trees in the district, and in the end the quartermasters were obliged to pull down empty houses in the villages, and to use the timbers for camp-fires.

The army was in touch with King Joseph's forces, but the infantry had not yet been engaged. Very few men knew why the

French continued to fall back, and only Staff-officers had any appreciation of the strategy underlying the march of Lord Wellington's three columns. The troops knew only that they were being hustled in a wide, north-westerly sweep, with the presumable object of turning King Joseph's right. That Lord Wellington, weeks before, had made plans to transfer his base from Lisbon to Biscay, abandoning his long, difficult communication-lines with the Portuguese coast, was his lordship's own secret. No one, least of all the harassed French commanders, connected the presence of a British supply fleet at Corunna with these carefully guarded plans. The ships were accounted for by the necessity of keeping the Spanish army of Galicia supplied with arms and stores. But from his headquarters at Melgar, on the 10th June, his lordship sent off a dispatch to an officer in charge of the British depôts in Galicia, informing him for the first time of the existence of these ships. '*I shall be much obliged,*' wrote his lordship, '*if you will request any officer of the navy who may be at Corunna, when you receive this letter, to take under his convoy all the vessels loaded as above mentioned, and to proceed with them to Santander. If he should find Santander occupied by the enemy,*' continued his lordship coolly, '*I beg him to remain off the port till the operations of this army have obliged the enemy to abandon it.*'

So his lordship, in spite of looking sometimes extremely anxious, as was natural in a General undertaking an advance of such magnitude, was in a mood of calm confidence. His army was in the best of health; with Murray as Q.M.G. every detail of the complicated triple march was exactly arranged; the supplies were keeping well-up with the columns; Clausel was still hunting guerrilleros in Navarre; and King Joseph's force was known to be hampered by the accompanying train of refugees (all with their carriages and impedimenta), civil administrators, ministers, his Majesty's private baggage, and a long line of treasure-carts.

The British officers thought that King Joseph and Marshal Jourdan would make a stand on the line of the Pisuerga river, but again the French fell back, this time on Burgos. King Joseph, very much in the dark as to his adversary's intentions, compelled by necessity (and the most stringent orders from his autocratic brother and mentor) to retain the great road to France that ran through Burgos and Vittoria, was nervous of the Pisuerga position, and found it, moreover, impossible to obtain food for his army there.

When it was realized in the Allied ranks that Burgos must be their objective, the prospect of having to engage upon a protracted siege damped everyone's spirits.

The Light Bobs had no doubt that they were destined to be employed on this labour. They would take the town, of course: no question about that; but they looked forward to it with gloomy feelings. Everyone hated siege-work; and everyone would rather fight in half-a-dozen open battles than take part in one storm of a fortified city. By all accounts, Burgos would be as hard a nut to crack as Badajos had been, and no one could think of that hellish business without hoping that he would never again be asked to go through such a hideous night. When, on the 12th June, the line of march took an abrupt turn eastwards, and the troops knew themselves to be marching on Burgos, there was less than the usual amount of cheerful talk in the ranks. Pessimists prophesied a month's trench-work under gun-fire, and when the division bivouacked that night at Hornilla, there was a faint atmosphere of depression over the camp.

But very early next morning the men were startled by the echoes of a terrific explosion. It was so loud that it brought many to their feet, and it was followed at intervals of a minute or two by three more. No one knew what had caused them, although the wildest hopes burnt in nearly every breast. It was said that Wellington had ridden off with the various divisional commanders to reconnoitre; he was seen returning a few hours later; and the news that Marshal Jourdan had evacuated Burgos, blowing up the Castle, and was in retreat towards the Ebro, spread quickly through the camp.

Shakos were flung up, and the air made loud with hurrahs. Orders to break camp and march towards the Ebro arrived, and were hailed by renewed cheers. Canteens were packed, fires stamped out, tents loaded on to the mules, and the division marched north-eastward in the best of good spirits.

Six

✣

VITTORIA

1

THE COLUMNS, LEAVING BEHIND THEM AT LAST THE VAST Tierra de Campos, with its miles of unbroken cornfields, plunged into a maze of rocks and towering hills; dropped from the mountains into the valley of the Upper Ebro; and thought themselves come suddenly upon the Promised Land. Giant cork trees gave shade from the sun's glare; fruit and flowers grew everywhere. From pretty little villages girls trooped out with garlands to throw over the heads of *los colorados*. They danced before them on the dusty road, and offered great baskets spilling with cherries and pears. The soldiers, disheartened by the waste of rocks amongst which they had forced a difficult way, revived at once; and as they crossed the Ebro the regimental bands struck up *The Downfall of Paris*.

On they went, hustled forward on long, hard marches for three sweltering days, sometimes panting up mountain-sides, sometimes plodding through the lush green valleys. Very few of them knew where they were going, or where any column other than their own was. There were troops (they were Graham's) some-where to the north, for the dull thunder of artillery-fire rolled and echoed one day round the hilltops. So it looked as though a

part of the army was thrusting northward, probably to outflank
the French. The Light division, ordered to leave its baggage and
artillery with the 4th, branched away from the road skirting the
foothills, and crossed the mountains by a track which everyone
but Lord Wellington would have thought impractical for troop
movements. They had their reward when they dropped down
into the village of San Millan, for there they came plump upon
a brigade of Maucune's, resting with piled arms and no pickets
posted. As luck would have it, Vandeleur's brigade was leading
and was the first to launch an attack upon the startled enemy.

Harry had no time to do more than shout to Juana to keep
back, as he galloped past her to bring the 52nd regiment up to
support the Rifle battalion. Vandeleur was deploying swiftly; a
cacophony of trumpet-calls blared through the village; and the
French, who had seen nothing of the Allied column's advance
along the hollow road, masked as it was by jutting rocks and
steep banks, tumbled into some sort of battle-order.

The Riflemen went down the slope at the double, firing as
they ran, and yelling: 'The first in the field and the last out of it,
the bloody, Fighting 95th!'

Juana had to dismount, and drag her horse out of the way of
the men coming up in support. An aide-de-camp went past her
in a cloud of dust to hasten the advance of Kempt's brigade,
closely following Vandeleur. The fight before the village rapidly
became a confused mêlée, the second French brigade, with the
baggage-train in its rear, suddenly appearing through a cleft in
the rocks, and being engaged by Kempt. The sumpter-beasts
broke loose and stampeded amongst the rocks; a rough-and-
tumble fight bickered all over the slopes of the hills; and the
French, ignorant of what troops the hollow road might still be
concealing, presently took to their heels, many of them throwing off their kit-bags to make their flight over the rocks easier.

When Juana, who had watched the fray in a state of bouncing excitement, rode down into the village, the dust kicked up by the skirmish was beginning to settle, and the ground was littered with scattered baggage and accoutrements. The whole of the baggage-train had been captured, and about two hundred prisoners. A very good day's work, was the verdict of the Light Bobs, counting the spoils, with only four dead men and a handful of wounded to offset the victory.

However, when the division halted at Pobes on the following day, and Alten ordered the French baggage to be sold by auction, a spurt of ill-feeling sprang up between the brigades, Kempt's men, in spite of having captured the train, being allowed no opportunity of bidding for the various goods. Feelings ran rather high for a time, but when it was discovered that the army had at last come up with the main body of the enemy, which was drawn up behind the twisting Zadorra river, on the undulating ground before Vittoria, such trifling considerations were forgotten, and nothing was thought of but the approaching engagement.

Lord Wellington spent the day surveying in person the various routes by which he meant to launch his force on to the French. He was in good spirits, but a little curt with his Staff. Some of these gentlemen had deprecated his rapid march north. They did not consider it safe to go beyond the Ebro, and the magnitude of his lordship's plans alarmed them. His lordship was unmoved by their disapproval. He had no opinion of King Joseph, not much respect for Marshal Jourdan; and he knew that although Sarrut had joined the King's army from Biscay, there was still no news of Clausel's advance. One or two critics said that his success at Salamanca had gone to his head; but they did not realize, as his lordship did, how crushing a blow to French morale that spectacular victory had been. He was, in fact, in a confident mood, though that did not prevent his snapping the heads off his personal Staff, said one of his rueful aides-de-camp, who had asked him a question which his lordship considered unnecessary.

It was misty on the morning of the 21st June. It even rained a little, but the weather prophets thought that the day would fair-up. The Light division was called to arms very early, and on their way up to their station before the Zadorra river they passed through the sleeping camp of the 4th division. But they were not destined to be the first to attack: that honour had fallen to Hill, and no one else was to be allowed to make the slightest move until it had been seen that he had gained his objective.

Harry knew all about it, of course; he had had a look at the ground too, and he knew that the Intelligence-officers were speaking the truth when they reported that the French were spread over too long a front, and had insufficient guards at the various bridges across the Zadorra. King Joseph was in the uncomfortable position of being quite in the dark about his adversary's intentions; and although his patrols had been feeling cautiously for the Allied army for some time past, they had brought in only the most confusing reports of the advance. He could get no tidings of Clausel, who, for all he knew, might still be hunting guerrilla-bands in the wilder parts of Biscay; and not only was the town of Vittoria crammed with civilian refugees, who were clinging to the skirts of his army, but amongst all the congestion of carts, caissons, and artillery-waggons were several fourgons from France, inscribed *Domaine extérieur de S.M. l'empereur*, containing specie to the value of five million francs. Like Lord Wellington's, King Joseph's soldiers had months of pay owing to them. The King had been very glad to see the long-overdue fourgons, but when faced with the imminent prospect of having to fight a battle he could have wished them otherwise.

The so-called plain of Vittoria, on which, after many heart-burnings, the King had determined to make a stand, was a stretch of rolling ground, about twelve miles long from north-east to south-west, and varying in breadth from six to eight miles. It was surrounded by hills, and drained by the Zadorra, a turbulent stream, affording, from its twisting nature, the very worst of fronts. Some of its bends were so sudden that the river seemed almost to double back on its course. It had several bridges, and, since the stream was easily fordable, these had been left intact. Vittoria, a town where five roads met, was situated some miles behind the Zadorra, on rising ground; and dotted over the land, in wooded valleys, were a number of villages.

A glance at the map spread out on the table at Alten's head-quarters was enough to show Harry that the field was a larger one than had yet been fought over. His lordship's plan was to launch his army in four masses upon the French, an operation requiring the nicest of timing. Hill, working round the outside of the French left, was to cross the Zadorra, and to storm the heights of Puebla, a range of hills almost at right angles to the Allied front; and from there to descend with his main body by a defile on to the plain, while his flank thrust its way along the heights. While these oper-ations were in progress, the Light and 4th divisions were to form before the two bridges of Nanclares, and to remain there, hidden from the enemy by the rugged nature of the ground, until Hill should have gained the Puebla heights. North-west of them, on the same front, the 3rd and 7th divisions would march over the high Monte Arrato, descending on to the plain near the Mendoza bridge, upstream from Nanclares, and just beyond a more than usually sharp bend in the river. Lastly, Graham's column, masked by Spanish infantry, was to fall on Sarrut's division on the extreme French right flank. In this way, the Allied army would, roughly, attack the enemy on three sides of a square.

Since the 20th June was spent by the army in getting into order, Harry was fully occupied, and had little time to spend with Juana. Brigade headquarters were in Pobes, a picturesque but filthy village which afforded nothing but bug-ridden cottages as billets for the Staff. There were so many fleas on the mud-floor in the Smiths' low-roofed room that Juana spread her bedding on the table, and curled herself up on it. A couple of centipedes, wandering out from under a cupboard, added nothing to her comfort. She slew them with the butt of her riding-whip, but they proved to be very tenacious of life, and the execution ended with Juana's feeling rather sick. When Harry came in to supper, it was late, and he was frowning over his orders. A grunt was the only answer he vouchsafed to a tentative remark, so Juana, who never took offence at being neglected in the army's cause, ate her supper in patient silence.

'What awful stuff!' Harry said, chewing some leathery beef.

'Yes,' Juana agreed. 'I could make an omelette for you, if you would like it.'

'No, it's of no consequence,' he replied, fork in one hand, and map in the other.

He went off to Vandeleur's headquarters after supper. When he returned, Juana was lying wrapped in a blanket on the table, wide-awake, and rather anxious. She smiled at him, but he was not deceived, and said at once: 'Hallo, there! Now, what business has that scared face in my quarters?'

Juana sat up. 'Don't be angry with me! I cannot help being a little afraid, I find.'

Harry hung up his wet cloak, and came over to the table. 'Afraid? You? *Qué dira la gente?*'

'I do not care.'

'Well, I hope you care for what *I* say! You are a bad, stupid child. How many actions do you suppose I have taken part in?'

'You know very well that has nothing to do with it. I wish you were a *Go-on*, and not a *Come-on!*'

'*Por gracia!* Do you? Do you indeed?'

'No,' sighed Juana.

'Just as well!' said Harry, kissing her cheek. 'Go to sleep now, *querida:* I must get some sleep too.'

There were a great many questions she wished to ask him, but he was still looking preoccupied, so she asked only the most important. 'When do we march?'

'What? Oh! – early. But you'll stay here with West.'

She sat hugging her knees, staring rather hard at a chair directly before her. 'It is a little melancholy, having to wait in the rear.'

He smiled, but shook his head. 'No use, Juana: you can't come on to the field with me.'

So when the Light Bobs moved off on the following morning, a disconsolate figure in a much worn riding-dress stood in the doorway of the cottage to watch them go.

The parting with Harry had not been at all romantic. He had been in a hurry, jumping up from the breakfast-table, after a glance at his watch, with his mouth full, snatching up his coat and cocked-hat from a chair, giving his wife a quick hug, and saying in a voice thickened by bread and meat: 'Take care of yourself! West will see to you.'

He had ridden off on the only one of his horses fit for duty, a nervous, obstinate animal, not yet accustomed to military service. Juana was thinking about that horse as she stood fluttering her handkerchief to the soldiers tramping past. If Harry had been riding Old Chap, the hunter James Stewart had given him, she thought she would not have felt so anxious.

She let her hand fall to her side, and stood leaning against the door-post, still watching the column go by. She felt very much oppressed, and began to wonder how many of the

Green-jackets moving down the road would be killed, and how many mutilated by horrible wounds. It seemed strange that they should be glad to be going to fight, but they were glad, nearly all of them, as you could see by the quickened look in their faces.

Suddenly she perceived Kincaid, and in case she should never meet him again, she ran out into the road. He was surprised to see her, for he thought that she would have gone farther to the rear. He was riding beside his company, and reined in at once, stretching down his hand, with an exclamation. She was unable to speak, but pressed his hand, looking up into his face with wet eyes. Before he could say anything, she had run back into the house. Kincaid told his horse savagely to 'Get up!' and rode on, a snatch of a poem, once read and almost forgotten, teasing his brain. But he could only remember one couplet, which ran: *So highly did his bosom swell As at that simple, mute farewell*, which sounded nonsensical, bereft of its context, but went on reiterating in his mind, as such jingles will.

2

By the time the Light division, traversing the high, rocky ground which dropped down to the Zadorra, reached the plain, the vapour had curled away, and the sun had come out. Every feature in the landscape became so sharply defined that distant objects could be discerned as well by the naked eye as by the help of spy glasses. The scene was oddly foreshortened, so that the spires of Vittoria, five or six miles away, looked to be much closer, and it was possible almost to distinguish the leaves upon trees a great way off.

The Light and 4th divisions took up positions about a mile back from the Zadorra, where it was spanned by the two bridges of Nanclares. They approached unseen by the enemy, and were ordered to pile arms, and to keep under cover of the hollow road, and the convenient outcrops of rock. They lay down, grumbling good-humouredly at old Douro for having given to Hill the honour of opening the engagement. From various posts of vantage, the officers were able to command a comprehensive view of the whole field, and even to pick out, upon a hill, the figures of King Joseph and his Staff.

For a long time, nothing but slight troop movements disturbed the stillness, but shortly after eight o'clock, Harry, who had gone a little way up the steep side of the Monte Arrato, to stare with puckered eyes towards the slopes of the Puebla heights, at right angles to the front, a mile or more away, saw puffs of smoke bursting all along the crest. He waited for a few minutes, and then, as the puffs grew more frequent, and tiny, dark figures appeared on the hill-side, like running ants, he scrambled down from his perch, mounted his horse, and rode back to Vandeleur. 'General Hill's come into action, sir.'

'He has, has he?' Vandeleur grunted. 'Where's my glass?'

It soon became apparent that a sharp struggle between the French skirmishing line and Hill's Spaniards was taking place on the Puebla heights; Hill sent forward reinforcements, and the gleam of scarlet could be seen beside the dark-coated Spaniards. Wellington, who had been standing in front of the Light division, rode forward to the river-bank to get a clear view of Hill's progress. A rumble of artillery fire began to echo round the hills; much larger bursts of smoke appeared on the right, and lifted lazily to disperse in black wisps across the sky.

Suddenly a vicious crackle of musketry in their front drew the attention of the Light Bobs away from Hill's battle. An aide-de-camp galloped up to Kempt, and desired him to advance his brigade to the bridge at Villodas, a few hundred yards to his left.

It was learned that a party of French voltigeurs, perceiving Lord Wellington on the river-bank, had rushed the bridge, seized a wooded knoll on the Allied side of the Zadorra, and opened a brisk fire upon his lordship. No one was hurt, but the shots kicked up showers of mud all round the Staff, and it was clearly necessary to dislodge these intrusive gentlemen. Kempt's men flung them back on to their own side of the river, and established themselves amongst the shrubs and trees on the bank. Fire flickered all along the line, and wounded men began to struggle to the rear.

'Catching it, aren't they?' remarked Billy Mein, of the 52nd. 'Hallo, Harry! Any orders?'

'Not yet. Hill has taken the heights.'

'Then what the devil are we waiting for?'

'The 3rd and 7th. They haven't come up.'

'God knows I hold no brief for old Picton,' said Mein, 'but it isn't like him to be backward in attack. Think anything's happened?'

'Dalhousie's in command, that's all,' said Harry.

'What?' Mein gasped. 'Dalhousie put over Picton? For God's sake, why?'

'Nobody knows.'

'Christ! I'm glad I'm not one of Picton's lot: he won't be fit to live with for weeks!'

At about half-past eleven, Kempt's brigade began to move off by threes to their left. The 2nd brigade watched this manoeuvre with jealous eyes. 'Here! if we don't get no sport we'll get no pie neither!' an indignant voice from the ranks announced.

'Hey, why the devil's Kempt moving?' demanded Tom Smith. 'When is it our turn to show our front?'

'Hell, how should I know?' said Harry, irritable at being kept for so many hours out of action. 'Some Spanish peasant came up to the Peer to tell him that there's no guard on the bridge of Tres Puentes. Kempt's to cross the river there.'

'And where,' enquired Billy Mein, 'might Tres Puentes be?'

'About a mile and a half to our left. It's round that sharp bend in the river. Where did you get that sausage?'

'Don't you wish you knew!' said Mein, taking a bite out of it.

Led by the Spanish guide, Kempt's men marched off under cover of the rocks, and, working round the hairpin bend of the Zadorra some time later, passed the bridge of Tres Puentes at the double, with rifles and firelocks cocked. They encountered no opposition, and soon gained a steep hill on the farther side of the river, which was crowned by a ruined chapel. 'Doesn't it give rise to some curious reflections?' panted George Simmons, gaining the summit, and shaking his head at the ancient building. 'You know, the Black Prince once fought here. One cannot but indulge one's fancy with the thought that he may have —'

'Take cover, George!' shouted Molloy, interrupting him without ceremony. 'Here it comes! Whew!'

A couple of round shots crashed amongst them, the second knocking the Spanish guide's head off his shoulders. His body stood for an instant, with the blood spurting up from the severed neck, and then fell, while the head was tossed through the air to bounce on the ground and roll away till it was stopped by a boulder. Someone laughed, and was clouted into silence by his comrades.

'Very nasty,' remarked Captain Leach, in a matter-of-fact tone. 'Do you like this position? I don't.'

The chapel-knoll, it was soon discovered, was commanded by a hill a few hundred yards distant, which was occupied by a large body of infantry. A shell followed the round shots, and burst almost under the nose of Kincaid's horse, kicking up a shower of dust and pebbles. A splinter struck his stirrup-iron, and his charger, squealing with fright, became almost unmanageable, capering and plunging in a mad struggle to bolt.

'Look to keeping your men together, sir!' snapped Wellington, riding up behind Kincaid at that unlucky moment.

Kincaid flushed scarlet, and gave his disobedient mount both whip and spurs. To be supposed by his lordship to be showing off his horsemanship, like any conceited Johnny Newcome, set him cursing under his breath, but he naturally could not explain the circumstances to Wellington, and was obliged to swallow his resentment.

The situation of the brigade was uncomfortable, since its rush across the river had isolated it from the rest of the army. The cover on the hill, however, was good, and after the first burst of artillery-fire, the French stopped shelling the position. 'We ought to advance, and take that village I can see over there,' remarked George Simmons, quite unruffled by having his shako blown off his head by the wind of a shot passing over him.

'Anything else you'd like to do?' enquired Molloy. 'I'm not happy. Damn it, I'm not a bit happy! Hi, you there, keep under cover!'

But while the Rifles were moving from Villodas to Tres Puentes, the 3rd division had been pouring down the defile of Monte Arrato, and by the time Simmons had decided that the village of Ariñez ought to be taken, Picton, an astonishing fig-ure in a blue coat, and a top-hat, with a brim to protect his inflamed eyes, was accosting every aide-de-camp who came in sight with a demand to know whether there were no orders for him. By noon, his temper had cracked badly, and he fidgeted up and down on his unhandsome cob, beating a tattoo on its hogged mane with the stick he carried. 'Damn it!' he burst out to his Brigade-Major. 'Lord Wellington must have forgotten us!'

Colonel Gordon came galloping from the direction of Tres Puentes, and reined in beside Picton.

'Well, sir, well?' barked Picton.

'I'm looking for Lord Dalhousie, sir. Have you seen him?'

'No sir, I have not seen his lordship!' said Picton, who had clean outstripped Dalhousie on the advance across Monte Arrato. 'But have you any orders for *me*?'

'None, sir,' confessed Gordon.

'Then pray, sir, what are the orders that you *do* bring?' asked Picton sharply.

'Why,' replied Gordon, 'that as soon as Lord Dalhousie shall commence an attack on *that* bridge –' he slewed round in his saddle to point out the Mendoza bridge in the distance to the left of the division – 'the 4th and Light are to support him.'

This was too much for Picton; he seemed to swell with indignation, and startled Gordon by saying in a thunderous tone: 'You may tell Lord Wellington from me, sir, that the 3rd division under my command, shall in less than ten minutes attack that bridge and carry it, and the 4th and Light may support me if they choose!'

He gave Gordon no opportunity of speaking a word, but wheeled his cob, and trotted off to put himself at the head of his men. 'Come on, ye rascals! Come on, ye fighting devils!' he roared at them.

If ten minutes was a slight exaggeration (for the bridge of Mendoza was two miles distant), the advance of the Fighting division right across the front of Dalhousie's 7th, which had at last arrived on the field, and halted there, was a spectacle quite as amazing as that presented by Picton himself, in his top-hat.

'God, will you look at Picton's division?' gasped one astonished spectator. 'Talk about meteors!'

One of Picton's brigades being directed on to the bridge, the other one to a ford farther upstream, the whole force hurled itself across the river in the teeth of a weak cavalry brigade, set, with three guns in support, to watch the bridge. The guns got into action, but Kempt flung Barnard forward with some Rifle companies, and the artillery-men, unable to stand the biting and accurate fire of the Green-jackets, limbered up, and made off.

As soon as he saw Picton safely over the river, Kempt advanced his whole brigade, forming it on the right rear of the 3rd division and putting to rout, on the way, the voltigeurs at the Villodas bridge.

'Now you'll be able to take your precious village, George!' grinned young Frere.

3

It was not until between two and three in the afternoon, when Kempt and Picton were hotly engaged with the defenders of Ariñez, that Vandeleur was at last ordered up. Dalhousie, whose advance had been delayed by two dilatory brigades, crossed the river some time after Picton, and directed his attack upon a village a quarter of a mile to the north of Ariñez. He succeeded in driving the French out of it, but became involved in a sanguinary struggle with five battalions of Germans, serving under the Eagles, who were formed behind a stream protecting the village of La Hermendad.

'What?' said Cadoux. 'Support the 7th? Well, of course we have *heard* that there is a 7th division, but we've never *seen* it!'

The brigade marched off, crossing the Villodas bridge, and passing behind the rising ground from which Picton and Kempt were launching attack after attack upon the walled village of Ariñez. As soon as the head of the column came under fire, Vandeleur sent Harry forward to report to Lord Dalhousie. Harry galloped off into the thick of the fray before La Hermandad, taking good care, as he went, to fix the lie of the land in his head. He came upon Dalhousie, talking earnestly to his Q.M.G., and saluted. 'Brigade-Major Smith, sir, sent by General Vandeleur for orders!'

The Q.M.G., a Rifleman, and an old friend of Harry's, exchanged a meaning look with him. Dalhousie said fussily: 'Yes, yes, wait now! This is a little awkward. Drake!'

An order to wait, while his lordship tried to make up his mind what to do, was not at all to Harry's taste. He made his horse fidget, himself in a fret of impatience, and words of advice on the tip of his insubordinate tongue. He could see that Drake was getting annoyed, and just as he was on the point of bursting into hasty speech, he heard Dalhousie say: 'Better to take the village, Drake!'

That was quite enough for Harry, who had decided, when he first rode up, that the village ought to be taken without loss of time. 'Certainly, my lord!' he said briskly, and wheeling his horse, dashed off, deaf to the voices of Dalhousie and Drake, who both shouted to him to wait.

'Take the village? Good!' said Vandeleur.

Harry, having seen the 52nd deploying into line, and the Rifles spreading out in deadly little parties of sharpshooters, galloped off to the nearest battalion of the 7th division, and thrust his way up to the officer in command of it. 'Lord Dalhousie desires you closely to follow this brigade of the Light division!' he announced.

'Who are you, sir?' demanded the Colonel, glaring at him.

'Never mind that! Disobey my lord's order at your peril!' Harry snapped back at him, in his most reckless fashion.

Off he shot again, to join his brigade in its rush upon the village. He reached the brook before it amongst the foremost, but there he suffered a check, his horse refusing to put a hoof over the bank. Twice Harry brought him up to it, and twice he came to a slithering halt. A beautiful bay went past Harry, down the steep slope, and Harry, with a furious oath, kicked his feet clear of the stirrups, and vaulted out of the saddle, snatching at the bay's tail. He was dragged across the brook, and up the farther bank, and found that the bay's rider was Cadoux.

'Well, if it isn't our esteemed Brigade-Major!' said Cadoux. 'And what might you have done with your horse, pray?'

'Abandoned the brute,' said Harry.

'How very like you!' Cadoux sighed. 'Now you'll have to walk.'

'Who cares?' retorted Harry. 'I'll go with your company.'

'Honoured, Captain Smith!' murmured Cadoux, bowing. 'But in that case I'm afraid you'll have to run, for you see we — er — we do like to be first in the field!'

First in the field they were, and in that furious rush upon the village, through ditches, over walls, in and out amongst the houses and the gardens, whatever doubts Harry had nursed of Cadoux's quality were put to rest. Wherever the firing was hottest, there was Cadoux, not a hair out of place, deaf to the whistle of shots all round him, encouraging his men in his calm way. 'Keep it steady, lads!' he said, when the rifle-fire grew momentarily ragged. 'Now, no untidiness! That's right — that's good shooting! We'll move on, Sergeant: I really think we must dispossess those noisy gentlemen in our front.'

Harry, himself hoarse from cheering on the men, left him driving a party of voltigeurs out of the garden, where they had ensconced themselves, and made his way to Ross's battery. He got a troop-horse from Ross, and plunged back into the fight for the village, catching a glimpse of Cadoux once, but not getting within speaking distance until they met on the farther side of the river, dusty, dishevelled, and intent only on getting the men into order again after their impetuous sweep through the village.

Cadoux removed his shako, and shook the dust off it. Harry rode his trooper up to him, his eyes very bright between their narrowed lids, and his lean cheeks still flushed with excitement. Cadoux looked at him with a flickering smile. 'Well, Captain Smith?' he drawled. 'Finished harrowing hell and raking up the devil?'

Harry laughed. 'Oh, by God, if we are to talk of harrowing hell – !' He stretched out his hand. 'Thank you for the loan of your horse's tail!'

Cadoux looked at him for an instant, his brows lifting in surprise. Then, with a little laugh, he held out his own hand, and shook Harry's sinewy one. 'Don't mention it!' he said, in his most finicking tone. 'I do hope you didn't pull any of his hairs out? Such a lovely creature, aren't you, Barossa?'

'Oh, is that the charger you got at Barossa?' Harry asked. 'Is it true you found the holster full of doubloons?'

'Rumour, my dear fellow, rumour!' Cadoux said, with an airy wave of his hand. 'It was a nice battle, though: a very nice battle. Dear old Graham stood in the river, up to his waist, shouting almost as loudly as *you*, until one of our fellows said: "Do go and take care of yourself, old corporal, and get out of our way!" '

Harry burst out laughing, and was still laughing when he got back to Vandeleur's side. Lord Dalhousie had arrived in a great bustle, with Drake beside him. 'Most brilliantly achieved indeed!' Dalhousie told Vandeleur. 'Where is the officer you sent to me for orders?'

Harry rode forward. 'Here I am, my lord.'

Dalhousie looked him over. 'Upon my word, sir! You receive and carry orders quicker than any officer I ever saw!'

Harry opened his eyes. 'You said, "Take the village," ' he protested. 'My lord, there it is, guns and all!'

Dalhousie put up a hand to hide a smile, but Drake grinned openly, and said: 'Well done, Harry!'

4

The brigade being allowed a breathing-space while it reformed, the men had leisure to notice the heavy roar and crash of artillery ahead of them, on their left flank, which they had not previously been aware of. It meant that Graham was in action to the north; and this fact, coupled with the very considerable advance all along the front, seemed to show that the Allied army was closing in on Vittoria. The battle was by no means over, however, for although the French were forced back, they fought with a great deal of stubbornness over every yard of the ground, their sharp-shooters taking advantage of every ditch, and every shrub. Vandeleur's brigade was fiercely engaged the whole afternoon, but in a running fight, over ground affording plenty of cover, the Light Bobs were unbeatable, never exposing themselves unnecessarily, nor massing in bodies large enough to provide good marks for the enemy. Where Kempt was, or how he was faring, no one knew, for the land was too undulating to allow of any very comprehensive view being taken of the rest of the field. But as the day wore on, the want of effective cavalry support began to be felt by those who had any time to think of anything but keeping up a steady aim.

The noise of the firing grew ever more deafening, till one had to shout to be heard above the appalling din. Smoke began to lie heavily over the plain; the air was so acrid with it that many men found it impossible to stop coughing. Through it, from a slight hill where he stood beside Ross's brigade of guns, Harry could see the dark mass of the enemy. Pencils of fire shot through it incessantly; shells screamed overhead, and burst in crash upon crash, sending up showers of mud, and stones, and scattering whole tree-branches, and splinters of rock, and often more horrible débris, over the lines.

'By God, if ever I saw such an inferno!' Harry exclaimed.

As he spoke, his horse fell under him, like a shot rabbit. He had just time to spring clear, and at once began to look for the wound. He had not been conscious of any missiles falling near enough to hurt the trooper, but in the middle of such a storm of bullets and shells it was possible that it had been hit without his knowledge. But although the horse was apparently dead, not a trace of a wound could he find upon it. He discovered that its heart was beating, and tried the experiment of giving it a kick on the nose. It answered admirably. The trooper gave its head a shake, and instantly scrambled to its feet. Harry jumped into the saddle again, and one of Ross's gunners shouted to him that he had seen the same thing happen before, the wind from one of the enemy's cannon-shot having acted on the poor beast like a knock-out blow.

It was dusk when Vandeleur's brigade passed Vittoria, over a plain at last free from the broad ditches which had made progress difficult. As far as the Light Bobs could judge, the French army was fleeing in a state of rout comparable to the disordered flight from the field of Salamanca. As the brigade passed on, leaving the town on their left, they found their advance checked by an indescribable confusion of abandoned baggage. Acres of ground were covered with every kind of conveyance, from fourgons to elegant private-carriages – these last often containing civilians in a state of the wildest terror. Horses had been dragged out of the shafts and ridden off into the gathering dusk; chests lay tumbled on the ground with the hasps broken, and art treasures spilling out of them; guns, caissons, artillery-waggons completely blocked the great causeway to Bayonne, and it was impossible to set one foot before the other without treading on a kit-bag, a burst portmanteau, a camp-kettle, a battered shako, or an officer's dressing-case. Everything seemed to have been abandoned by the French, even the precious treasure-chests from Paris.

As the brigade picked their way through the confusion, still in pursuit of the flying enemy, a swarm of French cavalry suddenly bore down upon them, and all but swept away Tom Cochrane's company. His men flung themselves down behind a bank, and met this onslaught with such an accurate fire that the cavalry was checked, and, by the time Harry had rushed some of his own company up in support, was making off, leaving a number of dead and wounded behind them.

Except for some desultory skirmishing, there was no more fighting in that quarter of the field. Some regiments were already plundering the abandoned baggage-train, and since cases of wine and brandy had been found, the night bade fair to be a merry one. Vandeleur received orders to join the 1st brigade with Alten's headquarters, and sent Harry on to take up the ground. Harry did not seem to be unduly fatigued by his exertions during the day, but he had quite lost his voice, as he generally did after a battle. When he approached the 1st brigade, the first thing he heard was a torrent of heart-broken Spanish lamentations.

'Oh, Charlie Eeles, *él no vendrà nunca! él no vendrà nunca! Muerto, muerto, muerto!*'

'But Juana, dearest Juana, only wait a little! There's no saying he's dead yet! Depend upon it, it was all a mistake! Pray, pray don't cry! We'll find him directly, see if we don't!'

Harry gave a cracked laugh, and spurred forward to where, dimly, in the twilight, he could see his wife. '*Hija!*'

It was the veriest croak, but she heard it, and came running up to him, stumbling over the tail of her riding-dress, which she had let fall in her start of joy. 'Enrique, mi Enrique! Oh, thank God you are not killed; only badly wounded!'

'Thank God, I'm neither!' said Harry hoarsely. 'But you, you little varmint! What the deuce are you doing here, in all this commotion?'

'I followed the 1st brigade, with West. I did not know our brigade was not with them! And then they told me that you were dead, for one of your men saw you fall! Oh, why do you lie to me? You must be wounded!'

Nothing would convince her that he was, in fact, untouched by so much as a splinter, and since he had neither voice nor time enough to spare for argument, he consigned her to Eeles's care, and rode off to find quarters for his General.

The brigade bivouacked in the stubble-fields beyond Vittoria, and the only habitation to be obtained for Vandeleur and his Staff was a large barn. Quartermaster Surtees reported that although he had located the division's commissariat-train, it was impossible to bring it beyond Vittoria, since the congestion on the roads was holding everything at a standstill. This was not such a serious business as it might have been, as anyone who chose to give himself the trouble of going for a stroll amongst the French baggage could be sure of returning with a ham, or some sausages, and a couple of bottles of excellent wine. It was unnecessary to post pickets, as the cavalry was already far in advance, pursuing the routed French into the darkness, so Harry was able to join his wife and General in time to share a supper of ham, Swiss cheese, and burgundy.

He brought in the news that one of the French Generals' wives, Mme de Gazan, had been found by Mr Larpent, stranded in a carriage from which the horses had been stolen, and loudly bewailing the loss of her little boy. Larpent had escorted her to Vittoria, of course, and as soon as she found that she was to consider herself Lord Wellington's honoured guest, her spirits revived, and she seemed to be in a fair way to forgetting the loss of her child.

'What's she like? Pretty?' enquired Vandeleur's A.D.C.

'I don't know, I didn't see her. Johnny Kincaid's in luck again: his fellows found a whole case of wine in some old gentleman's private carriage. I left Johnny drinking the old man's health. I've never seen anything like the mess all over the roads and fields! They say the whole of Joseph's private loot is lying about to be picked up by our plunderers. I myself saw a couple of fellows stuffing their pockets with doubloons.'

'Not ours?' Vandeleur said quickly.

Harry shook his head, and refrained from telling his General that one of these pilferers had been an officer.

It was growing dark, and as no one's baggage had come up there was no means of lighting the barn. The bâtmen had found some forage for the horses, and had procured a tin kettle, which was boiled over a fire kindled at one end of the barn. Supper was eaten by the flickering firelight, and everyone was so tired that as soon as the last mouthful had been swallowed, they all lay down amongst the horses, wrapped in their cloaks, and slept as soundly as if they lay on the best feather-mattresses.

Juana was entirely unembarrassed by a situation which would have made any English lady faint with horror. Having had no other experience of life outside convent walls than that which she had gained at Harry's side, she saw nothing out of the way in sharing sleeping-quarters with half-a-dozen horses, and several Staff-officers. If she had thought about it at all, she would have supposed that every married lady who followed the drum did the same. It would not, of course, be approved of by her own countrymen, but if one was married to an Englishman one's whole way of life was naturally peculiar. She was young enough to think it very good fun to comb out her tangled curls with the General's pocket-comb, to wash the dust from her face and hands in a tin pannikin, and to dry them on the A.D.C.'s hand-kerchief, which happened to be the only clean one to be found amongst the company.

By daybreak, the baggage, thanks to Surtees's indefatigable exertions, had arrived, and, the various canteens having been unloaded from the mules' backs, everyone, including Vandeleur, who tried to toast slices of bread on the end of his sword at a smoky fire, set about preparing breakfast. But hardly had the kettle begun to boil than orders came for the divisions to fall in. Everything had to be packed in a hurry, and the horses saddled-up, and led out of the barn. The General had already mounted, and Harry was shouting to Juana to make haste, when she sud-denly stopped in the doorway of the barn, and said: 'Listen! I am sure I hear someone moaning, like a wounded man!'

'Nonsense, come along!'

'But I *do* hear it!' she insisted.

'Better take a look round,' grunted Vandeleur.

Harry went back into the barn, and glanced about him rather impatiently. He discovered that there was a hay-loft over half the barn, which, in the dusk of the previous evening, no one had noticed. As he looked round for the ladder, a stifled groan sounded unmistakably. There did not seem to be a ladder, or else it had been hauled up, but with a little help from Vandeleur's A.D.C. Harry managed to scramble into the loft.

The most unexpected sight met his eyes. Upwards of twenty French officers, all badly wounded, and one poor devil dying fast, as Harry saw at a glance, lay huddled there on the heaped hay. A woman was bending over the dying man; when Harry hoisted himself into the loft, she looked up, putting back the hair from her brow with a shaking hand. Her expression was distraught; as she stared at Harry, a little pug-dog ran out from the shelter of her skirts, and began barking at him. Nobody spoke; several of the officers were lying in a state of semi-coma; and one, who was sitting up with his back against the wall, seemed hardly to be aware of Harry's arrival. The woman crouched over the dying man, as though trying to shield his body with her own. Harry stepped forward, addressing her in French. She answered in Spanish, and very disjointedly. He noticed that some of the men lying all around in the hay were watching him with wary, suspicious eyes, and spoke to them, assuring them of every attention. The lady, who seemed to be growing gradually less afraid of him, begged him to do something for her lover. Harry knelt down beside the man, but his face was livid, and his eyes beginning to glaze. 'I am sorry,' Harry said awkwardly.

She gave a moan of despair, and cast herself upon the dying man, passionately kissing his lips. The dog, which had been sniffing at Harry's boots, began to jump up at him, all the little bells on its collar tinkling merrily.

Harry got up, and, seeing the ladder lying near the edge of the loft, lowered it into the barn, calling to Juana to come up.

'Tell the General, Bob!' Harry said. 'We'll need a guard to take 'em in charge, but they're all of them wounded, and we ought to do something for them. Send a couple of fellows up to me, and West too!'

Juana, handed up the ladder, was dreadfully shocked by the sight of the wounded men, and the thought that they had lain there all night, stifling their groans for fear of the English officers beneath them. She ran at once to the Spanish lady, tears of sympathy springing to her eyes. The officer was dead, and for a little while it was impossible to coax the lady away from his body. She sobbed out that he had been so thirsty, and she had had no water to give him, which made Juana cry in great distress: 'Oh, señora, if we had but known! Alas, alas!'

The General having sent in a couple of orderlies, Harry was having the wounded men lifted down into the barn. They seemed at first very much alarmed, as though they dreaded their fates at the hands of their enemies, but when they had been given water and brandy to drink, they began to be better, and were able to reply with tolerable composure to Harry's assurances of kind treatment. They were all of them quite young men, hardly more than boys, and the dreadful defeat of the previous day, followed by a night spent in pain and thirst, had distorted their imaginations.

The breakfast, which had been stowed away in the canteens, was quickly unpacked again, and given to as many of the prisoners as were in a fit state to eat it; and the Spanish lady, seeing Juana bathing and binding an ugly wound on one officer's leg, roused herself from her grief, and tottered over to help her.

It was impossible for Harry to linger, but by the time the guard had arrived, the worst wounds had been roughly attended to, and several of the officers were sitting up, eating slabs of ham and bread, and feeling very much better. They were all of them embarrassingly grateful, particularly the lady, who caught up her little pug, and put her into Juana's arms, begging her to accept her in return for her kindness.

Juana was charmed with the dog, a pretty little creature with a coat like satin, and the most engaging tricks, but she hesitated to take her.

'No, no, I beg of you!' the lady insisted. 'She is very good, very intelligent. I wish you to take her! If you would give me pleasure, do not refuse!'

'Oh, Enrique, may I?' Juana said, turning a pair of starry eyes towards him.

Did it occur to Brigade-Major Smith that a lap-dog would scarcely be a welcome addition to his baggage? Not for a moment! Of course Juana might take the little thing, and a dozen more like her, if she chose!

'Now what in thunder have you got hold of there?' demanded the General, when he saw the pug-dog precariously mounted on Juana's saddle-bow.

Juana let the reins drop to hold up her pet for inspection. 'Oh, dear General Vandeleur, my *perrilla*! Look, is she not a darling dog? I am going to call her Vittoria! My little Vitty, are you not, *mi querida?*'

5

Although the division had been ordered to fall in by ten o'clock, they did not, after all, march until noon. There was much to be done to clear up the inevitable confusion resultant upon such a victory. The wounded had to be established in Vittoria; the dead had to be decently buried; and every regiment suspected of plunder was made to line up its kit-bags for inspection.

His lordship, whose plans to encircle and annihilate King Joseph's army had miscarried, owing partly to Graham's failure to push home a vigorous attack from the north, and partly to Dalhousie's dilatoriness, was in the vilest of tempers. Yet although over fifty thousand Frenchmen had managed to escape from the field, every one but two of their cannons had fallen into his lordship's hands, and not even Salamanca had been such a smashing victory. The King had fled, and his army was straggling after him, all the divisions but Reille's in a state of disastrous disorder; and their objective was France, where only the

King could think himself safe. But none of this made his lord-ship better-tempered. A large preponderance of his devoted troops had spent the night following the battle not in getting much-needed rest and food, but in searching the ground for plunder. The twinkling of many lanterns had made the stubble-fields beyond Vittoria look like a fair-ground, and naturally all the cases of wine had been disposed of, so that a number of good soldiers, when the order to fall-in was blared out on the trumpets, were sleeping the sleep of the totally drunk in ditches and under hedges. Some waggish souls, finding the uniforms of French officers amongst the baggage, had dressed themselves up in these, a jest not exactly calculated to appeal to their Commander-in-chief's sense of humour. But worse than these excesses was the disappearance of the greater part of King Joseph's treasure. Though priceless pictures, cut from their frames and rolled up in special containers, were to be found stowed away in the royal coaches, or spilled out of burst chests; though silks and brocades were packed layer upon layer in strong boxes; and silver chalices, candle-sticks, and pieces of gold plate were dragged out from under carriage-seats; though more than a hundred and fifty pieces of cannon had been cap-tured, an Eagle, a stand of colours, and no less a trophy than Marshal Jourdan's bâton (which his lordship sent off to the Prince Regent, with his humble duty); only one-twentieth of the money sent from Paris came into his lordship's custody.

'*The soldiers of the army have got among them about a million sterling in money*,' wrote his lordship bitterly, to Earl Bathurst.

The search through the kit-bags failed to discover the miss-ing treasure. His lordship said that the battle had totally annihi-lated all order and discipline. The rank-and-file were composed of the scum of the earth; the non-commissioned officers were as bad; and none of the officers performed any of their duties.

'*It is really a disgrace to have anything to say to such men as some of our soldiers are,*' wrote his lordship, but, happily, for Earl Bathurst's private consumption only.

But however much treasure his lordship's troops had plundered, and however many bottles of wine they had drunk, none offered the least violence to any of the distracted French and Spanish civilians, who had been abandoned by the flying army. There were many women and children amongst these, some of the children quite lost, and wailing dismally for their mothers. They were comforted by being fed on all the most unsuitable foods found amongst the French baggage-train; and the Comtesse de Gazan's little boy, not apparently at all dismayed by the loss of his parent, was actually adopted by one soft-hearted soldier. He was later discovered, and returned, protesting loudly, to his mother, who had, to do her justice, signified her complete willingness to relinquish him to his new protector.

When the division, which led the centre column, began their march along the Pampeluna road, their progress, like that of the rest of the army was slow. The soldiers were tired, and they had been gorging themselves on roast mutton, having captured some flocks of the enemy's sheep, and killed and eaten them. Nearly every man's haversack was found to be weighed down with pilfered flour, and large joints of fresh-killed mutton, and when this booty was thrown away, which it soon was, the brigades were able to march a little faster.

Ahead of the infantry, Victor Alten's horses were harrying the French rear-guard, and rounding up the stragglers. His lordship complained that his men were so fagged-out that he had no fresh troops to send forward to cut off the ragged retreat, but there were a great many Colonels who would have hotly refuted this accusation, had they known of it. The number of prisoners taken during the battle had been ridiculously small: a fault, said the infantry, to be laid at the cavalry's door.

The weather was appalling. Thunder rolled incessantly, and the rain came down in torrents, turning the causeway in some places into a swamp through which the swearing troops had to wade knee-deep. A steep climb, and a sharp descent through a defile led to Salvatierra, where all roads met, and the right and left columns were obliged to join the centre column. Ahead, the mountains of Navarre seemed to bar the way.

There was a change in the order of the march during the afternoon, his lordship, on his Quartermaster-General's advice, directing Graham, with the greater part of his force, to march north, towards the great Bayonne chaussée, cut during the battle by Longa's Spanish troops. Finding and diverting Graham's men on an afternoon of drenching rain and low mists was no easy task; there was a good deal of confusion; and some of the advanced cavalry did not receive the orders until nightfall. Wellington's temper, said his Staff, was getting worse. He was snapping at everyone, and before the day ended he had found a scapegoat. Through the damp bivouacs that evening, an incredible piece of news flew from camp-fire to camp-fire: his lordship had placed Norman Ramsay, his most brilliant artillery-officer, under arrest, for having misunderstood an order given to him by his lordship in person.

No one, from private to General, who had seen Ramsay burst through the mass of the French infantry at Fuentes de Oñoro, at the head of his battery, could hear such news unmoved. The army forgot its grievances in indignation. Nothing else was talked of, and the epithets used to describe his lordship were anything but flattering. Anson, to whose brigade Ramsay was attached, represented to his lordship what splendid work he had performed on the previous day, at

Vittoria; quite a number of senior officers took their courage in their hands, and interceded for him; but his lordship was implacable. The discipline of the whole army was lax, and he meant to make an example of Captain Ramsay.

6

All next day the army plodded and waded its way along the road to Pampeluna. Only Victor Alten's cavalry was in touch with the French rear, progress being delayed by the firing by the French of every village they passed through. Staff-officers, who had been privileged to hear Lord Wellington's opinion of his troops, thought privately that in the face of the ravages being committed by the enemy all along the line of the retreat his strictures might have been spared. The most dreadful scenes of desolation were everywhere seen. The country people had fled from their burning cottages to cower in the woods and orchards; farm animals lay bayoneted to death amongst the charred ruins of barns; and once the sad little corpse of a baby made the soldiers take firmer grips on their shouldered muskets, and march on at a quickened pace, in silence, and with gritted teeth. Very little was heard about hard going, wet clothes, and blistered feet. The army wanted only to come to grips with the enemy who had created this monstrous desolation.

The Riflemen of Kempt's brigade, supported by Ross, and Arentschildt's Hussars, came to grips with them on the following day, at Yrurzun. It was only a skirmish at the bridge of Araquil, but the Rifles felt much better after it. They captured one of the only two guns rescued from Vittoria, and the 2nd brigade said enviously that Kempt's fellows had all the luck. But the Enthusiastics, closely following the Light division on the march, damned all Light Bobs impartially, and said that it was time someone else had a chance to be first in the field.

The Light division bivouacked within sight of the walls of Pampeluna that night. The town looked rather imposing, situated on a hill in the middle of a treeless plain, on the left bank of the Arga, but no one had any opportunity of exploring it, since it was strongly fortified, and held by a French garrison. On the following morning, news that Clausel was in the vicinity, trying to effect a junction with King Joseph's force, reached Wellington, and the Light and 4th divisions were suddenly ordered to march south, taking the mountain road to Tudela.

Vandeleur's brigade reached the little village of Offala, after a difficult march, and as a sharp look-out had to be kept towards Pampeluna, Harry lost no time in finding a likely-looking guide. He and Vandeleur posted the pickets together, and the guide was found to be both knowledgeable and chatty. Since Vandeleur spoke no Spanish, Harry bore the burden of the conversation. The guide, like everyone else, was full of curiosity about the battle fought at Vittoria, and after asking Harry a great many questions, he whispered, with a jerk of his head in Vandeleur's direction, 'What's the name of that General?'

'General Vandeleur,' replied Harry, wondering what was coming next.

'*Bandelo, Bandelo,*' muttered the guide, apparently committing it to memory. 'Excuse me, señor!'

He bestowed an engaging smile upon Harry, and running forward to where Vandeleur was riding a little ahead, besieged him with a flood of conversation.

'Here, Harry, I want you!' called Vandeleur. 'What's the fellow saying?'

'He is telling all he heard from the Frenchmen who were billeted in his house during the retreat. He's full of anecdote.'

'Oh, is that all?' said Vandeleur.

The guide, his expressive eyes searching first Harry's face and then the General's, as though in an attempt to read the meaning of their English speech, said earnestly: 'Yes, they say the English fought well, but had it not been for one General *Bandelo*, the French would have gained the day!'

'Why does he keep staring at me?' demanded Vandeleur. 'What does he say now?'

Without as much as a quiver of a smile, Harry translated the guide's remark.

'Upon my word!' Vandeleur said, much struck. 'He must mean our going to support the 7th! Now, how the devil did he know?'

'Can't say, sir,' said Harry gravely.

'He's an intelligent fellow,' said Vandeleur. 'Here, you, catch!'

The guide caught the coin tossed to him with the most extravagant expressions of gratitude, and turning, winked broadly at Harry.

When they returned from posting the pickets, Harry discovered that the guide was his landlord for the night. He promised to provide an excellent dinner, and when Harry was hunting for a clean shirt in his portmanteau, he came up to tell him, with a great air of mystery, that he had some capital wine in his cellar, as much as Harry and his servants cared to drink. 'You come down and look at my cellar, señor,' he said. 'You will be surprised!'

'Yes, but I'm dressing,' answered Harry, rather impatiently.

'No, come!' insisted his host. 'I will show you what I have downstairs! You will be pleased!'

'What a strange man!' Juana said, in French. 'I don't like him. I wish you would send him away.'

'He's too damned civil by half. I suppose I shall have to go. I hope he really has got something worth having in his cellars.'

He followed the Spaniard out of the room, and waited at the head of the stone stairs leading down to the cellars while he lit a lamp.

'Now!' said the man.

The note of suppressed excitement in his voice made Harry look up sharply. He thought there was an odd expression in Gonsalez's face, but it was not until he was half-way down the stairs, and his host turned to speak to him, holding the lamp up, that he realized that the most extraordinary change had come over the man. His smiling countenance looked positively fiendish, and his eyes glanced sideways at Harry in the most sinister fashion imaginable. He was a big, muscular fellow, and Harry was unarmed, his servants out of earshot.

'Come, señor!' urged Gonsalez. 'You are about to see a wonderful sight! It will gladden your heart, and because you are English, I will let you feast your eyes on it.'

'Lead on!' said Harry lightly.

It was dank and chilly at the bottom of the stairs; Gonsalez fitted a key into the lock of one of the doors, turned it with a grating noise, and flung open the door, holding the lamp so that its beams lit up the cellar. 'There, señor!' he said, in a demoniacal voice. 'There lie four of the devils who thought to subjugate Spain!'

Harry checked on the threshold, frozen with horror. On the floor, stiff in their own blood, lay the bodies of four French soldiers.

'I am a Navarrese!' Gonsalez declaimed. 'I was born free from foreign invasion, and this right hand shall plunge this stiletto into my heart, as it did into theirs, ere I and my countrymen are subjugated!'

Out of the tail of his eye, Harry saw the glitter of steel, and knew that he was alone with a madman. He strolled forward into the vaulted apartment. 'Well done indeed!' he said coolly. 'This is more wonderful than I ever dreamed of!'

'I knew you would say so!' cried Gonsalez gleefully. 'Now we will drink death to all Frenchmen, eh?'

'By all means!' said Harry.

Gonsalez looked suspiciously at him. 'You are pleased? You like it?'

'Immensely!' Harry said fervently. 'A noble deed! a miracle!'

'Four of them!' Gonsalez pointed out. 'You see? I killed four with my own hand! It is a very good jest, is it not? Why don't you laugh?'

'Laugh? I don't laugh at such feats as this!' said Harry. 'Come, let's have a toast!' He sat down on a cask, his foot almost touching one of the corpses.

Gonsalez seemed satisfied. He set the lamp down, and began to draw off some wine into two mugs. While his back was turned, Harry took a look at the dead men. They were all of them dressed in dragoon uniforms, fine, big fellows, with their swords at their sides, and any one of them more than a match for their assassin. Each had been killed by knife-thrusts through the chest: a messy death, thought Harry, his nostrils quivering at the faint, creeping aroma of stale blood.

Gonsalez came up to him with the wine, stepping carelessly over the bodies of his victims. Harry took one of the mugs from him, and raised it. He was rather pleased to find that his hand was as steady as a rock, for a feeling of nausea was making his stomach turn over. 'Here's to your very good health!' he said.

'Death to the French!' cried Gonsalez.

The wine was of excellent quality, which helped to quieten Harry's stomach. He drank it all, and stood up. To his relief, Gonsalez made no objection to their leaving the cellar, but followed him out, locking the door behind him, and accompanying him up the stairs, to all appearances quite restored to his former good-humour.

'How were you able to overpower four big fellows like that?' Harry asked.

'Oh, easily enough!' replied Gonsalez, with a chuckle. 'I pretended that I was an Afrancesado, and I proposed, after dinner, that we should drink to the extermination of the English!' He paused, and Harry heard his teeth grind together. 'The French rascals! They little guessed what I meant to do! I got them into the cellar, and gave them wine, and more wine, until they became so drunk that they fell. Then I killed them. Thus die all enemies to Spain!'

'Shall you be going round to the General's house after dinner?' asked Juana, when Harry rejoined her. 'Because, if so —'

'I shall not,' said Harry.

Juana saw that he was looking rather pale. 'Are you ill?' she exclaimed. 'Tell me at once, is anything the matter?'

'Matter? Lord, no! nothing in the world!' said Harry.

7

The brigade left Offala next morning without Harry's host having shown any signs of returning madness. Harry did not feel that four dead French dragoons were any concern of his, and as he rather liked Gonsalez, in his sane moments, he said nothing about the gruesome remains in his cellar.

The day's march led the divisions into a beautiful, fruit-growing district, past the great, hundred-arched Pampeluna viaduct. Cherries, and pears, and big red plums were to be had for a penny a pound; there were olive-groves on every side; and plenty of pork to be bought in all the villages. Everyone was pleased when the orders to halt for a day's rest came. The divisions camped near the junction of the Tudela and the Saragossa roads, but nothing was seen or heard of Clausel's advance. However, towards the end of the day, one of the Riflemen went to Harry's quarters on a slim pretext, and asked: 'Sir, is the order come?'

Harry was used to such visits, for he was known to be one of the army's most accessible officers. 'For what?' he said. 'An extra allowance of wine?'

'No, sir, for an extra allowance of marching!' retorted the man, with a grin. 'We're to be off directly after these French chaps as expects to get to France without a kick up the backside from the Light division!'

'So that,' Harry said later to Cadoux, who had been invited to dine with the Smiths, 'means that we *are* going to get orders. Hang me if I know where the men pick up their information, but they always know long before we do when a move is coming!'

'Oh, what a bore!' said Cadoux. 'I was beginning to feel quite at home here.'

They had barely finished dinner when an orderly came in with a note from Vandeleur. 'I told you so!' said Harry. 'Old Douro's got wind of Clausel's division. We've got to try and intercept him.'

Cadoux picked up his shako, and fastidiously smoothed its jaunty green tuft of feathers. 'That will be very enjoyable,' he said. 'You need not tell me the worst: I know it. We're in for a night-march.'

'Correct!' said Harry.

The divisions reached Tafalla by dawn, a pretty town surrounded by olive groves; and, after a short rest, pressed on towards Olite, heading south all the way, towards the Aragon river. It began to rain again, and at Casada, where no cantonments were to be found for any but Staff-officers, everyone bivouacked amongst ploughed fields. 'Ha!' said Kincaid, eyeing the sodden trough which was to be his bed, '*Breathes there a man with soul so dead, who would not to himself have said, This is a confounded, comfortless dwelling!*'

At Olite, the direction of the march was changed suddenly, the divisions bringing up their right shoulders towards Sanguessa.

'Early up and never the nearer!' grumbled Tom Crawley. 'Damme, if the whole blurry division ain't chasing its own tail!'

They found themselves marching through a district of tall pine woods. The straight trunks gleamed in the wet, and the leaves dripped ceaselessly on to the thick beds of last year's needles. There was more night-marching, roundly cursed by the troops, who could not see a couple of yards ahead of them, and found the going painful.

'Too much breaks the bag!' said Humphrey Allen, ricking his ankle in an unsuspected pit full of water. 'That's done me to a cow's thumb!'

'Come on, Long Tom! We must be as near as be-damned to Johnny Crapaud, or Old Hookey wouldn't go hounding us about in the dark,' said a hopeful friend.

'That's right: we'll be up with Johnny before the cat can lick her ear!'

'Stow your gab, there's our Brigade-Major's lady!'

Juana, who was limping rather painfully along the rough road, had had to dismount from Tiny. She looked very wet, and her foot, which was by no means well, was evidently hurting her. Vitty was at her heels, the picture of misery, for the little dog hated rain.

'Here, missis!' called out Tom Plunket, in tolerable Spanish. 'You ought not to be walking with that foot of yours the way it is!'

'No, but poor Tiny has gone very lame, and it is better that I should walk, for he cannot carry me on such a bad road.'

'That's right, it's not safe, not when you can't see an inch before your nose,' said Sergeant Brotherwood. 'Only I was thinking one of us could help you along, señora, if you would condescend to take the loan of an arm.'

'No, no, you have enough to do without helping me! Besides, I can walk very well. Only I do not know where my husband has gone to. In fact, I have lost him.'

'He'll be around somewhere, don't you worry, señora! Just stay with the column. I wouldn't wonder if we was all lost, come to think of it.'

'I see the Brigade-Major going up to the head of the column a while back,' offered Josh Hetherington.

'Oh well, then, everything is all right!' said Juana.

No one in her audience, in however much esteem he held his Brigade-Major, could share her conviction that a knowledge of his whereabouts in any way improved the situation, but not even the sourest-tempered soldier said so.

Harry, contrary to his usual custom, was riding at the head of the brigade, which happened to be the leading one, in order to keep an eye on the guides. The column was approaching the Aragon river. There was a good bridge across the stream, but the approach to it was a little intricate, and as the first two battalions came across, Harry suggested to the General that the brigade should be ordered to form up, to be sure that all the battalions were present.

Vandeleur agreed to it. The first two battalions halted. Harry waited, but no column came in sight. He rode back towards the bridge hallooing, and heard a voice answering him from a long way off. In a few moments, he discovered that the voice belonged to Colonel Wade, an eccentric gentleman who was riding slowly along, with his bugler behind him. Harry galloped up to him. 'Colonel, form up your battalion as soon as you reach the brigade!'

'By Jesus, we're soon formed!' replied Wade casually. 'I and my bugler are alone.'

'Where's the regiment?' demanded Harry.

'Upon my soul, and that's what I would like to ask you!'

Harry gave an exclamation of impatience, and galloped on through the darkness towards the bridge. It was evident that an interval had been allowed to occur in the column, so that the rear battalion, losing sight of the van, had taken a wrong turning. Shades of Craufurd! thought Harry, reining in across the bridge, and peering about him. He could see nothing, but he thought be heard voices some way off. He rode on, along the road running beside the river, hallooing, and presently met the column, marching towards him.

'Is that you Smith? We missed the bridge, and had gone a good league out of our way before we found there had been a mistake.'

'Where's my wife?' Harry shot out.

'I don't know: I haven't seen her.'

Harry told him curtly to continue along the road till he came to a left-hand turning, and rode on. The road, which was little better than a mule-track, soon got so uneven that he was obliged to dismount, and to lead Old Chap. The column was straggling, and to keep out of the way of the infantry Harry led his horse on to the bank above the river. The first cold dawn-light was beginning to creep into the sky, but the rain kept coming down with unabated vigour. Part of the bank gave way suddenly under Harry's feet; a flicker of lightning showed him the river surging over the rocks thirty feet below him. He had the presence of mind to hold fast to the bridle, and Old Chap, frightened by the glimpse of the rushing waters below, reared up, and spun round on his hind legs, dragging Harry on to firm ground. As he was pulled up, he heard a shriek, and the next instant Juana was beside him, trembling with horror at the danger he had been in.

'No harm done!' Harry said. 'Thank God, you're safe! What's the matter with Tiny?'

'Oh, he is dreadfully lame again! And, do you know, we took the wrong turning, and I heard you shouting, oh, a long way off! And then I thought I had lost Vitty!'

'Never mind that now: go on and join Vandeleur! You'll find him across the bridge. I've no time to look after you until I get this infernal muddle straightened out.'

'*Muy bien!*' said Juana cheerfully.

It took Harry some time to collect his scattered brigade in the darkness, but the daylight soon made the task easier. Having delivered himself of some pithy comments on the battalions' un-Craufurd-like progress, he rode back to where he had left his General. He found Vandeleur and Juana sitting on a sodden bank, Juana holding her umbrella over the General's rheumaticky shoulder, and recounting to him in fluent French the tale of her adventures during the night.

'Hallo, Harry!' Vandeleur called. 'I hope you damned the lot of them!'

'I did, of course, but the fact is it was no one's fault,' Harry replied. 'The turn of the road to the bridge was very abrupt, and the road was too narrow to allow the Staff-officers to ride up and down the flank of the column, as they ought to. Juana, you're wet to the skin!'

'Yes, but never mind! Charlie Gore says he shall give a ball when we get to Sanguessa, because it is now certain that we shall never catch the French in this bad weather.'

'I wish I had you in Sanguessa now!' said Harry. 'How far did you walk on that foot of yours?'

'I don't know. *Nada importa!* But everyone wants to be in Sanguessa. Johnny Kincaid says that when we get there all our troubles will vanish.'

Sanguessa, an ancient town with rickety houses jostling one another in all the narrow streets, was reached later in the day, but although the Honourable Charles Gore, who was General Kempt's A.D.C., and a young gentleman of means, at once made the most lavish preparations for his ball, and reported that the girls of Sanguessa were an uncommonly handsome set, the division's troubles were not by any means over. Camps were pitched outside the town, and the usual difficulty of getting wood for firing arose. George Simmons, being sent out with a party to collect sufficient for the division, was obliged to ask the local authorities for permission to pull down a disused building. This being granted, a very strenuous time was spent by the party, gathering every scrap of timber from amongst the débris, and loading it on to the mules. As ill-luck would have it, on their return journey they ran plump into General Picton, coming up at the head of the 3rd division.

'You there!' Picton thundered, glaring at poor George. 'What have you got on those mules, sir?'

'Firewood for the Light division, sir,' replied George, saluting.

'Well, sir, you have got enough for my division and yours! I shall have it divided,' said Picton, who hated the Light division. 'Make your men throw it down! It is a damned concern to have to follow you cursed fellows! You *sweep* up everything before you!'

There was nothing for George to do but to obey. He gave the order to his men, while Picton sat his cob, looking the very picture of a burly ruffian. But as George's party began with black scowls to unload the mules, George caught sight of General Alten, and slipped off to report the matter to him.

General Baron Charles von Alten, a lean, hard-bitten warrior, bent his stern, bright gaze upon George. 'Vot's dat you say? General Picton takes our vood for his division? I dink *not!*'

Knowing Alten, George did not think so either. He fell in behind him, and followed him back to his mule-train. Alten rode past it, and straight up to Picton. George heard him say: 'Goot evening to you, General! Dere is von little mistake dat you make, I dink.'

'Quick, load up the mules!' George said to his men. 'Never mind staring! We'll be off while we may.'

The wood was hastily loaded again, while a battle-royal raged at a little distance from the party. Alten never shouted, but the echoes of Picton's roar pursued George's party for quite some way. What was the outcome of the encounter, George never learned, for he left both irate Generals in the middle of their altercation, but not another word did he hear about sharing his loads with the 3rd division.

'Such a time as I have had!' he told Kincaid, whom he found presently, superintending the erection of his tent.

'Such a time as *you've* had?' interrupted Kincaid. 'Such a time as *I've* had!'

'Why, what is the matter, old fellow?'

'I snatch the first hour off duty I've had in a week to write a couple of letters in my tent,' said Kincaid, 'and before I've had time to dip my pen in the ink, I find myself wrapped up into a bundle with my tent-pole and tent, rolling on the ground, mixed up with the table and all my writing utensils, and the devil himself dancing hornpipes over my body!'

'But how – why?' asked George, trying not to laugh. 'What devil?'

'It turned out to be two of 'em. Would you believe it, the whole scene – oh, don't mind me! You laugh! – the whole scene was arranged by a couple of rascally donkeys in a frolicsome humour, who had been chasing each other about the neighbourhood till they tumbled into my tent with a force which drew every peg, and rolled the whole lot over on the top of me! And it was I who said that our troubles would be over when we reached this rattle-trap of a town!'

Seven

❧

SKERRETT

1

BY THE MIDDLE OF JULY, THE LIGHT DIVISION WAS ENCAMPED on the Santa Barbara height above Vera, within ten miles of the French frontier. From Pampeluna, which they had left to the Spaniards, and a few British units, to blockade, they had marched north into the Pyrenees, plunging farther and farther into a wild, lovely country of valleys rich with olive groves and fruit-trees, and great stretches of Indian corn; and towering hills, whose lower slopes were thickly covered with chestnut-trees, feathery larches, and gray-stemmed beeches, and whose peaks were lost for six days out of seven in wreaths of cloud. There were rivers in the valleys, tumbling down from the mountain-sides, and purling over rocky beds; the villages were better than in Spain, with larger houses, owned by a people who spoke the queer, unintelligible Basque language. When the foothills were passed, marching became more difficult, and sometimes, when only narrow sheep-tracks led up the steep mountain passes, dangerous, since a false step would send one hurtling down a precipice on to craggy outcrops of rock hundreds of feet below. But nobody cared a penny for that when wild strawberries grew beside the way, and every step carried one nearer to the frontier.

The Johnny Petits had run back to France, and, by all accounts, their retreat had more closely resembled a rout than a retiring movement. It was said that King Joseph never drew rein until he reached St Jean de Luz. Poor Pepe Botellas! He had lost everything at Vittoria: his treasure, and his guns, and his love-letters, and even the support of his Imperial brother; and the last humiliation was not long delayed. Soult, the Marshal-Duke of Dalmatia, whom he had wanted the Emperor to disgrace, reached Bayonne on the 11th July to take command of the demoralized Armies of Spain, and with orders to place King Joseph under arrest, if the King should prove troublesome. There were to be no more separate commands in Spain, no more quarrels between jealous Marshals, no more vacillations of a puppet-king. Supreme, Soult was going to drive Lord Wellington out of the Pyrenees, over the Ebro, over the Douro, back to his Portuguese lines, just as soon as the great military storehouses at Bayonne could furnish him with artillery, ammunition, and fresh accoutrements for the troops.

But, meanwhile, Sir Thomas Graham was besieging the town and fortress of San Sebastian, on the coast; English convoys were landing supplies at Passages and Bilbao; and Lord Wellington's army held all the passes from the coast to Roncesvalles: a forty-mile front as the crow flies, with Sir Rowland Hill holding the right wing, from Roncesvalles to Maya, and Graham the left, and with the Light division between them, maintaining their communications.

It was an odd situation, Vera: not as pleasant as Santesteban, where the Light Bobs had camped for a week, amongst the most charming surroundings, but decidedly better than Lesaca, four miles to the rear, where his lordship had fixed his headquarters. Lesaca was pretty enough, lying in a cup of the densely wooded hills, but it had the reputation of being a damp, unhealthy town, and it was certainly very dirty. The headquarters Staff complained that you could actually see the fleas hopping on the floors in all the houses, while the racket in the overcrowded streets was appalling. When you tried to concentrate your mind upon your work, ten to one someone would start killing a pig under your window, your landlord would begin to thresh his garnered wheat in the loft above your head, or a shrill-voiced street-seller would linger under your window, calling interminably: '*Aqua ardente! Aqua ardente!*'

There was nothing like that about Vera. It was a small town on the twisting Bidassoa river, which ran fast there, through irregular and often precipitous banks to the sea, not ten miles away. When the Light division had chased the French out of it, the whole valley of Vera became more or less neutral ground, where foraging parties from each army met on terms of perfect cordiality in their search for corn and timber. The Light division placed advanced pickets in the town, but their main body camped on the Santa Barbara height, by the ruins of a convent. In front of the position, a steep hill was held by the French. English and French sentries stood within pistol-shot of one another, but there was never the least unpleasantness, either on the heights or in the valley. Only raw troops committed the folly of driving in pickets for no purpose: the English and French veterans never dreamed of fretting each other uselessly; and since each held the other in respect, they were able to meet on neutral ground without any appearance of animosity.

From Santa Barbara, the most extensive views could be enjoyed, when the hill was not enveloped in fog. When the Light Bobs had first climbed up the slope, it had been a clear day, and far away to the left, misty in the distance, they had caught a glimpse of the sea. Such a shout as had gone up when the first man, hardly able to believe his eyes, had gasped: 'Look!

Look!' Nobody knew why the sight of the sea filled him with sudden excitement. 'I suppose it makes us think of home,' said Captain Leach. 'Island blood, eh? My fellows have been snuffing the air and swearing they can smell the salt. Does it give you nostalgia, George?'

George shook his head. 'No. I often think that to be living in England after this wild, romantic existence would not give me half as much satisfaction. Campaigning is the life for me. I have never felt such happiness since I became a soldier.'

'The man's mad!' said Jack Molloy. 'George, old fellow, you've got a touch of the sun!'

'He's right,' said Harry.

'Nonsense, you're both mad! Jonathan, too, because he thinks one trout stream constitutes paradise.'

Leach smiled, but said seriously: 'Surtees tells me he saw a salmon, but failed to land him. If it had been anyone but Surtees, I should have disbelieved him, for *I've* never seen one. However, –'

'Now, that'll do!' begged Molloy. 'We've heard all about Surtees's salmon, and the enormous trout you got yesterday, and it's my belief you're both liars. If it was such a wonderful fish, why didn't we see it?'

'I gave it to the Smiths. Ask Harry!'

'Well!' said George, roused from his dreaming thoughts. 'Of all the treacherous things to do! Just you let those lazy beggars in the 2nd brigade fish for themselves!'

'Did you share it with your gallant Brigadier, Harry?' asked Molloy, grinning.

'Not I!' said Harry. 'I don't dine with my Brigadier these days unless I'm invited, I'll have you know!'

'You don't mean it?' George sounded quite shocked. 'Why, you used pretty well to live with dear Vandeleur!'

'Well, I don't live with Skerrett, make no mistake about that!' said Harry.

The 2nd brigade had had the misfortune to lose Vandeleur, who had been transferred at the beginning of the month to the command of a brigade of cavalry. In his room, the brigade had got General Skerrett, an officer of quite a different kidney. He came to the Light Bobs from the 4th division, but up till the time of the army's being quartered about Madrid he had been with the force in Cadiz, so that no one knew very much about him. Harry found him affable enough, but was given a plain hint, within three days of his taking up his command, that when the General wished to see his Brigade-Major he would send an orderly to summon him. Harry, who had been in the habit of walking in and out of his Brigadier's quarters as though they had been his own, and who had breakfasted or dined with him whenever he chose, could scarcely believe his ears when Skerrett's A.D.C. broke the news to him. 'By Jupiter, he'll never do for the Light division!' he said.

'He's not a bad fellow,' said Tom Fane apologetically. 'Only a trifle starchy. He keeps a very indifferent table, too.'

'Does he?' said Harry. 'You'd better come and share our quarters, then!'

'Oh, by Jove, wouldn't I like to!' said Fane, his pleasant, ugly countenance brightening.

So Ugly Tom, as the brigade promptly christened the new A.D.C., joined the Smiths' haphazard establishment, and shook down in it with astonishing ease, adoring Juana (who teased him unmercifully), taking a proper interest in Harry's hounds, and treating Vitty with due respect.

Everyone voted Ugly Tom a capital fellow, but no one looked upon General Skerrett with anything but the deepest suspicion.

'If he doesn't turn out to be a damned grenadier in action, I don't know the signs,' Cadoux said softly, looking through his lashes at the smart figure of the Brigadier in the distance.'I think we shall live to rue the day.'

Harry and Cadoux had become great friends. Always impulsive, naturally warm-hearted, Harry, confronted by gallantry, at once forgot the affectations of speech and manner which had previously irritated him. If a man could behave as coolly as Dan Cadoux in the thick of a fight, he was a good fellow, and might assume all the airs and graces he chose. His estimate of Skerrett was probably correct, Harry thought. Fane said that Skerrett had a reputation for personal courage, amounting almost to rashness: a tribute which merely made the critical Light Bobs say that if he was one of those officers who set themselves up for targets to be shot at by the enemy, he was no commander for troops trained never to expose themselves foolishly.

The brigade, except for the 52nd regiment, was, in fact, a little disgruntled. The 52nd, however, had got their beloved Colonel back, and they did not care a jot for anything else. He had been absent from the Peninsula for eighteen months, ever since the assault of Ciudad Rodrigo, and quite a number of his friends had taken the gloomiest view of his chances of rejoining the army. He had been on his back for ten months, suffering the most dreadful agony, but in the end the surgeons managed to wrench the ball out of his shoulder, and by July he had landed at San Sebastian, rather pale and thin, and with one shoulder falling away a little, and the arm stiff, but otherwise just the same as he had ever been. Everyone was delighted to see him back again, even Lord Wellington, who was not much given to demonstrations of welcome. 'By God, I'm damned glad to see you, Colborne!' said his lordship, in his blunt way. 'You see how we have rompéd the French!' He took a look at Colborne's handsome face, with its high-arched nose, and fine, dark eyes, and added: 'But I'm sorry to see you so pale and thin. Hope you've quite recovered? I hear I have to felicitate you.'

Colonel Colborne thanked him. No, he said, in answer to a quick question, he had not brought his bride out; he did not consider campaigning a suitable life for females.

'By God, you are right!' said his lordship forcibly.

His lordship had become a great man since Colborne had last seen him, but no trace of any added air of consequence was apparent in his manner. He did not seem to care a tinker's damn for any of the honours that had been showered on him; there was not a scrap of difference between Viscount Wellington of Talavera, and Field-Marshal the Marquis of Wellington.

The Prince Regent had made him a Field-Marshal. Upon receiving Jourdan's bâton from him, his Royal Highness had written one of his graceful letters. '*You have sent me, among the trophies of your unrivalled fame, the staff of a French Marshal, and I send you in return that of England,*' wrote the Prince Regent, regardless of the fact that no such staff was in existence. When his agitated ministers pointed this out to him, he could see no difficulty at all: he would design one himself.

This thought was horrid enough to make the gentlemen at the Horse Guards turn pale. While every effort was made to divert his Royal Highness's mind from his fell project, Colonel Torrens was told to get a bâton prepared with all possible speed. '*If I am not interfered with from* the fountain of taste, *I trust it will be found an appropriate badge of command,*' Torrens confided to Wellington, in a private letter.

But really it did not seem as though his lordship cared a button. All he said about his victories was that they had put him in the happy position of being able at last to do exactly as he chose. 'I have great advantages now over every other General,' he told the Judge Advocate, with one of his sardonic laughs. 'I have the confidence of the three Allied powers, so that what I say, or order, is, right or wrong, always thought right.' More seriously, and without a trace of affectation, he added: 'And the same with the troops. When I come myself, the soldiers think what they have to do the most important, as I am there, and that all will depend on their exertions. Of course, these are increased in proportion, and they will do for me what perhaps no one else can make them do.'

It was perfectly true. Yet you could not say that his men loved him; he had never been known to court popularity, and would very likely have greeted the suggestion that he was beloved with one of his chilling stares. 'But the fact is,' said Kincaid, 'we would rather see his long nose in the fight than a reinforcement of ten thousand men any day.'

2

The army, inactive above the mountain passes, wondered why his lordship was holding his hand. A bold advance into France, before Soult could drill his army into shape again, must surely have succeeded, thought many impatient gentlemen, paying little attention to the news from Germany, published in the *Gazette*. But his lordship was not so inattentive. The Armistice of Plässwitz was holding up operations in Germany, and his lordship knew that there was a lively possibility of a peace being patched up between Napoleon and the Allied Sovereigns. His lordship had not the slightest intention of marching into France while there was a chance of Napoleon's being in a position to send overwhelming reinforcements to Soult; nor did he want to advance a step before he had reduced Pampeluna and San Sebastian.

Pampeluna he was content to starve into submission; San Sebastian was a more pressing problem, and was proving as tough a nut to crack as Burgos. Officers, going off to the coast on a day's leave, reported that it was a bad place to have to take, the town and fortress being perched on a great sandstone rock, jutting up four hundred feet out of the sea, which washed it on three sides. Graham's force, they said, was welcome to the task of reducing it. But, all the same, when the news reached Vera that the assault by the 5th division had failed, the Light Bobs said that until they were called upon to storm the place it probably never would be taken. A most unjust rumour spread that the Pioneers had not acquitted themselves very creditably. 'Ah well!' said the Light Bobs, maddeningly indulgent.

The siege was raised on the day after the assault, news having reached Lord Wellington that Hill was engaged at Roncesvalles and at Maya, and had suffered some heavy casualties. Soult had moved at last, and rapidly, attacking the Allied right with the obvious intention of forcing the passes, and striking south to relieve Pampeluna.

'Be ready to march at a moment's notice!' Harry told Juana.

She had barely packed their portmanteau when an orderly brought her a hurried note from him: Stewart had lost the Maya pass, and the Light division was ordered to retire from Vera towards Yanzi, or even to Santesteban.

Off they went, the echo of gun-fire sounding on their left. No one, not even Alten, had any knowledge of the division's ultimate destination, nor could they obtain any very certain news of the fighting in the hills round Roncesvalles. They passed through Lesaca, finding all the headquarters Staff either packing-up, or already gone, and the whole town choked with pack-horses, and mules, and waggons. From Lesaca, they marched along a flinty road until nightfall, when they encamped on a height near

Sumbilla. Rumours were flying about: it was said that D'Erlon was over the pass of Maya with twenty thousand men, everything giving way before him, which made it seem certain that the division was being marched south to join in the defence of Pampeluna.

On the night of the 27th July, the division, marching again, blundered along craggy mountain-paths, with ghastly precipices lurking in the pitch-darkness to swallow up the unwary. Nerves were on the jump; men were heard shouting to one another, their voices sharpened by dread of being lost in this savage wilderness of broken hills, and deep, dangerous water-courses. Faggots were kindled for torches, but the darkness was like a smothering pall. Climbing a goat-track too narrow to allow of three men's walking abreast, the 2nd brigade was brought to a ragged halt by a yell of terror, and the sickening sound of a body's rolling and bumping away into the black void beside the path. It was a Rifleman, who had stepped unknowingly over the edge of the track; they could hear the clatter of the canteen on his back as it struck against the rocks, and the rattle of loose shale tumbling down the mountain-side. The man who had been plodding along beside him stood shaking as though he had ague, but when the noise of the fall had died away, suddenly, from a long way below, a voice floated up to the soldiers' straining ears. 'Hallo, there!' it shouted, quavering a little, but resolutely jaunty. 'Tell the Captain there's not a bit of me alive at all; but the devil a bone have I broken, and, faith, I'm thinking no soldier ever came to his ground at such a rate before! Have a care, boys, you don't follow! The breach at Badajos was nothing to the bottomless pit I'm in now!'

A burst of relieved laughter greeted this sally; he was retrieved from his pit, but the incident had shaken everyone's nerve, and progress grew slower than ever, so that when the dawn crept into the sky, the division found that it had covered barely half a league.

By the 30th of the month, they had reached Lecumberri, not much more than ten miles from Pampeluna. The sound of heavy cannon-fire to the east rumbled all day long, and even the sharper rattle of musketry could be heard. The knowledge that somewhere in the vicinity a battle was being fought kept the troops marching doggedly on, but although Alten sent out messenger after messenger to try to get news, nothing certain was learned, and no fresh orders reached the division from wherever Wellington had established his headquarters.

Harry, his wiry frame not much affected by the heat, the varying altitudes, or the hardness of the march, was, as usual in trying circumstances, a tower of strength. Neither his energy nor his cheerful rallying tongue flagged for a moment, but the lines in his sunburnt face might have been cut with a chisel, and even when he cracked a jest to encourage an exhausted private his eyes were strained with anxiety.

'Harry's learning what it is to worry,' said Colonel Ross.

'Poor devil!' Charlie Eeles muttered. 'Wonder what he'll do if she has to fall out?'

But Juana was not going to fall out. Not she! Tiny was so sure-footed that no one need concern himself about her, she said. As for the necessity of dismounting, and leading her horse up the steepest and roughest parts of the track, what was there to complain of in that? She assured solicitous enquirers that the broken bone in her foot was quite healed, and caused her no discomfort at all.

'*Nada me duele!*' she said. 'I think it is much better than our march to Rueda, because we were so thirsty then – *ti acordas?* – and here there are so many streams.'

'My poor little sister, you're so tired!' Tom Smith said, finding her leaning against Tiny's shoulder during a few moments' halt by one of the streams, and breathing in over-driven gasps.

'Don't tell Enrique!' she managed to say.

'No, no, but if only I could do something to help you!'

'It is nothing. It is only the mountains which make me pant so.'

Whenever Harry came riding down the column to the rear, she straightened her back, and greeted him cheerfully. He never uttered a word of pity; he seemed to take it for granted that she would keep up with the brigade, and spoke to her very much as he would have spoken to a young subaltern who needed encouragement; but between their puckered lids his eyes searched her face for the signs of exhaustion he dreaded, and in the bivouac he would roll her in her blanket as though she had been a baby, and sleep with her head pillowed on his shoulder, and his arms folded close about her.

They reached Lecumberri after dusk, and camped in a wood. It was chilly at night in the mountains, and the men built fires, and lay round them, within walls of pack-saddles, and bulky kit-bags.

'*Muy cómodo!*' Juana said sleepily, blinking at the flames. 'It is nice here, don't you think, Enrique?'

'If these damned mountain mists don't set you fast with rheumatism!'

'How foolish! Do you imagine I am like General Vandeleur?'

'Not a bit. Kiss me, *alma mia di mi corazón!*'

3

Not until late in the afternoon on the following day did any orders reach the division from Lord Wellington. Such news as

Alten's scouts brought in was vague, culled from the lips of peasants, and imperfectly understood. There seemed to have been heavy fighting somewhere north of Pampeluna, and there could be no doubt that Soult had made a big thrust through the mountains. Alten's hatchet-face was as calm as ever, but his Staff found him unusually curt, and when his messengers came back reporting failure to get into touch either with Wellington, or with Hill, a muscle twitched in his cheek, and he folded his lips as though to keep back a hasty word of censure. The troops, although they badly needed their enforced rest, could not enjoy it while rumours of an engagement were in the air, but fretted a little, wanting to know what they were doing, lying up in a wood while the rest of the army was fighting the Johnny Crapauds.

But at dusk, a cocked-hat, white with dust, was seen, and the word ran through the lines that one of the Squire's A.D.C.s had ridden into the bivouac, more dead than alive, and had fairly tumbled out of his saddle into Quartermaster Surtees's arms. He brought an order, dated the previous day, from Wellington, and had been hunting for the division until his horse almost foundered, and he himself reeled in the saddle from sheer fatigue. Soult had been defeated at Sorauren, after a very sharp engagement, lasting for two days, and the Light division was to retrace its steps at once to Zubieta.

Some hard swearing was indulged in, from the General down to the newest-joined private, for nothing was hated more than counter-marching. The Staff was blamed, of course, but it was, in fact, nobody's fault. With the Light division once set in motion through a maze of mountains and twisted valleys, it had been a difficult task to find it, and to halt it; and a running-fight, culminating in a two-day battle on the right wing, had not made matters any easier.

Alten issued his marching-orders immediately, and the division broke camp in the failing daylight. No more than nine miles was covered, for Alten, with the lesson of one night march along mountain roads behind him, halted the division at Leyza, as soon as darkness fell. Fresh orders from headquarters arrived during the small hours. Soult had retired by the Pass of Arraiz, and was making for Vera, and the neighbouring village of Echalar. His lordship desired Alten to head him off, if possible, at Santesteban; failing that, seven miles farther north, at Sumbilla; or at least to cut in upon his column of march somewhere. But his lordship had hoped to find the Light division at Zubieta, within five miles of Santesteban, not ten miles distant, on the other side of a difficult pass.

The division was under arms at dawn, and by noon had reached a point a few miles from Santesteban, after a hard march. 'George has the best of it after all,' said Molloy, mopping his brow.

George had had to stay at Leyza, in charge of a court martial. Harry had been half-inclined, foreseeing a gruelling day, to leave Juana with him, but the bare suggestion had made her so cross that he had given the notion up. Juana would suffer fatigue and hardships uncomplainingly, but the least hint of being left behind turned her from a gallant comrade into a disagreeable child with the sulks. A hunched shoulder, and glowering scowls were Harry's portion for three stormy hours.

'You will never see me again if you leave me behind, because I shall go back to Spain,' Juana announced.

'Don't talk nonsense!'

'I am not talking nonsense! You are unkind, and tired of me, and I expect you have seen some horrible woman whom you would like much better than me!'

'A Basque peasant, I suppose, all plaits and petticoats.'

'I don't care who it is, and I wish very much I had never married you, for you are brutal, and a tyrant, and I remember now a great many things you have done which I said nothing about at the time, but which wounded me very much for all that, and I can tell you this, that I would rather be taken by the French than stay with you another day!'

'Why I haven't wrung your neck all these months, I can't imagine!' said Harry.

'I should be very happy to have my neck wrung, for nothing could be worse than being obliged to live with you!'

'Oh, very well!' said Harry. 'Come, then: only you'll get no sympathy from me if you have to fall out on the march, mind!'

'*Mi queridissimo esposo!*' Juana breathed, casting herself into his arms, and passionately embracing him. 'Of course I won't fall out!'

After that, it became naturally a point of honour not to betray the least sign of fatigue, and when, after a full day's march, news reached Alten that the French had left Santesteban early, and he ordered the division to move on by the mountain path to Yanzi, Juana said nothing could please her more.

The day had begun by being misty, but for some hours past the sun had been beating down on the dusty troops. The supply column had been outstripped two days before, and the rations stowed in the soldiers' packs were running short. Everyone was tired, for the going was at all times difficult, and the labour of crawling up mountain-sides was nearly equalled by the strain of the inevitable descent, which some thought more wearing than the climb.

The long ascent of the Santa Cruz height cast into insignificance even the discomforts of the division's night-march. The sun was blazing overhead, and the path, little better than a sheep-track, grew ever more precipitous, until the officers had to dismount, to lead their horses, and the men struggled on, bent nearly double under the weight of their knapsacks. To make matters worse, large boulders were embedded in the track, and the loose shale slipped from under the men's feet. The altitude made the blood sing in their ears; one or two were actually sick; and all had to tear open their stiff jacket-collars to ease the throbbing of swollen throat-veins.

Kempt's brigade had the luck to form the leading column, but Skerrett's, choked by the dust raised by the troops ahead, suffering all the inevitable checks that fall to the lot of men marching in the rear, fared very badly. Man after man dropped out, literally unable to put one foot in front of the other. No one's pack weighed less than forty pounds, and some weighed much more; shakos seemed to tighten and tighten round sweating foreheads, and when a soldier tumbled down exhausted, and his shako fell off, it was seen that it had left a bright red line across his brow. Crawling up the abominable track, their heads almost on a level with their knees, the choking dust got into their lungs, and blinded their eyes, while the sun's rays scorched their backs. Juana passed a Rifleman stretched out beside the path, his face black, and froth on his lips. It was horrible to see him there, left to die, if he were not already dead, alone on the mountain-side. Her own heart was hammering as though it would burst her chest, and her head felt swollen. Terror blurred her vision; she could see only her own body, abandoned on the blistered rocks, with vultures circling and wheeling above it, as she had so often seen them on forced marches. She missed her footing on the loose surface, and stumbled, grazing her knees. The shock made her whimper, but it was fright, not the trifling pain, which dragged the sound out of her. Tiny's bridle was slippery in her damp clutch; his coat was streaked with sweat, and the sound of his breathing alarmed her. If Tiny were to fail, it

seemed to her as though she would have to die. A hand gripping her elbow helped her to her feet again, West's voice said
gruffly: 'All right, missus?'

She tried to wipe the mist out of her eyes, and smeared the
dust across her face. She could not tell West her fears; she whispered: 'Yes!' and gave Tiny's bridle a jerk.

The sweat from her body made the skirt of her habit cling
round her legs; she began to count her steps, keeping her head
bent so that she could see nothing but the stones and rocks at
her feet, and not the endless, climbing road ahead. She thought
that if she fell out West would probably sit by her till she was
dead, to keep off the vultures; only, big, strong men were sinking down every yard or so, and perhaps West would fail before
she did.

The column came to another jarring halt. West told her, in a
hoarse, parched voice, to sit down for a few minutes. It was too
much of an effort to answer him, and she said nothing. If she sat
down she would never get up again, so she stood still, leaning
against poor, patient Tiny, and trying to fill her lungs with the
thin, dust-laden air. It made her cough, and when she looked up,
sky, rocks, and men spun round in a giddy whirl. There was such
a roaring in her ears that she felt confused, and began to fear that
she would lose count of her steps. It was important not to do
that, she thought, so she said, 'Four thousand six hundred and
eighty-eight,' to herself, over and over again.

An insistent voice intruded upon her absorption. 'Open your
mouth! Juana, open your mouth, do you hear me?' it said.

'Four thousand six hundred and eighty-eight,' she said
huskily. 'Four thousand –'

'Stop that!' Harry said, in a rough voice. 'Drink this at once!'

She said in a vague, incredulous way: 'Enrique?'

'Yes, I'm here. Drink this up, and you will be better directly!'

He held an enamel mug to her lips, and she obediently swallowed the weak mixture of brandy and water it contained. The world steadied, and stopped whirling round her. She saw Harry's frowning face, and smiled. '*Nada me duele!*' she said.

'We are almost up,' he said. 'Can you go on?'

'Oh yes, only please, Enrique, will you tell West to keep away the vultures? I am sorry to be troublesome, but you mustn't let the vultures get me, if I fall out. Promise?'

'I promise,' he said, in a strangled tone. 'But you are talking nonsense. You are not going to fall out.'

'No, but I thought I would just speak to you about the vultures.'

'Very well, but you have spoken to me about them, and there is no need to think any more about such things.'

She agreed to it, and indeed, as soon as he was beside her, the phantasmagoria of nightmarish thoughts receded in her mind. The drink he had given her revived her; she said that she felt better, and even dared to look ahead towards the crest of the mountain. He was unable to stay with her; she was not the only cause of his anxieties, though she might be the most acute one. Two hundred men had been obliged to drop out of the column, so exhausted they could only stand leaning upon their firelocks, saying in sullen, bewildered voices that they had never fallen out before, not even on the road to Talavera. Scouts reported the enemy to be marching along the road beside the Bidassoa, and never was a brigade in worse fighting shape. To add to Harry's worries, Skerrett was fussing and fretting in a useless way which augured ill for his conduct of the brigade in action.

The leading brigade reached the crest of Santa Cruz at four in the afternoon, and was allowed to halt there. Several men who had accomplished the last few hundred yards only by dogged determination not to be beaten, no sooner reached the summit than they fell heavily on to the sun-baked rocks, lay writhing for a few moments of strange agony, and died there, black in the face, like the soldier Juana had seen, with froth on their lips, and their firelocks still grasped in their hands. Others, when the cry of 'The enemy!' penetrated to their brains through the drumming in their ears, raised their heads to show faces unrecognizable under the dust and sweat that covered them. Three thousand feet below them, the Bidassoa flowed through a deep gorge between the opposing heights of Santa Cruz and Sumbilla. Beyond the Bidassoa ran the road from Santesteban to Vera, following the river's course, and, as the weary soldiers looked, they perceived a dense mass of troops moving along the road. Even from where they were halted they could see that the column was in disorder, hurrying northward.

'Look at 'em, boys, look at 'em!' called out Tom Plunket, in a cracked voice. 'They're rompéd, by Gob! Now it's out with our muzzle-stoppers, and off with our lock-caps!'

4

The sight of the retreating column whipped up the division's spirits; men who, a moment before, had thought themselves unable to move, struggled to their feet again; and when Alten decided to force the march on for seven miles more in an attempt to intercept the retreat, almost the whole of the 1st brigade began to struggle down the steep track on the northern side of the mountain. As many of Skerrett's men as could still put one foot in front of the other followed, but thirty miles of marching in the rear of the column over heart-breaking ground had taken too big a toll of the brigade's strength. 'The men can't do it, General,' Harry told Skerrett bluntly.

'I believe you are right,' Skerrett said, in an undecided tone.

Harry, who knew he was right, bit his lip to keep back a hot retort. After a few moments, Skerrett seemed to make up his mind, and sent Fane off with a message for Alten. Fane came back presently with orders for the brigade to fall out at the foot of the hill, near a village where they had halted on their march to Lecumberri.

For himself and Juana, and Tom Fane, Harry took possession of the same cottage which they had occupied a few days before. It was a neat little building, and when they had last seen it it had stood in well-cultivated fields, with a garden full of vegetables behind it, and a yard teeming with poultry and goats. The passing of the French army had changed all that. The Indian corn had been seized for forage, the pea-rows stripped in the garden, all the fields trampled down, and the ducks and the hens commandeered. The owner seemed resigned, however. He told Harry that some of his corn had been taken by English Commissaries; but the English gave receipts for what they took, and paid for it, if one had patience; and even if they never paid, he would not care, since they had driven the villainous French out of the country. He still had a little bacon hidden away: enough, eked out with their own rations, to provide a supper for the Smiths, he said.

It was late when Harry joined Juana and Tom Fane in their billet. He found Juana asleep on the floor, with her cloak spread under her, and Tom Fane sitting on a stool, watching her. She looked small, and defenceless, so exhausted that neither the opening of the door, nor Harry's unhushed voice so much as stirred her eyelids.

When the farmer brought their supper in, Harry woke her. He made her sit up to the table; she still seemed half-asleep, but the smell of the food roused her, and she ate a very good supper. As soon as she had swallowed the last mouthful, she went to sleep again, and never moved until morning. She sat up, then, yawning, and stretching her limbs. 'Oh, how I have slept!' she said.

'Better, *querida*?' Harry asked.

'Oh, I am perfectly well, and so very hungry!'

'If only we had some more of that bacon we ate for supper!' said Fane. 'We ought to have saved some!'

'You ate bacon for supper?' exclaimed Juana. 'Oh, *malvado, bombre brutale*! Why did you not *wake* me?'

'But, Juana, Harry did wake you!'

'No! Never! It is not true!'

'Yes, it is,' Harry said, laughing at her. 'You ate a capital supper, too!'

'Enrique, it is a lie! I ate nothing, I tell you! *Estupido*, how could I have eaten supper when I remember nothing of the sort? I was all the time asleep.'

'My dearest heart, you may have been asleep, but upon my word of honour you sat on that stool, and you ate bacon, and eggs, and drank two cups of coffee!'

'Yes, you did really,' Fane assured her.

'Well, if it is true, I think it is worse than anything!' she said. 'Because it does not seem to me that I have had anything to eat since yesterday morning, and it would be very comforting just to *remember* eating bacon and eggs last night.'

5

They marched that morning, the brigade miraculously revived, and rejoined Alten at Yanzi. Kempt's brigade, reaching the banks of the Bidassoa on the previous evening under cover of thick woods, had taken the disorderly French column, on the other side of the river, by surprise, and had riddled the ranks with their fire. The prospect of 'knocking the dust out of the Frenchmen's hairy knapsacks' had spurred the brigade on, but after that first volley they had not attempted much more. Hemmed in the defile by the mountain behind them, horribly at the mercy of the Riflemen's accurate fire, the French had made signs asking for quarter, pointing to their wounded, whom they were taking with them. There was appalling confusion amongst them, and the bodies of dead men swirled away in the Bidassoa, while the cavalry, trampling over wounded infantrymen, tried to charge up the pass of Echalar.

On the march the next day, the weary Light division was cheered as much by the arrival of Lord Wellington in their midst as by the litter of abandoned French baggage all along the road. His lordship looked to be in excellent spirits. He touched his hat to the Light troops, and smiled, so presumably he was not dissatisfied with the results of their forced march. His lordship was, in fact, in a mood to be pleased with his men. He said in moments of exasperation that they were good for nothing but fighting. He admitted that they were very good at that, and it was reported that he had said of the action at Sorauren that he had never seen the army behave better. The men, as he knew they would, had got his lordship out of a scrape. General Cole had failed to send proper intelligence to him, and there had been, one way and another, a good deal of uncertainty amongst the various divisional commanders, so that Soult had been allowed to penetrate much farther than he ought to have done. The Pass of Maya had been lost rather unnecessarily, and by the time the army had retreated as far as to Sorauren the soldiers were grumbling and fretting, mistrustful of their Generals. But all that was changed the instant his lordship joined the army. He rode up quite alone, having sent Lord Fitzroy Somerset galloping off with despatches for the Quartermaster-General. He appeared amongst the skirmishers of some Portuguese Caçadores, and no sooner did the Caçadores clap eyes on that low-cocked hat, and familiar frock-coat, than they set up a shout of 'Douro! Douro!' by which title they were in the habit of hailing his lordship. The British troops pricked up their ears at the sound of it; a little later his lordship was amongst them, and such a roar of cheering greeted him that it reached Soult's lines, and even brought a tinge of colour into his lordship's cheeks. He saluted his troops in his stiff way, but although all he said was: 'No cheering, my lads, but send the French to the rightabout,' it could be seen that he was not unmoved by the demonstration. There was no more grumbling, there were no more pessimistic prophecies. When his lordship came himself, his men knew that the end was certain. You could not look at his calm profile without acquiring a feeling of boundless confidence, and he had a knack of appearing without warning amongst hardly-pressed troops which always turned the tide in favour of the Allied army. Nothing ever ruffled his calm in battle. You would not have known him for the same man who, in his office, displayed such alarming irritability whenever anything went awry. He could rally demoralized troops by merely putting himself in their midst; and if, in the stress of circumstances, their fire grew ragged, he could steady it just by saying in his loud, cheerful way: 'That's right, my lads: take your time! No hurrying now!' as though they were at target-practice.

The knowledge that Hill's force had done so well at Sorauren was naturally a little galling to the Light Bobs, remembering their abortive march to Lecumberri, but they were able to demonstrate what stuff they were made of when they reoccupied their original line of pickets above Vera, and found that the French were holding the heights of Echalar on their right. The men were so weakened by excessive marching and lack of food that some of them could scarcely stand. Some biscuit served out by the Commissary was eaten while they primed and loaded their pieces, and, weak or not, the division went into action on the French flank, while the 4th and 7th divisions launched an attack on the front. A brigade of the 7th carried off most of the honours of that day's fighting, but the Rifles and the 43rd regiment, under Colonel Barnard, won the peak of Ivantelly in dense fog, sweeping aside the French skirmishing-line, losing touch with their own main body, and fighting like devils in smothering cloud-wreaths. When the fog cleared, there was Barnard, established on the crest, so the army re-christened the peak Barnard's Hill, and the division was able to forget that it had not struck a blow at Sorauren.

Soult, with his centre smashed in, and his flanks routed in the bewildering mist, was now quite rompéd, the army thought. Men were said to be deserting from the French ranks by hundreds; and everyone knew how much valuable baggage had been lost on that disastrous retreat.

But there was still no news of the breaking of the Armistice of Plässwitz, so instead of pursuing the French into their own territory, Lord Wellington halted his army, and rearranged it on the line of the Pyrenees.

The whole of August passed quietly for the Light division. At San Sebastian, Graham had resumed the siege of the town and fortress, but the rest of the army enjoyed a well-earned breathing-space, the main preoccupation of the officers being the furnishing of their several messes with food and wine. It did not take Brigade-Major Smith long to discover that the Spanish Basques carried on a contraband trade with their French neighbours, and that brandy, claret, and even sheep were to be had easily, if one knew one's way about. Harry was besieged by his friends, and never once failed to procure for them what they wanted.

'You're wasted in the army,' Cadoux said. 'What a smuggler you would have made, to be sure! Should I soil my hands with these illicit bottles, I wonder?'

His Brigade-Major's activities came finally to Skerrett's ears. He complained to Harry that he could get no wine, and had not tasted mutton for months; and when Harry replied promptly that he could get both for him, he coughed, and looked sideways at Harry, and said: 'Well, I don't know how you manage, but if you *should* happen to hear of some decent claret, and some sheep, I wish you would procure them for me.'

'Nothing easier, General!' said Harry. 'I'll put my smugglers into requisition.'

He was quite as good as his word, and a few days later told Skerrett that he had got eight sheep, and a dozen of claret. Accustomed to Vandeleur's notions of hospitality, which were lavish, he thought the consignment rather meagre, and was just beginning to apologize for it when he was bereft of all power of speech by Skerrett's saying: 'I'm very much obliged to you, Smith! very much obliged indeed, and shall be glad of a whole sheep, and a couple of bottles of claret.'

That was too good a story to be withheld from the brigade. Skerrett's table became a standing joke, which spread through the division. As for seven sheep, and ten bottles of claret, Harry and Fane found them quite insufficient for the scale of their own hospitality.

The joke had barely had time to grow stale, when Skerrett announced his intention of giving a grand dinner. His A.D.C. and his Brigade-Major, when this news was broken to them, carefully avoided meeting each other's eyes. 'Whom do you invite, sir?' Harry asked.

'I must ask Barnard and Colborne, of course, and Blakeney, and some others. You and Fane will naturally be present, and I shall look to you to take care of everything,' said Skerrett.

They assured him that they would do so, but when Harry asked whether he should lay in provisions for the banquet,

Skerrett said No, he preferred to attend to that himself. 'One can't expect to fare very well in bivouac,' he said, 'but I daresay my cook can contrive a respectable dinner.'

Since he had the worst cook in the division, neither Harry nor Fane shared his optimism. Where were the supplies coming from? Where was the wine to be had?

'Barnard, of all people!' Harry chuckled. 'He's had a French cook ever since Salamanca, and oh, how he loves his dinner and a good bottle of wine! "Can't expect to fare well in bivouac!" Why, doesn't the old fool know that Colborne and Barnard are famous for their dinners? I'll tell you what, Tom: we shall sit down to steak and black strap!'

'He *must* mean to provide something better than black strap!' Tom said.

He was right. When Harry called upon his Brigadier for orders, on the morning of the feast, he found him dressed for travel. 'Where are you going, General?' he asked.

Skerrett, at first shocked by the free-and-easy ways of Light division officers, had become resigned to his Brigade-Major's lack of ceremony, and replied that he was off to Lesaca. This could only mean that he was going in search of supplies, so Harry promptly told Fane that they had misjudged the fellow, and he was actually going to buy suitable provisions from the sutler at headquarters.

Fane's rather simian countenance wrinkled in an effort of deductive reasoning. 'Headquarters' prices won't do for Skerrett,' he said. 'I believe you're wrong. It'll be steak and fowls – tough.'

'Then why has he gone to Lesaca?'

'I don't know,' said Fane, 'but I'll find out.'

He posted himself, accordingly, as a look-out, and arrived at the cottage he shared with the Smiths only just in time to get ready for the dinner-party. Harry heard him coming, and poked his head out of the door of his room. 'Well, did he buy supplies?'

'Yes!' replied Fane. 'Two bottles of sherry! And you're to be cautious with it! He had one in one pocket and one in the other, and he told me to warn you!'

Such a jest as this was naturally far too good not to be passed on, and when the party assembled in Skerrett's dining-room, both Barnard and Colborne were let into the secret.

The dinner was quite as bad as Tom had expected it to be, but everyone agreed that it was a splendid party, because no sooner had the company sat down to table than Colonel Barnard said: 'Come, Smith, a glass of wine!' in the blandest way. The sherry from Lesaca disappeared before the first course was served, and Tom Fane had to retire into the background to struggle with himself.

'Now, General, some more of this wine!' said Barnard. 'We camp fellows don't get such a treat every day!'

Colborne's grave, fine mouth twitched, for he had dined with Colonel Barnard. Skerrett, glaring at Harry, said: 'I very much regret to say that is the last of an old stock, Barnard. What I must now give you, I fear, won't be so good.'

It was, in fact, black strap. Barnard said: 'No, that won't do, but let us have some brandy!'

But black strap was all they got, and no brandy made its appearance, even when some very bad coffee was served to round off General Skerrett's first and last dinner-party.

'You are wicked fellows, all of you,' Colborne said afterwards, with the smile that only lit his eyes. 'If ever I get a brigade, I hope they don't send me you for my Brigade-Major, Smith.'

'*When* you get your brigade, I hope I *may* be your Brigade-Major, Colonel!' replied Harry quickly.

6

On the 25th August, the regiment's birthday, the officers of the 95th Rifles held their first regimental dinner, a very different affair from Skerrett's memorable feast. No less than seventy cheerful gentlemen sat down to dinner, and since the whole division was in bivouac, and there was no house in the vicinity with a room large enough to accommodate such a party, it was decided to hold a strictly alfresco entertainment. Two long, deep, parallel trenches were dug; the gentlemen sat on the ground with their legs in these, and the greensward between them served as a table. Anything less solid, Molloy said, would have collapsed under the weight of food and drink spread upon it. It was a noisy, cheerful party, with plenty of toasts, and a good deal of singing; and the French outposts, on the height over-looking the scene, watched it all with the keenest interest.

A few days later, volunteers were called for to help in the second assault on San Sebastian. It was rumoured that Lord Wellington had said that he would send troops to San Sebastian who would show the 5th division how to carry a town by storm: a remark not calculated to please soldiers who had failed to accomplish an impossible task. Lord Wellington wanted a hundred and fifty men from the Light division, besides several hundreds from other divisions; but when forty volunteers were asked to step out from one battalion, the whole battalion took a pace forward. In the end, the forty were selected, but there was a good deal of quarrelling between the men; and officers, clam-ouring in vain to be chosen, nursed bitter grievances for days. However, the successful volunteers got a very cold welcome from the Pioneers, when they reached San Sebastian; and General Leith said roundly that so far from showing the 5th

how to mount a breach, they should act as supports, not as the
forlorn hope. The date of the storm was fixed for the last day of
August, but it was expected that Soult would make an effort to
relieve the town. His army was known to be concentrated
between the coast town of St Jean de Luz, and the village of
Espelette, so Lord Wellington was quite ready for him, on the
western side of the Bidassoa. Near the coast, there were fords at
Irun and Behobie, but everywhere else in the district the river
was very inaccessible, with steep, rocky banks, affording no facil-
ities for the crossing of an army. On the Upper Bidassoa, at Vera,
the Light division still held the town with pickets, the body of
the division being encamped on Santa Barbara, looking slant-
ways down upon the town, and the barricaded bridge. The
Portuguese attached to the 4th division were guarding the fords
lower down the stream, but when Souk moved in force, very
early on the morning of the 31st August, one of the all too frequent mountain fogs hung heavily over the river, so that nothing could be seen of an enemy advance. Four divisions, under
Clausel, attacked the Portuguese before seven o'clock, and
crossed the river in the dense haze. This lifted about an hour
later, and a French battery began at once to shell Vera, from
which the Light division withdrew its pickets. The division,
drawn up in battle array on the commanding ground above the
town, expected to be attacked in force, but it soon became evident that the main attack was being launched on the Lower
Bidassoa, where General Freire's Spaniards (with two British
divisions in support) had the honour of receiving the frontal
onset. By ten o'clock, that affair was at an end, the Spaniards
behaving very well, but losing heart a little towards the end of
the struggle. General Freire, very nervous, went in person to
Lord Wellington to beg for reinforcements, but his lordship
replied coolly: 'If I sent you British troops, it would be said that

they had won the battle. But as the French are already retiring, you may as well win it by yourselves.'

Meanwhile, some miles farther upstream, at Vera, the Portuguese continued to be engaged all day, in the most miserable weather. It rained incessantly, and some threatening growls of thunder, and sudden squalls of wind, indicated that a tempest was brewing. The river was rising rapidly, a circumstance which soon made Brigade-Major Smith uneasy, for if the fords became impassible it was obvious that the French must, for safety's sake, try to possess themselves of the bridge at Vera. When the heavy cannon-fire drove back the British pickets from the town, Harry galloped at once to where Skerrett was standing, in a most exposed position, beside his horse, and pointed out to him the preparations being made by the enemy for an attack upon the cluster of houses, held by some Riflemen, at the bridge head. Harry, who was already exasperated by Skerrett's apparently fixed habit of choosing a dangerous place to stand in while his men cleverly concealed themselves in every available scrap of cover, spoke impetuously, and with a good deal of impatience. 'General Skerrett, unless we send down the 52nd regiment in support, the enemy will drive back the Riflemen! They can't hold those houses against the numbers prepared to attack. Our men will fight like devils, expecting to be supported, and when they're driven out their loss will be very severe!'

He had to shout to make himself heard above the noise of shell-bursts, and, indeed, expected to be hit momently, since every kind of shot was peppering the ground all round his General. Skerrett seemed to be as unconcerned at his warning as at the gun-fire, and laughed. 'Oh, is that your opinion?' he said.

'And it will be yours in five minutes!' retorted Harry insubordinately.

He was so angry that he would have said much more, had Skerrett given him an opportunity. But Skerrett, without seeming greatly to resent his hasty rejoinder, began to argue the matter. It was a moment calling for action, not discussion, and before Skerrett had had time to elaborate his views, a cloud of voltigeurs, supported by a large column, descended upon the bridge-houses.

'*Now* will you move?' shouted Harry.

No, General Skerrett would not move. He considered it would be unwise to hazard any troops merely to defend the bridge-houses; he wanted advice, and time to think the matter over, and he feared that his Brigade-Major was a very reckless young man. While he argued, and fidgeted, the French possessed themselves of the houses, and consequently the bridge itself, and the Riflemen, after putting up a spirited resistance, had to retire, with even heavier losses than Harry had feared.

To one who was a Rifleman himself, and knew, as though he had been amongst them, how implicitly the men posted in the houses had trusted in the support of their comrades, it was maddening to see this faith, built up by so many hard fights, destroyed by wanton stupidity, and lives uselessly sacrificed. Bitter reproaches sprang to Harry's lips, but he suppressed them, because the harm was done, and nothing could be gained by reproaches. The houses could be retaken, and must be retaken. From their position, the French could not hope to hold them, unless they drove the Light division back from its commanding position above them. He said: 'You see now what you have permitted, General. We must retake those houses, which we ought never to have lost.'

'Well,' Skerrett said, 'I believe you are right.'

Harry waited, but no order to advance any part of the brigade was given him. Skerrett seemed more undecided than ever, and losing any shreds of patience or temper remaining to him, Harry wheeled his horse, and galloped off through a storm of shot, to where the 52nd regiment was drawn up. He rode straight to Colborne, who greeted him with a very stern look, and an unusually grim: 'Well, Smith? Pray, what are you about?'

'Sir, General Skerrett will do nothing!' Harry burst out. 'We must retake those houses! I told him what would happen!'

'Oh!' said Colborne. 'I'm glad of that, for I was angry with you. Very well, we'll retake them at once.'

It did not take many minutes to reoccupy the houses, the French retiring as soon as they saw that the British were in earnest. Harry could not help wondering what Skerrett must feel at seeing a part of his brigade go into action without any order from himself, but when he presently rejoined them, Skerrett made no comment. This did nothing to advance his claim to Harry's good opinion. 'Only fancy old Vandeleur, if one had taken the law into one's own hands!' he said scornfully.

'Wouldn't have had to,' said Brother Tom, Adjutant, tersely.

The firing ceased during the afternoon, but the weather grew steadily worse. Vedettes reported six feet of racing water in the Bidassoa, and the rain was all the time falling in torrents. The streams trickling down the mountain-sides had become cascades, carrying stones with them in a roar audible above the incessant rumble of thunder. George Simmons, who was on picket-duty in the valley, was not only drenched to the skin, but was nearly knocked down by a branch, torn from its tree, and tossed through the air by a wind like a hurricane.

It was known that the French had everywhere crossed the Bidassoa, and as it could not be doubted that Lord Wellington would fling them back before nightfall, the swollen state of the river began by dusk to cause Harry grave anxiety. He proposed to Skerrett that the whole of the 2nd Battalion of the 95th

Rifles should be posted by the bridge-houses, with the 52nd regiment near to them, in support; and that no time should be lost in barricading the bridge itself.

Skerrett, lulled into a false feeling of security by the inaction of the French during the afternoon, and the disappearance towards the Lower Bidassoa of Clausel's force, only laughed at him. 'Upon my word, Smith, you make me think of a cat on a hot bake-stone! You may leave a picket of one officer and thirty men at the bridge.'

'General Skerrett,' said Harry, 'the French are on our side of the river, and they will have to recross it. The fords are already impassable, and I submit that it is of the utmost importance to hold the bridge!'

Skerrett, who was about to sit down to supper in his house on the Santa Barbara hill, reddened, and said angrily: 'Have the goodness to do as you're told, sir!'

'Very well!' snapped Harry. 'I am to order the battalion to retire to these heights.' He pulled his memorandum-book out of his pocket, and, for the first time in his life, jotted down his General's orders in it. 'Is that correct, sir?' he demanded, showing Skerrett what he had written.

'Yes, I have already told you so!'

'We shall repent this before daylight!' Harry said, and flung out of the house before Skerrett had time to censure his impertinence.

He galloped down to the bridge through the blinding rain. The wind was so violent that he seemed to be riding through a maelstrom of leaves, sticks, and the rubbish cast out of the cottages in the village, all whirled about in the gusts and eddies of the storm. He ordered the battalion to retire to the Santa Barbara position, and called up the Adjutant. Colonel Norcott said: 'Have you gone mad, or have I misunderstood you?'

'Neither,' said Harry curtly. He found Tom Smith at his elbow. 'Call me a picket of an officer and thirty men for the bridge!' he said.

'By God, you are mad!' Norcott exclaimed. 'I'll have no hand in this!'

'Do as you please! Your orders are to retire to the heights.'

'Harry, you can't mean to leave one picket to hold the bridge!' Tom said urgently. 'It's murder!'

'I don't need your comments!' Harry rapped out. 'What the hell are you standing there for, when you're given an order? Call a picket to me at once, damn you!'

'Cadoux's company is for picket,' Tom said, startled by the savagery in Harry's voice.

Harry vouchsafed no answer. In a few minutes, Cadoux came riding up on Barossa. 'What nice weather we do have, to be sure!' he said. 'Ah, is that you, Harry? I have been wanting a word with you ever since this morning. I should not like to be thought impolite, but what the *devil* did you mean by not supporting us in our little affair?'

'Scold away! no fault of mine!' Harry replied, with an ugly little laugh.

'Oh, was it not? You'll have to pardon me: I thought you were our Brigade-Major. Do you know, we held on in the expectation of being supported? We are not loving you much, Harry. My company is reduced to fifty. Did you know *that*?'

'You fool, Dan, do you suppose it was my doing? But come: no time for jaw! The picket!'

'Oh, so that was true, was it?' said Cadoux. 'A picket of an officer and thirty men for the bridge! Well, with your kind permission, we'll make it the whole company, and I'll stay with them.'

'Of course you have my permission!' Harry said. 'And, Dan, keep a strict watch: you'll be attacked before daylight, for

Clausel's somewhere this side of the river, trying to find a safe way over it.'

'Most certainly we shall be attacked,' Cadoux said coolly. 'I'll block up the bridge as well as I can, and if possible I'll hold it until I'm supported. But I *should* like to find myself still with a company by morning, so when the attack begins, send the whole battalion down to me, will you?'

'You know I'll do everything I can!' Harry said. 'But that damned fool – !'

'Well, please God I'll hold the bridge! Oh, and – er – Harry?'

Harry looked back. Cadoux, his wet cloak whipped about him by the wind, was sitting nonchalantly, a hand on his hip, Barossa sidling uneasily beneath him. Harry could not distinguish his face very clearly in the dusk, but he knew that he was smiling. 'Well?'

'My love to General Skerrett,' said Cadoux.

'May he rot!' growled Harry.

Leaving the battalion getting ready to retire, he rode off, not to report to Skerrett, but to find Colborne, and to show him the order in his memorandum-book.

It was just as well that he had made a note of the order, for Colborne, incredulous of such folly, was almost inclined to believe that he must have mistaken Skerrett's meaning.

'I've left Cadoux with his company to hold the bridge, sir,' Harry said. 'But this morning's wicked muddle has so reduced him he has only about fifty men left. I know him: he'll hold the bridge to the last man, but he must be supported!'

'Of course he must be supported,' said Colborne, his calm voice in odd contrast to Harry's impetuous tone. 'The whole battalion should move down into Vera.'

'Move down into Vera! I had them there, and they are even now retiring up the hill!' said Harry bitterly. 'Cadoux expects them to go to his support, but, oh, Colonel, Skerrett is callous to anything! I fear I shall never prevail on him to move!'

'Well,' said Colborne, 'you must do as you can. When the attack comes, the 95th must move to the support of the picket without an instant's loss of time. As soon as I see the battalion in motion, I will move down the hill on your flank. You had better go back to the Brigadier now.' He added, with a slight smile: 'And if I were you, Smith, I would not lose my temper with him.'

'No use, sir, it's lost already. If he lets Cadoux's company be cut to pieces, I don't care how soon he breaks me, for by God, I'll be no Brigade-Major of his!'

He found Skerrett sitting over the fire in his quarters. When he reported the arrangement he had made with Colborne, Skerrett merely laughed, and said he should be glad to know who was in command of the brigade: himself, Colonel Colborne, or a young whipper-snapper of a Brigade-Major.

'Cadoux will be attacked before dawn,' Harry replied shortly.

'Nonsense!' said Skerrett. 'I don't expect anything of the sort. If he is attacked, it will certainly not be in force. I've no more orders for you tonight, so you may go back to your own quarters. I should advise you to go to bed, and forget all these alarms of yours.'

'With your permission, General, I will stay here,' said Harry.

'Oh, do as you please,' shrugged Skerrett. 'But don't fancy you can succeed in putting me into a panic! I have a great deal more experience than you, strange though you may think it. If I did not know you for a well-meaning young hothead, I should have something to say about your behaviour tonight. However, you are a good boy, in your way, and we'll let it pass.'

Since he was unable to force his tongue to reply civilly to this speech, Harry said nothing. Skerrett presently lay down on his bed, and went to sleep; but Harry stayed wakeful by the fire, listening to the scream of the wind round the corners of the house, and the lashing of the rain on the window-panes. The night was very dark, lit only by occasional flashes of lightning. Some time after midnight, a messenger arrived from divisional headquarters with a dispatch from Alten, informing Skerrett that the enemy were retiring across the river; that it was to be apprehended they would before daylight try to possess themselves of the bridge of Vera, and that every precaution must be taken to prevent this.

'Now, General!' Harry said triumphantly. 'Let me move the battalion down to the bridge at once!'

'Oh, pooh, you are a great deal too hasty! Ten to one the French will never reach Vera in this storm! Why, it is so dark you cannot see your hand before your face! A nice thing it would be for me to march the men off on such a night, for no good reason!'

'General Skerrett, every minute that you delay puts that picket in worse danger! What have you to lose moving the regiment forward in support?'

'What have I to lose indeed! Why, you young fool, I should have half the men down with ague through exposing them unnecessarily! No, no, I know my business better than that!'

No argument, and Harry used many, had the power to make him alter his decision. The matter was still being discussed, on Harry's part most intemperately, when the sound of trumpets penetrated the racket of the storm. Harry leaped to the window, and forced open the rickety casement. The wind whistled into the room, scattering the papers on the table, and making Skerrett swear. 'Quiet! For God's sake, listen!' Harry said.

His straining ears caught the sound of the all too familiar cry of: '*En avant l'Empereur recompensera le primier qui s'avancera!*'

The faint echo was drowned by the sudden staccato rattle of rifle-fire. Harry shut the window, and turned to snatch up his hat and boat-cloak. 'Now, General, who is right?'

Skerrett was struggling into his coat. He looked chagrined, and muttered something about hoping that it would be found to be nothing but an attack by skirmishers. Harry ran out, shouting for his horse, which he had directed West to keep ready saddled in the barn, and galloped recklessly through the darkness to where the 2nd Rifle battalion was bivouacked. The men had been lying by their arms, and no urging was necessary to hasten the falling-in. They advanced downhill, guided more by the sound of the firing by the bridge than by the faint light creeping through the storm-wrack. It was obvious from the din that Cadoux was hotly engaged, and reports received confirmed Harry's fears that the bridge was being assailed by overwhelming numbers. Clausel himself, with two brigades, had succeeded in crossing the river during the afternoon, before the fords became impassable, but his rear brigades, stranded on the western bank, had been groping about all night in search of the bridge of Vera. Cadoux had posted double sentries, but the noise of the storm had smothered the sound of the French column's approach; and the sentries were fallen upon, and bayoneted, because the rain had damped their priming powder, and the rifles missed fire. But Cadoux was on the watch, and instead of passing unmolested across the bridge, the French met the determined charge of fifty Riflemen. Had the rest of the battalion been posted in the village, the French column must have been overcome, but though they made charge after charge, rallying in dwindling numbers about their Captain, the Riflemen could not stand against the waves of Frenchmen that were launched upon them. The battalion, making all possible speed to the bridge, was too far distant to arrive there in time to save its being lost. The Rifles reached it in the first gray dawn-light, and fell upon the French rear-guard, but the leading column was already on the eastern bank, and Cadoux's company driven back, half his little force either killed or badly wounded.

When Harry galloped down to the bridge, there was light enough for him to see how desperately the picket had defended its position. The bridge was choked with dead, and many bodies, hurled into the river, were being tossed and churned in the swollen waters. Llewellyn, Cadoux's lieutenant, was lying with a shattered jaw; he tried to call to Harry, and could not. Harry saw one of the Sergeants attempting with a broken leg to get upon his feet, and shouted to him: 'Captain Cadoux? Where's Captain Cadoux?'

'Dead, dead!'

A groan burst from Harry. He had no time then to search for Cadoux's body, but when the bridge was once more in British hands, and the corpses of the enemy were being pushed over the parapet into the river, he found it, lying where the fight had been most fierce. A bullet had pierced the brain; Cadoux must have died instantly; perhaps had felt nothing. His face was calm, with the shadow of his lazy smile on his lips. The little remnant of his company, bearing his body to the grave dug to receive it, wept as they shovelled the wet, cold earth on to him, for his men had loved him dearly.

'If he hadn't of fallen, we'd have held the bridge, so help us, we would!' a wounded private said, dragging his cuff across his eyes.

But Harry's grief was more acute, because he knew that Cadoux had trusted to being supported; and although it was not his fault that support had come too late, it seemed as though the faint, mocking smile on the dead lips reproached him for betraying a trust.

COLBORNE

1

IN WHAT TERMS SKERRETT REPORTED THE DISASTER AT THE bridge of Vera to Alten, his officers did not know. It was thought that he had somehow managed to excuse himself, but to whatever extent he might be able to put himself right with Alten, no future deed of heroism or of skill would ever win for him the forgiveness of the Riflemen. The news that the town, though not the fortress, of San Sebastian had been carried, that the French had everywhere been repulsed, was received by the regiment in sullen silence. The most unhappy spirit prevailed in the brigade, the men of the 52nd openly sympathizing with the Riflemen, and even the Caçadores inveighing against the stupidity of the Brigadier. The death-toll, out of the already depleted company, was so appalling that no one spoke of it. Wherever Skerrett went, he was met with glowering looks.

'It can't be very pleasant to be held accountable for sacrificing the lives of one's men,' said tender-hearted Fane.

'Let him resign his command, then!' was all Harry had to say.

He did resign it. Officially, he went home on sick leave, but those who knew him best said that he had come into a fortune on the death of his father, and was off to enjoy it. Whatever was the real reason behind his retirement, he had left the Pyrenees before the dead men choking the Bidassoa had been washed away.

The Rifles, who had cast the mounds of dead Frenchmen into the river, expecting the fast waters to bear them away, had ample time to regret their impetuosity. For many days the corpses lingered, setting up the most appalling stench. Trout were seen feeding upon them (Captain Leach was not fishing these days, thank you); and a young subaltern from another division, much farther down the river, had experienced a horrid shock when, as he knelt down to drink, he had seen a blackened arm, with some of the nails rotted away from the finger-tips, sticking up out of the water.

Everything, in fact, was wrong with Skerrett's brigade, even the weather, which had begun to get colder, with incessant fogs and rain-storms. The prospect, apparently an unending one, of remaining inactive on Santa Barbara disgusted everyone almost as much as the thought of being led into battle by Skerrett alarmed them. But Skerrett departed, and while pessimists were betting on the chances of another incompetent General's being appointed to fill his place, the news that Colonel Colborne was to assume temporary command of the brigade sent the spirits of the men soaring upwards.

No one was more delighted than Harry. He flung his hat in the air when he heard the tidings, and shouted 'Hurrah!' Quite a number of people wondered how he would go on with Colborne, for no two men could have been more unlike, the one quiet and undemonstrative, rather reserved in manner; the other hot-natured, emotional, and impulsive to a fault. But no one need have worried. From the moment of Colborne's taking up his command, he had Harry's whole-hearted allegiance.

'Well, and so I have you for my Brigade-Major after all, Smith,' said Colborne, half-smiling.

'Yes, and thank God for it!' replied Harry.

To the day of his death, Harry maintained that all his knowledge of outpost-work he learned from John Colborne. Certainly, no man knew the duty of light troops better than this pupil of Moore. During the month the division remained in bivouac on Santa Barbara, Harry seemed to be always in the saddle, conning every yard of the ground in their front. He learned how and where to post pickets to the best advantage; how to strengthen every post by throwing up obstacles to prevent night-rushes; how to save men undue fatigue; and how to anticipate the enemy's intentions. Colborne, who already knew him for a tireless Brigade Major, found him an apt pupil, laughed at his extravagances, and liked him very much. He liked Juana too, and got on with her even better than Vandeleur had done, since he spoke Spanish as fluently as Harry. Whatever he thought of women in camp, he never gave the least sign of wishing Juana otherwise, but was always glad to see her in his quarters, taking it for granted that if Harry dined with him she would too. He was a much younger man than Vandeleur, only thirty-five, in fact, and consequently rather shy of Juana at first. But no one could be shy of Juana for long, and by the time she had mended a tear in his jacket, darned his socks, sewn several missing buttons on to his shirts, and scolded him for allowing MacCurrie, his servant, to neglect him, he had grown so accustomed to her presence that she seemed to him quite like a young sister. 'Dear Colborne,' she called him, which made him smile.

'*Colonel* Colborne, you insubordinate varmint!' said Harry.

'*Coronel* Colborne,' said Juana obediently.

'If I were you, I would not pay too much attention to Smith,' interposed Colborne. 'I don't think I like *Coronel* Colborne, and you will never get your tongue round *Colonel*.'

The news of the breaking of the Armistice of Plässwitz reached Wellington on the 3rd September, with rumours of the battle at Dresden, but the siege of the fortress of San Sebastian dragged on for another week. A corps of Sappers and Miners had arrived in the Pyrenees, but they had come too late to be of much assistance. A bad business, San Sebastian: just like every other siege his lordship had engaged on. As for the taking of the town, best draw a veil over that, said those who had seen something of the sack. The fortress surrendered at last on the 9th September, and the army began to talk hopefully of an advance. It was already obvious that there were to be no regular winter-quarters this year, and everyone except Lord Wellington was itching to set foot on French territory.

His lordship was not quite so anxious to lead his mixed force into the enemy's country. It was one thing for them to plunder in Spain; quite another for them to do so amongst a hostile population. Already the Judge Advocate had a case to try of a soldier who, arrested for rape at Urdug, pleaded in extenuation of his crime that he had thought himself in France, and that there it was all regular. This kind of thing did not augur well for the army's future behaviour; but far more harassing than the British soldiers' probable misdemeanours was the prospect of the Spaniards revenging themselves upon the French as soon as they crossed the frontier. There was little doubt that they would conduct themselves damnably, thought his lordship; more especially since their supply columns were so badly organized that the greater part of their forces were half-starved, and ragged.

His lordship was receiving information out of France which he mistrusted. He was assured that Napoleon had become very unpopular in the south; that there was a strong Royalist party there; that the country people would welcome the advance of the British. 'H'm! I daresay,' said his lordship, unimpressed.

But by the middle of the month, a full report of the battle at Külm had reached him, and he began at last to prepare for the advance.

The French, meanwhile, were working like swarms of ants to render their positions more secure. Colborne and Harry used to ride out to watch them building their redoubts and entrenchments. There were two heights in front of Vera, called La Grande Rhune, and La Petite Rhune, which were separated one from the other by a narrow gorge through which the Nivelle flowed. La Grande Rhune, its steep slopes studded with gorse bushes, and rocky outcrops, made the Scots remember their Highlands. Secondary heights, like tongues of land, formed a part of the great mass; two of them, called the Bayonette, and the Commissari, loomed above Vera, and were extensively protected by entrenchments and forts.

The advance across the Bidassoa was held up for longer than had been expected by the state of the fords on the lower river, which, until October, were still too deep to allow Graham's force, now commanded by Sir John Hope, to pass; but on the 6th October, the impatiently awaited orders were brought to the Light division by Colonel Barnard, from headquarters. There was much dancing and singing that night, for the division, having come to regard itself as a superb fighting unit, was never quite happy unless on the move. That the task allotted to Colborne's brigade looked, to say the least of it, to be extremely unpromising, worried no one. Colborne himself had reconnoitred the French position, and the brigade had no doubt that under his leadership they would do all that was expected of them. The Rifles were happy, because theirs was to be the honour of opening the attack; and the men of the 52nd were happy because under cover of the skirmishing screen of Rifles they were going to storm the redoubt on one of the three hill-tongues above Vera.

The attack by the Light division, with Lowry Cole's 4th division in reserve, was to be made in two columns. Kempt's brigade, striking to the east, after driving in the outposts in the Pass of Vera, was going to outflank the Rhune behind it; while Colborne, attacking the trenches above the town on the Bayonette and the Commissari heights, would turn the hill from the south-west. Since the Bayonette was a steep, narrow spur, blocked by three successive forts, it was plain that Colborne's brigade had been given the harder task to accomplish. Colborne would not allow the pickets to be changed at daybreak, but ordered them to move on, so that the whole brigade was in Vera town before the French were aware of the impending attack.

The advance began a little after seven in the morning, Colville's division distracting the enemy by noisy demonstrations at Urdax, away to the east; but the Light division, which was the most forward unit of all, did not come into action until the head of Cole's column appeared, at about two in the afternoon.

'Now, Smith, you see the heights above us?' said Colborne.

'Yes, and I wish we were there!' replied Harry.

Colborne laughed. 'Well, when we are, and if you are not knocked over, you shall be a Brevet-Major, if my recommendation has anything to do with it.'

2

From the window of the cottage which had for so long been the Smiths' quarters, Juana was able to watch the whole attack. The cottage was hardly out of musket-range, but nothing would induce her to retire from it. She said she wanted to see a battle, and if Harry sent her to the rear she would return the instant his back was turned. She was excited, and nervous, not for herself but for Harry, and West could not prevail upon her to move away from the window. She kept thinking that she could pick Harry out amongst the mounted officers, and although it was impossible that she could recognize him at such a distance, this conviction very soon put her into a fever of anxiety. The Rifles, dark-habited troops in advance of the red-coats, seemed to be swarming all over the slope of the Bayonette. Spurts of fire from behind bushes and crags of rock showed that they were availing themselves of every bit of natural cover, but the Bayonette looked to be so precipitous that it did not seem possible for any troops to scale it.

'It's safer shooting uphill than down,' said West comfortably. 'Nor master isn't with the skirmishers. It's not likely he would be, in his position.'

'Oh, he is always in the most dangerous place!' said Juana, wringing her hands. 'I wish I had not stayed! This is terrible!'

'Well, now, missus, do but let me saddle Tiny, and I'll take you away!'

'No, no, not for anything in the world! How could I possibly go away?' she replied, not stirring from the window. 'I am glad he is riding Old Chap. It is better to be mounted on a good horse, isn't it, West?'

West assured her that it was half the battle, but she hardly attended to him, crying out suddenly that the Rifles were being thrown back. This brought him to the window, and he saw that what she said was true, the French having rushed out in great numbers from the redoubt on the spur of the hill, and driven the skirmishing line back. They had, in fact, mistaken the Riflemen, in their green uniforms, for a detachment of Caçadores,

and were considerably discomposed when they discovered their
mistake. For the 52nd had come up behind the Rifles, and as
these fell back, Colborne led his regiment forward in a grand
charge which carried the first of the redoubts.

From the cottage window, it was hard to see anything but
confusion on the hill-side. There was a great deal of noise, and
the struggle, swaying uphill and down, looked to be such a desperate business that Juana involuntarily covered her eyes. Upon
West's pointing out to her a little knot of persons visible on a
hill-crest overlooking the whole, and telling her he could clearly
detect Lord Wellington in their midst, she looked up again,
childishly hoping that his lordship would send instant help to
Harry's brigade.

She would have been indignant had she known that at that
very moment an A.D.C. had galloped up to General Alten with
a message from Kempt, a mile away, and out of sight round the
flank of the Grande Rhune, to ask if the 52nd regiment could
give him some assistance.

'Colonel Colborne gif him some assistance!' said Alten. 'If
he could see der hill Colborne's Prigade is on, he'd see dat
Colborne has quite enough to do himself!'

The dropping of men upon the slope of the Bayonette was
a sight too heart-rending for Juana to bear. She turned away
with a shudder, begging West, however, to keep a sharp look-
out. He was able, presently, to tell her that the 52nd had reached
the first redoubt, and that the Rifles and the Caçadores were
fair murdering them Frenchies on their retreat to the top of the
ridge.

She ran back to the window, but had scarcely reached it when
a chestnut hunter came galloping to the rear, his saddle empty,
and his rider, caught by one foot in the stirrup, dragged over the
ground beside him.

A shriek of the wildest despair burst from Juana. 'Old Chap!'
'My God, it is!' West muttered.

Juana ran out of the cottage, her desperate fear lending her
such speed that West, though he ran as fast as he could, was not
able to catch up with her. The dead man, his foot freed from the
stirrup, was lying in a heap some distance away, but the chestnut
still came on, bolting in terror away from the battleground.
Colour and marking were the same as Old Chap's, but as he galloped past her Juana recognized him, and stopped running.
West, pounding up behind her, gasped out: 'Missus, it's not Old
Chap! It's that Portuguese Colonel's horse that's the living spit
of master's!'

She was deathly pale, her chest labouring. She tried to smile,
to speak, but the shock had been too much for her, and to West's
dismay she fell at his feet in a deep faint.

She did not come round until he had carried her back into
the cottage, and laid her on her bed. He was in a great state of
anxiety about her, and between splashing water over her, and
shouting to Jenny Bates to get some feathers to burn under her
nose, seemed in danger of becoming quite distracted. But in a
few moments, Juana recovered consciousness, and tried to sit up.

Jenny Bates, elbowing West out of the way, pushed her back
on to her pillow. 'Now, you lie still, missus, do! That's enough
of watching nasty battles! If some people had the sense they
was born with, they never would have let you go agaping out
of the window!'

'Not Old Chap!' Juana said in a husky voice. 'I saw. It was
poor Algeo! Oh, West, look out and tell me what is happening!'

'He'll tell you our men are safe on top of the hill, and no need
for any of us to worry our heads over them!' said Jenny, in such
minatory accents that West took the hint, and reported the
brigade to be in possession of the heights.

'Oh, is it true?' Juana said. 'Are you sure?'

'Why, where else would they be?' demanded Jenny scorn-fully. 'You don't want to fret about master, for he's enjoying him-self, same as my man will be, if I know them! Men! Yes, there's nothing they like better than to go mixing themselves up in a nasty, bloody battle, fair frightening the wits out of decent women, and themselves like a set of pesky lads out of school! You lie quiet now, and see if the master don't come bounding in presently, as right as a ram's horn, and telling you what a rare day's fighting he's had!'

'If you are sure it is all over!' Juana said, with a shudder. 'But I can still hear firing!'

'Ay, but it's not our men,' West assured her. 'Of course it's all over! I daresay master will be standing there, atop of the hill with the Colonel, at this very moment.'

3

But the brigade, in spite of having possessed themselves of the first redoubt, had still some way to go before they reached the defences on the ridge of the Bayonette, and Harry, so far from standing there with his Colonel, was riding back as hard as he could to Cole's supporting division.

The Enthusiastics had pushed forward up the slope of the hill, and as soon as Cole heard that Colborne meant to press on, he said in his quick way: 'Rely on my support! By God, you'll need it, for you have a tough struggle before you! Magnificently done, sir! magnificently done, indeed! Everyone is talking of your charge!'

Harry turned, and spurred Old Chap up the hill again. As soon as he was assured of Cole's support, Colborne threw out a screen of Riflemen in skirmishing order, and advanced the whole brigade under a murderous fire from the ridge. Many of the shots, however, went over the heads of the men, while the Riflemen, firing uphill, found their marks with awful precision. The French continued firing from behind the parapets until the British, advancing steadily all the time, were almost upon them. A very short hand-to-hand fight followed, but instead of defending their rather formidable position with the determination the British had expected them to show, the French suddenly abandoned it, rushing away down the steep side of the ravine in their rear.

Colborne, Harry, Winterbottom, the Adjutant of the 52nd, and Tom Smith were in the forefront of the fight, and upon the Frenchmen's flight into the ravine, they all four of them pushed on in pursuit, with some ten of the swiftest-footed men in the brigade racing after them. On the opposite side of the ravine, they saw a small detachment of the Riflemen from Kempt's brigade, who had reached the crest of the opposite spur, and were pushing forward.

'Where are you going to, Colonel?' shouted Harry, his eyes blazing with excitement.

'Why, to reconnoitre a little, to be sure!' replied Colborne.

The ravine expanded rather unexpectedly, and a column of quite four hundred Frenchmen was suddenly exposed.

Harry began to laugh. 'For God's sake, Colonel, take care what you are about! You have clean outstripped our own column! What shall we do?'

'Oh, there's nothing for it but to put a good face on the matter!' said Colborne. 'I daresay they will think Kempt's fellows on the other ridge the head of the column. Come on!'

He clapped his spurs into his horse's flanks, and galloped up to the officer at the head of the enemy column. 'You are cut off,' he said, in French, and for all the world (thought Harry) as though he were supported by ten thousand men. 'Lay down your arms!'

The officer, though taken by surprise, remained perfectly cool. He glanced up at the Riflemen on the ridge, and for a moment Harry thought that he had guessed that the ten men in sight comprised the whole force. But apparently he supposed them to be the head of a large column, for he turned back to Colborne, and, presenting the hilt of his sword, said: 'I surrender to you a sword which has ever done its duty, monsieur!'

Colborne received it, bowing gravely. The three officers behind him, taken as much by surprise as the Frenchman, wondered what he would do next, but with his usual presence of mind, he said: 'Face your men to the left, and move out of the ravine.'

His tone was so calm, his bearing so assured that Harry was not at all surprised that the order was immediately obeyed. He was extremely glad to see the Frenchmen separated from their weapons, but while he stood, trying to suppress the laughter that was consuming him, Colborne turned, and said: 'Quick, Smith, what are you doing there? Get a few men together, or we are yet in a scrape!'

Harry, recalled to his duty, said hastily: 'Yes, sir!' and rode off to hasten the march of the men behind Colborne. He found them on the ridge, forming up, and soon brought them down to where Colborne was exchanging civilities with the French officer. Young Cargill, a very Scotch subaltern of the 52nd, marched the prisoners off to the rear under escort, while the rest of the column pushed on into French territory.

By this time it was growing dark, and Harry was sent to halt the brigade, just as one of Lowry Cole's A.D.C.s came riding up to ask Colborne, with General Cole's compliments, how much farther he intended to go. 'For Sir Lowry says, sir, that he don't intend to go any farther!'

'Oh, I have gone quite far enough!' replied Colborne.

The brigade bivouacked on the ground it had won, the

men lying by their arms, and a fine drizzle of rain falling all
night. No baggage having come up, conditions were miserable, but everyone seemed to be in excellent spirits. Fires were
laboriously kindled, rum washed down the ration of biscuit,
and Colborne had the satisfaction of overhearing a private of
his own regiment sing out: 'The Colonel's health! and damn
the man who gets a shot into him!'

Morning brought young Cargill back to the brigade. Having
marched his prisoners to the rear, he had spent the night snugly
in Vera, a piece of intelligence which made his fellow-officers,
rubbing cramped limbs, swear at him. He went off to make his
report to Colborne, whom he found toasting sausages with his
Staff.

'Well, you look very spruce, Mr Cargill,' said Colborne,
himself unshaven and dirty. 'Get those prisoners safely to the
rear?'

'Yes sir. And I met Lord Wellington on the way, sir, just about
dusk, it would be.'

'You did, did you?'

'Yes, sir. His lordship called out to me, "Hallo, sir, where did
you get those fellows?" and I told him, "In France: Colonel
Colborne's brigade took them!"'

'Oh, that's why you're looking so confoundedly pleased with
yourself, is it?' said Harry.

'Well, it was his lordship himself,' replied Cargill, with simple
pride. 'And he said to me, "How the devil do you know it was
France?" Och, I knew *that*! "Because I saw a lot of our fellows
coming into the column with pigs and poultry, which we had
not got on the Spanish side," I told him.'

Colborne started up, a very black look on his face. 'Why Mr
Cargill, you were not such a blockhead as to tell his lordship
that, were you?'

'What for would I not? It was true as death!' said Cargill, round-eyed.

'You young fool, don't you know better than to talk about the men's plundering to Wellington? Get back to your regiment, sir, get back to your regiment!'

Cargill withdrew, very crestfallen. Harry was laughing, but Colborne said: 'I shall hear more of this.'

However, when he rode off to headquarters a little later, he found his lordship in a very good humour.

'By God, Colborne, your fellows did damned well!' said his lordship energetically. 'But you know, though your brigade have distinguished themselves even more than usual, we must respect the property of the country.'

'I'm fully aware of it, my lord. I can rely on the discipline of my soldiers, but your lordship well knows that in the very heat of action a little irregularity will occur.'

'Ah, ah!' said his lordship. 'Stop it in future, Colborne!'

Such a mild reproof, accompanied as it was by a smile and a nod, quite staggered Colborne. He told Lord Fitzroy Somerset, whom he applied to on Harry's behalf, that he had never known his lordship to be in such excellent temper.

'Oh, he was watching your little affair yesterday!' replied Fitzroy. 'There was nothing ever like it, Colonel! I wish you might have heard his lordship: he said the charge of the 52nd was the finest thing he ever saw. You'll be mentioned in the dispatch.'

'Well, I don't care about that, but I want a brevet-majority for Smith.'

'I don't think there will be any difficulty about that,' said Fitzroy. 'I'll see to it.'

So back went Colborne to the brigade, and, finding Harry presently, said: 'Well, give me your hand, Major Smith!'

But a disappointment was in store for Harry. Colonel Barnard, hearing of the Brevet, went immediately to Fitzroy to demand it for one of his own captains. 'Damme, you can't give it to young Smith!' he said. 'I'm very fond of the boy, and I daresay he deserves it, but he can't be made a major over the heads of twenty other fellows in the regiment!'

There was no getting over that, of course, and Fitzroy had to break the sad news to Harry. He softened the blow by telling Harry that his lordship, when the difficulty had been explained to him, had said forcibly: 'A pity, by God! If he will go and serve as Brigade-Major to another brigade, I'll give him the rank after the next battle.'

'You had better do so, Smith,' Colborne said, angry and mortified.

'No, dear Colonel!' said Harry, swallowing his own chagrin. 'Not to be made of *your* rank!'

4

The baggage arrived during the morning, and with it Juana, still so much upset by the shock of mistaking Algeo's horse for Old Chap that she was quite unlike herself, subdued enough to make Harry anxious, and starting at every unexpected sound. Several days passed before her spirits recovered their usual buoyancy, but, happily, having won the Grande Rhune, Lord Wellington condemned his army to another month of inactivity, so that no further alarms occurred to set her back again.

The division now took possession of the great ridge of hills. It was a wonderful position, if you had a fancy for long views and morning fogs. On a clear day, even Bayonne could be seen in the distance, while St Jean de Luz seemed to be like a toy town below the division. The waters of the Bay of Biscay sparkled to the west, with little ships dotted everywhere along the coast. They were British cruisers, and great was the excitement when one was seen chasing a French brig-of-war. Thousands of soldiers, straining their eyes from the top of the Grande Rhune, burst into wild cheering when the brig blew up.

'How delighted the tars would be if they knew that so many of their countrymen were observing and applauding them from the tops of the Pyrenees!' remarked George Simmons, beaming with pleasure.

'Oh, George, George!' chuckled Tom Smith. 'How are your horn-players?'

George's company had captured a couple of French horn-players at the Pass of Vera. He shook his head. 'Oh, no good at all! We tried to get 'em to play us the latest French songs, but the poor fellows were so scared they made wretched work of it.'

George's horn-players were a great joke, of course, but Juana could not quite understand how George was able to laugh so light-heartedly, for he had just come back from San Sebastian where he had been visiting a close friend, who had been desperately wounded in the storming of the citadel. So many friends had fallen there, and at the Crossing of the Bidassoa, that she herself felt such an oppression of the spirits that laughter, for many days, seemed impossible.

However, a diversion soon occurred which made her forget such gloomy thoughts. In the redisposition of the forces on the ridge, the extreme right of the division became the left, and the Smiths had to pack up and move their ground. When the brigade reached the new position, they found the first battalion of the Rifles just evacuating it. Major Gilmour, in command of the battalion during the temporary absence of Barnard, had built a mud hut for himself, and as soon as Juana came riding up, he hailed her, and pointed to this grand erection with a flourish of his hat. 'Jump off my dear, and come into your own castle, which I in perpetuity bequeath to you!' he declaimed.

Juana slid off Tiny's back at once. She was delighted with the hut, and clapped her hands at its elegant appointments. 'Oh, a chimney, and a fireplace! Oh, how did you contrive to make a door? It is the dearest house!'

'Quite a gentleman's residence, I flatter myself,' said Gilmour. 'Ten foot square, you observe: door of the best wattles and bullock-hide: situation commanding unrivalled views! Bless you, my child: may you find it watertight! Where's Harry?'

'Oh, he has gone to post the pickets! He will be so astonished when he sees our lovely house! Dear Gilmour, I am so grateful! It is horrid in our tent now!'

By the time Harry and Fane came in, a fire was burning brightly in the hut, supper was ready, and the servants had set up the tent for their own use.

'By jove, nothing was ever so snug!' Fane exclaimed, warming his chilled hands at the fire. 'What a good fellow Gilmour is! Only to think of sleeping in the warm!'

After the rigours of damp autumn nights under canvas, the hut did indeed seem the height of luxury. As soon as supper was cleared away, they stoked the fire, spread a couple of mattresses on the floor, and lay down under their blankets in quite a glow of content. Snuggled in the crook of Harry's arm, Juana said drowsily: 'Listen to the wind! It will rain soon. How sorry I am for West and Kitchen in my horrid tent!'

She was right about the rain. She had barely dropped into her first sleep when a sudden storm rose. Harry, still awake, heard the rain pelting down, and was just congratulating himself on his dry quarters when a clod of earth fell on to his face. Before he had time to do more than look up at the roof of black sods, the rain was pouring between the cracks, crumbling away the sods, and smothering everything in the hut with mud.

Fane started up with a shout of dismay, but Juana, rudely awakened by a shower of rain and slime, broke into peals of laughter. In a few seconds the hut seemed to be full of water. The fire, extinguished by the rain, belched clouds of smoke, and the hut's unfortunate owners tumbled out of it, quite drenched, and as black as mudlarks.

'Oh, *wasn't* it nice of Gilmour?' said Harry. 'Just wait till I see him! My poor darling, are you very wet?'

'Oh, I am soaked, but wasn't it funny, Enrique? Oh, look at Tom's face! He is just like a blackamoor!'

They spent the rest of the night in the despised tent, dispossessing the servants without ceremony, and never again braved the dangers of Gilmour's mud-hut.

The weather was becoming very cold, and as the convoys were late in arriving from Portugal, the soldiers began to be sorry they had been parted from their overcoats. A disagreeable feature of the district started to manifest itself in the sudden springs which broke through the ground in all the most unexpected places, and transformed reasonably dry bivouacs into swamps. Kincaid, who had made a most ingenious fire-place in his tent by digging a hole, and carrying the smoke out under the canvas wall to a turf chimney, returned from dining in a friend's tent to find a fountain springing out of his fireplace, and playing over his bed and all his baggage.

'It couldn't have happened to anyone else!' said Charlie Eeles, trying, as well as he could for laughing, to help Kincaid to remove his belongings to a dryer spot.

'No, because no one else had the sense to think of such a fine invention,' retorted Kincaid.

The morning fogs grew thicker. It was a beautiful sight, George said, to watch the peaks emerge, like islands, from the clouds, while the dense vapour, iridescent with the rays of the sun, hung heavily over all the valleys.

'Ugh!' said Molloy, shivering. 'We shall have the whole division down with ague, that's all I know.'

Oddly enough (for frequent hail-storms alternated with the fogs) the health of the men was good. They grumbled a great deal, for it was not only cold and wet on the Rhune, but the sight of the rich plains of France below them was tantalizing, and they all longed for the order to dislodge the French from the opposite height of La Petite Rhune. Moreover, while the Allied army remained inactive, every French soldier seemed to be busy casting up fortifications, so it looked as though they meant to defend their front pretty desperately. When the weather was at its worst, pickets at the foot of La Petite Rhune used to call hopefully to the British outposts: 'You can't remain in these bleak mountains much longer. We suppose you will soon retire into Spain for the winter?'

'Very likely we may, if we are ordered to,' was all the answer they got.

'Spain or France, it's all the same to me,' said fat Johnny Castles, crawling out from under the wet folds of a collapsed tent. 'Hail brings snow in its tail, and it's time we came down from the clouds.'

'Ah!' remarked a Scot. 'I was hearing that Hill's fellys are under a gude twa feet of snow the noo, so set that doon on the backside o' your count-book!'

'The way our Colonel's spying out the land looks to me like we'll soon be knocking Johnny Petit off his perch there,' said a private from the 52nd, with a jerk of his thumb towards the Lesser Rhune.

It was quite true: Colonel Colborne, imparting his wisdom to Harry, was reconnoitring every yard of ground in his front, for with the surrender of Pampeluna, at the end of October, orders for a general advance were daily expected. From the commanding heights of the Grande Rhune, all the French lines could be seen. Colborne and Harry used to watch the progress made on the enemy's fortifications, and often Wellington would join them, walking about on one of the northern ridges of the hill, and staring in his high-nosed way over the rich terrain below him. He used to talk to Colborne, sometimes with a good deal of animation, more often in staccato sentences. He said he would be obliged to send the greater part of the Spanish troops home before venturing into France, and even Colborne, who, from having served with the Spaniards in the past was always inclined to defend them, could not deny that it would be hazardous to march them into France. As for the British, discipline must be strengthened, said his lordship; and indeed, between them, he and the Judge Advocate were imposing the stiffest punishments for plundering.

One day, when his lordship rode to Colborne's outpost, he stayed for longer than was usual, and after walking about for some time, lay down on the ground, supporting himself on his folded arms, and looking meditatively towards the Petite Rhune. His Quartermaster-General, Sir George Murray, was with him, Fitzroy Somerset, and one of his A.D.C.s; and an orderly was walking their horses about a little way behind them. Besides Colborne and Harry, Alten and Kempt had joined the party.

Wellington was silent for some time, but presently he turned his head towards Colborne, and said abruptly: 'Those fellows think themselves invulnerable, but I shall beat them out, and with great ease.'

'That we shall beat them, when your lordship attacks, I have no doubt,' replied Colborne. 'But for the ease – !'

'Ah, Colborne, with your local knowledge only you're perfectly right!' interrupted Wellington. 'It appears difficult, but the fact is the enemy have not men to man the works and lines they occupy. They dare not concentrate a sufficient body to resist the attacks I shall make upon them. I can pour a greater force on certain points than they can concentrate to resist me.' He turned towards Murray, seated beside him, and, dropping his voice to an earnest undertone, began to talk to him.

Alten, collecting the eyes of his Brigadiers, got up, as though to move away, but his lordship broke off his conversation to say: 'Oh, lie still!'

He went on speaking to Murray, in his quick incisive way, out-lining his plan for an attack of the whole army. Murray listened attentively, once or twice interpolating a question. When his lordship had finished speaking, he pulled writing materials out of his sabretache, and began methodically to set down the plans on paper. The chill wind rustled the sheets, and whipped the plume in his cocked-hat. It must have been very uncomfortable, Harry thought, sitting on damp ground, and trying at once to write with cold fingers, and to hold down the corner of the paper, but Sir George seemed to be quite unperturbed. When he had transcribed his chief's plans, he read them aloud, while Wellington, with his telescope to his eye, scanned the French lines.

Harry had heard it said that, after Wellington's, Murray's was the best brain in the army, and by the time the Quartermaster-General had finished reading his notes aloud, he believed it. It was wonderful, he thought, that Murray had not missed one point, but had got it all down, almost precisely as Wellington had spoken it.

'Is that your desire, my lord?'

Wellington had listened in silence to his orders being read, his cheeks a little sucked in, and his lips pursed. He put his telescope down, and smiled. 'Murray, this will put us in possession of the fellows' lines. Shall we be ready tomorrow?'

'I fear not, my lord, but next day.'

Wellington nodded, and sat up. 'Now, Alten,' he said, 'if, during the night previous to the attack, the Light division could be formed on this very ground, so as to rush at La Petite Rhune just as day dawned, it would be of vast importance, and save great loss. And by thus throwing yourselves on the right of the works of La Petite Rhune, you would certainly carry them.'

Alten looked meditatively across the ravine at the jagged ridge of the Lesser Rhune, with its scarped front, and redoubts overhanging the steep slopes. His lordship's tone was confident, but anyone with the smallest knowledge of the ground must have known how desperate a task he was asking of his crack troops. Alten's lean, dark countenance gave nothing away; after a few moments' consideration, he said calmly: 'I dink I can, my lord.'

'My brigade has a road,' said Kempt. 'There can be no difficulty.'

'For me, there's no road,' said Colborne, 'but Smith and I know every bush and every stone. We've studied what we've daily expected, and I think we can engage to lead the brigade to this very spot on the darkest night.'

'Well then, Alten,' said his lordship briskly, 'when you receive your orders for the attack, let it be so.'

5

Harry was agog with excitement at the prospect of the coming attack, but not even the hope of moving to dryer and warmer

quarters could make Juana think of it with anything but misgiving. Harry had trained her so well that she did her best to conceal her fears from him. When Colborne, whose deep-set eyes
saw so much more than Harry's, talked reassuringly to her, she
controlled a quivering lip, and said that indeed she was not
going to be silly, and he must not on any account tell Enrique
how afraid she was that she would never see him again.

When, at nightfall, on the 9th November, the brigade moved
forward from its encampment, Harry had gone a short distance
when he suddenly reined in, and exclaimed: 'Oh, by Jupiter, I
forgot to say good-bye to my wife!'

'You had better go back, then,' said Colborne.

'I had, indeed!' Harry said. 'I don't know how I came to forget, but she will certainly box my ears!'

'Well, I daresay it will serve you right. Be off with you, and
make haste!'

Juana heard the thud of Old Chap's hooves galloping up to
the wooden hut which Harry had had built. She was sitting
with her hands tightly clasped in her lap, and instead of greeting Harry with a storm of abuse, which he quite expected, she
flung herself into his arms as soon as he came in, and clung to
him in silence.

He felt how her heart beat against his, and said remorsefully:
'*Hija*, forgive me! I was so busy, right up to the last, that I clean
forgot!'

Only a deep sigh answered him. He held her away from him,
and tilted up her chin. 'Hallo, what's the matter?'

'Enrique!' she said, her throat painfully constricted, 'either
you or your horse will be killed tomorrow! I know it, *here*!' She
pressed a hand to her breast, looking mournfully up at him.

He laughed. 'Well, of two such chances, I hope it may be the
horse!'

'You don't believe me.'

He took her face between his hands, and kissed her. 'Sweetheart, no!'

'I should not have said it. But it is true.'

'Nonsense! There, I must go! Take care of yourself, and be sure I'll take good care of *my*self!'

He gave her another kiss, rather a rough one, because her eyes were full of tears, and ran out again to jump on Old Chap's back, and ride off after the brigade.

The night was very dark, and as there was no road over the mountain-ridge, leading the column to the appointed place was a ticklish business. But Colborne's lessons stood Harry in good stead, and he found that even in the darkness he was able to recognize the boulders and bushes he had been made to study so minutely. Since quiet was essential for the success of the movement, Colborne remained near the brigade, and sent Harry on from point to point before he would allow the men to march forward. Even when Harry found his landmarks, he was not always satisfied, but several times rode up himself to make sure that no mistake had been made.

All talking in the ranks was forbidden, and the men were warned to tread carefully when they marched down the northern slope of the mountain. Once or twice a small boulder, dislodged by an unwary foot, went rolling and bounding down the hill, but the brigade finally crept up behind their advanced picket, a hundred and fifty yards from the enemy, without having betrayed their approach by any more serious noise.

Halting the column, Colborne and Harry rode forward to the picket, knowing that the French, if they heard them, would think that they were merely visiting outposts, in the usual way. They found the picket sitting round a camp-fire, their rifles across their knees, and every man quite as alert as the sentry posted a little in advance. Colborne was pleased, and commended them for their vigilance. The Sergeant said softly: 'Well, sir, it don't seem to be quite the time to be lying snoring, as you might say. But there's nothing stirring in our front.'

Satisfied, Colborne returned to the brigade; and Harry, having seen the men all lying down under their blankets, snatched a couple of hours' sleep himself. Fane, who had chosen to remain with him rather than go to the rear, tried to sleep too, but could not. He sat huddled in his greatcoat, keeping the cold out with frequent nips of brandy from his flask, and wondering how Harry could drop off so easily, and sleep so peacefully. 'You are a callous devil, and I'm sure I don't know why I like you so much,' he said softly and sadly, tucking the boat-cloak under Harry's unconscious form.

Harry was jerked awake, an hour before daylight, by the sudden report of a musket. He was up in a minute, an oath on his lips, but although some anxious moments had to be lived through, no alarm sounded from the French outpost. The soldier who had accidentally fired his piece was silently and scientifically kicked by his friends, and all was still again.

There was not much sleep after that. The men lay watching the dim crests of the mountains for the first signs of dawn. While they had been eating a meal of meat and biscuits at two in the morning, Kempt's brigade had arrived after a long march by road, and had silently taken up its position beside Colborne's. Once again the brigades were going to engage the enemy separately, Kempt's business being to get across the marsh in his front, and to assail the narrow hog's-back ridge, two-thirds of the way up the side of the Rhune; and Colborne's to work round the extreme west of the mountain, and to rush the table-land beyond the hog's back, with its strong forts. To the right of the division, Giron's Spaniards, and the Enthusiastics were to attack the Rhune on its eastern side.

The advance was to be a general one, but no one in the Light division had much thought to spare for the proceedings of any other part of the army than that massed for the main attack on the French centre. The weakest point in the enemy's defences was the opening between the two Rhunes and the Nivelle river, but the lesser Rhune formed an effective bar to an approach along this line. A wag, looking at the impregnable front of the mountain, said: 'It's a pity them fine new Sappers and Miners wot didn't do any good at San Sebastian don't blow up that bloody mountain, then we wouldn't 'ave to go scaling up it.'

'We won't ever get up it, will we?' asked a young soldier, trying not to let his teeth chatter.

'Ho, so that's wot you think, is it? 'Ow the 'ell are we going to get at Johnny Petit's lines if we don't take the Rhune first?'

'It looks an awful place!'

'Don't talk so cork-brained! Nice thing if the Light Bobs couldn't kick the Crapauds off of their perch any day they felt like it!' said the veteran scathingly. 'You give over, now, and keep your eyes skinned for the dawn!'

'I wish it would come quick!'

'Well, it won't come no quicker for your wishing. Stow your gab!'

The signal for the attack was to be three gun-shots fired from the top of the Atchubia mountain, away to the east of the division. Some firing was heard to the west a little before dawn, and the young soldier started at the sound of it.

'Keep quiet, that's 'Ope,' growled his companion. 'False attack. If you're alive this time tomorrow, you won't be so green as wot you are now, that's one comfort.'

All heads were turned towards the east. The dark mass of Mount Atchubia could be seen against the gray sky, but it was not until six o'clock that the first rays of sunlight stole over the summit. Almost at the same instant, the signal shots were fired. Orders ran down the lines; the men leaped to their feet, and formed up; and two companies of the 43rd regiment, of Kempt's brigade, surged forward to plunge through the marsh, while the rest of the regiment advanced against the crags of the Rhune in their front.

Seven columns were launched against the Rhune, and so successful had the night-marches been that the attack took the enemy completely by surprise. During the rush from the lower slopes of the Grand Rhune, across the difficult ravine to the base of the Petite Rhune, the French were seen flying to man their formidable defences. A few pieces opened fire, and from the top of the Grand Rhune were immediately answered by the mountain artillery placed there.

Colborne, advancing simultaneously with Kempt, passed along the dead ground of the ravine on the southern side of the Rhune while the skirmishers of the 1st brigade were engaging the attention of the French on the lower slopes, and penetrated beyond the western end of the defences. The 52nd regiment, sweeping aside all opposition, went up the slopes of the Mouiz hill in an impetuous charge, to take in flank the breast-works and fortifications which the Riflemen were assailing.

Never had the Light division engaged on a more glorious action. The speed of their advance, and the bravery of their several attacks must have satisfied great little Craufurd himself. By eight o'clock, the key of the French position was won, and the way lay open for an attack against the main position on the Nivelle. Major Napier, with his pantaloons torn and singed by gunfire, had led the 43rd regiment up on to the hog's back in spite of every effort made to repulse him. Gun-fire, musketry, and great boulders rolled over the craggy sides of the position were not enough to check the advance of the 43rd. Up they came, climbing over places that looked inaccessible, and one after another the three forts on the ridge fell into their hands. The casualties were appalling, but nothing could check the swarm of redcoats. A seven-foot wall protected the first of the redoubts, but it was scaled in the teeth of a murderous fire from the defenders. Major Napier was all but bayoneted as he tried to hoist himself over the top from a precarious foothold on a projecting stone half-way up, and was dragged down, much to his rage, by a couple of his subalterns.

The men were so exhausted by the time the French fled from the redoubt, that they flung themselves panting on the ground, heedless of the fire from the second of the redoubts. As soon as they had recovered their breath, they rushed forward again, like so many scarlet devils, stormed the Magpie's Nest redoubt, and surged on, leaving their dead and wounded in mounds behind them, and formed up in some sort of order for an attack upon the Donjon, the last of the redoubts along the ridge.

From the Magpie's Nest, a fine view of the whole field of battle could be had. Below it, a ravine separated the spur from the Mouiz height, which the 52nd regiment had reached. Up the ravine, Kempt was leading his Portuguese reserve, but it was Colborne's swift advance which decided the day. Finding their flank turned, and themselves in peril of being cut off, the French on the Mouiz hill abandoned their trenches, and fled northwards in considerable confusion. The troops opposing the Portuguese caught the terror, and followed suit; and when the garrison in the Donjon fort on the Lesser Rhune saw the disordered retreat of their comrades across the ravine, they deserted the fort before Napier had finished forming his men up for an attack upon it.

On the Mouiz height, Colborne was re-forming his men for an attack upon the main French position, north of the Lesser Rhune. All along the forty-mile front, guns were pounding the lines. It was a brilliant day, without a trace of fog in the valleys; Hope's divisions could be seen threatening the French lines from the coast to the Rhunes; and on the sparkling waters of the Bay of Biscay the distant ships were so clearly etched against the sky that they looked like miniatures. Eastward, fifty thousand men were pouring down the slope of Mount Atchubia, their bayonets flashing in the sunlight. On the Mouiz ridge itself, the only French troops left were those manning a strong star-redoubt, placed on the edge of a steep hill. Colborne, approaching it along a narrow neck of land, halted the 52nd under the brow of the hill, for his experience told him that since it was isolated from the rest of the French army there was no need to waste men's lives in an assault upon it. Kempt's brigade was already turning it on the left, and Cole was coming up with the Enthusiastics to the rear; while Giron's Spaniards, to the right of Colborne, closed in on the eastern side.

Harry, who had just changed Old Chap for his thoroughbred mare, joined Colborne on the neck of land below the redoubt. He had been in the thick of the fighting, but was unscathed. 'Barnard's been hit,' he said. 'I don't know how badly: Simmons has taken him to the rear. Kempt's wounded too, but they say he's still on the field. By Jove, sir, there was never such a day! Do you mean to assail the redoubt?'

'I see no need. It can't hold out, and we should lose men for no purpose,' Colborne replied, looking up at the steep hill above him.

The Spaniards on his right chose, however, at that moment, to make a demonstration against the fort. The defenders sent them quickly to the rightabout, and just as Colborne was observing their proceedings with a good deal of annoyance, Charles Beckwith rode up with orders from Alten for the brigade to move on.

'Move on?' said Colborne. 'What do you mean by that? Does General Alten wish me to attack the redoubt? If we leave it to our right or left, it must fall as a matter of course. Our whole army will be beyond it in twenty minutes.'

'I don't know,' said Beckwith, who was looking tired and harassed. 'Your orders are to move on.'

'Charlie, am I to attack the redoubt?' demanded Colborne.

'I tell you, I only know you are to move on!' replied Beckwith, wheeling his horse, and galloping off.

'What an evasive order!' said Colborne.

'Oh, sir, do let *us* take the last of the works!' Harry said, his eyes sparkling. 'It will be done in a few minutes!'

'It seems that we must do so. Advance in column of companies!'

No sooner was the 52nd in motion, climbing the hill under the fort, than it was made plain to them that the French meant to defend the place. Such a murderous fire met the troops that the leading ranks were mown down. The regiment struggled on, Colborne at their head, and gained the crest, only to be brought up short by a deep, well-palisaded ditch cut in front of the redoubt. They recoiled before the fire of the defenders, and sought cover in a little ravine. As soon as they could be re-formed, Colborne led them forward again through a rain of shot and shell. Within twenty yards of the ditch, Harry's mare was struck. He turned her quickly, so that as he jumped off, her body should be between him and the enemy's fire, and as he swung a leg over another shot hit her, and she fell, pinning Harry under her, her blood pouring on to his face.

Colborne saw Harry go down, but was too busy encouraging his men to pay much heed. Shells were bursting all round him, and the 52nd were suffering shocking losses without being able to make any headway against the redoubt. Tom Fane, dismounting from his horse, ran to him, and shouted: 'Pray get off, sir, pray get off! You will be killed in an instant!'

'No! This is absurd! They must surrender!' Colborne exclaimed, and pulling out his handkerchief, rode forward, waving it above his head. As he approached the ditch, the fire slackened. He spurred right up to the brink, and seeing an officer within the works, called out: 'What nonsense this is, attempting to hold out! You are surrounded on every side! There are Spaniards on the left; you had better surrender at once!'

He spoke loudly, and the French officer, thinking that he was trying to urge the men to surrender, leaned over the wall, saying indignantly: 'You are speaking to my men!'

'That is all nonsense: you must surrender!'

'You incite my men to desert me! Retire, or I will shoot you!'

'If a shot is fired now that you are surrounded by our army,' said Colborne, 'we'll put every man to the sword! Come now, or you will have the Spaniards here directly.'

The dread of falling into Spanish hands had a decided effect upon the defenders of the redoubt, as Colborne knew it would. The officer hesitated, but his situation was hopeless, and after a moment he asked Colborne to come into the fort to arrange terms.

Meanwhile, Harry, crushed under the body of his mare, but miraculously unhurt, was shouting to some soldiers near at hand to come and pull him out. They ran towards him, astonished to find him alive.

'Why, damn my eyes if our old Brigade-Major is killed after all!' one of them exclaimed.

'Come, pull me out!' said Harry. 'I'm not even wounded: only squeezed!'

'Lor', sir, you're as bloody as a butcher!' said a stout private, hauling him out from under the mare.

Harry did not trouble to wipe the blood from his face, but ran to join Colborne, who had pulled out his note-book, and was writing in it, in French, *I surrender unconditionally.*

'Hallo, Smith! I thought you were dead. Give this to that fellow, and tell him to sign it,' Colborne said.

The French officer burst out laughing when Harry went into the fort. 'One would say you were a walking corpse!' he said. 'You are literally covered with blood!'

'Nevertheless, I'm very much alive,' replied Harry, giving him Colborne's paper to sign.

The officer grimaced at the words Colborne had written, but since there was no help for it, scrawled his name, and gave the paper back to Harry.

'That's right,' said Colborne, when Harry brought it to him. 'Find yourself a fresh horse, and take it to Wellington.'

'Here, have mine!' Fane said, thrusting his bridle into Harry's hand. 'What a sight you are, to be sure!'

Harry was, indeed, such a mask of blood that when he rode up to Wellington, his lordship demanded: 'Who are you, sir?'

'The Brigade-Major, 2nd Rifle brigade, my lord,' replied Harry.

His lordship stared at him. 'Hallo, Smith! Are you badly wounded?'

'Not at all, sir: it's my horse's blood,' said Harry, giving him Colborne's paper.

'Well!' said Wellington, taking it, and running his eye over it. 'Tell Colborne I approve. Did you lose many men in that affair?'

'Yes, my lord, very many.'

'I'm sorry for it,' said his lordship, looking down his nose. 'No need to have attacked the redoubt.'

'Our orders were to move on, sir.'

'Dey were not mine! Dere is some mistake!' Alten said angrily. 'I sent no order to Colborne! I dink Colborne understands his pusiness fery well widout such orders from me.'

'Ah – h'm! I wish Staff-officers would learn to know their duties better!' said his lordship, with one of his frosty glares.

6

By two in the afternoon, Clausel's troops were retreating across the Nivelle in confusion; at dusk, Wellington crossed the river with two divisions; and the Light, the 4th, and Giron's Andalusians bivouacked on the reverse slope of the original French position.

Here Juana rejoined the brigade, coming up with the baggage early on the following morning, and almost swooning with horror at the sight of Harry's blood-stained garments. That he was not wounded seemed to her incredible; she could not believe that he was not concealing some dreadful hurt from her. He took her by the shoulders and shook her, saying: 'Will you have sense, *estupida*, or must I strip to show you that I have nothing but a few bruises? It was the mare who was hurt, not I.'

She exclaimed at once: 'I knew it! Did I not tell you what would happen? You are not wounded at all?'

'No, I tell you!'

Her terrors laid, she suffered an instant reaction. 'Oh, you are abominable to frighten me so! I won't speak to you till you have washed yourself, and taken off those horrible clothes!'

'As though I had not been longing to take them off all this time!' said Harry. 'Won't you kiss me, my hateful darling?'

'No! Your face is smeared with blood! I would sooner kiss Ugly Tom!' she declared.

She went off to visit one of his friends, who was wounded. He did not see her again until much later, and then it was she who was in need of a change of clothes, for out of two hundred men of the 52nd regiment returned as killed and wounded, a hundred, suffering from flesh wounds, had refused to go to the rear. Quite a number of these needed attention, and Juana, who had become expert in the washing and binding up of hurts, was busy all the morning. When Harry, very spruce in his best jacket and sash, encountered her, he recoiled, his narrow eyes gleaming with laughter, and said: 'Oh, you horrid little thing! Don't touch me!'

'Oh!' Juana cried. 'One little bloodstain! How nice you look! Kiss me quickly, for I must go and wash my hands!'

'Not till you have washed, and taken off those clothes!' murmured Harry wickedly. '*I'm* going to find out how many of my friends were hit yesterday!'

'Well, I can tell you that all our particular friends are safe, only Johnny Kincaid is quite wretched about poor Colonel Barnard, for he fears he will die.'

This was very bad news, and had the effect of sending Harry off immediately to find Kincaid, who was Barnard's Adjutant. The Colonel had been knocked off his horse by a musket-ball through the lung, and by the time Kincaid had reached him he was so choked by blood that he could not speak. His men gathered round him in the greatest distress, for he was very much beloved, but Kincaid, seeing George Simmons not far off, had the presence of mind to shout to him to come to Barnard quickly. George washed the blood out of Barnard's mouth, felt the wound, and looked grave, but upon Barnard's regaining his senses, and saying to him: 'Simmons, am I mortally wounded?'

he had replied in his honest way: 'Colonel, it is useless to mince the matter: you are dangerously wounded, but not immediately mortally.'

'Be candid!' Barnard had said. 'I'm not afraid to die.'

'I am candid,' George said steadfastly.

Four men had carried the Colonel off on a blanket, George accompanying them. It was expected that George would return to his regiment on the following day, but just before the brigade moved on, Joe Simmons got a message from him that he was staying in Vera for the present, in charge of Barnard, who was going on remarkably well, and had placed himself in George's sole care.

'Dear old George, how he must be enjoying himself!' said Kincaid.

The brigade moved on that day, descending into the fertile French plain, and reaching Arbonne. After the wild mountains they had been amongst for so long, the sight of neat farmsteads, and tilled fields, intersected by hedgerows, pleased everyone. Hay was obtainable for the horses, too, which relieved mounted officers of one of their most pressing anxieties. The weather, however, was bad, and it was evident that a great deal of rain had fallen on the plains, since all the ways were spongy with soaked clay. Tiny sank in this sticky mud to his knees, a circumstance which made Harry Smith think poorly of the army's prospects of continuing the drive into France.

He was quite right. The condition of the ground made the passage of the artillery almost impossible, nor could the heavy cavalry be brought up from their quarters in Spain. Had the weather been clement, and the Spanish troops better fed, there was no saying how far Wellington might not have thrust Soult. He had forced him to evacuate St Jean de Luz, which town he made his own headquarters, but he might have been able to do more. '*I despair of the Spaniards,*' he wrote to Lord Bathurst, ten days after the battle. '*They are in so miserable a state, that it is really hardly fair to expect that they will refrain from plundering a beautiful country: particularly adverting to the miseries which their own country has suffered from its invaders. If I could now bring forward 20,000 good Spaniards, paid and fed, I should have Bayonne. If I could bring forward 40,000, I do not know where I should stop. Now I have both the 20,000 and the 40,000 at my command, upon this frontier, but I cannot venture to bring forward any. Without pay and food, they must plunder; and if they plunder, they will ruin us all.*'

It was some consolation, while Freire's and Longa's men were sacking Ascain, and Miña's wild guerrilleros were rapidly approaching a state of open mutiny, that his lordship was able to tell Bathurst that the conduct of the British and Portuguese troops was being exactly what he wished; but the atrocious behaviour of the starved Spaniards came at the worst possible moment. Never was the time riper for a bold thrust. 'Where are your Emperor's headquarters now?' Wellington asked one of the French officers, who had been taken prisoner.

'*Nulle part,*' the Frenchman had answered sadly. '*Il n'y a point de quartier général, et point d'armée.*'

It was not every Commander, advancing into enemy territory, who would have been able to bring himself deliberately to dispense with 40,000 men out of his whole force; but Wellington's cold judgment convinced him that delay in completing his operations would be less harmful to the Allied cause than the depredations of the Spaniards in a country which it was vital to conciliate. Having hanged an astonishing number of the marauders without achieving any improvement in the conduct of the rest, his lordship deliberately sent every Spanish division except Morillo's back to Spain.

The weather grew worse. The Light division, bivouacking near Arbonne, in hourly expectation of being ordered to advance, was moved forward only as far as the town, and quartered there.

It was an uncomfortable situation, for it rained incessantly, and although the French inhabitants of the district were as friendly towards the British as Wellington had been assured they would be, there were bickering fights going on with Soult's forces, entrenched before Bayonne; and every day seemed to bring skirmishes with outposts all along the line of the front.

As soon as the rain stopped, and the sodden ground was dry enough to make an advance possible, the division was moved forward, nearer to Bayonne, and quartered in two large châteaux. The first brigade was at Arcangues, the second at Castilleur, in which Colborne packed the 52nd regiment, Harry said, as close as cards.

It was December by this time, and they began to think of Christmas. Colborne's Staff had bought a goose, and if it did not die from surfeit, Colborne said, they would give a grand dinner on Christmas Day.

'But of course it will not die!' said Juana. 'We are fattening it in quite the proper way.'

'Well, that's what you say,' answered Colborne, with his lurking smile. 'But there's reason in everything, and I think the bird will very likely burst. Whenever I want Fane or Harry, I find them stuffing it with most unsuitable food. In fact, the goose is beginning to embarrass me, for you all watch my plate so jealously at dinner, to see what I shall leave that can be scraped up to be given to the creature, that I am becoming quite shy.'

'Oh come, now, sir!' protested Fane. 'Who tried to make the goose eat a hard-boiled egg? Addled, too!'

'But you are not to make it eat eggs!' exclaimed Juana. 'It is very bad of you, Colborne, very wrong indeed, and I am quite shocked!'

'I merely offered it,' said Colborne. 'Heaven forbid that I should compel that obese bird to eat anything against its will!'

But, in the end, all their anxious care of the goose was wasted. On the 9th December, the 1st and 7th divisions moved close up to the rear of the Light, which made everyone feel sure that some action was contemplated.

'Whist, whist, I smell a bird's nest!' said Tom Plunket.

'Yes, and so does Johnny Crapaud!' replied the Bombproof Man caustically. 'This mousetrap smells too strong of cheese. Johnny's up to snuff all right. Every man-jacket of them's been standing to his arms ever since the Gentlemen's Sons showed their front. I wouldn't wonder if we had a pretty batch of trouble before the day's out.'

It was soon learned that the 1st and 7th had moved up for the purpose of crossing the Nive. The Light division received orders to drive back the enemy's pickets towards Bayonne, by way of creating a diversion. They effected this after a little desultory skirmishing, and at dusk resumed the usual line of pickets.

It was generally thought that nothing further would come of the demonstration, but news filtered through that Hill was moving up to St Pierre, near Bayonne, and Harry, always very alert, was uneasy. He was convinced that the French would create a diversion on the left of the Allied army, and was in the saddle before dawn next day, visiting the advanced pickets, a mile in front of the main body of the brigade. He was joined as soon as it was daylight by Beckwith, who stared with puckered eyelids towards the French lines, and said: 'What do you think of it, Harry?'

'I don't like it. They mean something.'

'Why, so I think!'

Colborne came up while they were watching the movement in the French camp. Harry rode a little way to meet him. 'The enemy are going to attack us,' he said abruptly.

'No; they are only going to resume their ordinary posts in our front,' replied Colborne.

'But look at the column in our immediate front!' Harry said. 'There's a column over there, if I am not much mistaken, evidently moving on the 1st division!'

His tone was impatient. Colborne knew that he was always uneasy if there was any possibility of a sudden attack, on account of Juana; and paid no attention. He had pulled out his glass, and was looking through it at the enemy's lines. He detected some flashes in the distance, and said: 'Those must be some men discharging their pieces.' The next instant he saw a large body of men advancing, a good way away.

'By God, the whole army's in movement!' Beckwith said, his glass also trained on the column Colborne had seen.

'Yes, you're right,' Colborne said.

'Come, something must be done!' Harry burst out. 'What are you going to do?'

'Gently, I must think a little first,' Colborne replied.

Old Chap began to sidle and fidget, as though infected by Harry's impatience. 'At least let me order the brigade under arms!' begged Harry.

'Oh, do be quiet, Smith!' said Colborne, trying to think out his dispositions.

'I can't be quiet while nothing is done! We shall be attacked immediately!'

'Go and order the brigade under arms, and bring up the 52nd. You had better tell your wife to leave the château at once, for I imagine an attack will be made upon it.'

Harry went off at a hand-gallop, just as the French opened fire on the advanced pickets. Juana was ironing shirts when the alarm sounded, and had barely time to put the iron down in the hearth before West came running in to tell her that he had seen Master for a hurried moment, and that the orders were to evacuate the château immediately.

Juana caught up the shirts, but West said: 'No time to pack anything, missus: we shall be under fire in a minute!'

'Go and saddle Tiny then, and I will come directly!' she said, pulling her riding-habit out of the cupboard. 'And West, West! Find Vitty! She ran out a little while ago!'

She had only just scrambled into her habit when the first shots rattled about the walls of the château. The 52nd were forming up in battle-order, and there was so much noise and confusion that she had some difficulty in forcing her way to where West had the horses waiting. She was on Tiny's back in an instant, but demanded in a sharpened tone where Vitty was?

'I can't find her, missus! It's no use, we daren't stay for her!'

'Oh, I won't go without my poor little dog! No, no, she may get killed! We must find her!'

West said roughly: 'Missus, you heard Master's orders! It's my business to get you to where you'll be safe, and if you don't come willingly I shall lead Tiny!'

Her eyes flashed, but a musket-ball whistling above their heads made her see how unreasonable it would be to insist upon remaining in such a perilous situation; so, swallowing a sob, she said humbly that she was sorry, and would not be troublesome any more.

The thunder of gun-fire on the left showed that an action was being fought near Bayonne, but although the French made a vigorous attack upon both Castilleur and Arcangues, they did not follow it up by anything more than some rather vicious skirmishing.

West had had Juana's tent loaded on to the pack-mule, and pitched it for her as soon as they got to the rear of the division. She tried not to let herself think about Vitty's fate, but when Harry came in at the end of the day, tired and harrassed, he was met by such a woebegone face, that he said in an attempt to rally Juana's spirits: 'Hallo, what's the matter now? Are you mourning the loss of our goose?'

'Vitty!' Juana said, with tears rolling down her cheeks.

'Oh, has she been snapped up? Poor little Pug! Whew, what a day! What's for supper?'

Such callous disregard for Vitty's plight was more than Juana could bear. 'You are cruel and cold and you don't care what becomes of my darling! All you think of is food!'

'I'm sorry,' said Harry. 'Of course I care about Vitty, *querida*. Only, to tell you the truth, I haven't had a bite to eat all day, and I'm dog-tired besides.'

She flushed scarlet, and dashed the tears out of her eyes. 'Oh, I am such a bad wife, mi Enrique! Forgive me! Look, I brought away the bacon we had this morning, and West stuffed some bread into his pockets, and besides that he found some very good vegetables here, so I made a stew. It does not matter about Vitty. *You* are safe, and that is enough for me!'

She began to serve out the stew. Just as she sat down to share it with Harry, Kitchen put his head into the tent, and said that one of the buglers of the 52nd regiment wanted to see her.

'Hallo, one of your odd friends?' said Harry. 'Send him in, Joe!'

'But I do not know any of the buglers in the 52nd!' objected Juana. 'He cannot want to see me. It must be you he asked for, only Joe is so stupid!'

But when the bugler came in, grinning broadly, he addressed himself to Juana, not to Harry. 'Beg pardon, missus!' he said in rough Spanish. 'I've got something in my haversack for you.'

'What then?' Juana asked, surprised by his air of mystery.

'Something you'll be glad to have, I'll be bound. I saw her in the scuffle, back there at the château, and whipped her up, for it won't do to lose you, I said to myself!'

'Vitty!' cried Juana, jumping up.

'That's right, missus,' said the bugler, hauling the unhappy little pug out of his haversack, and putting her into Juana's arms.
'She's been in there all day, as good as you please, barring a bit
of whimpering on and off!'

7

With the recovery of her pet, Juana's spirits rose mercurially. The
discomforts of bivouacking for several days without the least
vestige of baggage became at once very good fun, and when the
French were finally driven back, and the brigade returned to
Castilleur, not even the discovery that some of her belongings
had been stolen had the power to depress her. Tom Fane was
loudly and indignantly condemning the French thieves who
had rifled the contents of his portmanteau, and Billy Mein was
bewailing the loss of the goose, 'just as he was fattening up!' but
Juana said that although it was a great pity Ugly Tom had been
robbed, she was not at all sorry the goose had gone. 'For I don't
think we *could* have eaten him, do you?' she said seriously.

'Oh, couldn't we just!' said Mein.

'No, Billy, because we had become too fond of him, and
besides, the *Coronel* gave him bad things to eat.'

'Shame!' said Colborne, looking up with a twinkle in his eye.

'Good-bye to our grand dinner!' said Mein.

'Not a bit of it!' said Harry briskly. 'I know how we can contrive to make up for losing the goose.'

'You would, of course,' said Fane. 'Found some more smugglers?'

'Devil a one! But we'll invite the Commissary to the party!'

'Harry,' said Colborne, 'if you're not cashiered for impudence,
you ought to go far. I foresee a brilliant career.'

'Well, I hope we may still be here at Christmas,' said Fane, somewhat pessimistically.

There did indeed seem to be some doubt about the matter, for the French in their front showed enough liveliness to keep them continually on the alert. Officers responsible for posting pickets found the frequent alarms wearing, and Harry, never one to take his duties lightly, began to look red-eyed again from lack of sleep.

On one occasion, when he was posting the night's sentries after a day of skirmishing, he encountered a French officer performing the same duty. Harry thought he was placing his vedettes too close to the British advance-posts, and as he had no notion of withdrawing his own pickets, he walked over to remonstrate with the Frenchman.

'Hallo there, I want to speak to you!' he called out.

The officer seemed to be a little amused, but came to meet Harry without the smallest hesitation. 'But certainly, monsieur! What is it, then?'

'Your vedette,' said Harry. 'There's mine, over there, and if you post yours so far in advance, it will lead to nothing but alarms being given when they're relieved. I wish you will retire a little way!'

The Frenchman raised his brows. 'I do not see that, monsieur, but if you will point out to me where you wish my vedette to be, I shall be enchanted to oblige you by moving him.'

'Very good of you,' said Harry. 'Let us take a look at the ground!'

This they did. The Frenchman moved his vedette to a place of Harry's choosing, and before they parted company, offered Harry a drink of his excellent brandy. Harry accepted it gratefully, for it was a cold night, bade his new acquaintance good-bye, and rode back to Château Castilleur.

It was late when he arrived, and he found Colborne asleep on a mattress before the fire. He was fully clothed, even to his boots, for there had been so many alarms since the brigade's arrival at Castilleur that neither he nor Harry ever thought of undressing at night. Harry, himself dog-weary, did not wake him; but after wondering whether it was worth while to go to forage for some supper, decided that it was not, and lay down as he was on the mattress which he kept in Colborne's room. He dropped asleep almost immediately, but whether from fatigue, or from lack of food, the rest which he so badly needed was disturbed by a dream vivid enough to wake him with a terrific start, and a shout of: 'Stand to your arms!'

Colborne woke, and was on his feet in an instant. The flickering firelight showed Harry standing in the middle of the room, blinking as though still half-asleep.

'Oh, I beg your pardon, sir! I've been dreaming,' he said in an uncertain voice.

'Never mind,' said Colborne. 'It's near daylight, and it shows anyway that asleep or awake you're intent on your duty. Did you dream that we were being attacked?'

'No,' Harry said. 'Not us. I – Damn it, it has taken such possession of my senses I can't throw it off! I thought the enemy were attacking my father's house. There's a door at the back which leads into the garden. My father had my mother in his arms; I saw them as plainly as ever I did in my life: he was carrying her through the Black Door, as we always called it when we were children, and calling out: "Now, someone shut the door! She is safe and rescued." Then I woke. Such nonsense! And to have roused you, too, sir!'

He lay down again, but could not sleep, the dream oppressing him to such an extent that every time he closed his eyes the picture of it returned to him. When morning came, he looked rather haggard, and was quieter than usual, and very brittle-tempered.

It was a tiresome day, with incessant skirmishes of outposts. The Caçadores had the advance, and were attacked early in the morning. Harry said he had not seen the French as daring since the retreat to Corunna. 'I don't know what the devil we've got in our front to-day!' he said, when Colborne came riding up to the advanced posts. He added irritably: 'Don't stand there! You will be shot in a moment!'

Colborne laughed, but, sure enough, a minute later a ball went through his hat. He did not seem much disturbed, but he moved to a safer place, remarking: 'Look at the fellows! It's evident it's no general attack, for the troops in the bivouac are not under arms. They want this post.'

'Which they will have in ten minutes,' said Harry, 'unless I bring up the 2nd Rifle battalion. The Caçadores aren't equal to the task.'

'Fetch them!' said Colborne, inspecting the hole through his hat. 'What a narrow escape, to be sure!'

Harry only said, as he prepared to ride off: 'You should not expose yourself so, sir!'

'What *is* the matter with Harry?' demanded Mein, after three days of the Brigade-Major's moodiness. 'There's not a laugh to be got out of him! What's worrying him?'

Nobody knew; but not many days later the English mail arrived, bringing a letter for Harry, from his father. When he saw the writing, Harry turned pale. 'I know what it is,' he said, breaking the seal with trembling fingers. 'I have known ever since that dream!'

Juana watched him timidly as he read his father's letter. A groan broke from him; she said: 'Is it – is it your mother, Enrique?'

'Yes,' he answered. He stood still for a moment, then quite suddenly flung himself on his knees beside Juana, and wept and wept, with his face buried in her hands.

She did not know how to comfort him. His grief frightened her, because he had always seemed to her so strong that she had not known that he could be broken to pieces like this for any care in the world. She cried a little, too, because she was so sorry for him. Later, when the cloud did not lift from Harry's brow, she cried for herself, because the repressed, silent man who shared her bed was not Harry, who loved and bullied her, but a stranger too sad to quarrel with her, too listless to ask even how she had spent her day.

Harry found her crying once, and stopped dead upon the threshold. '*Hija!*'

She started up, trying to hide her face, stammering: 'The toothache! It is nothing!'

He came across the room, not slowly as though he were worn-out, but with his own quick tread. 'My darling! What is it?'

She said: 'Enrique, I have lost father and mother, and my brother died of his wounds in my arms. You still have your home and your father left. I – I live alone for you, my all!'

He held her tightly against his breast. 'And I for you! There is no one else.'

'I cannot comfort you, Enrique,' she said sadly. 'It is not enough, that you have me.'

'Yes, it *is* enough,' he replied. 'This is nonsense! Why, you bad little varmint, are you telling me I don't love you? What do you think you deserve for that?'

She flung her arms round his neck, overjoyed at hearing the teasing note in his voice. Later, pondering the matter, she saw that her efforts to be good, and patient, and sympathetic, had not helped Harry to recover from his grief nearly as much as the weakness she had tried to hide from him. So when next he sat staring into the fire, with his head propped on his hand, she picked a quarrel with him over a trifle; and when he was abstracted, sighing heavily at his own thoughts, she treated him to such an exhibition of sheer naughtiness, that after a week of wondering from hour to hour what dangerous prank she would play next, Harry was in a fair way to forgetting his unhappiness in worrying over his wife's abominable behaviour. By the time he had descended to the most ferocious threats of what he would do if Juana risked her neck and his horses by trying to ride up a flight of stairs, Brigade-Major Smith was himself again, and Mrs Harry Smith judged it to be time to hang a meek head, and promise to be good.

Nine

❦

BARNARD

1

THE END OF JANUARY FOUND THE LIGHT DIVISION AT Ustaritz, where, being ten miles to the rear of their posts at Arcangues and Castilleur, they for a time lost sight of the enemy. This, said Harry, was just as well, since the pickets of both armies were getting much too friendly. An officer, visiting outposts one night, had actually found his picket, with the exception of one sentry left on guard, fraternizing with the French picket in a ruined house whose cellars were full of wine-casks. Upon his arrival, all the men had jumped up, the French saluting him with particular flourish, and had gone back to their posts. It was one thing, Harry said, to signal to the enemy that one was in earnest, by tapping the butts of the rifles in a peculiar fashion, when one sallied forth in force to seize a lightly-held advance-post: it saved unnecessary bloodshed, and gave the enemy a chance to retire in good order; but it was quite another to send a messenger across to the French lines on Christmas Eve to buy brandy from the enemy. That, he said, was the outside of enough.

The Riflemen who had subscribed for the brandy were in agreement with him. Each man had contributed half-a-dollar, and the French had produced the brandy readily enough.

Unfortunately, the messenger sent to bring away the brandy had thought it proper to sample it before returning to his comrades, with the result that the French sentry had had to shout to the Riflemen to come and rescue their friend from the ditch into which he had fallen. It had taken three of them to carry him back to his own lines, and both bottles of brandy had been found to be empty.

Life at Ustaritz was comparatively dull, although there was plenty of hunting and shooting for those officers who could afford to indulge in these pastimes. Lord Wellington, whose headquarters at St Jean de Luz were only about fifteen miles away, had sent for his hounds out of Spain, and was often to be seen, riding in his bruising style across country, and generally dressed in the sky-blue coat of the Salisbury Hunt, with a little black cape over it. His lordship left his cares behind him when he rode to hounds. He became as accessible as you please, laughing at his own and other men's tumbles, and conversing with everyone with the greatest good-humour.

He still had his cares, of course, though not as many as poor Marshal Soult complained of to his Emperor. Soult said indignantly that all the inhabitants of the south were welcoming the British with open arms. It was quite true. As soon as the marauding Spaniards had been sent back to their own country, people who had fled from their villages in terror of these invaders, came nervously back again. They found the British, and even the Portuguese, not only well-behaved, but unmistakably friendly. But the popularity of the Allied army was not due so much to these causes as to the incredible discovery that what the Commissaries took, they paid for. To a people accustomed to being preyed upon by their own armies, this honesty on the part of the British seemed too astonishing to be at first believed in. But the word spread that officers billeted in cottages and inns called for the reckoning before they left; and that Commissaries, haggling over loads of hay, gave promissory notes in exchange for everything they commandeered. *'Vivent les Anglais!'* shouted the peasants gratefully, whenever they saw a company of redcoats on the road.

That was all very well, and certainly relieved his lordship's mind of one of its cares. But the war-chest was still in a bad way, and promissory notes were hard to meet, while the long-suffering infantry was six months in arrears of pay. *'I can scarcely stir out of my house on account of the public creditors waiting to demand what is due to them,'* wrote his lordship, never one to understate a grievance.

It was annoying, but neither the Basques nor the French could be induced to accept Spanish or Portuguese silver, which was all the loose cash the war-chest held. His lordship published notices informing the mistrustful people how much the dollar and the real were worth, but they continued obstinately to refuse dollars. So his lordship wrote a private letter to Colonels commanding battalions in the army, promising, in the coolest way, indemnity and good pay to all professional coiners in the ranks who would step forward. He got about fifty of these gentlemen, spirited them away to St Jean de Luz, set up a secret mint there, and put them to work on the Spanish silver in the war-chest. The dollars disappeared, and excellent Napoleonic five-franc pieces began, mysteriously, to circulate in their place.

The weather, throughout December and January, continued to be shocking, and made troop movements impossible. The army remained in cantonments, fretting a little at inaction. But his lordship, for once in his life, was not altogether displeased at the inclemency of the season. He did not wish to advance much farther into France until he should be informed of the Allies' intentions. Did they contemplate making peace with Napoleon? Did they mean to support the Royalist claims? Or were they considering the possibility of setting up a new republic? His lordship could not discover that there was much enthusiasm for the Royalist cause, but was inclined to think that if he were a Bourbon prince he would come to France, and take his chance. He said that the people of southern France, though heartily sick of the Bonapartist régime, did not seem to care much what form of government was to succeed it.

So the Duc d'Angoulême came incognito on a visit to head-quarters. He was rather an odd person, and his lordship's personal Staff, who dubbed all distinguished visitors to headquarters Tigers, promptly christened him the Royal Tiger. He found the Field-Marshal's headquarters quite devoid of any pomp or ceremony, no one, from the youngest A.D.C. to the Field-Marshal himself, putting on any of the airs of a great man. It was rather disconcerting at first to find Lord Wellington's family composed of very young gentlemen with a flow of inexhaustible high spirits, and a nice taste in fancy waistcoats; and most bewildering to hear his lordship and all the big-wigs in the army joking and laughing with these sprigs from the Universities, just as though they were all members of one big, jolly, family, but the Duc soon grew accustomed to it, and settled down quite happily.

2

In January, upon its becoming known that General Skerrett was not going to return to his brigade, Colonel Colborne's temporary command came to an end. He went back to his regiment, but the blow was a good deal softened by the appointment of Colonel Andrew Barnard in Skerrett's room.

Colonel Barnard, who had commanded the entire division during the siege of Badajos, was a splendid soldier, and the most

cheerful, hospitable fellow in the world, said his officers, affec-
tionately welcoming him back. The wound in his chest was not
by any means healed, but he said that he was in the best of
health, and owed his life to the devoted attention of George
Simmons. No one but George had been allowed to doctor
him, and as soon as he could stand on his feet he had taken
George with him to St Jean de Luz, where he had stayed for
some time. George had actually dined at Lord Wellington's
table, so that it was a wonder, said his messmates, that he
deigned to consort with his humbler friends any more. George
received all the chaff with his placid grin, but said seriously that
to gain the friendship of a man of Colonel Barnard's ability
would always be of use. Colonel Barnard had presented him
with a handsome gold watch, especially sent from London,
which George showed proudly to everyone; and in the New
Year George was appointed to superintend the new Light division telegraph, at the Château d'Urdanches.

'George, you're becoming a great man!' his friends told him.

'No, no!' protested George. 'Only I am determined to make
my way in the army, and I cannot but be grateful for the chance
which led to my being singled out.'

Brother Maud, returning from St Jean de Luz, whither his
battalion had been sent to get new equipment, visited George
in his log-house by the telegraph-post. He ate a tight little beef-
steak with him, and went off with George's good mule in
exchange for his own broken-down pack horse. George's
friends thought that Maud's visits closely resembled the descent
of locusts upon the plain, but George was always glad to see his
graceless brother, and could be relied upon to find any number
of excuses for his predatory habits.

With the appointment of Barnard to the command of the 2nd
brigade, the 1st Rifle battalion, of which he was Colonel, changed

places with the 2nd, an alteration which could not be other than
agreeable to Harry, who belonged to the 1st battalion, and was
delighted to have his particular friends in his own brigade.

In February, the weather improved, and his lordship began to
complete his arrangements for driving Soult out of Bayonne. His
manœuvres were very bewildering to Soult, a much harassed
man. His Emperor had demanded three divisions from him, and
Soult obediently sent them off. This left him in the uncomfortable position of being numerically inferior to Lord Wellington.
He had been drilling conscripts throughout January, but even
conscripts were hard to come by, since the young Gascons fled to
the woods to escape being forced into the army. The Emperor's
advice to him was not at all helpful, and consisted largely of
instructions to him to make the best of his situation.

It seemed to Soult that his adversary's thrust must come
somewhere between Bayonne and Port de Lanne, some thirty
or more miles farther up the Adour; and he began to move
troops eastward, with the intention of striking at Wellington's
flank when the attempt to cross the river should be made. That
Wellington meant to cross below Bayonne, right at the river's
mouth, never occurred to him. When Wellington began to
move eastward, with the greater part of his army, leaving only
Hope and 18,000 English and Portuguese troops round Bayonne, the Marshal thought his reading of the situation correct,
and obligingly drew off yet more of his troops from Bayonne.

Wellington had been forced to call up Freire's and Carlos de
España's Spaniards to reinforce Hope. He had to feed them, of
course, which he could ill-afford to do, but even that drain
upon his magazines was preferable to letting them subsist on
the country.

On the 12th February, his lordship began his movement, with
the object of pushing the enemy back from river to river until

he should have manœuvred him too far eastward to permit of his returning to the Adour.

It was not, however, until four days later that the Light division, forming, with the 6th, the rear of Beresford's force, broke up from cantonments. They marched without the 1st Rifle battalion and the 43rd regiment, which had both gone off to St Jean de Luz to get new equipment, and they were extremely disgusted at not being in the van of the army. 'A Rifleman in the rear is like a fish out of water,' said Kincaid once.

Hill's flanking force, on the left of the Allied line, had the honour of beginning the movement; and it was not until the French General Harispe, retreating first to Le Palais on the line of the Bidouze, and then to the line of the Saison, at last was driven to a position behind the Gave d'Oloron, that Beresford received orders to march. The 2nd division, and old Picton's 3rd, advancing north of Hill, were having all the sport, said Beresford's men.

But everything was working out just as his lordship had meant it to. The whole of Clausel's force had been obliged to fall back behind the Gave d'Oloron, from Peyrehorade to Narreux, a front of thirty miles; and on the 18th February, it was learned that two out of the three divisions left to guard Bayonne had been ordered to march east.

Beresford was told to push on. He marched with Vivian's and Lord Edward Somerset's cavalry brigades flung out in front of his infantry. The Enthusiastics, and the 7th (whom men of the older divisions unkindly called the Mongrels), followed the cavalry; the Light division came next; and the 6th, bringing up the extreme rear, had not as yet overtaken the force.

The Light division, ordered to halt for a day at La Bastide Clarence, on the Joyeuse, heard of Hill's fights at Garris, and Arriverayte, and growled. Hill was rolling up the French in famous style; Picton was pressing forward; *The* Division, the very spearhead of attack, was kept kicking its heels twenty and more miles in the rear.

The weather was stormy, and very cold. Lord Wellington, snatching a day to visit Sir John Hope, found big seas breaking on the coast-line, and Admiral Penrose unable to bring his chasse-marées, which were to form a bridge across the Adour, into the mouth of the river.

That was vexatious, but his lordship remained calm, unlike Marshal Soult, who was talking rather wildly of being opposed by an army of a hundred thousand men. The Marshal, very much puzzled by his lordship's manœuvres, had already made up his mind to abandon the line of the Gave d'Oloron, and to fall back behind the Gave de Pau, with the strong position of Orthez in his rear.

On the 21st of the month, Wellington was with Hill, at Garris; on the following day, the Light and 6th divisions were directed to fall in with Hill's force.

Soult, who had expected Beresford to attempt to cross at Urt, was still more puzzled by the news of this change. What, he demanded fretfully, did Wellington intend? Did he mean to march on Toulouse by way of Pau and Tarbes? The augmentation of Hill's force pointed to such a movement, but it would be very rash, and would gravely imperil his communications with his coastal base. 'I am astonished at the idea!' said the Marshal. 'Whatever happens, I have made arrangements to mass my troops and attack him if a favourable opportunity offers.' That his lordship had never yet offered anyone a favourable opportunity for attacking him, occurred to more than one of the Marshal's Staff; but that his lordship was intending to do nothing but to roll up the French army, and to possess himself of Bayonne, no one seemed to suspect.

On the 24th February, the heads of the Allied columns appeared before the Gave d'Oloron, on a fifteen-mile front. The water in the river was waist-high, and icily cold, but by evening four out of the five divisions had crossed with no other loss than a few deaths by drowning. Only Picton pressed on too far, and lost eighty men in an unnecessary skirmish, a circumstance not altogether displeasing to the Light division. 'Old Picton attacking where he ought not!' said the Fighting division's bitterest rivals scornfully.

Soult fell back behind the Gave de Pau, concentrating his army at Orthez, a position Lord Wellington himself might have chosen, since it was admirably placed on a height, and easily defensible.

Hill detached the 1st Caçadores from Barnard's brigade, and threw them into the suburb of Départ. 'Orthez,' said Harry, 'will remain in my memory as the battle where I lost the Caçadores, and couldn't find them again.'

The next day was spent by the Allied army in moving into position. Beresford, whose divisions had become, instead of Hill's, the flanking force, was ordered off on a long march, to turn the French right, and the Light Bobs were once more told to follow him.

'Follow?' said an indignant private in the 52nd. 'What does old Hookey take us for? A set of St Anthony's pigs?'

At daybreak the division crossed the river by a pontoon bridge, and marched over ground which seemed to be made up of banks and ditches and occasional quagmires. As they moved on the right of the 3rd division, Picton rode up to Barnard on one of his cobs, and demanded roughly: 'Who the devil are you?'

'We,' said Barnard, who was perfectly well known to Picton, 'are the Light division.'

'If you are *Light*, sir, I wish you'd move a little quicker!' snarled Picton.

'Alten commands,' replied Barnard in the coolest of voices. He added kindly: 'But the march of infantry is quick time, and you cannot accelerate the pace of the head of the column without doing an injury to the whole. Wherever the *3rd* division are, Sir Thomas, *we* shall be in our places, depend upon it!'

Picton looked as though he would burst a blood-vessel, but since Barnard had really left him nothing to say, he contented himself with swearing loudly enough to be heard by several interested privates, and rode off.

'Too hot to hold, *he* is,' remarked one of these. 'He'd swear through an inchboard!'

'Ah, well! Got his men cut up, he did, poor old bastard!' said a more tolerant gentleman. 'No wonder he's hot!'

By the time the division reached its post by a Roman Camp facing the village of St Boes, over a mile to the west of Orthez, the battle had been in progress for some while, and the Light Bobs, for a long time, had nothing to do but to watch the stubborn fighting on the ridge. That Wellington, who was observing the battle from a commanding knoll in their immediate front, might be keeping them in the rear on account of both brigades being short of a regiment, occurred to no one; and by the time the Enthusiastics, having won a part of St Boes after a very sanguinary struggle, were driven back in a little disorder, the weakened Light division was fairly dancing with impatience. However, just as everyone had reached the stage of explaining to his neighbour how the action ought to have been fought, General Alten rode up to Colborne, who was talking to Kempt, and told him to go on and attack.

The 52nd regiment, moving forward in columns of threes, was naturally delighted, but Kempt, demanding: 'And I, General? am I not to go on?' was so mortified that he growled to Colborne: 'Confound the old fellow! God forgive me!'

'Hallo, Colborne!' called out Wellington, when the regiment passed him. 'Ride on, and see if artillery can pass there!'

Colborne galloped towards the marsh, and returned presently with the news that anything could pass.

'Well, then, make haste!' said his lordship. 'Take your regiment on and deploy into the plain. I leave it to your disposition.'

So the 52nd went forward until they reached the ridge, where they met the 4th division, in disorderly retreat. Sir Lowry Cole, looking for support, and rather agitated, hustled his horse up to Colborne, saying: 'Well, Colborne, what's to be done? Here we are, all coming back as fast as we can! What's to be done, eh? What would you do?'

'Have patience, and we shall see what's to be done,' replied Colborne, who, never losing a jot of his own calm, had very little sympathy to spare for more excitable men.

Picton's division was scattering on the left: one of his Adjutants came riding up, quite as flustered as Cole, to know what he was to do. Colborne said: 'Deploy into the low ground as fast as you can.'

While this was being done, the 52nd marched down the hill as though on parade, waded through the marsh under a heavy fire which, happily, passed mostly over their heads, and went up the hill in famous style.

'The most majestic advance I've ever seen!' Harry declared.

Foy's men certainly agreed with him. Even as Marshal Soult was reported to be slapping his thigh, and exclaiming gleefully: 'At last I have him!' Foy began to fall back before the 52nd's irresistible advance. The 4th and 3rd divisions, united by Colborne's operations, recovered from their repulse, and surged forward; the French were dislodged from the height, leaving open the narrow pass behind St Boes, and Wellington flung into it the 7th division, with Vivian's horse, and two brigades of artillery.

3

His lordship wrote in his dispatch that the attack led by the 52nd regiment had given the Allies the victory.

'He could not help saying that,' Colborne remarked, with rather a wry smile.

Indeed, his lordship's unenthusiastic dispatches, with their coldly favourable mention of senior officers (whether they had acquitted themselves well, or had behaved in a fashion which led his lordship to give it as his private opinion that they were mad) were a source of much discontent in the army. The fact was that his lordship, whose censure was masterly, had never learnt how to praise.

But the army forgave him his grudging approval on this occasion, for his lordship had actually been hit during the battle. As he always exposed himself in the most reckless fashion, it was surprising that he had never been hit before; but he had not, so that his men had come to think him invulnerable. But at Orthez, just as he was laughing at General Alava for being unseated by a hit from a spent shot, he himself was badly grazed on one hip. General Alava said that it served him right, and that he deserved to be wounded, for mocking at the misfortunes of others.

'Wounded? Pooh! Nothing of the sort!' said his lordship.

However, the abrasion made him very lame for several days, and it was evident that it hurt him a good deal to mount his horse. He would not admit it, of course; and so far from lying up for a time, he undertook a long ride, which he need not have done, to visit Lord March, desperately wounded, and carried off to the rear in the middle of the battle.

The 52nd were mourning March as dead already, and were heartily sorry for it. They had not much acquaintance with him, since he had always been employed on Lord Wellington's personal Staff; but in the New Year he had made up his mind that it was time he learned his duties as an officer of the line; and had given up his Staff appointment to join the regiment. He was a charming young man, and when he fell, Major George Napier was so distressed that, leaving his brother William to hold March's head on his knee, he dashed off to tell Colborne, who said unemotionally: 'Well, I can't help it. Have him carried to the rear.'

Harry, meanwhile, had raced off to bring up a surgeon. He thought March pretty far gone, and was horrified to see the surgeon poking his finger into the wound to trace the course of the ball. Fitzroy Somerset had ridden up with March's brother, Lord George Lennox, and was very much upset, but March, digging his nails into the palms of his hands, said faintly, but with great firmness: 'Maling, tell me if I am mortally wounded, because I have something I wish to impart to George.'

'If you will be very quiet, you will do very well,' replied the surgeon gruffly.

But he told Harry that he did not see how March could recover, a piece of intelligence which eventually reached Lord Wellington's ears, and sent him off on that imprudent ride.

'People who say the Peer has no heart know nothing of the matter!' Harry told Juana. 'Only fancy his riding all that way to visit poor March! Dr Hare, who has March in charge, told me that the Peer came in in the middle of the night, limping awfully, and upon hearing that March was asleep, just kissed his brow, and went away again, taking care not to waken him!'

'Well, that was very kind of him, certainly,' said Juana in a practical voice, 'but tell me, Enrique, have you found the Caçadores yet?'

'Oh, my God, no!' groaned Harry.

He did not find them for two days, so inextricably mixed with the 6th division had they become. Barnard (the best of Brigadiers, Harry swore) only laughed; and when Harry came in wet, and cold, and triumphant one evening, and said: 'Eureka!' he replied in the most unceremonious way: 'What, have you found those damned Portuguese at last? By God, we must crack a bottle on it!'

He, and Bob Digby, his A.D.C., and the Smiths, crammed themselves into a tiny inn that night, which was owned by an old soldier who had lost a limb in one of Napoleon's Italian campaigns. He knew just what an officer wanted for dinner, and dished up a splendid meal. He was a wag, too, and he told Barnard that war was no longer what it was when he first served. 'I see that now the cavalry give way first, then come the artillery, and then follow the infantry in disorder,' he said.

This unflattering picture of Souk's retreat from Orthez at once endeared him to his British guests. They won his heart next day when Barnard called for the bill.

'The bill?' he repeated.

'Yes, for our lodging, and food, and wine.'

The old soldier gaped at him. '*Mon colonel*, you mean to *pay* for what you have had?'

'Of course I do! Come now, what's the figure?'

'*Eh bien, monsieur! comme vous voulez!* But I see that war is not *at all* what it used to be!'

The baggage came up with the division that morning, and in the afternoon they forded the Adour. News had reached the army of Sir John Hope's crossing at the mouth of the river, and everyone was in splendid fettle.

'By Jesus, if we don't kick the Frogs all the way to Paris!' swore a Rifleman, just returned to the brigade in all the glory of a new uniform.

Juana, on her way to join Harry, had been obliged to ride over the battlefield, and had found it covered with dead and dying men. She said that nearly everyone had been wounded in the head, a circumstance attributable to the high banks which had afforded cover for the men's bodies; but she was particularly distressed by the plight of an artillery-man, who had had both arms shot off while he was ramming down the cartridge into his own gun. He would accept neither food nor drink from Juana: he told her quite roughly to go away; and when she had begged him at least to sip a little brandy and water, he had spat a very impolite name at her, and had said with all the failing strength he could muster: 'You'd like me to drag out me life with both me arms gone, wouldn't you? Ah, leave me be, you bloody little fool!'

'He was right,' Harry said decidedly, when the sad little tale was told him. 'Better dead than crippled like that!'

The incident, however, clouded Juana's day. It was clouded for the army by the bitter cold, and the necessity of undertaking an arduous march to Mont de Marsan, north of St Sever. The men had been so tired after the battle that whole regiments had slept in the open rather than give themselves the extra exertion of pitching tents. The result was cramped and rheumaticky limbs. A tot of rum, served out at dawn, improved matters a little; and after some hours of hard marching all but the worst sufferers had tramped off their rheumatism.

The Light division reached Mont de Marsan after dark, and were ordered to take up quarters for the night. It was a large, busy town, but was already so full of Marshal Beresford's Staff, and a brigade of cavalry, that Harry had the greatest difficulty in finding a billet even for his Brigadier. Frost was hardening the ground, and sleet had begun to drift before he got his wife under cover. He had found a little house owned by a widow, who no sooner saw Juana's white face, and shivering limbs, than she set about lighting a fire. Juana was tired, and so cold that she had to clench her teeth to prevent their chattering. The widow stripped her wet clothes off, and rubbed her body with a warm towel, until Juana begged for mercy. Jenny Bates had unpacked Juana's portmanteau, but the widow, forming the poorest opinion of such an uncouth handmaiden, told her to be off and leave her mistress to those who knew how to wait on ladies.

Jenny, who wanted to find her man, readily went away; and the Frenchwoman, dressing Juana in dry clothes, put a pot of bouillon on the fire, and sat down to look her guest over.

'But you are a child!' she exclaimed.

'No, I am sixteen,' said Juana, spreading her hands to the blaze in the hearth.

'My poor little one, you are a baby! And Spanish? One would not have credited it! But your man, he is English?'

'My husband. I have been married since two years.'

'Is it possible? *Mon Dieu*, what you must have seen!'

'Only battles,' said Juana sleepily.

'Only! *Ma pauvre*, have you no mother, no father?'

'No. I have no one but my husband. It is quite enough,' she added, seeing the pity in the widow's eyes.

'But an Englishman!'

'Do you dislike the English? I forgot that perhaps you might hate us,' said Juana, a little nervously.

'No, no, my cabbage! The English are freeing my country from the usurper; how should I hate them? I am a Royalist! I am proud to have our deliverers in my poor house. Sit still, and rest yourself; presently you shall have your bouillon.'

She bustled away, and when she came back it was with a pretty Sèvres bowl, into which she ladled the broth. The bowl, she told Juana, had been one of her wedding gifts, and had never been used since her husband's death.

Juana admired it very much, and by the time Harry came in, shaking the wet off his cocked-hat, she could have given him a minute account of their hostess's life, with the details of every illness she had suffered over a period of forty years.

They spent the night lost in the billows of a feather-bed, and parted from the widow next morning with every expression of gratitude and regret. The division was ordered back to St Sever, a town on the high road to Toulouse; and as the weather was showery and cold, they had a miserable march of it, over one of the worst roads they had ever encountered. When darkness fell, the best accommodation Harry could find for Barnard was a tiny cottage by the wayside, into which Barnard, and Digby, and the Smiths all managed to squeeze themselves. The baggage having been left to follow the division, wet and muddied garments could not be changed, and although Juana got a tiny bedchamber under the eaves for her exclusive use, the three men were obliged to sleep on the floor downstairs, wrapped in their cloaks, and using their sabretaches as pillows. An order to march at daybreak was expected, but it did not come, so the party sat down to breakfast, Barnard and little Digby loudly envying Harry his boyish lack of beard. Barnard, passing a hand over his bristly chin, said that he wondered Juana would consent to sit down with such a ruffianly-looking fellow, but Juana assured him that she did not mind at all.

'You know, my dear, you ought by rights to be in bed with an inflammation of the lungs,' said Barnard severely.

'*Qué absurdidad!* I am never ill. You are like General Vandeleur, and that nice woman at our billet last night, thinking that I must be very weak and delicate. It is not true.'

'By the way, did you find a good billet?' Barnard asked. 'Harry put me in a hole of a place with a smoking chimney.'

'Oh, we were so comfortable! Our hostess was a Royalist, and a widow, and, do you know, she gave me some bouillon to drink out of the prettiest Sèvres bowl, which she had not used since her husband died! *Muy patético!* And she told me about her baby that died, and about −' She broke off, as Joe Kitchen came in. 'Oh!' she cried, tears springing to her eyes. 'Oh, Enrique!'

Harry turned, and saw that Joe, considerably taken aback by his mistress's sudden agitation, was standing in the threshold, agape, and with the identical Sèvres bowl, full of milk, in his hands.

'Where did you get that?' demanded Harry angrily.

'Why, from the widow's house, sir!' faltered Joe.

'You mean you stole it! How *dare* you, sir, do anything of the sort?'

Barnard, made uncomfortable by Juana's tears, delivered himself of a tirade against the plundering habits of the army, which made poor Joe shiver in his shoes. Upon being ordered to explain what the devil he meant by his conduct, he plucked up enough courage to say: 'Lord sir, why, the French soldiers would have carried off *the widow*, if she'd been young, and I thought it would be so nice for the goat's milk in the morning! She was angry, though, because I took it,' he added honestly.

Barnard, who had a very ready sense of humour, could not help letting his lips twitch at this. Joe saw it, and thought that if he made himself scarce he would escape a flogging, so he put the bowl down, and, with a pleading look cast in Juana's direction, effaced himself.

Barnard went off to headquarters as soon as he had swallowed his breakfast, but came back at ten o'clock with the news that the division would not move that day. Juana, who had been unwontedly silent since the discovery of the Sèvres bowl, slipped out, and went in search of West. West was a little startled at being told to saddle his own horse and Tiny, and to put up a feed of corn in his haversack, but Juana said grandly, if untruthfully, that Master knew all about it.

Harry was on the point of setting out for his brigade when Juana came up to him, dressed for riding, and said in a careless tone that she was going to visit one of the wounded officers.

He never interfered with such excursions, and merely nodded now, and told her to take West with her.

'Oh yes, of course! But do not be alarmed if I am not back till late.'

'No, very well,' Harry said absently, frowning over his order-book.

Digby, coming round the corner of the cottage, overheard this interchange, and not being preoccupied, like Harry, wondered why Juana, going to visit a sick man at ten in the morning, should expect to be back late. He was still puzzling over it when West brought the horses round to the door. He heard Juana ask West if he had remembered the feed of corn, and jumped up, exclaiming: 'By Jove, the little monkey is up to some mischief!'

It did not take him long to get his own horse saddled, and he was soon riding after Juana, in a northerly direction. He overtook her about a mile from the cottage, and ranged alongside, demanding: 'Where in the name of heaven are you off to, Juanita? This is no way to take to visit any wounded of ours!'

Juana looked very much put-out, and said crossly: '*Fuera!* I don't want you!'

'No, but only listen! You are going in the wrong direction, really you are!'

'I am *not*! I am going to Mont de Marsan, and I know the way very well.'

'Mont de Marsan!' he ejaculated. 'My dear girl, you can't!'

'I must. *Un caso de necesidad*,' said Juana mysteriously.

'What need can you possibly – Don't tell me it is because of that wretched bowl!'

'It's not a wretched bowl! It is the prettiest bowl in the world, and that poor woman's husband used to drink out of it, and I do not care what you say: I am going to take it back to her!'

'Dearest Juana, I do feel for you, indeed I do, but you mustn't – I'll tell you what! Give it to me, and I'll take it for you!'

'*De ningún modo!* I must *myself* take it to her, and beg her pardon.'

'It's fifteen miles there, and there are enemy patrols about!'

'I am not in the least afraid of enemy patrols,' said Juana scornfully. 'No French dragoon could ever catch me on my Spanish horse Tiny. Besides, I have told West to keep a sharp look-out.'

'Oh dear, what an obstinate little wretch you are!' said Digby. 'Very well, if you *will* go, I must come with you.'

'A *voluntad*! But will not Barnard need you?'

'He'll have to do without me,' said Digby. 'But what Harry will say when he hears of this – !'

'Oh, never mind that!' said Juana cheerfully. '*Adelante!*'

4

Brigade-Major Smith's duties kept him busy until after dusk. When he came back to his billet, Barnard was pulling off his muddied boots before the fire, and an agreeable aroma of cooking pervaded the cottage.

'Is that you, Harry?' Barnard said, turning his head. 'Shut the door: there's a devilish draught blowing in! Have you seen that scamp Bob?'

'No, sir. I thought he was with you,' replied Harry, hanging up his cloak.

'I haven't set eyes on him all day.'

'I daresay he went off to see how poor March is going on. Where's Juana?'

'I don't know. Your rascally servant said she went off this morning to visit a wounded friend.'

Harry looked a little startled. 'So she did, but she ought to be back by now.'

'I hope to God nothing has happened to her!'

'Oh no! She has far too much sense to get into a scrape. I remember now: she said she might be back late. Will you dine, sir?'

'No, no, we must wait for Juana!' said Barnard. 'The baggage has come up, so you had better change those wet clothes, or I shall have you laid-up on my hands, no good to anyone.'

By the time Harry had followed this piece of advice, Barnard's French cook, who had arrived that morning with the baggage-train, had bounced into his master's presence to remonstrate with him in person. 'The dinner he is spoiled!' he announced tragically.

'Go away, sir, go away!' said Barnard testily. 'We wait for madame.'

'The dinner he will not wait!'

'Well, it must wait! Keep it hot, and don't come waving your hands at me!'

'*Ah, mon Dieu!*' groaned the cook in anguished tones. 'Keep it hot, you say! What a pleasantry!'

'I wish you will have your dinner, sir,' said Harry, who had just come back into the room. 'There is no need for you to wait, after all! If only I knew in which direction she had gone!'

'Now, don't begin to get into a fret!' said Barnard, who had been looking at his watch every other minute since Harry had gone to change his clothes. 'She will be in directly! Of course we shall wait for her!'

Hearing this, the cook said: 'It is the death-knell!' and tottered away to the kitchen, presumably to mourn over the ruin of his art.

'If that fellow weren't such a devilish fine cook, I'm damned if I'd put up with him another hour!' said Barnard. 'Don't fidget about the room! Sit down, and be quiet!'

'I can't sit down and be quiet!' said Harry irritably. 'If it were your wife, a nice way you'd be in!'

'Nonsense! What should have happened to her? Depend upon it, she is perfectly safe! And don't be an impudent young dog, Harry! I may have to swallow that damned cook's impertinence, but I'll be hanged if I'll swallow impertinence from my Brigade-Major! What in the world can be keeping the child?'

'I don't know, but if she doesn't come in within the next quarter of an hour, I shall go and look for her.'

'In the dark? I never heard such folly! You would miss her for a certainty! Besides, I am convinced there is not the slightest need!'

However, when fifteen minutes had lagged by, and Harry said insubordinately: 'You may say what you like, Colonel: I am going in search of my wife!' he did not attempt to dissuade him, but replied in a worried tone that it was very disturbing, and he did not know what to do for the best.

Harry reached for his cloak, but before he had time to take it off the peg, the door opened, and Juana came in, very cold and wet, and splashed all over with mud. She raised her brows at sight of the bare table, and said with a little laugh: 'Well, why did you wait dinner? Order it: I shall soon have my habit off!'

'Where have you been?' demanded Harry and Barnard together, in such explosive tones that Juana was quite startled.

She said coaxingly: 'Oh, don't be angry! I am not taken prisoner, as you see! I've been to Mont de Marsan, to take back the poor widow's basin.'

'To Mont de Marsan!' Harry exclaimed.

'Upon my word!' said Barnard. 'Well done, Juana! You're a heroine! Why, the Maid of Saragossa is nothing to you!'

She laughed, but stole rather an anxious glance at Harry's face. 'Oh no! Only I could not be comfortable until the bowl was given back, so I thought it would be nice to take it myself. I was so glad! She cried with joy when she saw me, and she wanted me very much to keep the bowl, but of course I would not do that.'

'Juana, you have never deceived me before!'

'No, *mi querido*, but I did not think you would let me go if I told you the truth,' she explained ingenuously.

'Little devil!' Harry said. 'Little abominable varmint! You might have been taken prisoner! Weren't you afraid of that?'

'No, because we kept a good look-out, and I had my dear Tiny. And Bob came with me too, so I was quite safe.'

'Oh, so that's where he's been!' said Barnard. 'A fine Staff I have, I must say! Where is the rascal?'

'He went to see the horses stabled. He will be in directly. He thought you would wish him to go with me. Don't be angry, will you?'

'Get along with you, and take off those wet clothes!' Barnard said. 'Don't think to coax *me*! You are a bad child, and a great deal more trouble than the rest of the brigade put together.'

This stricture, however, failed to impress Juana, who knew that Barnard, quite one of her oldest friends, could be twisted round her finger whenever she chose. She blew him a kiss, and ran off to change her clothes.

Barnard was, in fact, so delighted with her exploit, that he spread the story through the division, so that Juana became quite embarrassed by the congratulations she received next day, and instead of accepting these gracefully, as a heroine should, scowled dreadfully, and threatened to throw the *panella* at the next person who dared to mention her ride to Mont de Marsan.

The Light division remained in cantonments about St Sever, where Wellington had fixed his headquarters, for eight days, no one having any very clear idea of what his lordship's next move would be. Soult, retiring eastwards, and desperately trying to reorganize a much-shaken army, had plainly decided to fall back on Toulouse rather than to protect Bordeaux, the approach to which lay through sandy, bare country, sparsely populated, and intersected by the difficult Garonne river. To defend Bordeaux would be to leave the whole of southern France open to the invaders; much the better plan would be to draw Wellington off towards the Pyrenees, for it was not to be supposed that that most wary of Commanders would march on Bordeaux, leaving his flank exposed to an attack from the east.

The Marshal was not aware that there had arrived at the Allied headquarters, from Bordeaux, a very respectable old gentleman of Irish Jacobite extraction, who proposed, surprisingly, to raise the White Banner of the Bourbons in Bordeaux. Jean-Baptiste Lynch, a lawyer by profession, and Mayor of Bordeaux, was so extremely unlike the general run of gentlemen who plot risings, that Lord Wellington was inclined to look on him with a favourable eye. The obvious course was to set up the Duc d'Angoulême, still haunting headquarters under his official title of Comte de Pradel, at Bordeaux; but unfortunately the Allied powers had still not made up their minds whether or not to conclude a peace with Napoleon. Lord Wellington was forced, therefore, to proceed with great caution, but he let it be known that although he should take Bordeaux for military and not political reasons, he had no objection to the Royalists' declaring for Louis XVIII. Only Beresford, whom he meant to send to Bordeaux, with the 7th and 4th divisions, must on no account allow himself to be implicated in such a rising. Jean-Baptiste Lynch's legal mind fully appreciated his lordship's difficulty. He expressed himself as being perfectly satisfied, and went back to Bordeaux, presumably to distribute white cockades.

Meanwhile, Hope, investing Bayonne, was finding the task of reducing that town unexpectedly difficult. Lord Wellington, having under his hand a force of no more than forty thousand men, was obliged to call up two of Freire's Spanish divisions from the siege, and to send for all his heavy cavalry out of Spain.

On 9th March, these reinforcements, having come up, and Beresford being well on his way to Bordeaux, the army broke up from cantonments, and pushed forward to engage once more with Soult. The Light division moved to Gée, where they saw the 2nd division, under the leadership of that intrepid but somewhat erratic warrior, Sir William Stewart, win fresh laurels for themselves by a very pretty little affair at Aire. One Rifleman was engaged in the skirmish, Sir William's improvident nephew, Lord Charles Spencer, who was acting as his uncle's A.D.C. Lord Charles had lately bought himself a superb hunter, far beyond the means of his purse. It was shot dead in the town, on the bank of a muddy horse-pond, and into the pond went Lord Charles, over its head, a misfortune which drew from his uncle nothing but a mild: 'Ha! there goes my poor nephew and all his fortune!'

Sir William had the reputation of being the bravest man in the army. He could be very testy upon occasion, but no one had ever seen him moved from his calm upon the battle-field. 'Damn the old ruffian!' said one shaken officer, wiping the sweat from his brow. 'A shell fell right between us when I was speaking to him just now, frightening me out of my wits! Would you believe it, all the old fire-eater said was, "A shell, sir! Very animating!"'

Harry's brigade remained at Gée for several days. He had taken a large house for Barnard, Digby, himself and Juana, and they all thought themselves on clover, until the housekeeper, finding Juana alone one day, suddenly seized her with the grip of a madwoman, and swore she would put her to death for being an accursed Spaniard. Juana, for all her wiriness, was helpless in the woman's grasp, and, seeing a hideously sharp carving-knife brandished before her eyes, nearly swooned with terror. Fortunately, Joe Kitchen walked in at that moment, with a message from Harry, and promptly closed with the madwoman. She soon grew quiet and a few enquiries elicited the information that such fits were only temporary. But Juana was not in the least comforted by this news, and would never afterwards stay in the house without Jenny Bates to protect her. Jenny, hearing of the adventure, folded her massive arms, and, looking the Frenchwoman up and down, delivered herself of one scathing monosyllable. 'Ho!' said Jenny awfully.

After the combat of Aire, the army halted again for twelve days, while his lordship rested his troops, and observed the progress of Beresford and Dalhousie at Bordeaux. Jean-Baptiste Lynch had been as good as his word, and the English, marching into the town without the least opposition, had found the White Banner flying in place of the Tricolour. '*A bas les aigles! Vivent les Bourbons!*' shouted the populace, waving little white flags. That was all very well, but his lordship was anything but pleased when the Duc d'Angoulême, collecting a few noted Royalists, abruptly left his headquarters, and appeared in Bordeaux, announcing that he had the support of the Allies. He actually had the effrontery to write to Wellington, desiring him to instruct Marshal Beresford to place himself at his Royal orders. All he got by that was one of his lordship's coldest letters. His lordship sent for Beresford to rejoin the army with the 4th division, and left only Dalhousie, with the 7th, to keep a watch over Bordeaux.

When the army moved again, there was a good deal of skirmishing, but the Light division was not engaged, until Soult, drawing Wellington ever southwards, reached Tarbes, at the foot of the Pyrenees. Here the division experienced what many of its officers considered to be its hardest day's fighting. All three Rifle battalions were engaged in a bitter, up-hill struggle, and the loss of life was very heavy. No less than twelve officers were killed and wounded, and great was the distress of his many friends when it was discovered that George Simmons was one of the casualties. Poor George was wounded in the knee-pan, and had only been saved from having another shot put into him by his servant's standing over him until Colonel Barnard himself rode up, and had him carried off the field.

So George had to be left behind at Tarbes, suffering a great deal of pain from his fractured knee, while the army pursued Soult on his retreat to Toulouse. Those of his friends who could spare the time visited him before they left the town. They found him invincibly cheerful, and apparently deriving much consolation from the fact that a part of his brother's regiment was being left to guard the wounded. Maud had been appointed Town-Major, and had found George a good billet. He was sharing it with him, drinking George's allowance of wine as well as his own, and enjoying himself very much. He did not think that George would see any more fighting, but George, subjecting his own knee to a keen examination, said that he felt sure he would soon be well enough to rejoin his regiment. He was delighted to hear how Barnard, on the day after the battle, had persuaded Lord Wellington to ride over the hill and see the ground the Rifles had fought over. No one, Barnard swore, could ever have seen the dead lie more thickly. Lord Wellington went with him in the end, saying: 'Well, Barnard, to please you I will go, but I require no new proof of the destructive fire of your Rifles.'

'Oh, did he say that?' exclaimed George, rather faintly, but with a beaming smile of gratification. 'Why, that makes everything worth while!'

5

If the truth were told, Lord Wellington was by no means satis-fied with the result of the action at Tarbes. Having driven Soult from every position during the three days of the Allied advance, with the intention of forcing him back against the barrier of the Pyrenees, it was exasperating to find that one road of retreat had been left open. Soult, keeping his army intact, escaped by the St Gaudens road, which, running along the line of the Pyrenees for some fifty miles, took a northward turn towards Toulouse at St Martory.

His lordship, deciding that it was of more importance to strike at Toulouse than to pursue Soult in force, detached Hill to follow him, and himself led the main body of his army to Toulouse by the direct road running through Trie, Castelnau, and Lombex.

Weather conditions were appalling. The whole of the sur-rounding countryside was water-logged, and the road was worse than a Spanish mule-track. The artillery stuck fast in mud; the waggons foundered in deep pits and ruts; even his lordship's barouche, with General Alva in it, had to be man-hauled out of clinging slime. The army's progress was slow, partly owing to the state of the roads, partly owing to his lordship's mistrust of the French population. This was soon discovered to be unfounded. Although Morillo's Spaniards left a trail of rapine in their wake, the Allied army was welcomed with open arms. Every kind of food-stuff was offered for sale, from bales of corn to cackling geese. The army, in spite of having outdistanced its supplies, had never fared so well. It behaved well, too: there was really very little unpleasantness, although at Castelnau a vociferous female loudly and insistently demanded vengeance on a handsome young Rifleman, who, she said, had seduced her daughter. No evidence was forthcoming, and it was generally felt that fat Johnny Castles had summed the matter up very justly when he remarked, slicing a hunk of bacon on to his bread, that if the mother had never been in the oven, she would not have looked for her daughter there.

But this was an isolated incident, the behaviour of the French people as a whole being so enthusiastic that an indignant *sous-préfet* wrote to inform Marshal Soult that the whole population had ceased to have any national spirit.

Soult, leaving five thousand stragglers along the route of his march, reached Toulouse two days ahead of Lord Wellington: a remarkable feat, considering the deplorable condition of his troops, and the fifty extra miles he was forced to cover. The country people reported that the French soldiers had worn out their boots, but as Toulouse was the main depôt of military stores for southern France, this, and every other deficiency of equipment, could very soon be made good.

Toulouse, a mediæval fortress, lay, from Lord Wellington's point of view, on the wrong side of the Garonne; and was protected, in addition to its bastioned walls, by a very wide ditch, like a moat. On the northern and eastern sides, the Royal Canal made any approach next door to impossible; on the west the Garonne presented an even more difficult problem; and the only feasible way into the city, to the south, was guarded by the well-fortified bridge-head of St Cyprien. Between the canal, and the Ers river, on the east, the commanding heights of Mont Rave dominated the city, and had already been extensively entrenched.

The heads of Lord Wellington's columns appeared before Toulouse on the 26th March, and for the next fortnight his lordship's temper was worn thin by a series of unsuccessful attempts to get his army across the Garonne. The fact that a certain measure of this unsuccess was due to his own refusal, at St Jean de Luz, to listen to the advice of his senior Engineer, did nothing to improve his temper.

His first plan, rather a risky one, was to force a passage at Portet, south of the city. He succeeded by some clever demonstrations, in convincing Soult that he meant to cross downstream, north of Toulouse, but when the Marshal had obligingly drawn off four of the seven cavalry regiments patrolling the Garonne to watch the banks to the north, leaving the southern reaches almost wholly unguarded, the plan failed owing to there not being sufficient pontoons to span the swollen river. After they had been laboriously laid down on the bank, and launched, it was found that the bridge fell short by as much as eighty yards; a contingency long foreseen by Elphinstone, the Engineer. In a black rage, his lordship, clinging to his plan of crossing south of the city, had the pontoons moved three miles upstream, just above the junction of the Ariège with the Garonne. The bridge was thrown over during the night of the 30th March, at Pinsaguel; and in the morning Hill's corps passed without encountering any opposition.

Soult, busy strengthening his fortifications, did not discover the move for a whole day; but Hill, finding the ground sodden with rain, and the Ariège impassable, was forced to abandon his position, and to countermarch on Pinsaguel.

Up came the pontoons again, back on to their travelling-carriages. 'Lummy, who'd be an Engineer?' said the rest of the army.

By the 2nd April, his lordship had made up his mind that he must cross, after all, below Toulouse. By the 4th April, the cursing Engineers had succeeded in transporting the pontoons to a point eleven miles to the north of the city, and there, at last, they threw a bridge over the river by which the army could pass.

There was still no opposition from Soult; and by the afternoon, Beresford was across with three divisions of infantry, three brigades of cavalry, and some artillery.

Then the rain came. The Garonne, filling fast, swayed the pontoons this way and that, until the last of the cavalry were obliged to dismount and lead their horses over the perilous bridge. By dark, some of the moorings had broken, and one pontoon, in spite of every effort made by the drenched Engineers to save it, went bobbing away down the river. Freire's Spanish divisions, the dragoons of the King's German Legion, the Light division, and all the reserve artillery were left on the western bank and Marshal Beresford, separated from this force by a swollen and angry river, felt himself to be in such a hazardous position that even a visit from Lord Wellington, who had himself rowed across in a small boat, failed to convince him that he was not in the utmost danger. 'You are safe enough, Beresford!' said his lordship bracingly. 'Two such armies as Soult's could make no impression on you with that ravine in your front!'

To everyone's surprise, Marshal Soult made no effort to drive Beresford's force into the river. The Marshal, reinforced by conscripts, was either suffering from nervous dread, thought the English, or he did not know how few men Beresford had with him.

The rain stopped; and by the 7th April the floods began to fall. The lost pontoon was miraculously recovered, the bridge once more thrown across the river, and all but the Light division passed over to join Beresford. The Light division, moving upstream to Seilh, maintaining communications with Hill's force, did not cross until dawn on the 10th April, and by that time his lordship had moved his troops forward to the outer defences of Toulouse, and Vivian's cavalry had started hostilities by engaging in a brief but glorious skirmish with the French dragoons.

6

'The worst arranged battle there could be: nothing but mistakes!' That was Colonel Colborne's verdict on the battle of Toulouse.

It began at five in the morning, with a demonstration by Hill against the outer lines beyond the St Cyprien bridge; and it did not end until five in the afternoon, when the daylight was failing. Freire's Spaniards, having demanded the place of honour in the attack, failed to carry the Mont Rave heights; Picton turned a false attack into a real one, and once more got his division cut up; and Beresford, playing the chief part, was forced to undertake a long, arduous flanking movement, with his columns exposed all the way to the French artillery-fire from the heights.

'I think Lord Wellington almost deserved to have been beaten,' Colborne said.

The Light division of course thought that the battle would have been won much sooner had they been more actively employed, adding a rider to the effect that if Picton had refrained from attacking (as usual) where he ought not to have done, it would have been helpful.

The Light Bobs were drawn up rather more than half a mile from the Matabiau bridge across the Royal Canal, with General Freire's divisions on their left, by the hill of Pujade. This hill, beyond which, to the east, Beresford's flanking movement began, was dominated by the northern end of the Mont Rave heights, upon which the French General Villatte was strongly entrenched. General Freire having, after the customary Spanish fashion, claimed the right of holding the place of honour, Lord Wellington rather surprisingly gave him the task of storming the slope of Mont Rave, and dislodging the French from their redoubts and entrenchments. The attack was not to be made until Beresford had come up on the Spaniards' left, but General Freire, a trifle elated, launched it before even the head of Beresford's column had shown itself. He led the attack himself, and so gallantly did the Galicians charge up the hill that sceptical observers in the Light division said that they really looked as if they intended to do the thing handsomely.

Barnard's brigade was the nearest to the Spaniards' right flank, and from the start Colonel Colborne expected nothing but disaster. 'I should be sorry to have to do it with two Light divisions,' he said, when an optimistic officer cried, by God, Freire would do the business after all!

A withering fire from the heights met the Spanish advance, but they struggled on with great courage, until the sunken road leading to Peyrolle was reached.

'Oh, the devil!' exclaimed Harry, his glass fixed on the slopes of Mont Rave. 'Their officers will never get 'em out of that!'

He was quite right; the hollow road was the Spaniards' undoing. Scrambling down into it, they found that its high banks protected them from the artillery-fire. They lost the impetus of their first gallant rush; courage had time to cool: and not all the exertions of the officers could force them to face the murderous fire again. As soon as Villatte saw that they were not going to continue their advance, he sent his infantry forward from the trenches to pour a deadly musketry-fire into the hollow road. This was more than the Spaniards could bear. One regiment only, of Morilla's division, stood its ground; the rest flew back pell-mell to the slopes of the Pujade.

Major George Napier, of the 52nd, seeing the rout descending upon his regiment, shouted: 'Stop them! Stop them! Don't let them go!'

Colborne, himself slightly wounded in the flesh of his arm by a splinter of shell, called out: 'Yes, yes, let them go, and clear our fronts! Quick George! Throw the regiment into open column of companies, and let the Spaniards pass through!'

This was done; Barnard flung his brigade forward to cover the retreat, and the French, seeing the Light division moving to the attack, abandoned the pursuit, and retired again to their entrenchments.

'By God, won't old Douro be in a rage!' exclaimed Charlie Beckwith.

But his lordship, watching the rout of the Spaniards with his brother-in-law, the Adjutant-General, beside him, had given a whoop of sudden laughter, and slapped his thigh. 'Well, damme if ever I saw ten thousand men run a race before!' he declared. 'Now, what's to be done? There I am, with nothing between me and the enemy!'

'Well, I suppose you'll order up the Light division now!' said Pakenham.

'I'll be hanged if I do!' replied his lordship.

It took the Spaniards two hours to re-form, but re-form they did, and, to their credit, attacked the heights again. Freire led them in person, but they were repulsed with a good deal of loss, while the Light Bobs swore long and fluently at their own inactivity.

'By God, I can't stand this!' Harry said, in a fret of impatience. 'If we were pushed forward *now*, on the Spaniards' flank, they would succeed! It's murder to send 'em without support! Damn Alten!'

'Wellington's orders,' grunted Barnard.

'Serve Freire right for clamouring to be allowed to start the battle!' said Digby unsympathetically. 'They always do it, and they've never yet finished anything they've begun. To hell with 'em!'

By the time the Spaniards fell back for the second time, Beresford, having completed his long march at the foot of the eastern slopes of Mont Rave, was fast winning the battle from the south. He forced his way up on to the heights, defeating Harispe, and began to shell Villatte's position from the rear, just as Barnard's brigade was at last moved forward to support the Spaniards.

Soult ordered Villatte to retire. It was not yet dark, but after twelve hours of fighting both armies were tired out, and the Allied artillery was temporarily exhausted. French and British bivouacked where they stood, Beresford and Freire occupying the heights of Mont Rave, and the French having retreated behind the barrier of the Royal Canal.

7

Those who expected Lord Wellington to launch a final offensive early on the following morning were disappointed. The ammunition-park being upon Hill's side of the river, it was some time before fresh supplies could be brought up. The French showed no disposition to sally forth from Toulouse, and the day was spent by the Allies in succouring their wounded, and exchanging views on the engagement. Lord Wellington, encountering Colonel Colborne during the morning, called out to him, with a wave of his hand towards the northern slopes of Mont Rave: 'Well, Colborne, did you ever see anything like that? Was that like the rout at Ocaña?'

'Oh, I don't know!' Colborne said, never willing to condemn the Spaniards. 'They ran to the bridge, I believe.'

'To the bridge, indeed! To the Pyrenees!' said his lordship sardonically. 'I daresay they are all back in Spain by this time!'

There was no more fighting at Toulouse. At dusk, Soult

withdrew his army from the town by the Carcassonne road; and very early on the 12th April, a deputation of citizens arrived at Lord Wellington's headquarters with an invitation to him to enter the city. Toulouse, it seemed, was delighted with the result of the battle.

His lordship rode in later in the day, accompanied by his Staff. All the inhabitants of the town wore the white cockade, and waved white flags; and as his lordship entered the Capitol, the great statue of Napoleon was thrown off the roof, and smashed into fragments on the cobble-stones.

At five o'clock in the afternoon, Colonel Ponsonby rode in from Bordeaux with definite news of Napoleon's abdication; so his lordship, who had been finding the situation a little awkward, was able to rise to his feet during the dinner he gave that evening, and at last drink to the health of King Louis XVIII. There was quite a riot of cheering, and General Alava, carried away by the enthusiasm, leaped up and called for a toast in honour of Wellington: liberator of Portugal! – of Spain! – of France! – of Europe!

The cheers crashed again and again. His lordship, looking down his bony nose, bowed stiffly, and called for coffee.

The news of the abdication was conveyed at once to Soult by one of his lordship's A.D.C.s, but not until the arrival of envoys from Paris would the Marshal believe that it was true, and that there was nothing left to fight for.

Everyone found that hard to believe. Pickets were still posted, but there were no more sudden calls to arms; no more cavalry vedettes riding in circles to signal the approach of an enemy column; no more forced marches over heart-breaking roads; no more bivouacking in sodden fields. It seemed incredible at first, and Colonel Arentschildt disbelieved in the armistice so profoundly that he was discovered going to bed in his clothes, just as though he expected a night-alarm. 'Air-mistress or no air-mistress, by Gott, I sleeps in mein breeches!' he swore.

The Light division was moved into the suburb of Toulouse, and cantoned there. Harry requisitioned for himself and a select party of his friends, a positively luxurious château, engaged a French cook, borrowed some money from the Quartermaster, and spent it all on what George Simmons, restored to his regiment, called riotous living.

Theatres, balls, and fêtes were the order of the day, and of course it was imperative to buy dresses and ornaments for Juana, besides new boots and sashes for himself, and a splendid collar with silver bells for Vitty.

There were so few duties to be performed that all the unattached officers busied themselves with falling in love with the girls of Toulouse.

'But I,' said Harry, guilty of sliding his arm round a seductive waist, 'have a safeguard in my lovely young wife!'

'You are shameless, and faithless, and altogether good-for-nothing, besides being a great liar!' said his lovely young wife hotly. 'It is quite plain to me that you like Frenchwomen better than Spaniards, and I am not at all angry, or hurt, only extremely sorry that you have such abominable taste!'

'Not at all!' said Harry. 'I adore Spanish women: I always did!'

An indignant face was turned towards him. 'Yes! You have loved hundreds besides me, I daresay!'

'Oh, thousands!' agreed Harry. 'I nearly married one once. *Ay de mí!* She was a dear little creature, pretty as paint too, and with the gentlest ways!'

'Enrique! It is not true!' gasped Juana.

'True as I stand here!'

'When?' she stammered. 'Where?'

'Oh, when I was at Monte Video, with Whitelocke! I was billeted in her house, and was devilish ill there, with fever.'

She drew a breath of relief. 'All that time ago! You were nothing but a schoolboy! I don't believe she was pretty at all, or had gentle ways!'

'Oh, but she had! Eyes like a doe's, too.'

'If she had eyes like a doe's she was probably foolish. She does not sound to me the sort of wife one would choose for a hard campaign.'

Harry made a kissing-face at her. 'Not a bit, General Juana!'

8

At the end of the month, the division was moved away from Toulouse, to Castel Sarrasin, a circumstance which was fortunate for the gay Light Bobs, however loudly they might regret it, since the social life at Toulouse was fast ruining them. The Smiths were billeted in the house of a middle-aged widow of good family, who had lost all but one of her sons in Napoleon's wars. She was very kind to the Smiths, happy, she said, to have young people under her roof again.

They were not destined to remain there for long. Hardly had they had time to settle down, when Harry was sent for one morning by Colonel Colborne, who took his breath away by saying abruptly: 'Smith, you've been so unlucky, after all your service, in not getting your Majority, that you mustn't be idle. There's a force – a considerable one – going to America. You must go with it.'

'Go with it?' Harry repeated, in rather an odd voice.

'Yes,' said Colborne. 'I know what you're thinking, but you have your whole future to consider, remember! You and I will ride to Toulouse tomorrow: you had better send a horse on tonight; it's only thirty-four miles. We'll go there to breakfast, and ride back to dinner.'

Harry did not answer for a moment. He had whitened under his tan, for he knew very well that such a change in his fortunes would mean separation from Juana. As soon as he could trust his voice, he said: 'Thank you, sir: I'll be ready. This is – this is very kind of you!'

'You'll think so one day, I promise you, even though you don't now,' said Colborne, smiling faintly.

'Yes,' said Harry. 'Of course!'

He went slowly back to his own quarters. Juana was playing with Vitty in the garden; she looked up as Harry came towards her, and the laughter vanished from her face. She jumped up from the grass, saying anxiously: 'You have had bad news! What did Colborne want you for?'

'No, no, not bad news! At least – oh, by Jupiter, I don't know whether it's good or bad!'

Juana stood quite still. 'You are going to leave me,' she said, in a frightened voice.

'Yes – no! Nothing is certain yet! I daresay nothing will come of it! I hope to God it won't, though I suppose I ought not to wish that!'

'Enrique, *en nombre de Dios*, tell me!'

'Colborne wants me to put my name down for the expedition that's going to America.'

'America! Oh, Enrique, *mi esposo*, no, no, no!' she cried, throwing herself into his arms.

'Don't cry! *alma mia*, don't cry! I'll tell Colborne I can't! God knows I don't want to!'

But when the first abandonment of her despair was over, Juana said: 'You must go. It is your duty. I am sorry I cried. You see, I – I had never thought that perhaps we might be separated.'

'I daresay I haven't a chance of being chosen,' Harry said.

She tried hard to smile. 'You would like to go, would you not, mi Enrique?'

'If I were not married! But to be parted – No, it's not to be thought of! I'll tell Colborne.'

'You know you could never, never tell Colborne such a thing,' said Juana mournfully.

She cried herself to sleep that night, but in the early morning she saw Harry off with a smile on her lips. Madame La Rivière, their hostess, put an arm round her waist, and told Harry he must not worry about her, since she would take care of her till his return; but when Harry joined Colborne he was looking so haggard that Colborne took him to task, and reminded him that he himself had not seen his bride for over a year.

Juana spent the day trying not to cry, and hoping desperately that Harry's application would be refused. One glance at his face, when he returned at four in the afternoon, told her that it was all settled. She had made up her mind that she would be calm, and reasonable, and she said at once, with only the smallest quiver in her voice: 'You, are going. I am – I am *glad*, Enrique, because it is for your advantage, and neither of us must repine. Tell me – tell me what happened?'

He sat down beside her, drawing her head down on to his shoulder. '*Hija*, what shall I do without you?'

'You will do very well. You did, before I knew you. You will m-make love to all the American women,' she said, with a forlorn attempt at a joke.

'That I swear to you I will not!'

'Yes, but you are a bad, faithless one. Don't let us talk about it! What did you do at Toulouse?'

'We went at once to the A.G.'s office, and found that someone had already put my name down on the list of Majors of

Brigade wishing to serve in America. It was rather high up – third, I think. We asked old Darling who had done it, and what do you think? – he said, Colonel Elley! Wasn't it kind of the dear old man? He used to know my family very well, but I never expected him to do a thing like that for me. He actually mentioned me to Pakenham! Then Colborne said: "My friend Ross, who commanded the 20th when I was Captain of the Light Company, is going. I'll go and ask him to take you as his Brigade-Major." Ross knew me, of course, on the retreat to Corunna. He is to command a force consisting of three brigades. I'm to be Deputy-Adjutant-General.'

'It is very comforting to think that Ross was so ready to take you,' said Juana carefully. 'All your friends have been so kind in – in arranging everything so satisfactorily.' Her tears fell on to the wings of his jacket. 'Oh, Enrique, you have friends everywhere, but I have no one, no one in the world but you, and you are sending me to live with strangers, in a strange country!'

He gave her a convulsive hug. 'You will have Tom. He will go with you. And my father, and my sisters will welcome you –'

'Oh, I can't, Enrique! I can't! Not without you! What will they think of me? How can I face them, without being able even to speak their language? No, no, if I must go to England without you, I will be alone, not amongst people who are strangers, and will perhaps despise me!'

'They would not!' Harry said, but although he spoke stoutly his imagination could not quite see Juana in sleepy Whittlesey. 'If only my mother were alive!' he said, with a deep sigh. '*Hija*, I have been a bad husband to you, not to have made you learn to speak English!'

But when Madame La Rivière heard this, she said: 'Well now, that is excellent, for it will give the little one something to do while you are away. She will learn to speak your tongue, so that when you come back she will be able to astonish you.'

'Yes,' agreed Juana doubtfully.

Brother Tom, who was being sent home on account of an old wound, which had been troubling him for weeks, said: 'I don't see why you shouldn't stay in London, I must say. I wouldn't send her to Whittlesey, if I were you, Harry. Let her take lessons in English from a good master in town. She'd find it devilish flat at Whittlesey, besides being cut-off from all our friends. I'll keep an eye on her. And really, you know,' he added, dropping into his own tongue, 'it isn't fair to thrust her into the family when she can't make herself understood in English, nor they in any language she speaks.'

Juana looked so much more cheerful at the prospect of being allowed to await Harry's return in London, that in the end that was how the matter was arranged. Any doubts Harry might have nourished of the propriety of sending a sixteen-year-old to fend for herself in London were outweighed by the consideration, bluntly expressed by Tom, that: 'She will do very much better amongst our fellows (for there are bound to be several of us fixed in London for a few months) than being cosseted and fussed, and very likely lectured by Eleanor, and Betsy, and Mary. You know, Harry, *we* all love her, but there's no denying she's not at all like the girls at home.'

No, Harry thought, remembering long marches under molten skies, bivouacs in streaming woods, the fording of swirling rivers, mattresses spread in filthy, flea-ridden hovels, the washing of gangrenous wounds which would have made an English miss swoon with horror: she was not like the girls at home.

Fortunately for them both, they had not much time to waste in dwelling on the miseries of separation. Not only had arrangements to be made for Juana's voyage to London, but Harry had to settle his affairs: no easy matter, with nine months' regimental pay owing to him, and no time to get a private draught from England. He did it, in the end, but only through the staunchness of his friends, who forwent the greater part of their first issues of pay in order to make Harry's up to the requisite amount.

His own regiment gave him a farewell dinner, and so did the 1st and 3rd Caçadores, themselves very sad at the imminent prospect of being sent back to Portugal. 'Ah, my friend, you are more fortunate than we are!' said the Commander of the 3rd Caçadores with a shake of his head. '*You* will return to your comrades, but we, never!'

'Oh, don't say that! It doesn't bear thinking of!' said Harry.

'Alas!' said the Portuguese, a look of melancholy spreading over his homely countenance. 'When, I ask myself, shall I again hear my English name on English lips?'

That made Harry laugh, for, the Colonel's name being Manuel Terçeira Caetano Pinto de Silvuica y Souza, he had very early in his career in the Allied army been dubbed, much more simply, Jack Nasty-Face. 'By Jove, Jack, I should think that would be an advantage, at any rate!'

'I regard it as a name expressing the most gratifying affection,' said Souza sadly.

When the day of leaving Castel Sarrasin came, Harry nearly broke his heart. Much more affecting than the parting with his friends, was the send-off he got from the rank-and-file. His own battalion, a thousand strong when it had embarked for the Peninsula just before Talavera, now reduced to five hundred, lined up to cheer him. There was hardly a man amongst them who had not been wounded; not one, Harry swore, whose knowledge of outpost duty had not been brought to perfection.

'Come back to us, Mr Smith!' shouted the veterans, who never, all their lives, gave him any other title.

'By God, I will!' Harry choked.

'He's true-blue: *he'll* never stain!' said Tom Crawley. 'Lordy, I'd give a month's pay to be by when he starts in to damn this new brigade of his into shape! *They'll* learn a thing or two once they gets *our* Brigade-Major amongst 'em!'

Accompanied by Tom, and by little Digby, who had got leave to go with them to Bordeaux, the Smiths embarked in a skiff, and journeyed to the coast down the Garonne, anchoring each night, and putting up at inns which, after the *posadas* of Spain, seemed the height of luxury to them. If the black cloud of separation had not hung over their heads, they would have enjoyed their river-voyage immensely; as it was they pretended to each other that they were delighted with everything they saw, and thought secretly that they would surely never live through unhappier days.

They found Bordeaux quite the most beautiful city (except, said Juana firmly, Madrid) that they had ever seen. They put up at one of the best inns, and desperately crammed their days with sight-seeing, and theatre-going. Harry was to embark on the *Royal Oak*, a 74, anchored off Pauillac, under the command of Rear-Admiral Malcolm; and Juana was to remain with Tom in Bordeaux until the next transport sailed for England. Quite a number of their friends, who were suffering from the effects of wounds, were going to England too; and since Harry was taking West with him to America, Digby was sending his own excellent private servant with Juana, with orders not on any account to leave her until she was safely installed in London, and had no further use for his services. He was a very capable man, and could be trusted to look after all her baggage, and Tom's too; not to mention Tiny, and

Harry's greyhounds; and would be of much more use to her than the female attendant whom Madame La Rivière had wished her to engage.

Four days was all the time granted to the Smiths in Bordeaux. Harry sent West on ahead of him with his horses to Pauillac, and himself remained with Juana until the last possible minute. She bore up with wonderful courage, but her face grew steadily more pinched, and her eyes blacker-rimmed; and when the dreadful moment of parting came, she clung convulsively to Harry for an instant, trying to speak. His face swam before her anguished eyes; her throat worked; she tried with all the resolution left to her to smile at him, but as he kissed her, the suffocation in her breast overcame her, and she sank mercifully into a deep swoon.

Digby, taking her forcibly out of Harry's embrace, thought that in another minute Harry too would be in a swoon, so deathly white had he become. 'She's all right! Go now, Harry, before she comes round! She can't stand any more of this, or you either!'

'For God's sake, Bob, take care of her!' Harry said hoarsely.

'Yes, yes, of course I will! Good luck to you, old fellow! and don't worry! I'll send you word how she goes on!'

With a last, wild look at Juana's pale, inanimate countenance, Harry turned, and strode out of the inn. His horse was being held for him in the street; he jumped into the saddle, and rode off, his face so grim that the ostler stood gaping after him, wondering what could be the matter with the cheerful young Englishman.

9

Harry did not reach Pauillac until the following day. He found West waiting for him there, and the *Royal Oak* riding at anchor a few miles below the village. West greeted his master in a matter-of-fact way, but when he had conducted him to the billet he had found for him, he could not help directing one or two earnestly enquiring looks at him. Harry could only shake his head.

West began to unpack a clean shirt from the portmanteau. Clearing his throat after a few minutes, he said: 'General Ross hasn't shown his front yet, sir.'

'Oh!'

'I took a look at that there *Royal Oak*,' persevered West. 'I reckon she's a fine ship.'

'We shall have to mind our P's and Q's aboard her,' said Harry, trying to speak lightly. 'They say the etiquette on a man-of-war's so strict that there's no keeping up with it at all.'

'Ah, I daresay!' said West gloomily. 'I never did hold with them Navy chaps.'

They were kept kicking their heels for two days at Pauillac, but Harry had the satisfaction of getting a note from Digby, through the military post-office, which assured him that Juana was well, and trying hard to be brave.

On the afternoon of the second day, Harry, having seen his horses off with West, embarked in a small boat with his portmanteau, and was rowed out to the *Royal Oak*. He really was a little nervous of boarding a man-of-war, having heard the most chilling tales of the rigidity of all naval rules and regulations, but as soon as he came over the side he was met by the officer of the Watch, who asked him bluffly what his name was; said he was happy to welcome him aboard; and at once escorted him aft, to the Admiral's cabin. 'The old boy wants to see you,' he confided. 'Your General hasn't come aboard yet. You're a Rifleman, aren't you? I'll wager you've seen some fights in your time! Were you at Salamanca? I say, what a hiding you fellows gave the Frogs at Vittoria! We heard that poor old Joseph never stopped running till he got to France! Here's the Admiral's cabin: you'll find him a nice old dog.'

There were two gentlemen in the cabin: Malcolm, and Captain Dick. As he paused on the threshold, Harry thought that if the Admiral was the personification of a British sailor, his companion might well have sat as a model for a portrait of John Bull.

Both men got up at once, and welcomed Harry so warmly that he began to realize that during his years of service in the Peninsula the Navy's opinion of the Army had undergone a change. Nine years before, when Harry first joined, nothing was talked of but Nelson's victories; now, as he shook hands with Malcolm, he was conscious of a marked look of respect on that weather-beaten countenance. The Army had become glorious, even in the eyes of the Navy.

'Very glad to welcome you aboard, sir!' said the Admiral. 'Captain Smith, aren't you? This is Captain Dick. Come and sit down, and have a glass of grog! Your General don't mean to haul his wind till tomorrow.'

Harry returned some sort of an answer. The idea that in a few hours this gently swaying ship would be bearing him thousands of miles away from Juana had taken such strong possession of his mind that he hardly knew what he was doing. Upon the Admiral's pushing a bottle towards him, he half-filled his glass with gin, added a splash of water, and tossed the whole off without a blink.

If anything had been needed to convince Malcolm that the officers in the army were a good set of fellows, this absent-minded action would have been enough.

'Well done!' he exclaimed. 'I've been at sea, man and boy, these forty years, but damn me if I ever saw a stiffer glass of grog than that in my life!'

He insisted on showing Harry to his cabin himself, and told him what his hours were. 'I breakfast at eight, dine at three, have tea in the evening, and grog at night, as you see; and if you're thirsty, or want anything, my steward's name is Stewart – a Scot, like myself. Tell the Marine at the cabin door to call him, and ask him to bring you everything you want.'

Such easy, friendly manners, and so much kindness, had the effect of cheering Harry, who began to think that once the pangs of separation from his wife had grown less acute, he might enjoy himself very well aboard the *Royal Oak*.

General Ross arrived next morning, with his A.D.C., Captain Tom Falls, of the 20th, and his A.Q.M.G., Lieutenant De Lacy Evans. Both these young gentlemen took an instant liking to Harry, and he to them. 'I say, we're all frightened to death of you!' said De Lacy Evans, grinning. 'They tell us you're the devil of a fellow!'

The General, a mild-looking man in the late forties, said that he was very glad to have Harry with him, and favoured him, as he shook hands, with an appraising look.

'He's a hot-tempered, emotional young dog,' Colborne had told the General. 'He'll very likely damn your eyes, if he thinks you're making a mistake, and he'll command the brigade, if you give him rope enough. He thinks the devil of a lot of himself; but so does every man who was ever in his brigade. He'll very likely drive you mad with his restless ways; and you'll probably be shocked if you hear him on a field of battle; but you'll never have a better Major of Brigade, sir, nor one who spares himself less.'

General Ross thought that his new Staff-officer looked rather fine-drawn; he hoped he was not ill?

'Not a bit, sir! I'm never ill,' said Harry briskly.

'Good!' said Ross. 'I've heard a great deal about you from Colonel Colborne.' He added, with a twinkle in his eye: 'I understand you'll take the command out of my hands, if I'm not careful.'

'Oh, that's too bad, sir!' protested Harry, blushing. 'At least I never did so with dear Colborne!'

'Ah, *we* know what you Sweeps are!' murmured Tom Falls.

Harry laughed, and began to think that he would go on very well with his new General, and his Staff.

Soon after Ross's coming aboard, the *Royal Oak* weighed anchor, and stood out to sea. Harry remained motionless on deck, watching the coast of France dwindle in the distance, until nothing but the line of the horizon could any longer be seen.

Ten

ENGLAND

1

JUANA'S FIRST SIGHT OF LONDON WAS BY LAMPLIGHT. PARTING from her friends on board the convoy at Portsmouth, she had spent an hour or two at the George Inn, while Tom saw Tiny, and Old Chap, and all the greyhounds ashore, and arranged with Digby's servant for their conveyance to Whittlesey. Tom was in tearing spirits, quite forgetting the pain in his knee in his delight at being in England again. He was not an exile of such long standing as Harry, who had not been in England for five years, but his last visit, in 1810, after the battle of the Coa, had been made in such unpleasant circumstances that it seemed as though it hardly counted. He had been carried off the ship then, suffering the most dreadful agony, and had been so ill that the noise and bustle of the port had hurt his head, and he had not cared even to look out of the coach window at the familiar countryside. All was different now. It was true that his old wound was troubling him a good deal, but it was not bad enough to prevent his walking about the town, and revelling in being in his own land again. It seemed strange, and delightful, to be able to walk into a shop and speak to its owner in English. So accustomed had he become to the use of Spanish or Portuguese, that he found himself addressing a bewildered haberdasher in the most fluent Castilian, and quite burst out laughing at his own forgetfulness.

Juana had declined going to walk about the town with him. Harry had so often drawn pictures of what they would do together as soon as they set foot in England, that the thought of being in Portsmouth without him for some time threatened to overpower her. She had promised to be good, however, and knew enough about men to realize that Tom would like nothing less than to be obliged to escort all the way to London a sister-in-law who was labouring under all the miseries of homesickness and grasswidowhood. When he returned to the inn, he found her sitting by the window in the parlour, watching the busy quay-side. Her eyes were rather red, but he was too excited to notice that, and he found nothing to complain of in her demeanour, which was subdued, but perfectly cheerful.

He had hired a post-chaise-and-pair to carry them to London, and the question now occupying his mind was to which hotel he should take Juana.

'You know, we shan't get to London until late,' he said. 'I daresay Harry would wish me to take you to Grillon's, or Fenton's, for he said you were to have everything of the best, but the thing is that we haven't much money, until I can see my father, and those grand hotels are devilish dear.'

'Oh, don't take me to a grand hotel!' begged Juana. 'I have been watching a party of ladies, and I know my dress is quite out of fashion.'

'Well, I must say I should prefer to go to a good inn, but the thing is, would you be comfortable?'

That made her laugh. 'Oh, Tom, how foolish of you! Do you remember the cottage at Pobes, when I slept on the table because of the bugs?'

'Well, *that* you won't have to do, at any rate!' grinned Tom. 'The post-boy says the coaches set down passengers at the Angel, at St Clement's-in-the-Strand, a tolerable sort of a place. Shall we go there for a night at least?'

She was quite agreeable, so the post-boy was told to carry them to the Angel, and off they set.

The Angel was found to be a busy, cheerful inn, its proprietor too well-accustomed to having shabby, sunburnt officers from the Peninsula set down at his door to think the arrival of a gentle-man in a green jacket and a black shako in any way remarkable. The discovery that the gentleman's companion was a Spanish lady was something entirely out of the way, however, and Juana found herself being stared at so hard that she began to blush. Then Tom had to explain that she was not his wife, but his sister-in-law, whose husband had gone to America; and the landlord evidently thought it all very odd and said that he for one didn't hold with this American war, dragging on and on, and, if anyone wanted his opinion, the sooner it was over the better. From having been in the habit of accommodating foreign visitors for many years, he was able to speak a little bad French, but as none of the chambermaids could understand anything but the few English words Juana knew, she was obliged to make known her wants by signs; and began to wonder, with a sinking heart, how she would fare in London, once Tom was no longer at hand to act as her interpreter.

They spent the following morning looking for suitable lodgings. Juana was quite bewildered by the size of London. Every street seemed to be full of traffic, chairs, hackneys, elegant barouches, and sporting curricles seeming to jostle one another on all sides; while nattily-dressed gentlemen on horseback picked their way through the crowd of vehicles. The shops seemed very fine, particularly in Bond Street, where Juana and Tom encountered the élite of fashion promenading, and Juana felt herself to be quite a dowd. However, chancing to see a very pretty hat of satin-straw trimmed with pomona-green ribbons, in one of the shop-windows, she prevailed on Tom to go into the shop with her to buy it. He said he felt a fool in milliners' shops, but Juana reminded him with paralysing frankness that he had not seemed to feel a fool in Toulouse, when he had bought an Angoulême bonnet of white thread-net for the lady then living under his protection.

'Now, Juanita, for the Lord's sake don't talk so!' begged Tom. 'You know, it won't do in England! People wouldn't understand! You must forget all those bits of muslin, really you must!'

'Well, I don't want to remember them,' said Juana. 'I thought *your* bit of muslin was a very vulgar person.'

'You never clapped eyes on her!'

'Yes, I did. I saw you with her at the theatre, and Harry told me she was your Cyprian.'

'Well, upon my word! There's a brother for you!' said Tom indignantly. 'You won't go and tell my family, will you?'

'No, of course not, stupid! But can I have that hat?'

'Oh, very well!' Tom replied. 'But it's three o'clock already, and we still haven't found an eligible lodging for you, and now here you are wanting to buy hats!'

But Juana's desire to buy a hat turned out to be a most fortunate circumstance, for, upon entering the shop, she discovered that the milliner was a Frenchwoman, and at once fell into conversation with her. Madame Céleste was much affected by her story, and, learning that she was in search of a lodging, at once recommended her to go to Panton Square, where, at No. 11, a French *émigrée* resided, a most respectable widow, with five children, who eked out her slender means by boarding one or two select visitors.

The prospect of lodging with a woman who would be able to converse with her made Juana feel much more cheerful.

Tom, discovering that Panton Square was situated quite close to St James's, pronounced the locality to be unexceptionable – indeed, a most fashionable quarter – so as soon as the satin-straw hat had been paid for, and packed into a band-box, a hackney was called for, and they drove off hopefully to Panton Square.

When the hackney turned into the Square, it was found to be a quiet little cul-de-sac, rather than a square, surrounded on three sides by flat-fronted, narrow houses built mostly of weathered bricks, each with its area guarded by iron railings. Some of the houses were larger than others, with their front doors flanked by sash windows; and some had been covered with stucco, in conformity with the prevailing fashion; but No. 11 was found to be a modest, three-storey residence, with a row of dormer-windows set in the roof, and a green front-door with a bright brass knocker on it. The shallow door-step was gleamingly white, and the curtains in the windows clean, which had not always been the case in the lodgings Juana had seen.

As luck would have it, Madame Dupont was able to offer Juana a pair of tolerable rooms upon the first floor. Her terms, to the wife of an officer engaged for seven years in helping to bring about the ruin of the Corsican Monster, were most reasonable. She was very sympathetic when she heard of Juana's temporary widowhood, and privately assured Tom that he need have no qualms at leaving his sister-in-law in her charge.

Since the Angel, being situated in the Strand, was a noisy inn where it was almost impossible to sleep at night, it was arranged that Juana should remove to Panton Square without loss of time.

Tom, who was obliged to report his arrival in England to the army medical authorities, was relieved to have found a safe harbourage for Juana. He promised to visit her frequently, if the doctors did not clap him into hospital; warned her that she would very likely receive a visit from his married sister, who lived just out of London, at Clapton; bade her be a good girl; kissed her in a brotherly fashion; and took himself off.

He was not condemned to a hospital, but as Juana seemed to be quite comfortable in her lodgings, he thought he should take a journey into Cambridgeshire to visit his family. Feeling very much as though her one sheet anchor were being taken away from her, Juana said bravely that of course he must go. Being well aware of his besetting sin, she added that considering he had not written to his father or sisters for years, the least he could do was to visit them without an instant's loss of time.

'You know, if you cared to come with me they would be delighted to see you,' he suggested.

'Oh no! Please, no, Tom!' she said. 'You have such a large family, and it quite frightens me!'

'Well, I daresay you're right, but there are only eleven of us, besides Grandmamma and my aunts. And Stona's married now, you know, as well as Alice; and my sister Eleanor writes that Charlie lives with my Uncle Davie almost entirely.'

But even this assurance failed to persuade Juana to go with him. She sent instead her humble duty to her father-in-law, and the trifles Harry had purchased for his sisters in Bordeaux, and sped Tom on his way with adjurations to explain to his family what her reasons were for remaining in London.

2

With the departure of Tom for Whittlesey, Juana, having enjoyed the luxury of crying bitterly in the privacy of her bed-chamber, resolutely bathed her swollen eyes, and determined at once to occupy herself in learning to speak English. Madame Dupont not unnaturally thought that a female would be a better teacher for her young guest than a man, but after enduring several depressing hours in the company of a genteel spinster, employed for many years at a Seminary for the Daughters of Gentlemen, Juana announced that she liked men better than women, and begged Madame to look about her for a suitable professor. Miss Price bridled when Juana's excuses were conveyed to her, but she was really quite relieved to be rid of a pupil whose unconventionality bordered, she thought, on impropriety. Since the few English phrases at Juana's command had been mostly picked up from the rank-and-file of the Light division, it was no wonder that the poor lady should feel a certain degree of dismay. The circumstances were explained to her, of course, but the notion of a female's following the drum was so repugnant to her, that she could not rid herself of the belief that Juana must be a very ungenteel young person.

Madame Dupont next found Mr Frederick Stone for Juana, an elderly gentleman with a sense of humour, with whom she professed herself very well satisfied. He made her read Thomson's *Seasons* aloud to him, and while her tongue struggled with the difficult English words, her imagination followed Harry across the Atlantic, or dwelt again amongst the Pyrenees. She could almost hear the challenge to Portuguese sentries: '*Sentre alert? – Alerte soy!*' and came back to the unhappy present to find Mr Stone correcting a mispronunciation.

Several wounded acquaintances from the Light division were in England, and she received visits from those who were well enough to go about town; but most of them had gone on leave to their homes in different parts of the country; nor were any of them, with the exception of Colonel Ross, of the 3rd battalion, close friends.

She soon learned to find her way about the bewildering streets of London; and she would very often accompany Madame Dupont on her shopping-expeditions. She would not admit that London was comparable to Madrid, but secretly she was much impressed by it, and quite gasped when Madame took her to the Pantheon Bazaar, in Oxford Street. Hyde Park she thought very pretty, but when she went for walks there, and saw the smart London ladies floating along in their diaphanous gowns, on the arms of dandies who would have put to shame all the Counts in the army, she felt very lonely, and sometimes had to wink hard to stop the tears coming into her eyes.

When Tom came back from Whittlesey, she greeted him in English, saying proudly: ''Ow do you do?' which made him laugh at her.

'Do not queez me!' she scolded. 'I spik very well already! And now we will talk in Spanish, please. Was your father well? Were your sisters glad to see you?'

Yes, Tom had received a much warmer welcome than such a neglectful son deserved, but he said it had been melancholy to see his home without his mother. However, Betsy was a famous housekeeper; Eleanor, dear, dreamy soul! was the same as ever; and little Anna had grown out of all knowledge.

'She's rather like you, only older, of course. They all sent their love to you, and Eleanor – she's our scholar, you know – gave me a letter for you, written in French. My father wishes so much that you would go down to live with them, but I said there was no chance of that. My sisters would give their eyes to see you! They would have me describe you to them over and over again, and Betsy said she was convinced of your being a female of the noblest character! Such a good joke, Juana! – they are quite afraid of your being like the haughty Spanish dames one reads about! Nothing will make them believe all Spaniards are not so! Then they *would* pronounce your name wrong, sounding the J as we English do. It sounded quite odd, and not a bit like you. And now I have to go out to Clapton to visit my sister Sargant! It is a great bore, but I promised my father I would do so.'

'Yes, of course, but tell me, Tom: are the horses at Whittlesey? Is Tiny well?'

'Oh, by Jove, if I was not forgetting! My father told me to say that Tiny is in famous shape, but he wonders that Harry should mount you on such an unmanageable horse! Old Chap is still poorly. My father fears he will never be good for much again, but never mind! he has his eye on just such a hunter as would suit Harry.'

'And the hounds? Are they well?'

'Yes, and Lola has whelped again, and my sisters are quite wild about the puppies. I tell them they will spoil them if they fondle and cosset them so much, but they don't heed a word I say, of course!'

He went off again soon afterwards to visit his sister, but not before he had squired Juana to watch the procession of the Allied Sovereigns, who had come to London on a visit to the Prince Regent. Tom hired a window, but he agreed with Juana that it was hardly worth the expense, not one of the magnificent persons bowing so graciously to the cheering crowds being able to hold a candle to old Hookey.

His lordship had had a dukedom conferred on him, and had been appointed, besides, Ambassador to the Court of King Louis XVIII. Napoleon having retired to Elba, under polite supervision, it might have been supposed that his lordship's troubles were at an end. Nothing of the sort! Ferdinand VII, restored to his kingdom, had no sooner been established in Madrid than he began to behave in the most tiresome fashion, dissolving the Cortes, setting up the Inquisition again, and pursuing the *Liberales* with the most relentless persecution. If Ferdinand was determined to rule as a despot, there was naturally only one thing to be done: Field-Marshall the Duke of Wellington must be sent as plenipotentiary to Madrid to reason with him. The Duke, whose rigid sense of duty never permitted him to decline to perform any service demanded of him for the good of the state, accepted the charge, but thought, at the end of a visit full of flattery, banquets, and processions, that he had done very little good.

Returning to France, he took leave of his army in a General Order, dated 14th June, at Bordeaux. He arrived in London on the 23rd of the month, and joined the Prince Regent, the Emperor of Russia, and the King of Prussia, not to mention Marshal Blücher, at Portsmouth, where they were engaged in reviewing the Fleet.

Laboriously spelling out this news in the *Gazette*, Juana said that of course it was gratifying to think that the war was over at last, but that the thought of the Squire's taking leave of the army was so melancholy that it made one almost wish that peace had not been concluded.

'The Squire?' said Mr Stone.

'Oh, that is what *we* call Lord Wellington!' said Juana superbly.

A faint smile hovered on Mr Stone's lips; he had never seen his pupil so animated, for she was generally rather listless, and given to heaving deep, sad sighs. He saw that when the conversation turned on army matters her mournful eyes brightened, and he drew her out a little, asking her what the army thought of all the new peerages. 'Lord Niddry, for instance: Sir John Hope!' he said.

A shrug of the shoulder disposed of Niddry. 'We do not know very much about Hope, but it is a fact he was taken prisoner at Toulouse, which naturally made us Light Bobs laugh a good deal. And as for Cotton, whom they have made Lord

Combermere, everyone knows that he wanted a peerage months and months ago, and was very angry because it was not given to him. We call him the Lion d'Or, you know, but he leads our cavalry very well. And everyone says Graham deserves anything, because he is an excellent soldier, though not, of course, to be compared with Wellington, who, I assure you, would *never* have allowed himself to fail at Bergen-op-Zoom! But poor Sir Thomas – I mean, Lord Lynedoch – left us because he was going blind, and it was not at all fair to send him to Holland in charge of that expedition. As for Daddy Hill, my husband says he is a most capable General, and I expect he will be glad to hear of *his* peerage. But I know he will say that dear Colborne deserves more than just to be made an A.D.C. to the Prince Regent! For there is *no-one* like Colborne!'

Her expressive eyes sparkled, but the mere mention of Harry and Colborne immediately reminded her of the change in her fortunes, and she was obliged to turn away to hide her sudden rush of tears from her instructor.

Such persons as delight in hearing of the mildly scandalous activities of Royalty, were edified, in July, to read of the Princess Charlotte's sending her suitor, the young Prince of Orange, to the rightabout. Not having the smallest interest in the Princess, Juana merely said that the Prince of Orange was a wispy creature, with a startled expression, and no chin; and that she for one did not blame Charlotte for refusing him.

There was no news yet of the arrival of Ross's expeditionary force in North America. Dreams of shipwreck began to disturb Juana's night. She felt herself so entirely cut off from Harry that sometimes a dread of never seeing him again would haunt her to such an extent that she could not shake it off. At every turn she missed him, so that sometimes she could fancy herself but half-alive.

That was the impression Mrs Sargant formed of her, when, towards the end of July, she had herself driven to town for the express purpose of calling upon her sister-in-law.

Mrs Sargant was only twenty-five years old, but a decided manner, and the natural air of consequence belonging to a young matron, made her seem much older. She had a great look of Harry, and something of his quick way of speaking. When she was ushered into Juana's parlour, in her best pelisse, and gown of French muslin, clasping in one hand an absurdly small parasol, she found her unwilling hostess shrinking instinctively behind the table, and looking so young and frightened that she could scarcely bring herself to believe that she was really confronting Harry's wife. She exclaimed in astonishment: 'Is this possible? Can you be my new sister?'

'I am Juana Smith,' said Juana, conscious of her plain, round morning-dress, and uncovered head.

'My dear! You must forgive me! I had pictured you – different! though why I should, I'm sure I don't know! You must let me make myself known to you: I am Harry's sister Alice. I daresay he may have spoken of me!'

Juana murmured Yes, but it was Tom, not Harry, who had spoken of Mrs Sargant. 'Alice,' had said Tom, 'is the only person Harry stands in awe of!'

Not a very encouraging introduction, nor did Mrs Sargant's brisk, competent manner do much to allay Juana's nervous qualms. The two ladies, having embraced, sat down opposite to each other, on either side of the empty fireplace, and embarked on a laborious conversation, which, since Juana's command of the English tongue was negligible, rapidly deteriorated into questions and monosyllabic answers.

Mrs Sargant, trying in vain to kindle a spark in her timid-looking hostess, privately wrote her down as insipid, and wondered what Harry could have seen in her. She was pretty, she supposed, but lacked animation. Her voice was certainly good, very low and musical; her figure decidedly elegant; her ankle particularly well-turned; but what was there in all this to make Harry tumble head over ears in love with the child? Allowance had to be made, of course, for her inability to express herself in English, but Mrs Sargant thought she might have exerted herself to answer more fully questions put to her about Harry. She detected a certain stiffening when she mentioned her brother's name, and did not guess that it concealed a bursting heart.

Just as she was wondering whether she could with propriety take her leave of this disappointing sister-in-law, the serving-maid opened the door, announcing the arrival of two gentlemen. The next instant, a very tall officer, followed by a shorter and much stouter one, both dressed in Rifle green, entered the room, and Juana had flown up out of her chair with a shriek of joy.

'Oh, Johnny! Oh, George! Oh, my dear friends! To see you again!'

In considerable amazement, Mrs Sargant saw the prim girl of a moment earlier transformed into a creature glowing with animation. Such a babel of Spanish broke out that Mrs Sargant felt stunned. She was startled to see Juana actually embracing the visitors, throwing her arms round their necks, and shedding tears down the frogs of their pelisses.

'Poor little soul! There, there!' said George, patting her shoulder.

'Now, Juanita, what would Enrique say if he could see you crying?' said Kincaid. 'This won't do at all! A pretty way to welcome old friends!'

'Oh, do not heed me! I am so overjoyed!' Juana said, mopping her eyes. 'When did you land? How is the regiment? Tell me everything, everything!'

'Of course we will, but you have a visitor,' said George, becoming aware of Mrs Sargant.

'Oh, how I forget my manners!' Juana turned remorsefully towards her sister-in-law, saying in her broken English: 'Please forgive! I must present Señor Kincaid, and Señor Simmons, of ours. This is Enrique's sister, Johnny, Señora – I mean, Mrs Sargant!'

In spite of having been a good deal shocked by the manner of Juana's reception of her friends, Mrs Sargant shook hands graciously with them, and soon had George sitting beside her on the sofa, conversing most amiably, while Juana plied Kincaid with eager questions. Were all her particular friends well? Was Charlie Beckwith in town? Had the 52nd come home with the Rifles? Was Kincaid heartbroken at leaving behind that French girl he had fallen so desperately in love with, or had he brought her home on his arm?

'No, no, would you believe it, I was cured upon our last day at Castel Sarrasin? Positively cured, my dear! I overtook her and her sister, strolling by the river's side, and instantly dismounting, I joined in their walk. My horse was following at the length of his bridle-reins, and while I was doing the polite with the sister, the other dropped behind, and when I looked round, I found her mounted *astride* upon my horse! And with such a pair of legs, too! It was rather too good: "Richard was himself again!"'

Juana's delighted trill of laughter made Mrs Sargant break off in the middle of what she was saying to George, to interpolate: 'It must be most gratifying to my sister to receive a visit from old friends. To see her suddenly so lively makes me realize how much she must feel her separation from the regiment.'

'Well, I don't know about that,' George answered, in his honest way. 'She don't really care a button for anyone but dear Harry. I must say, I don't know how she contrives to go on without him. But, then, she is equal to anything.'

She perceived that he knew a Juana other than the shy girl who had received her; watching the sparkle in the large eyes fixed on Kincaid's face, the fluttering movements of Juana's hands, she saw why Harry had fallen in love with her. She wondered whether Juana's reserved manner with her arose from pride. One heard such tales of the Spaniards! Harry had mentioned, in one of his letters, hidalgo blood; and had written, in his vile scrawl, a name so long that one could not but suppose the child to be oppressively well-born. Did her reluctance to visit her husband's family signify a grand lady's contempt for a country surgeon? Mrs Sargant hoped that there might be no such nonsensical notions in that little curly head, and decided, as she rose to leave, that judgment must, for the present, be suspended. She got a shy kiss from her sister-in-law, a stammered apology for being able to speak only a few words of English, and went away reflecting that when the child smiled she was really enchantingly pretty.

'Now we can be cosy!' said Juana, when the door had shut behind Mrs Sargant.

3

Both George and Kincaid were going home on leave, Kincaid to shoot partridges in Scotland, George to renew his acquaintance with all his numerous brothers and sisters; but before they left London they were determined to form a pleasure-party to Vauxhall, in Juana's honour. 'Only we must have another female,' said George.

'Oh, Johnny will find one easily!' said Juana. 'He always does!'

'No, no, that won't do at all!' replied George. 'You do say such things, Juanita! It must be a respectable female, of course.'

'But you don't know any!' objected Juana.

It seemed for a time as though the Vauxhall plan would come to nothing, but fortunately Juana had the happy notion of inviting Madame Dupont to join the party. Madame professed herself charmed with the idea, and two days later they all four sallied forth to spend a delightful evening across the river, watching a grand firework display, and sitting down in a box to a cosy supper of ham-shavings and arrack-punch. Never having seen fireworks before, Juana was so excited by the bursting rockets, and clapped her hands so hard at the set-piece, that, as George confided to Kincaid, it made one happy just to watch her pleasure.

When these two faithful friends left town, Juana felt dreadfully sad at parting with them, but was soon diverted by the arrival of Charlie Beckwith on her doorstep. Beckwith was such a close friend of Harry that she was even more delighted to see him. They enjoyed some long discussions on the probable progress of the *Royal Oak* across the Atlantic, Charlie asserting stoutly that she might soon expect to receive tidings of Harry.

Not to be outdone by her first visitors, Beckwith took Juana to Astley's Royal Amphitheatre, to see a Grand Romantic Spectacle of the Cataract of the Ganges, supported by a Double Tight-Rope performance, and various feats of equestrianism; so that Juana began to think that if only Harry were with her, London would not seem such a big, dull city after all.

The home station of the 95th was in Kent, and it was expected that the regiment, all but the few companies with Graham in Holland, would winter in Dover. But meanwhile there were always one or two officers to be found at the London barracks, besides those who were undergoing medical treatment for wounds.

London was beginning to be very thin of company, even to Juana's inexperienced eye. When she took Vitty for walks in

Hyde Park, there were hardly any perch-phætons to be seen bowling along, no barouches, no sporting curricles driven by noted whips. Even the promenaders seemed to come from a different class of society. The Upper Ten Thousand, beginning as early in the year as June to drift away from town to Brighton, or Worthing, or Cromer, had by the end of July quite disappeared from London.

The Princess of Wales disappeared too, much to the relief of the Regent. She had decided to travel abroad for a space, and embarked from Worthing on the 8th August. The Regent hoped that by the exercise of a little ingenuity it might be found possible to prevent her ever returning to England. You could hardly blame him, for what with her peculiar personal habits, the questionable nature of her ménage at Kensington, the subversive influence she exercised over the Princess Charlotte, and the deplorable way she had fallen into of appearing in the opposite box to his at the theatre, her continued presence in England had become a serious embarrassment. The Prince Regent was certainly not a model husband, but when the British public, moved by the spectacle of a deserted wife, took Caroline to its great, throbbing heart, and actually hissed him when he made a public appearance, he felt that injustice could go no farther. If reports were to be believed, Caroline had taken to favouring the interested with a scandalous description of their wedding-night; while she made no bones at all at bastardizing her daughter by announcing that she had always considered Mrs Fitzherbert to have been his only wife.

Madame Dupont, who, from being able to remember how handsome the Regent had been before he grew so fat, was inclined to sentimentalize over him, and Juana grew quite tired of having items of Court news read to her from the *Gazette*. She was more interested to hear that Lord Fitzroy Somerset had lately been married to one of the Duke's lovely nieces, the Lady Emily Wellesley Pole, but the only news that could be really welcome to her was news from America, and of that there was none.

She did not see Mrs Sargant again, because her sister-in-law had gone away to Cromer for the month of August. London had become insufferably hot and dusty; the flies were as numerous as in Portugal; and the meaner streets were so malodorous from the rubbish accumulating in the kennels that everyone longed for a day of heavy rain to wash away the filth. There did not seem to be anything for a foreigner to do in London but to wander about the hot streets, looking in at shop-windows; to stroll in the Park; to visit the Bayswater Tea Gardens; or the Botanical Gardens; and these were amusements which soon palled. Juana thought how much more enjoyable it was to spend the summer campaigning under scorching Spanish skies, and wondered drearily how many years it would be before she saw Harry again. Madame Dupont pooh-poohed such melancholy notions, but Juana knew that it was now more than five years since Harry had set foot in England. If the war with America dragged on, five more years might lag by without a sight of him.

I shall be twenty-one years old, Juana thought, seeing middle-age creeping upon her.

September came without bringing a letter from Harry. He was receding into a past that was beginning to seem dream-like. Only the periodic visits of their friends still made the Peninsular years real to Juana. They noticed that she no longer recalled the old days; she explained simply that she was silly, and found that talking about the past made her cry.

But Harry came swiftly back into the present when a packet arrived in Panton Square from Whittlesey. It was addressed in her father-in-law's hand, but when Juana opened it, out tumbled a letter from Harry.

It had been sent off in August, from Bermuda, where the *Royal Oak* had been delayed through having had her mizzen-top blown away in a terrific gale. Harry was well, but he missed his *queridissima muger* every moment of the day, through all his dreams at night. His scrawl covered pages of thin, crackling paper, which soon grew limp through being kept in Juana's bosom, and constantly drawn out for re-reading.

He was enjoying a capital passage; Admiral Malcolm was the best fellow in the world; one of the lieutenants, called Holmes, was his particular friend: Juana must picture him pacing up and down the deck, talking of her to Holmes – always so sympathetic! Ross was very affable and fatherly, but Harry could not say that he inspired him with the opinion that he was the officer Colborne regarded him as being. He was very cautious in responsibility – awfully so! Harry thought he would be found to lack that dashing enterprise so essential in a soldier. He was organizing his force into three brigades, and Harry had been put in orders as Deputy-Adjutant-General. Admiral Cochrane, commanding one hundred and seventy pennons of all descriptions on the coast of America, had proposed a rendezvous in Chesapeake Bay as soon as possible. Prices were very high in Bermuda: what did Juana think of fifteen Spanish dollars for one miserable turkey?

There was no word in all this of a possible return to England. Indeed, how should there be, when Harry had not yet arrived in America?

Tears watered the thin sheets, and had to be carefully wiped away. Vitty jumped up on to Juana's lap, licking her hands, and begging her with flattened ears and wagging tail not to cry.

'Yes, yes, Vitty, a letter from Master! Oh, my little *perrilla* when shall we see Master again?'

4

During the afternoon of the 20th September, the *Iphigenia* anchored off Spithead, and pretty soon the rumour that there were three officers aboard her, bringing home dispatches from the *Chesapeake*, began to circulate through Portsmouth. A Naval Captain, and two military Staff-officers, one of them apparently a sick man, came ashore in the Captain's gig, and went to the George inn. The news reaching the ears of one Mr Meyers, general agent, tailor, and outfit-merchant to the army, that gentleman meditatively bit the tip of one finger, announced mysteriously to the wife of his bosom that there might be a little profit in the news, and sallied forth to nose out the names of the officers at the George.

He found that they had already bespoken a chaise-and-four to carry them to London. 'I wonder who they are?' he said invitingly.

The landlord knew exactly who they were. 'Captain Wainwright of the *Tonnant*; Captain Smith, attached to General Ross; and Captain Falls of the 20th,' he replied.

'Ah!' said Mr Meyers, brightening. 'If it is Captain Harry Smith of the 95th, I know him. I will step into the coffee-room.'

He did so. Captain Wainwright was not there, but one military gentleman was standing by the window, holding an unmistakable box under one arm, while the other sat in a chair, wrapped in his cloak.

'Good afternoon, sir!' said Mr Meyers politely. 'I am very glad to see you safely in England again. Dear me, sir, I do believe I have not laid eyes on you since I had the honour of supplying you with some necessaries to take to South America! A long time! It quite makes one think!'

Harry turned. He had a very good memory, and after frowning for a moment at Mr Meyers, his brow cleared, and he said: 'Meyers! That's who you are!'

'Always at your service, sir,' bowed Mr Meyers. 'Hearing that you had landed from the *Iphigenia* – from the *Chesapeake*, I apprehend? – I took the liberty of coming to pay my respects.'

'Devilish civil of you!' said Harry, alert with suspicion.

He encountered an absurdly roguish look. 'That little box under your arm contains, I see, dispatches,' suggested Mr Meyers.

'Well?' said Harry. 'What of that?'

'If,' said Mr Meyers coaxingly, 'you will tell me their general import, whether good news or bad, I will make it worth your while. Your refit, now! An expensive business, sir, as I well know.'

'I'll see you damned first!' exclaimed Harry, controlling a strong desire to knock his visitor down. 'Of what use, pray, would such general information be to you?'

'I could get a man on horseback to London two hours before you,' replied Mr Meyers, in a persuasive tone. 'Good news or bad on 'Change is my object. Now do you understand, sir?'

'Perfectly!' said Harry. 'And when I return to America I shall expect a capital outfit from you for all the valuable information I have afforded you! Good-bye, Meyers!'

Not, apparently, in the least put out of countenance, Mr Meyers bowed himself out.

'Well, if that don't beat all!' said Tom Falls. 'Old fox! Do you mean to get to London to-night?'

'By Jupiter, I should just think I do! That is, if you can stand the journey?'

'Oh lord, don't worry about me! I shall do very well. What a curst thing this dysentery is!'

Ten minutes later, Captain Wainwright, bearing naval dispatches for my Lords at the Admiralty, came back to the inn; and by five o'clock he, Harry, Tom, and West were bowling out of Portsmouth on the London road in a post-chaise-and-four.

'I wish to God I hadn't come in the same chaise with you!' said Wainwright, when Harry let down the window to shout to the post-boys to drive faster. 'There's no need to crowd all sail, you young madman!'

'Oh, but there is!' Harry said, drawing up the window again, and showing his companions a thin, burnt face in which his narrow eyes seemed to be on fire with impatience. 'My wife, Wainwright, my wife!'

Captain Wainwright caught at an arm-sling to steady himself as the chaise bounced over a shocking patch in the road. 'To be sure, yes! Is she in London?'

'I don't know,' said Harry. 'I parted from her in Bordeaux, four months ago! I don't know where she is, whether she's well, or – or alive, even!'

Wainwright could see no reason for supposing that Juana should be either unwell or deceased, but as it was plainly useless to expect the least degree of rational thought from Harry, he attempted no argument, but merely grunted, and said that he fully expected the chaise to lose a wheel before they had accomplished as much as half their journey.

This gloomy prophecy was not fulfilled, but by the time the chaise had reached Liphook, a couple of hours later, Wainwright, bitterly regretting that no accident had befallen them, climbed stiffly down at the Anchor inn, and announced his irrevocable intention of partaking supper.

'We shan't have above another hour of daylight,' objected Harry.

'My abominable young friend, here's where I haul to. Damme, if I don't spend the night here!'

'Oh, sir, don't say that! Think of your precious dispatches!' Harry begged.

'Who's going to read dispatches in the middle of the night? Stop fidgeting about, or I will sleep here!'

Harry's face of scarcely curbed impatience, however, touched the Captain's heart, and after consuming a quantity of bread-and-butter, and several cups of tea with plenty of good English cream in it, he consented to resume the journey to town.

'I must say, I wish you wouldn't insist on driving so fast,' he remarked, not with any hope of being attended to, but in a tone of resignation. 'After the scenes we've witnessed, I like to feast my eyes on a placid countryside.'

'By God, and so do I,' Harry responded quickly. 'No burning villages, no starving, wretched peasants! I have had seven years of that. The excitement bears a soldier happily through it all, but *this* makes one realize the damnable, accursed thing war is!'

'No burning citadels either,' murmured Tom from his corner.

The two soldiers exchanged fleeting glances. Wainwright said: 'Well, I didn't order that!'

'No. But if it hadn't been for Ross, your precious Admiral Cockburn would have destroyed the whole of Washington!' said Harry.

Wainwright grunted, and the conversation lapsed.

When the daylight faded, the pace had to be slackened, but the moon presently rose, and once more the post-boys were bidden to spring 'em. Captain Wainwright, remarking that he would rather be beating off a leeshore in a gale with the tide against him than travelling in Harry's company, wedged himself into his corner, shut his eyes, and remained dead to human intercourse until the chaise drew up in Downing Street. He took leave of the two younger men there, and made off to the Admiralty. The chaise was paid off, Falls insisting that he was quite well enough to walk to a coffee-house; Harry lodged his dispatches; West picked up the portmanteaux; and they all three set off to find a suitable lodging for the night. As it was by this time past midnight, the quest was not easy. Every inn near Downing Street was full; and Harry, fearing that Tom's state of health was not good enough to permit of his walking about town any longer, was considering the advisability of calling up a hackney, when they came upon the Salopian Coffee-house, in Parliament Street. It looked to be a clean, comfortable place, but the waiter who met them said that he was very sorry, there was only one spare bedroom: nothing more!

'Oh, plenty!' said Harry. 'All we want is an hour or two's sleep!'

The waiter looked doubtful, but he handed them over to a chambermaid.

'Only one room, sir!' said this damsel.

'Plenty!' declared Harry.

'But, gentlemen, only one bed!'

'Plenty!' said Tom, with the croak of a laugh.

So up they went, West following with the portmanteaux; and, finding the one bed well furnished with blankets, proceeded, under the scandalized eyes of the chambermaid, to haul half the clothes on to the floor.

'But what are you doing, sir?' she demanded, trying to rescue a chintz-quilt from this fate.

'Making a second bed,' replied Harry. 'Be off with you, there's a good girl!'

'But you can't sleep on the floor, sir!'

'Can't I, by Jupiter! I've done so for seven years!' said Harry, setting his hands on her shoulders, and running her out of the room.

5

Harry was up long before Tom Falls in the morning, and ate a hasty breakfast in the coffee-room under the eye of a depressed-looking waiter, who was engaged in dusting the chairs, and setting the furniture straight for the day. As soon as he had swallowed his eggs and bacon and coffee, Harry ran up to take his leave of poor Tom, still snug in bed, called for a hackney, bundled himself and West into it, and drove off to the barracks where he knew he would find some Rifle comrades quartered.

The porter there seemed surprised to see an officer abroad so early. He was not a quick-witted man, and when Harry accosted him with a demand to know the names of any officers in the building, he stood gaping until Harry said impatiently: 'Come on, man, come on! You must know who's inside!'

'Yes, sir, for sure I do. There's – let me see now – there's Mr Dixon, and – and Captain Logan.'

'No, no good. Think again!'

'Yes, sir. Well – well – Mr Fry, and Captain Macnamara, and Colonel Ross, and young Mr Milligan.'

'Hold a minute! Colonel Ross? What regiment?'

'He had a green jacket when he came up,' said the porter.

'John Ross!' exclaimed Harry. 'Where's the room?'

'Oh, but, sir! don't disturb the gentleman: he's only just gone to bed!'

'My friend,' said Harry, 'I've often turned him out, and he shall be broad-awake in a couple of minutes! Come now, show me his room, and be quick about it!'

'Well, sir, if you say so!' said the porter.

He conducted Harry to Colonel Ross's room, but when he would have tapped discreetly, Harry elbowed him aside, flung open the door, and bounced into the room, calling out: 'Hallo, Ross! Stand to your arms!'

The Colonel, who had come in after a very late night, and was peacefully sleeping, leaped up at this all too familiar shout, realized where he was, and demanded: 'Who the devil are you?'

'Harry Smith: fall in!' said Harry, drawing back the blinds with a ruthless hand.

'Harry!' exclaimed Ross. 'Well, upon my soul! You old ruffian, where do you spring from?'

'The Chesapeake, with dispatches. How are you? Is the regiment home? By God, it is good to see you again!'

Ross, wringing him by the hand, began to pelt him with questions. He was quite as excited as Harry, and there was a great deal of laughing, and back-slapping, until Harry said: 'Well, John, but quiet! Is my wife alive and well?'

'All right, thank God, Harry! In every respect as you would wish! I was with her yesterday.'

'Where, John, where?'

'In Panton Square, No. 11.'

'Oh, thank God!' Harry exclaimed, and burst into tears.

'Now, Harry! now, Harry!' Ross said. 'I tell you she's safe and well!'

'If you knew what I've suffered! The anxiety – not knowing where she was – her youth – her dependence on me! But that's enough! I'll see you presently, John: I can't wait now!'

He left as abruptly as he had come, jumped into the waiting hackney, and shouted to the coachman to drive like mad to Panton Square. The hackney rattled over the cobbles in fine style, and had no sooner turned into the little square than Harry leaned forward eagerly, his hand on the door. He expected to find Juana breakfasting, if not still in bed, but just as he was scanning the numbers over the doors on one side of the square, a shriek reached his ears.

'*Oh Dios! la mano de mi Enrique!*'

'Stop!' shouted Harry to the coachman. Almost before the hackney had pulled up, he had thrust open the door, and jumped out, just as Juana, who was walking along the opposite side of the square, came running across the broad road.

She was sobbing with mingled joy and shock; he flung open his arms, and she fell into them, right in the middle of the square, under the interested gaze of the coachman, two errand-boys, and a chambermaid who happened to be leaning out of an upper window.

'My soul, my darling!' Harry said, holding his wife so close that the breath was almost squeezed out of her.

West, who had descended more sedately from the hackney, and was observing the grins of the errand-boys with great disfavour, coughed apologetically. His employers paid no heed to him. Oblivious of their surroundings, they clung together in such an ecstasy of joy that not even the arrival on the scene of a coal-heaver's cart penetrated their consciousness.

'Hey, soldier! Sweetheart and honey-bird keeps no house!' shouted the coal-heaver, grinning broadly.

'*Mi Enrique, mi esposo!*' Juana sobbed, arms locked round Harry's neck.

'*Alma mia de mi corazón!*'

'Ah!' said the coal-heaver, shaking a waggish head. 'Free of her lips, free of her hips!'

'Here!' said West menacingly. 'You be off out of this, or I'll make you!'

'Gip with an ill-rubbing, quoth Badger, when his mare kicked!' retorted the coal-heaver.

It seemed for a moment as though the quiet square would be

further enlivened by a brawl, but happily Harry lifted his head just then, and became aware of his audience. 'Oh, the devil!' he said, bursting out laughing. '*Hija*, where do you live? Take me in!'

'Ho, a furriner!' remarked the coal-heaver, who had by this time descended from his cart.

'As English as yourself!' said Harry. 'Hallo, Vitty! I declare she remembers me as well as you do, Juanita!'

Vitty, who had been leaping up at him quite unheeded, began to bark shrilly; several heads were poked out of windows, and Juana, blushing and laughing, seized Harry by the hand, and fairly ran with him through the open doorway of No. 11.

'Well, there's a light-skirt for you!' remarked the coal-heaver.

'If you want to have your cork drawn, say the word!' said West. 'She's my master's lawful wedded wife!'

'You don't say!' gasped the coal-heaver. 'No offence, I'm sure!'

Meanwhile, in the narrow hallway of No. 11, Juana, encountering Madame Dupont, stammered out the joyful tidings, allowed Harry just time enough to shake the good lady's hand, and then swept him upstairs to her sitting-room. She was so overcome by the shock of having him unexpectedly restored to her that for a time she could scarcely speak, or believe that she was not dreaming. A storm of tears shook her; she lay in his arms, gripping his coat with both hands, sobbing out disjointed exclamations. But presently she grew calmer, and was able to lift her head from his shoulder, and to release her clutch on his coat. 'I can't believe it! I can't believe it!' she said, stroking his tanned cheek. 'Oh, mi Enrique, you have grown thinner! How did you come? Is the war over at last?'

'No, not over, but please God, it soon will be! Poor Tom Falls – Ross's A.D.C., you know – was sent home on sick leave, so Ross gave the dispatch to me. Oh, *querida*, do you know you are more beautiful than ever? Have you been well? Has Tom taken good care of you? Have you seen my father?'

'No, no, I would not go to your home until I could speak English!'

'Oh, you bad child, can't you do so yet?'

'Yes!' she said. 'I speak it very well: it is quite estraordinary how well I speak it!'

He kissed her, laughing at her. 'Indeed, it is most *estraordinary* how *oo-ell* you speak it!'

'Don't queeze me, *espadachín!*' she said, pinching the lobe of his ear. 'Ah, Enrique, *tirano odioso*, I have been so unhappy!'

'And I! You don't know!'

'I shall never let you go again, not a step out of my sight!'

'Oh, by Jupiter!' Harry said, recalled to a sense of his duties. 'My poor darling, you'll have to! I must be off to wait on Lord Bathurst!'

'It is your duty? Then of course you must go. I do not forget that I am a good soldier! But, Enrique, tell me, is all well in America?'

'I hope to God it is! But oh, the times I have sighed, "Oh, for dear John Colborne!" Ross is the kindest fellow in the world, but he is no more fit for a command – But, there! I should not say so! Yet if you could have seen our battle at Bladensburg, General Juana, with all we learned from old Douro given in full to the enemy, you would have been shocked!'

'Oh, Enrique, we were not defeated?'

'No, we licked the Yankees, and took all their guns, but lost upwards of three hundred men in the engagement. Colborne would have done the same thing with a loss of forty or fifty at most! However, we entered Washington, with Admiral Cockburn.'

'You entered Washington!'

'Yes, for the amiable purpose of burning the city to ashes! Never was there anything so barbarous! To those of us, fresh from Wellington's methods of warfare, it was too shocking to be borne! Ross felt it: it was thanks to him the flames stopped where they did. That damned Admiral would have set fire to everything! As it was, all the public buildings were set light to. Oh, it was melancholy to see the elegant Capitol and the President's House being destroyed in such a way! It made one ashamed to be an Englishman. We felt more like a band of Red Savages of the woods! However, you won't spread that about, remember! Juana, this won't do! I must be off!'

She would not hear of his going to Downing Street until he had brushed his hair, changed his shirt, and put on his best sash. To see him tossing the contents of his portmanteau all over her bedchamber brought home to her the realization of his return far more than anything else could have done. The quiet house seemed to be full of his energetic personality; his voice shouting to her for God's sake to come at once, because he could not find his neckcloth, was the sweetest music she had heard for months. She ran in, and found the neckcloth without the least difficulty, of course; and ten minutes later was waving good-bye to him from the window.

On his arrival in Downing Street, Harry had reason to be grateful to his wife for insisting on his furbishing up his person, for after receiving him very kindly, and putting a number of questions to him, Lord Bathurst said: 'Well, Captain Smith, the intelligence you bring is of such importance that the Prince Regent desires to see you. We'll go immediately.'

'What, my lord, to Carlton House?' exclaimed Harry.

'To be sure,' smiled Bathurst.

'Then be so good as to allow me to take the map I brought

you,' said Harry, recovering his poise with considerable aplomb.

'A very good notion: I have it here,' approved Bathurst.

The summons to the Regent's presence was not, of course, quite unexpected, but never having been in such exalted circles before Harry, for once in his life, felt extremely nervous. When the carriage drew up behind the colonnade, and he and Bathurst were admitted into Carlton House, the magnificence of his surroundings at first exercised a most oppressive effect upon his naturally vivacious spirits, and he could almost have wished that Tom Falls had been well enough to have been the bearer of the dispatch. But upon being shown into a large apartment, and left there for half-an-hour, while Lord Bathurst went off alone to confer with the Regent, he soon recovered his self-possession, in spite of the stunning effect of the Regent's taste in house-decoration, and reflected that never having quailed under the piercing eye of old Douro there was no need for him to be afraid of meeting even the Prince Regent.

'Anyway, General Ross begged me to talk, if I were asked to!' he told an unresponsive gilt chair, just as Bathurst came back into the room.

'Come along!' said his lordship. 'The Prince will see you.'

Harry got up, but said frankly: 'My lord, if we were in camp, I could take your lordship all about, but I know nothing of the etiquette of a court.'

'Oh, just behave as you would to any gentleman!' Bathurst replied. 'Call him "Sir," and don't turn your back on him.'

'No, I know *that*!' said Harry, following him out of the room.

'You'll do very well. His Highness's manner will soon put you at ease. And don't be afraid to talk! He is for ever complaining that the bearer of dispatches will never do so. Now, here we are: Captain Smith, Sir!'

The Prince Regent had, for a number of years, been providing the British public with a surfeit of scandal. His debts, his matrimonial affairs, his quarrels with his daughter, the vulgarity of his expensive tastes, his succession of mistresses, were all perfectly well known even to a young officer from the Peninsula. He was the subject of the grossest caricatures in the newspapers; his treatment of his wife; his predilection for the bottle; the way he had done his best to hound his father into a madhouse; his countless follies: all these were subjects bandied from lip to lip, but when Harry stepped into his dressing-room he straightway forgot them.

The Regent, who was seated before an opulent dressing-table, rose at once, and came forward, holding out his hand in the most natural way. 'I am very glad to see you, Captain Smith. General Ross has strongly recommended you to my notice as an officer who can afford me every information of the service you come to report – the importance of which,' he added, with an unexpectedly charming smile – 'is marked by the firing of the guns you can now hear.'

Harry quite blushed to think of all London being in an uproar at the news he had brought, and himself actually shaking hands with his future sovereign. The Regent drew him over to a table, and begged him to be seated, and to spread out 'that map I see you have under your arm.'

In a few minutes, Harry was perfectly at his ease, securely mounted on his own hobby-horse. He was astonished at the grasp of military affairs shown by the Regent. The most pertinent questions were put to him, and he found his Royal interlocutor so knowledgeable, so sincerely interested in the conduct of the war, that he spoke out with the greatest frankness, even saying bluntly that it was to be regretted a sufficient force had not been sent out to hold Washington.

'What do you call a sufficient force?' asked the Regent.

'Fourteen thousand men, Sir.'

'On what do you base such an opinion?'

If the Regent thought to convict Harry of speaking at random, he soon discovered his mistake. Harry had no hesitation in stating his reasons. He asked about the present state of affairs in America, and was told that Harry had left half the army sick from dysentery, which made him look grave.

'Then there can be no attempting Baltimore!' he exclaimed.

'Captain Smith has told me, Sir, that General Ross assured him, when he left the country, that he would not do so,' interposed Bathurst, forbearing to add that Harry had also told him that Admirals Cochrane and Cockburn had done their utmost to urge Ross to move against Baltimore.

'We induced the enemy, by a ruse, to concentrate on Baltimore, Sir,' said Harry. 'A *coup de main*, like the conflagration of Washington, may be effected once during a war, but can rarely be repeated. The entrance to the harbour, moreover, will be effectually obstructed.'

The Regent seemed to appreciate this reasoning; he asked Harry a great many more questions, drawing him out so skilfully that Harry presently found himself recounting one or two funny episodes, which made his Royal Highness roar with laughter.

When he at last backed his way out of the room, the Regent came after him to ask if he were a relation of his friend, Sir Edward Smith, of Shropshire. He looked disappointed upon being told No, but shook hands with Harry again, saying graciously: 'I and the country are much obliged to you all. Ross's recommendations will not be forgotten; and, Bathurst! don't forget this officer's promotion!'

6

As though a reunion with his wife, and a visit to Carlton House were not enough to cram into one day of an obscure officer's life, Lord Bathurst, as he and Harry drove back to Downing Street, invited him most cordially to dine with him at his house on Putney Heath that evening. There was no refusing such an invitation, however much Harry would have preferred to have spent the evening with Juana. Nor, when she presently learned of it, did she raise the least demur. She said, on the contrary, that it was most fortunate that she had had the forethought to press out his mess jacket and to launder his muslin neckcloths.

Bathurst's secretary, a lively young gentleman owning to the name of Charles Cavendish Fulke Greville, but answering equally readily to the more simple nickname of Punch, had offered to drive Harry out in his tilbury. He called for him in Panton Square just after seven o'clock, and regaled him all the way to Putney with a flow of the most amusing conversation, most of it far too scandalous to be seriously attended to.

When they were ushered into the drawing-room of Lord Bathurst's house, they found a large party assembled, amongst whom were Lord Fitzroy Somerset, and his bride. Fitzroy moved across the room to shake hands with Harry at once, congratulating him on the success achieved in America, and introducing him to his wife, whom Harry presently took in to dinner.

Lady Fitzroy, a gentle creature with a decided look of her famous uncle in her rather long but handsome face, accorded Harry a flattering degree of attention. To his surprise, he discovered that he was the lion of the evening, his host being at pains to draw him out, and every one quite hanging on his lips. Lord Fitzroy being placed opposite to him, it was not long before the conversation turned on the late campaign in the Peninsula. Well-fed, and well-wined, Harry was not a bit shy of talking before such a distinguished company, and upon a gentleman's saying, from the other end of the table, that the Duke of Wellington was certainly unequalled *in defence*, he picked up the cudgels without an instant's hesitation, and said, that in his army's eyes the Duke was unequalled in any form of warfare.

Fitzroy laughed. 'Well done!'

Seated beside Harry was an elderly gentleman, with very dark brows arched above large, lustrous eyes, and a skin so white that it might have been lacquered. He inclined his head courteously, saying in a deep, soft voice: 'You entertain a high opinion of the Duke, Captain Smith?'

'All who have had the honour of serving under him must do so,' responded Harry. 'To *us* he is elevated beyond any other human being!'

The gentleman smiled. 'I am very glad to hear you speak in such raptures of him. He is my brother.'

Harry realized that he was sitting beside the Marquis Wellesley, and blushed, but said, with a laugh: 'I have not exceeded in anything, sir, to the best of my judgment!'

After dinner, when they rejoined the ladies in the drawing-room, Fitzroy came over to Harry, and they had a long talk. Fitzroy had gone to Cadiz with the Duke, after the armistice, and had naturally had a good deal of conversation with him about the late war. 'You know, Smith, the Duke often said to me, "The Light, 3rd, and 4th divisions were the *élite* of my army, but the Light had this peculiar perfection: no matter what was the arduous service they were employed on, when I rode up next day, I still found a *division*. They never lost one half the men other divisions did."'

'No! Did he indeed say that?' cried Harry, quite delighted. 'Oh, famous, for that was what we so prided ourselves on! I have actually heard our soldiers bullying one another about the number such-and-such a company had lost, always attaching discredit to the loss!'

Altogether, Harry, in spite of being separated from Juana, spent a charming evening. He got back to Panton Square after midnight, and found Juana waiting for him, with such a beaming look in her eyes, such a welcoming smile on her lips, that he caught her up bodily in his arms, exclaiming in a sudden thickened voice: 'To know that I shall find you when I get back to my quarters! *Mi muger! mi queridissima muger!*'

She took his face between her palms, pushing back his head so that she could look into his eyes, her own full of mischief. 'Ah, ah! Do you think I shall believe that there have been no beautiful American women, mi Enrique?'

'Never one! *Siempre tu fiel, fiel Enrique!*'

She laughed, but kissed him. 'I don't believe you, because I know you for a bad, wicked man, but I love you, I love you!'

Later, dropping asleep in his arms, she roused herself to murmur: 'Now I can go to your home!'

'So you shall, as soon as we get back from Bath,' he responded.

'Bath?' she said, bewildered.

'Didn't I tell you, *hija*? I promised Ross I would go to call on his wife there, and take her a letter from him. Shall you mind going?'

'I mind nothing,' said Juana, tucking her head under his chin. 'When do we march?'

They 'marched' the very next day, travelling all the way in a private chaise, an extravagance justified, they thought, by the prospect of Harry's promotion.

'Oh,' said Juana, leaning back luxuriously against the squabs of the chaise, 'we have journeyed so many miles together, but never like this before! I feel so grand! Did you remember to write to your father?'

Yes, Harry had done all that a dutiful son should, even to begging Mr Smith to come up to town in a few days to meet him on his return from Bath. There was nothing, in fact, on his conscience, and he was able to give himself up to a week's bliss.

They found Bath a delightful town, and Mrs Ross very amiable and hospitable. A few days crammed with sight-seeing were spent there, and then off the Smiths set for London again, quite astonishing Mrs Ross by such meteoric movements.

They reached Panton Square again in the highest fettle, Juana having read in a newspaper bought at the last stage, of Harry's promotion to the rank of Major. 'The reward of our separation!' she called it.

Madame Dupont met them at the door of No. 11, with the intelligence that Mr Smith had arrived in town the day before, and was actually upstairs in the parlour at that very moment.

Juana had told Harry of how Tom had found his family living in dread of her being a haughty Spanish dame, and as soon as he heard of his father's arrival, he was seized by a mischievous desire to tease him a little. He would not hear of Juana's going straight in to Mr Smith; he wanted to show her off, not tumbled from a long journey, but looking her best.

'Do, do put on your Spanish dress!' he coaxed. 'I shall tell my father you're as stately as a swan and about as proud as a peacock! It will be a famous joke!'

So Juana slipped upstairs to her bedchamber, while Harry went in to his father.

It was easy to see from where Harry got his long, narrow eyes, and aquiline nose. The resemblance between Mr Smith and

his favourite son was most pronounced. Even the upward tilt of
their mouths at the corners was the same; the only difference
was in expression. John Smith's was a milder face than Harry's.
His chin was not so aggressive; his lips not so close-gripped; nor
had he that look of scarcely curbed energy.

When Harry opened the door, he looked round, and stayed
for a moment, grasping the arms of his chair, and gazing at his
son. 'Harry!' he said. 'My boy!'

Harry reached him as he rose from his chair, and caught both
his hands. 'Father!' he said, flushing with a quick surge of emotion. 'My dear, dear Father!'

John Smith found it difficult to speak for a moment. He had
last seen his son upon his return from the horrors of the retreat
to Corunna. Harry had been worn down by dysentery, shuddering continuously with ague, his clothes verminous, his slight
frame a pitiful skeleton. It had taken all his father's skill in medicine, and all his mother's cosseting, to set him on his feet again
in time to join Sir Arthur Wellesley's expedition to the Peninsula; and John Smith had never been able to rid himself of the
last glimpse he had had of him, waving good-bye from the window of the chaise. He had only been twenty-two, and he had
looked, in spite of his three years of strenuous service, much
younger. Somehow, John Smith had gone on picturing him as a
thin scrap of a white-faced boy. Well, he was still thin, but not
boyish any longer, and certainly not white-faced. The bones of
his face, more sharply defined than ever, gave him a look of
maturity. There were little lines at the corner of his eyes,
induced by constant narrowing of the eyes against the glare of
sunlight; and deeper lines which made him look sometimes a
little sardonic.

'I should hardly have known you!' John Smith managed to say
at last, still holding him tightly by the hands.

'I should have known you anywhere!' Harry declared. 'You haven't altered – not a scrap!'

'Well, I don't know that you've altered so much either, now I come to look at you again,' said John, releasing him to draw out a handkerchief, and blow his nose with unnecessary violence. 'If your mother were alive, how proud she would be!'

Harry's lip trembled. 'Don't! Don't speak of that! I cannot *bear* to!' he said sharply. 'When I think – But, come! *You* are well, sir! And my sisters?'

'Yes, yes, all of us! But you will be sorry to hear about that horse you had from Stewart!'

'Alas! Old Chap! Not dead?'

'Yes. There was nothing to be done, my boy. I knew you would feel it, and a lovely creature he must have been before he took ill! But never mind! Your wife's horse is in famous shape. But how came you to mount a lady on such a varmint, Harry? I am surprised you should do such a thing!'

'Oh, she manages him to perfection, sir, I assure you! She is a splendid horsewoman!'

'She must be indeed! You know, we were very sorry she was so resolute in refusing to come to Whittlesey. I am afraid she will find us very simple people, and our way of living not what she has been accustomed to.'

'True, very true!' Harry said, casting down his eyes to hide the laughter in them. 'She has been used to a *very* different life!'

'I hope she will be comfortable,' John said doubtfully. 'Your sisters are quite frightened to meet her, you know! They feel sure she must be very proud.'

'Oh, well, you know how it is with Spaniards of the hidalgo class!' said Harry airily. 'They are all a trifle stiff, to be sure, and devilish particular in matters of etiquette, but one grows accustomed to it! Don't be surprised if she is a little stately at first: I am persuaded you will soon come to like her.'

A very little of this kind of teasing was enough to make John Smith look forward to making Juana's acquaintance with a sinking heart; and by the time she came into the room, dressed in full Spanish costume, he had reached the stage of dreading her arrival.

She paused for a moment on the threshold, looking so beautiful that she took Harry's breath away, and so haughty that John Smith wondered what in the world had possessed his son to marry such a stiff-necked young woman.

'Juana, my love! Allow me to present my father!' said Harry.

'My dear —' began John, and stopped.

The play broke down. The doubtful, rather wistful look in John Smith's face was too much for Juana. The fan she was waving was shut with a click, and tossed aside. 'Oh no! I cannot!' she cried, and ran across the room, straight into her father-in-law's arms. 'I am not at all proud — not a bit! It was Enrique's fault! He is a villain, a wretch, altogether abominable! *No vale nada!*'

'Well, Father?' said Harry, wickedly grinning. 'Do you like my little peacock?'

7

Did he like her? He adored her. She was his little dove, and his pretty rogue, and by the time he got her down to Whittlesey he so doted on her that it began to be quite a question whether he would ever be able to let her out of his sight again. The sisters — sedate Mary, playful Eleanor, brisk Betsy, and lively little Anna — confided to Harry that they had not seen their father so cheerful since Mama's death. They were such good girls, Harry's sisters: they never thought of being jealous of his wife. They were tolerably handsome, all of them, but Juana cast them in the shade, for if Eleanor had more classical features, Juana had the glow and sparkle Eleanor lacked; and if Anna's teeth were seen to be more even when she smiled, Juana's were the whiter.

As for the brothers, they used to sit and watch her shyly, quite fascinated by her quick little movements, and her pretty, broken English. Grave Samuel, who was going to be a surgeon, like his father, said in his slow way that his new sister was just like a boy; but Charlie, living with his Uncle Davie, but spending a large part of his time at home, laughed such a notion to scorn. She was not in the least like a boy, he said. She was like – well, he didn't quite know what, but he thought Harry the luckiest devil going. Charles was plaguing the life out of his father to let him join the army as a volunteer; William, the staidest of the brothers, said it was a piece of nonsense, and he would do better to attend to his books.

There were so many aunts and uncles and cousins living in Whittlesey that Juana was quite bewildered at first. They used to call in St Mary's Street, on the slimmest of pretexts, Grounds and Moores, and sit looking at Harry's Spanish wife as though she were a strange animal on show. 'You must not mind them, Jenny dear,' Eleanor said. 'You see, they have never seen a Spanish lady before.'

Mary offered to help Juana with her studies of the English tongue, but the brothers cried out against it. Why, she would not be half as jolly if she did not set them all laughing at the funny words she used, or break into a flood of swift, fierce Spanish when they teased her more than she liked. 'Whew! What a spitfire!' Charlie said admiringly, the first time she rounded on him.

'I must say,' Betsy conceded handsomely, 'one would never have supposed Jenny had not been used to living in a large family!'

'No,' agreed Eleanor. 'Does it not bring home to one our shocking ignorance of other lands and peoples? I am sure I shall never again be prejudiced against foreigners. Why, only think how we feared she would be stiff and prim, and always wanting to have a duenna with her!'

'The most remarkable thing about her,' said Mary gravely, 'is that she should have gone through such adventures with dear Harry without losing the delicacy of mind which I must hold to be a female's chief attribute. I own, I had dreaded to detect a certain degree of impropriety; for, you know, to be obliged to live amongst soldiers for so long is enough to blunt the keenest sensibility. The very thought of all the evils of such a situation quite makes one shudder.'

'Oh, does it, though!' cried Anna, distressingly tomboyish still. 'Wouldn't I just love to follow the drum, and have a Spanish horse to follow me like a dog, and eat acorns, and all the rest of it!'

If anything had been needed to win John Smith's heart, it would have been supplied by Juana's handling of Tiny. The little horse had been so unmanageable, even with John, who, Harry said, was the finest horseman he knew, that when Juana led him out of his stall, and loosed him, poor John was quite alarmed, expecting him to bolt into his cherished flower-garden. But Tiny minced delicately behind Juana, with Vitty trotting beside him, right up the neat path, and into the drawing-room. The Smiths could hardly believe their eyes. Then of course nothing would do for Harry but to make his wife change into her habit, and show off herself and the horse, figuring him as well as any Mameluke.

Harry was allowed just three weeks at home before letters reached him from the Horse Guards. The first he opened ordered his immediate return to London; the second drew from him a shocked groan that brought Juana quickly to his side.

'Ross!' he said. 'Oh, the fool, the dear, kind fool! I might have known it!'

'*John* Ross?' she cried. 'Oh, what?'

'No, no! Poor General Ross! He let them persuade him – De Lacy Evans and those damned Admirals! – and attempted Baltimore on the 12th September, failed, of course, and lost his life there! Good God, he was dead when we were congratulating his poor wife on his success at Washington! It does not bear thinking about!'

Juana's eyes were fixed on his face. 'And that other letter?'

'I am to return instantly to London. Pakenham is appointed to succeed Ross, and I go with him as A.A.G.'

Nothing could soften such a blow, not all the caresses of her new family. Juana's white face brought tears of sympathy to the sisters' eyes. Everyone tried to be helpful, and so many people assisted in packing Harry's portmanteau that it was wonderful that it was ever induced to shut. Aunts and cousins brought all manner of unsuitable comforts for an officer about to set out in the middle of the winter to cross the Atlantic; and Grandmama at the last moment tried to fit in a jar of her own apricot preserve.

There was no question this time of Juana's living alone in London. John Smith was going to take her up to see the last of Harry, and bring her back to Whittlesey when he had gone.

They all three of them went to Panton Square, and, fortunately for Juana, time was so short, and the things to be done so many, that there was no opportunity for indulging in melancholy reflection.

Harry went at once to see Pakenham, who greeted him most warmly, and told him that they must sail in a few days from Portsmouth, on the *Statira* frigate. Harry knew Pakenham of old, and already entertained a great respect for his talents. His reputation in the army was high, for whether he was leading another man's division in a spectacular charge, as at Salamanca, or performing the duties of Adjutant-General, as he had done after Vittoria, he was always cool, competent, and unfailingly light-hearted.

To Harry's delight, he found that the 3rd battalion of the Rifles was destined for America, and that his old friend, John Robb, of the 95th, had been appointed Inspector-General of Hospitals. He and Robb arranged to travel down to Portsmouth together, sending West ahead with their baggage; and at three o'clock on a grey November Sunday, Harry once more said farewell to his wife.

For him at least it was not so painful a separation as at Bordeaux, for he had the comfort of knowing that he left her in his father's tender care; but for her it meant more months of anxiety, more searching of the newspapers for dread tidings from America. She behaved with great courage, trying hard to show a smiling face at the last, but he left her, half-fainting, leaning her forehead against the mantelpiece, and pressing her handkerchief to her lips to force back the sobs that crowded in her breast.

'Good-bye, my dear boy, good-bye! You know I will look after her as though she were indeed my own daughter!' cried John, quite overcome.

'God bless you!' Harry said hoarsely, and fairly dashed out of the room.

Eleven

⅗

WATERLOO

1

BACK AGAIN IN WHITTLESEY, LIFE LOST ITS ZEST FOR JUANA. SHE rode with her father-in-law, paid morning calls with Mary, and learned how to make apple-jelly from Betsy; but although she never repined it was sad to see how her buoyancy left her when Harry was not by. Everyone felt his absence, of course. There were seven young persons in the house in St Mary's Street, but with Harry's departure quiet seemed to descend upon it. Anna, yawning, said that life was abominably flat, and although Mary reproved her for using such unconventional language, she admitted that it did seem a little dull.

The weather grew very cold. An icy wind cut across the Cambridgeshire flats, howled round the corners of the house at night, and whistled under the doors, lifting all the carpets. Eleanor's fingers were swollen with chilblains, Mary developed a streaming cold, and Betsy complained that do what she would she could not exclude draughts from the house. Only Juana did not seem to feel the cold. When the sisters pointed out the stupid position of the windows, the disagreeable habit the dining-room fire had of smoking when the wind blew from the north-east, and the impossibility of warming the hall and stairway, she opened her eyes at them in surprise, and said she thought the house *muy cómodo*. They exclaimed, but when she described her winter quarters at Fuentes de Oñoro, and the mud hut Major Gilmour had bequeathed to her on the Grande Rhune, they owned that there could be no comparison.

Snow fell from a leaden sky in December. The bleak countryside seemed to shiver under it, and the farmers prophesied a white Christmas.

'Your first English Christmas, dearest!' Eleanor said, bringing a prickly armful of holly into the house. 'If only our dear traveller could be here to share it with us!'

'Never mind!' Juana said. 'There will be a letter from him soon now.'

She was so sure that Harry would write; the sisters hoped that she would not be disappointed; but they said, sighing, that neither Tom nor Harry was a very regular correspondent. 'He promised me,' Juana replied, with impressive simplicity.

She began to be rather restless about a week before Christmas, because she thought that the *Statira* must have reached America by then, and perhaps already Pakenham's force was engaged with the enemy. Her interest in the Christmas preparations was dutiful, but a little perfunctory, and she did not much enjoy the party itself. It was soothing to her present mood to accompany the family to Church in the morning, and to pray for Harry's safety, (for she had not the smallest hesitation in entering a Protestant Church), but the big dinner-party in the evening she found rather overwhelming. There were so many relatives present, all chattering about family affairs, and laughing at old jests, that she felt herself a stranger, and would have slipped away had not John seen the disconsolate look in her face, and moved over to sit beside her, and to talk to her about the subject nearest to both their hearts.

In the New Year, John had business in London, and he took Juana and Anna with him, travelling post all the way. There had been heavy snow-falls, and once they came up with a stage-coach which had strayed off the road into the ditch, and lay there with two wheels cocked up in the air.

They said in London that it was the hardest winter within the memory of man. Never had there been such a frost! Sand had to be scattered in the streets to prevent the horses sliding on the glass-like cobble-stones; ladies pulled snow-boots on over their kid shoes, dug their hands deep into fat little muffs, and, in defiance of fashion, wore fur-lined coats over their foolish muslin dresses. Actually, the Thames was frozen, and fairs were being held on it. Charlie Beckwith, and Jack Molloy, on leave from Dover, where the regiment was quartered for the winter, took Juana and Anna to see the fun there one evening. A capital time they had, but it was not at all the kind of entertainment of which Mary would have approved. They bought roast potatoes, and held them in their muffs to warm their hands; they paid their groats to see the Fat Woman, and the Calf with Five Legs; they even tried their luck at the cock-shies; just like all the vulgar cits, declared Anna joyously.

Beckwith and Molloy had plenty of regimental gossip for Juana, and oddments of news about the troops stationed in Holland. Beckwith said he had it on the best of authority that ever since his father's restoration to the throne, the young Prince of Orange, who had been made Commander of the British forces in the Netherlands, had been giving great offence to the Dutch by associating almost exclusively with the English in Brussels. Colborne, a full Colonel now, and a K.C.B. besides, was his Military Secretary: no sinecure, thought Beckwith.

Jack, drawing the grimmest picture of the bleak barracks at Dover, wished the 95th had been ordered to the Netherlands.

Brussels seemed, by all accounts, to have become the gayest city in Europe. The English, delighted at being at last able to travel out of their own island, were flocking to Belgium in hundreds. Jack knew a fellow who had the luck to be stationed there; he said that London was nothing to it. 'Better even than Madrid!' Jack said, teasing Juana.

When they went home to Whittlesey, no sooner had the chaise drawn up in St Mary's Street, than Sam ran hallooing out of the house to tell Juana to come inside quick, and see what a surprise was awaiting her. A surprise could mean only one thing; she picked up her skirts and ran in; and there, sure enough, was Eleanor, clutching a shawl round her shoulders, and holding out a letter from Harry.

Such a long letter it was, written like a journal on board the *Statira*, and sent off from the mouth of the Mississippi, on the 25th December. Only fancy! The *Statira* had taken all that time to reach her rendezvous with the fleet. But Harry said that was on account of her captain's being one of the old school, and making all snug each night by shortening sail.

It did not seem, though, as if Harry had chafed much at the delay. He had enjoyed the voyage, in spite of the frigate's being so crowded that most of the Army officers had had to sleep in cots in the steerage. There were many Peninsular comrades on board, and Sir Edward Pakenham, '*one of the most amusing persons imaginable*,' inspired Harry every day with increasing respect and affection. '*I never served under a man whose good opinion I was so desirous of having*,' he wrote.

He had found time to scrawl a few lines after landing in America. Owing to the *Statira*'s leisurely voyage, he said, they had arrived three days after the disembarkation of the Army, under Major-General Keane. The force had sustained a sharp night-attack; Stovin, the Adjutant-General, had been wounded in the neck; and Harry was promoted to his room.

This was naturally very good news; but the announcement that the army was assembling for an assault upon New Orleans quite superseded it. The reflection that the engagement must by this time be over, for good or ill, chased away the smiles from the sisters' faces, and made Juana clutch Harry's letter to her breast, exclaiming: 'He may be dead! He may be dead! *Ah Dios*, how can I bear to wait and wait for the news?'

A most painful period of anxiety had indeed to be lived through before any further tidings came from America. The snow that covered the fens had turned to slush, when, upon a dull February day, Brother William brought in the *Gazette*. He was looking so grave that Eleanor, who met him at the door, uttered a muffled shriek, and said hoarsely: 'Harry?'

'No, thank God! He is safe! But the news is shocking! We have suffered a terrible reverse.'

'Oh, what does *that* matter as long as dear Harry is safe and well? Quick, come in at once to Juana!' She paused. 'But how do you know?' she asked. 'Is there a letter from him?'

'No, something better than that: General Lambert mentions him in the Dispatch!'

She could not forbear to seize the *Gazette* from him, and to direct her gaze towards the few lines his finger pointed out to her. '*Major Smith of the 95th Regiment, now acting as Military Secretary, is so well known for his zeal and talents, that I can with great truth say that I think he possesses every qualification to render him hereafter one of the brightest ornaments of his profession,*' she read and at once cried out: 'Oh, what joy! How Juana will feel this! Our Harry! Military Secretary! His zeal and talents! Oh, I must find Juana directly!'

This was soon done, and it was not until she had exclaimed over the tribute to Harry, flying up out of her chair, and dancing about the room like the child she was, that William could get anyone to attend to the rest of the Dispatch. But as soon as Juana heard that the Dispatch had been written by Major-General Lambert, her jubilations were checked in an instant, and she said sharply: 'Lambert? You mean Pakenham, our dear Sir Edward!'

'No, alas! Pakenham was killed. Our arms have met with a reverse, my dear sister.'

'Killed!' Juana cried, turning pale. 'Reverse! It is not possible! Give me the *Gazette* immediately! I do not believe you!'

But it was quite true. The assault upon New Orleans had been repulsed with shocking loss, and Pakenham's body, enclosed in a cask of spirits, had been actually brought home to England for burial.

Juana burst into tears. Not even Harry's safety and promotion could alleviate her distress at hearing of a British defeat. She said over and over again that it could not be: 'Never, never did we lose a battle! Oh, why was not Lord Wellington in command? It could not then have happened!'

Upon the following day, a packet arrived from Harry, enclosed in a very civil note from Wylly, Pakenham's Military Secretary, who had brought home the dispatch.

Harry's letter was written again in the form of a journal, but it was a hurried, disjointed scrawl, showing plainly how busy and how harassed he had been ever since his landing in America. He had been dissatisfied with several of the regiments from the start; he discovered early that the American Riflemen, though slow, were excellent shots; and it was plain that he considered the enemy to have been very strongly placed. Only on one subject did he write with his usual enthusiasm. '*I am always with Sir Edward. . . . I am delighted with Sir Edward; he evinces an animation, a knowledge of ground, of his own resources and the strength of the enemy's position, which reminds us of his brother-in-law, our Duke. . . . I do believe I am more attached to Sir Edward, as a soldier, than I was to John Colborne, if possible!*'

The last lines of Harry's letter were more disjointed than ever, evidently written in great agitation. Before the assault, on the 8th January, Harry had had to give up his post of Adjutant-General to a senior officer arrived to fill Stovin's place. Lambert's brigade having landed, he had been sent to it as A.A.G. He expected Juana would remember Lambert at Toulouse: a gentlemanlike, amiable fellow, very much a Guardsman. Harry had known, twenty-five minutes before the fall of Pakenham, what the end must be. '*I said, in twenty-five minutes, General, you will command the army. Sir Edward will be wounded and incapable or killed. The troops do not get on a step. He will be at the head of the first brigade he comes to.*'

That was what had happened. Pakenham had fallen, the attack had failed. Never since Buenos Ayres, wrote Harry, had he witnessed a reverse: that was what made it doubly hard to bear. He was so busy that Juana must forgive him for writing only a short letter. In spite of his detestable scrawl, Lambert had made him Military Secretary; he had been sent with a flag of truce to General Jackson; he would be going again, to propose an exchange of prisoners. Wretched work, but thank God he had found a most liberal, clear-minded man to deal with in Jackson's Military Secretary, Lushington! He could give Juana no more news, except that the army would shortly re-embark. She would read the rest in Lambert's dispatch.

2

Hardly had England had time to recover from the news of the reverse in America than she was stunned by a far more shocking event. On February 26th, Napoleon Bonaparte escaped from the island of Elba.

Consternation reigned in London; it spread swiftly over the country, and nothing was anywhere talked of but the Ogre's landing in the south of France. Pessimists prophesied that with half the army in America, and Wellington far away with the Congress in Vienna, there would be no stopping Napoleon. He would overrun France, and Europe too, very likely; there would be no more peace for anyone.

John Smith looked grave, and shook his head, but Juana said: 'Oh, *basta*! The Duke will come back from the Congress; yes, and Enrique will come back from America, because you know it is certain now that the peace will be signed; and again we shall be on the march, with all our friends! Oh, I am happy, I am happy, I am happy!'

'How can you talk so?' Mary exclaimed.

'My little tent – the columns marching – West leading Enrique's spare horse – the camp fires – Oh, you do not know, you cannot understand how much I want it all again!'

'Well!' Mary said. 'To wish to plunge Europe into war again, for any consideration in the world, is something I hope I may never understand!'

'You know nothing about the matter!' said Charles. 'I know what you mean, Jenny, and if anyone tries to stop my joining now, I'll – I'll –'

'Well, and what will you do?' enquired John, with rather a melancholy smile.

'Oh, sir, I am persuaded you cannot be so unfeeling as to stand in my way! It's all I care about, to be a soldier, like Harry and Tom! You must let me go!'

'Yes,' said John, sighing. 'I suppose I must.'

For the next month, the newspapers reported day by day Napoleon's leisurely progress towards Paris. When Marshal Ney went over to him, there were gloomy headshakes, and a great deal of talk about treachery. On March 20th, Napoleon entered Paris, Louis XVIII having packed up his court in a hurry and fled over the border to Ghent. The British army began to collect in Belgium still under the generalship of the young Prince of Orange: a circumstance which made Juana most indignant. She said it was a very good thing he had dear John Colborne to guide him, for he knew nothing more about war than how to behave as Wellington's A.D.C.

It might have been expected that with Napoleon in power again the English visitors in Brussels would have gone home, but hardly any of them did so. Far otherwise, in fact: it was said that all the packets were crowded with rich idlers on their way to Belgium, all anxious to see something of the brewing war.

With the news of the signing of the peace treaty with America, Juana every day expected Harry to arrive in England. Nothing, however, was heard of him, and when she reflected that between the assault on New Orleans and the signing of the treaty there had very likely been more fighting in America, she began to dread hearing that he had been killed. The prolonged silence affected her nerves so badly that it was noticed that any sudden noise would make her start violently, while a knock on the front-door drove the colour from her cheeks, and brought on one of her distressing fits of breathlessness. Anna told Eleanor that she wondered how such a nervous little thing could ever have braved the dangers of campaigning.

March, a month of alarums and excursions, passed without news from Harry. It passed also without bringing tidings of the Duke of Wellington's return from Vienna. Really, everyone said, he ought to be with the army! No one could feel the least degree of safety while he was absent. Just supposing Napoleon were to strike at our forces while he was still at that stupid Congress! It was nonsense to say that Napoleon was not ready to strike: he was probably planning some shattering *coup*, while the Allies continued to dilly-dally, and to haggle over subsidies.

Nothing had ever been so ill-managed from start to finish! What with Wellington in Vienna, and many of his Peninsular veterans in America, it would be wonderful if Napoleon did not succeed in winning back everything he had lost.

On April 5th, however, the Duke arrived in Brussels, and even confirmed pessimists began to feel that all was not yet lost. But Harry's Uncle Davie said gloomily that depend upon it, we should make wretched work of *this* campaign, for he had heard from a friend of his, who had had it from a man who had been in Belgium, that our army there was composed for the most part of quite raw troops. Moreover, the Dutch–Belgian soldiers were said to be a disaffected lot, and Blücher's Prussians were at logger-heads with them already.

'All will go well now that the Duke is with the army,' said Juana confidently.

'Ah, my dear, I wish you may be right!' said Uncle Davie, shaking his head. 'But everything has been so bungled! I said from the start they should never have let Bonaparte go to Elba; and I always knew how this wretched American war would end! It won't surprise *me*, if we learn of a fresh disaster from that quarter!'

'Oh, do not say so!' Juana exclaimed.

'I think it very ominous, very ominous *indeed*,' said Uncle Davie, ignoring frantic signs made to him by his nieces, 'that nothing has been heard of Lambert since that last dispatch that told of the embarkation of the troops after the disaster at New Orleans. Here we are, in the middle of April, and still Harry has not come home! Mark my words, there is something behind which we don't know about!'

'Do you think that indeed?' Juana said, fixing her eyes upon his face.

'I hope I am not lacking in the proper respect which I owe

to my uncle,' said Betsy roundly, 'but I declare I never heard such nonsense in my life. If you take *my* advice, Jenny, you will not pay the least attention!'

But Uncle Davie's tactless words had only expressed the fear which Juana carried everywhere with her; and although she forced herself to smile at Betsy, it was plain that to do so was an effort.

The sisters became quite worried over her loss of colour, and of spirits, and of appetite. Nothing seemed to do her any good! Nothing, John Smith said, appealed to by his daughters to prescribe for poor Jenny, would do her any good until Harry came back to her. 'Such devotion,' said Eleanor, with a deep sigh, 'is a lesson to us all! Do you know, papa, when she goes with us to Church, and I see her gazing before her, with *such* a look in her eyes, and her hands clasped so tightly over her heart, it affects me so that I am sure I do not know how I keep from bursting into tears!'

Juana went with the sisters to Church every Sunday, and afterwards for a sedate walk with them. On a Sunday, late in April, the sun was so bright, and the sky so clear, that even prudent Mary thought they might venture a little farther than usual without running any risk of being caught in a shower of rain. They were strolling along, with William and Sam to bear them company, when they suddenly perceived the gardener's boy, a new servant, running towards them, and waving to attract their attention.

They hastened their steps to meet him, wondering what he could want, and were astonished to find that he seemed to be labouring under a strong sense of excitement. William asked him rather sharply if anything were amiss, and got the mysterious reply that he did not know, only that Master desired the Misses Smith to return directly to the house.

'Good God, is my father ill?' cried Eleanor.

No, Master was very well, but there was a strange gentleman arrived at the Falcon Inn in a post-chaise-and-four, who had sent for him. 'And Master said as I must go to find the young ladies and to tell them quietly as how he wanted them to come home at once.'

'Oh!' said Anna thoughtlessly. 'Can it be that someone has brought us news of Harry?'

Juana gave a queer little sigh, and fainted.

'Anna, how could you?' exclaimed Eleanor, dropping down on to her knees beside Juana.

Capable Betsy was already slapping Juana's death-like cheeks, and while the two brothers, quite distracted, were still trying to think where they could most quickly procure some water, she recovered consciousness.

'*Mi Enrique! Está muerto! El no vendrà nunca, nunca!*'

'Dearest Jenny! Dearest sister! See, it is your own Eleanor!'

'Oh!' Juana pressed a hand to her head. 'I am sorry – *un acto de locura!* – but someone said – oh, how dreadful of me to behave so! Please give me your arm, for I am quite well, I assure you! We must go home instantly!'

'Are you sure you are able to walk?' Mary asked. 'Sam can run back and fetch the carriage, you know.'

'No, no, I cannot wait! Someone has come with news of Enrique!'

Since the others were almost as anxious as she to reach home, they did not try to dissuade her, but set off at once for St Mary's Street. When the house came in sight, Juana let go of William's arm, and ran ahead. The gate was standing open; as Juana reached it, a figure there was no mistaking came out of the house. '*Mi esposo, mi esposo!*' sobbed Juana, and flung herself into Harry's arms.

3

He had meant it all for the best, of course. So afraid had he been of startling Juana, that he had stopped his chaise at the Falcon, and had sent privately to call his father to him. How could he have foreseen that that stupid lout of a boy would blurt out his message in such a way?

'Oh!' said Eleanor playfully, 'I do not know which was the greater goose, you or Papa! As though it could hurt Juana to see you, whom she has been daily, nay, hourly, expecting! Such a fright as you gave us all! We have been in a fever of anxiety, fearing you might be dead, or badly wounded!'

'*This* little varmint should have known better at least!' Harry said, holding Juana tightly in the crook of his arm. 'Nothing ever hurts me!'

'But you have been so long in coming!'

'By Jupiter, I should think we have! You can blame Admiral Cochrane! No proper provisions on the ships – we had to put in at Havana for a full week, to take stores aboard! – and to crown all, he delayed communicating the news of the peace to Lambert! Oh, how I have cursed the Admirals! All of them but Malcolm, that is! But never mind! Here we are, in time for a last brush with Boney! Do you know, we hadn't a notion of what had been happening in France until the *Brazen* was nearing the Bristol Channel? We had just run into the usual thick weather when we shot past a merchant-man. "Where are you from?" roars our Captain. "Portsmouth." – "Any news?" – "No, none." Would you believe it, the ship was almost out of sight when we heard someone shout from her: "Ho! Bonaparter's back again on the throne of France!" Such a hurrah as I set up! "I'll be a Lieutenant-Colonel yet before the year's out!" I said.

Lambert could not bring himself to believe it! I never knew a fellow with such faith in the Government! It wasn't until we got to Spithead that he could be convinced; but the sight of all the bustle there, and the men-of-war, was enough even for him.'

'When did you anchor?' John asked.

'Yesterday. Sir John and I started for London in a chaise at night, but got only as far as Guildford. I soon found that his rate of progression would not do, so I asked his leave to set off home. He didn't know my romantic story till then! When I told him about you, *hija*, I never saw his affectionate heart so angry before – for he has treated me like his own son. He positively scolded me, told me he would report our arrival, bade me write to him, so that he might know my address, and packed me off straightway! So West and I got a chaise, reached London this morning, and drove straight to Panton Square. Madame assured me you were well, *querida*, and had quite lately ordered a new riding-habit. So first I got a post-chaise, and then I ran to Week's in the Haymarket, for I was not going to come home empty-handed again! See what I've brought you!'

Improvident Harry! He had bought a heavy gold chain for his Juana, and a dressing-case, fit, Anna declared, for a duchess! He had a cartload of Spanish books for her, too, from Havana; and West had got a couple of the little curly white dogs they bred there, and had brought them home especially for Missus! 'Not much in my line,' said Harry indulgently.

He had much to tell about his last weeks in America: how he had been sent to demand the surrender of Fort Bowyer; how the army, pending the ratification of peace, had been disembarked on Isle Dauphine, at the entrance of Mobile Bay, and what difficulties they had had there in getting fresh provisions; how they could bake no bread, for want of ovens, until Harry, with Admiral Malcolm's ready help, had made mortar for ovens by burning oyster shells, and had surprised the Generals by producing a column of hot loaves and rolls for breakfast; how West had run into Harry's tent one morning, and had exclaimed: 'Oh, sir, thank the Lord you're alive! A *navigator* has been going round and round your tent all night! Here's a regular road about it!' He had meant an alligator, of course: there were a great many on the island; the soldiers used to eat the young ones, which tasted rather like coarsely-fed pork. The sandflies had been appalling; Harry, who hated tobacco, had given his orderly as much as he could smoke, and had bade him sit under the table in his tent, while he wrote his reports. 'If you please, sir,' had said the orderly, a Peninsular veteran, poking his head out with a very knowing look, 'this is drier work than in front of Salamanca, where water wasn't to be had and what's more, no grog neither.' So Harry had sent West for rum and water, and the orderly had said contentedly, 'Now, your honour, if you can write as long as I can smoke, you'll write the history of the world, and I'll kill all the midges.'

When the ratification of the treaty arrived, Lambert, and Harry, and Baynes, the A.D.C., had embarked on the *Brazen* sloop-of-war, and had sailed for Havana. They were entertained there by a Mr Drake, a wealthy merchant who had married a Spaniard. But all Harry's spare time had been spent in the Governor's house, for the Governor had a daughter so like Juana that Harry could hardly tear himself away from her.

'Yes! You need not tell me that!' said Juana. 'You are altogether abominable, *mi querido! Muy perfido!*'

At Havana, Harry had met Woodville, the cigar manufacturer, a most extraordinary man, who had told Lambert that he had a sight to show which few men could boast of. He had put his fingers in his mouth, and had whistled up forty-one children, of a variety of shades of colour, and not one above thirteen years of age. 'Report says, Sir John, and I believe it,' he had told Lambert, 'that they are every one of them my children.'

'I thought Stirling and I – Stirling is the *Brazen's* captain, you know, – would have died of laughing! For dear Sir John, one of the most moral men in the world, said in the mildest way: "A very large family indeed, Mr Woodville."'

Then, in the gulf of Florida, the *Brazen* had encountered the most terrific gale, and had lain-to for forty-eight hours. At one time, Harry had wondered whether he would ever see his Juana again, but there was never a captain like Stirling, and here he was, after all, never better in his life, and agog to join the army in Belgium.

'Oh, to be under old Hookey again!' he said.

'And me, Enrique? And me?' Juana demanded, shaking his arm.

'Of course you, my darling! I told Lambert I should bring you, and he desired his kind compliments, and bade me tell you that he was looking forward to meeting my little Spanish heroine. I did not tell him what a varmint you are, *hija*!'

'Oh, Harry, you will not take Juana to Belgium with you?' cried Mary.

'Oh, won't I, by Jupiter!' said Harry. 'No more separations for me, I thank you!'

4

It was not many days before Harry heard from Lambert that he was to be employed with the army in Belgium, and that Harry had better be prepared to join him at a few hours' notice. He would go as Major of Brigade again, a situation which suited him very well. The sisters shed tears, but Juana and Harry danced a fandango, in such wild spirits that sighs and tears were felt to be out of place. The house in St Mary's Street was transformed suddenly into something very like a military depôt; and Anna, seeing tents overhauled, canteens restocked, riding-habits, boots, and boat-cloaks spread out for inspection, was so envious of Juana that she could scarcely bring herself to face her own humdrum future.

The most urgent need was for horses. Harry pronounced both Tiny and his own mare too old for further military service, and went off to Newmarket, with Juana and his father, to procure a stud. He bought two good horses there, two more in Whittlesey, and, from his brother Stona, a beautiful mare of his father's breeding, for Juana. They called her The Brass Mare, and a fine, strong creature she was: a perfect lady's mount – provided that the lady was a perfect rider.

Betsy declared that Harry's promotion to the rank of Major had quite gone to his head. She said he would very soon be ruined, for besides the bâtman he would have as soon as he joined the army, he was taking West, a young groom to look after Juana's horse, and a lady's maid. How, she demanded, did he mean to transport himself, his wife, his brother Charles, three servants, five horses, and a pug-dog to Ostend?

'Oh, I shall contrive somehow!' said Harry carelessly.

Charles, a trifle self-conscious in a brand-new Rifleman's uniform, was going to accompany Harry. He hoped he would be given a chance to distinguish himself in the coming campaign, because within one hour of putting on his Volunteer-jacket, he had only one ambition: to exchange his shoulder-straps for a pair of Rifle-wings.

Hardly had all the preparations been completed, and the sisters dissuaded from pressing on Juana all manner of comforts which they could as well have carried, said Harry, as the parish Church, than another letter arrived from Sir John Lambert. Sir

John was starting for Ghent immediately, and recommended Harry to proceed via Harwich for Ostend to join him.

West and Jenkins were sent off at once to Harwich with the horses, Harry arranging to follow with his wife and brother by post-chaise. On their last day at home, he and Juana went riding with John and the sisters, and Harry very nearly put an end to his career by taking a last jump on his old mare. She fell with him, pinning his leg to the ground under her shoulder. For one dreadful minute, the rest of the party expected to see Harry either dead or crippled. No such thing! He was not hurt, and as soon as he found he could not drag his leg out, he passed his hand down till he got a short hold of the curb-rein, gave the mare such a snatch that she made a convulsive effort to rise, and he was able to draw his leg out. He staggered up, bruised, shaken, and faint, but with no bones broken. 'Good God!' he said, with an unsteady laugh, 'there was nearly an end to my Brigade-Majorship that time!'

He was not a penny the worse for the accident next moring he did not even seem to be very stiff, which was the least, his father said, he deserved to be. At three in the morning, the post-chaise was at the door, and all the misery of parting had to be faced. Poor John, sending three of his sons to the war, was dreadfully upset. 'Napoleon and Wellington will meet; there will be a battle of a kind never heard of before. I shall not see you all again,' he said mournfully. All the sisters showed red eyes, and clutched damp handkerchiefs. Juana was kissed again and again; Harry was bidden to take the greatest care of her; a basket of refreshments for the journey was handed into the chaise; Matty, Juana's country-bred maid, climbed in after it, clutching an armful of cloaks and parcels; and at last they were off.

They reached Harwich in the afternoon, and went at once to the Black Bull, where Harry had stayed years before when he had embarked with Moore for Gothenburg. Mr Briton, the landlord, remembered him at once, but said rather dampingly that unless he freighted a craft he had no chance of embarking from Harwich. Every packet was full to overflowing, every ship of any tonnage at all had been commandeered by the Government for the transport of troops.

Charles was much cast-down by this intelligence, but Harry, always at his energetic best when there were difficulties to be overcome, at once set about finding a suitable craft. He got wind of a sloop of a few tons' burden, and next day, after long and noisy bargaining, came to terms with the skipper, who, with one boy, formed the entire crew of the vessel. Careful measurement satisfied Harry that there would be just room enough for the horses, with a little hole left over, aft, for himself, his wife, and his brother to crowd into. Charles, inspecting the ship in dismay, blurted out: 'This will never do for Jenny!'

'Not do for me?' said Juana, coming out of the tiny cabin on to the deck. 'Why not?'

'It's so dingy! There is no room for a lady!'

'*Basta!* I am not a lady, but, on the contrary, a good soldier. When do we sail on this dear little boat, Enrique?'

That was the trouble: they could not sail until the wind was fair on account of the horses, and, by ill-luck, a spell of foul weather had set in.

It kept them kicking their heels in Harwich for a fortnight, but at last it wore itself out, the horses and all the baggage were got aboard, and they set sail on an afternoon of sunshine.

A gentle breeze carried them over to Ostend in twenty-four hours. They had to land the horses there by slinging them, and lowering them into the sea to swim ashore. When the Brass Mare was in the slings, she saw the land, and neighed loudly, an omen of success, Juana declared.

They stayed for three days in Ostend, putting up at the great inn there, which was teeming with visitors, both civil and military. Harry soon found an English horse-dealer, and bought a couple of good mules and a Flemish pony from him, for the baggage. They met several acquaintances in Ostend, and learned that the 1st battalion of the Rifles was at Brussels, and the whole army concentrated behind the frontier, in the closest touch with the Prussians.

When they reached Ghent, they found that Sir John had arrived there only a day before them. Sir John received Juana in the kindest way, and soon began to treat her as though she had been his daughter. His brigade consisted of four old Peninsular regiments: the 4th, 27th, and 40th, and the 81st, which was employed on garrison duty at Brussels. He told Harry that they must be ready to take the field at an instant's warning.

'No trouble about that!' said Harry.

'Not for my brigade,' Sir John agreed, 'but I can tell you this, my boy: the Duke has no such army here as we have been accustomed to. The only way he can make anything of it is to scatter the old troops amongst the raw battalions. I've learned already that some of the Generals are pretty sore at having their old numbers taken from them. Alten has the new 3rd division; Picton gets the 5th; Colville has the 4th. What's left of you Light Bobs are spread amongst the rest. Colborne is with the 52nd in Clinton's 2nd division – Adam's brigade – and so are your 2nd and 3rd battalions. Barnard, with the 1st battalion, is in Picton's division, under Kempt. Then there's Lord Uxbridge commanding the cavalry instead of Cotton: everything seems topsy-turvy to us old stagers.'

The brigade continued to be stationed at Ghent, but as the French King's court was established there, it was quite a centre of activity, and was very often visited, not only by Wellington, and the other great men in the army, but by any officer who could get leave, and had a fancy to visit Ghent instead of Brussels. Tom Smith, who was stationed near Ath, came to pay a flying visit to Harry. He laughed when he heard that Charlie had got himself into the regiment as a Volunteer, but wished that he had been in his battalion. Charlie had gone off to join the 1st battalion in Brussels, where there was no doubt that Harry's friends would make him welcome.

The Smiths had a very good billet in Ghent, and as soon as their particular cronies heard of their arival, they received so many visits that it seemed as though they had come to Belgium to enjoy a social round rather than to take part in an arduous campaign. But Charlie Gore, who had once given a ball in Sanguessa, after Vittoria, and who was still Kempt's A.D.C., told them that they had missed all the best of the fun. 'Nothing but parties and balls and picnics, I give you my word!' he declared. 'We don't go so far afield now. Old Hookey don't like it. There's a good deal of movement on the frontier. They say Boney's still in Paris, though. By Jove, Harry, you are in luck to have got home from America in time for this affair!'

That was the opinion held by everyone: to be out of this campaign would be the greatest piece of ill-luck imaginable. But Kincaid, riding to Ghent from Brussels, said that they wanted Harry back with them as Brigade-Major.

'Hi, you long, lanky devil, what do you mean by that?' demanded Charlie Eeles indignantly. 'Aren't I good enough for you?'

'You do your best, little man,' said Kincaid, with odious patronage. 'You certainly aren't as noisy, which I admit is an advantage.'

'No fighting in my expensive billet!' Harry called out. 'I'd rather be with Lambert than in old Picton's division. It's too melancholy to see *The* Division broken up like this! How do you go on with the other fellows in your brigade? Whom have you got?'

'The Slashers, the 32nd, and the Cameron Highlanders: couldn't be better!' replied Eeles.

Kincaid sighed. 'We don't mix with 'em much,' he said. 'Speaking for myself, I miss our old friends the Caçadores. They do say that old Douro tried to get 'em sent back to us.'

'Never mind! We've always got the Dutch-Belgians,' said Eeles unctuously.

'What are the Prussians like?' Harry asked.

'Don't know: don't see anything of 'em. I suppose you know we've lost the Lion d'Or, Harry?'

'Nothing to grumble about in that,' replied Harry. 'I never thought so much of Cotton. If we've got Uxbridge, we've got a damned good man: we knew him when he was with Moore.'

'But tell me!' interrupted Juana. 'Where is dear Charlie Beckwith?'

'Oh, still on the Q.M.G. staff! Hasn't he been to see you? The fact of the matter is, they're devilish busy in the Q.M.G.'s office. That's what makes us think we shall soon be on the move. What's it like, being quartered in Ghent? Do you see much of the French troops? Are they any good?'

'Lord, no!' said Harry. 'Never saw such a set of fellows in my life! The King's impressive enough, but he can't set eyes on one of us without saying how delighted he is to see us, and how much he is indebted to our nation. He's told me so twice.'

'Listen to this!' said Kincaid admiringly. 'Court circles and all! Just fancy our Major Smith!'

'Yes, the King leaned on Enrique's shoulder!' said Juana.

'I *thought* he seemed even more pleased with himself than usual, didn't you, Charlie?'

'Yes, but I put it down to his promotion,' Eeles replied promptly.

'Oh, Charlie, no! Johnny, how could you say such a thing?' cried Juana, quite distressed.

'Don't let them roast you, *hija*!' Harry said, grinning.

5

Harry used to wait on Sir John Lambert every morning after breakfast for orders, while in Ghent. There were always plenty of orders, for Sir John, a Guardsman, held parade after parade, and was very fussy over the details of guard-mounting, sentry-duty, and correct garrison-procedure. Harry laughed, but admitted that the brigade was in splendid trim.

He was with Sir John one morning when a voice was heard calling for him in stentorian tones in the passage. 'Lambert! Lambert! Hallo there, where the devil's the door?'

'Who in heaven's name can that be? Go and see, Harry!' said Lambert.

Harry went, and walked, to his surprise, straight into Admiral Malcolm, who hailed him in a genial bellow, and wanted to know where Lambert had stowed himself. 'The house is as dark as a sheer hulk!' he declared, rolling in, and seizing Sir John by the hand. 'Come, bear a hand, and get me some breakfast, Harry! No regular hours on shore, as in the *Royal Oak*!'

Where had he sprung from? Oh, he had brought over some troops from America, including the 27th regiment of Lambert's own brigade, and had been appointed to the command of the coast. He didn't see why the army should have all the fun; from what he could discover from his friend Wellington a rare time they had been having! Nothing but balls and picnics!

But the army was not long to be left in peace to enjoy these festivities. Orders reached Lambert from De Lancey, the Quartermaster-General, on the night of the 15th June, and one hour later, at dawn, the brigade, assembling at the alarm-posts, marched out of Ghent along the road to Brussels.

By the afternoon they had reached Assche, and the noise of continuous firing from the south put the veterans on their toes with eagerness.

'It is like old times!' Juana said. She slid off the Brass Mare's back, her habit powdered with dust, but her eyes like stars. 'Any orders, *mi amigo?*'

'No, General, none! We bivouac,' responded Harry promptly.

'*Muy bien!*' she said, stripping off her gloves.

Lambert was afraid she must be tired, and said solicitously that he hoped the march had not been too much for her, which made Harry burst out laughing. 'What, that little way, sir? You don't know her!'

'No, indeed!' said Juana, smiling up into Lambert's face of kindly concern. '*I* marched with the division from Lecumberri to the top of Santa Cruz, in the Pyrenees! And I did not fall out! *Absolutamente no!*'

'Well, you are a wonderful woman,' said Lambert. 'Will you give me the pleasure of dining with me now?'

'Yes, please!' said Juana. 'I am very hungry, and you have a very good cook!'

No certain news reached the brigade that night, but the noise of the firing, which had been incessant all day, died down with the coming of darkness. It was evident that a sharp engagement had taken place somewhere to the south, but they did not learn where precisely until the following day, when they reached Brussels. They halted in the town, and found everything in a state of the greatest confusion, droves of civilians trying to escape to Antwerp by chaise, on horseback, by canal-barge, even on foot. Rumours were flying about: it was said that there had been a battle fought at Quatre-Bras on the 16th; that Napoleon had taken the Duke by surprise, marching to the frontier from Paris with the Imperial Guard, with incredible celerity; that the Prussians had suffered a heavy defeat somewhere near Quatre-Bras, and were in full retreat; that the French would be in Brussels at any moment. A dramatic Belgian described the march of the British troops out of Brussels all through the small hours of the previous day. They had formed up in the market-place, regiment after regiment: Brussels had never before witnessed such a scene. There had been a grand ball given by the Duchess of Richmond: all the Generals had been present, even the Duke himself, and the Prince of Orange, commanding the 1st Corps. When the news had come of the Prussians' retreat from Charleroi, young officers, in all the splendour of mess-jackets and white gloves, had ridden back to join their various regiments, already on the march through the placid Flemish countryside. The Duke had ridden out of Brussels in the morning, saying, with his loud laugh, that very likely Blücher would have finished the business by that time, and he would be back in Brussels to dinner.

But he had not come back, and the aspect the town had worn all day was, the Belgians assured Harry, *triste* beyond compare! After teeming for so long with English and Scottish soldiers, and with lovely ladies tripping along the streets in ravishing toilettes to pay morning calls, it was strange indeed, and melancholy, to see the town quite deserted by the usual frivolous crowd. People had gone to the ramparts, and a good many had fled to Antwerp. Then, in the night, a dismal cortège had borne the poor Duke of Brunswick's body into Brussels: as though one had not been gloomy enough before!

'Brunswick killed?' Harry exclaimed. 'That ought to make the Death-or-Glory boys killing-mad!'

Fresh orders arrived from the Quartermaster-General, directing Lambert to move on Quatre-Bras. In the afternoon, they marched out of Brussels by the Namur gate, along the chaussée leading south through the Forest of Soignies to Charleroi. All the baggage was left in the market-place, and, with it, Juana's two servants.

The march south was a little disturbing. The chaussée was in a state of such wild confusion that progress, at all times difficult, became sometimes impossible. Flemish carts, baggage-waggons, wounded men, and deserters were all retreating in such scandalous disorder that the Peninsular veterans stared with shocked, incredulous eyes. Here and there a cart would be found in the road with a wheel off, blocking the way; horses who had fallen and broken their knees on the pavé had been shot, and left to stiffen where they lay; once a squadron of some foreign cavalry galloped by, shouting that the French were on their heels.

At about half-past two, the day, which had been brilliant, suddenly clouded over. Inky clouds rolled up, and almost before Juana had time to unclasp her boat-cloak from the saddle, the most terrific thunderstorm broke over their heads. Great splinters of lightning shot through the black clouds; the thunder crashed deafeningly, and within a few minutes the rain began to fall in torrents. 'It is worse than that night before Salamanca!' Juana screamed to West, above the appalling racket. 'Poor Vitty is so afraid!'

The storm seemed to heighten the confusion on the road, for some of the baggage-horses moving towards Brussels took fright, and careered about in a state of snorting terror. An orderly came riding along, plastered with mud. He brought yet another dispatch from De Lancey, this time directing Lambert to halt his brigade at the village of Epinay, short of the great forest. Questioned, he said that the army was in retreat from Quatre-Bras upon Waterloo; he did not think there had been any fighting that morning, but the previous day's losses had been shocking.

This was very bad news, but, a few minutes later, riding ahead to clear the road, Harry encountered a small party of wounded Highlanders, making their painful way to Brussels. They said yes, it had been a hard day's fighting at Quatre-Bras; the Highland brigade had been fair cut to pieces, and Kempt's too; but as for defeat, it was no such thing! The French had not gained an inch of ground.

'Depend upon it, the Duke has been forced to retreat to maintain his communications with the Prussians,' said Lambert. 'We'll push on, if you please.'

There was not much accommodation to be had at Epinay, but Harry put his General and his wife into a tolerable cottage, and left them there while he went off to see the brigade bivouacked for the night. More foreign troops came galloping from the front, spreading a story that the enemy cavalry was actually threatening the Duke's communication with Brussels; bugles began to blow; the soldiers hastily stowed away the rations they had not had time to eat, and ran to the alarm-posts in front of the village.

Harry rode back to Lambert's headquarters, and found him sitting quietly down to dinner with Juana and his A.D.C.

'Well, Smith, what's all the commotion?'

'Some Belgian troops who have just passed through the village, Sir John, say that the enemy's cavalry are threatening the Duke's communication lines.'

'Oh, do they?' said Lambert. 'A pretty set of fellows! Let the troops dismiss: it's all nonsense! Depend upon it, there is not a

French soldier in the rear of his Grace! Sit down to dinner! My butler bought a fine turbot in Brussels, and we are just about to eat it.'

'Save some for me, sir. I'll go and reconnoitre a little.'

'If that husband of yours doesn't wear himself out before he's thirty, he'll make a very fine General one of these days,' remarked Lambert, as the door shut behind Harry. 'I never knew such an energetic fellow in my life! Are you sure that habit of yours is quite dry, my dear?'

It was some time before Harry returned. He reported that he had ridden through the forest to the village of Waterloo, just beyond it, and had found a long line of baggage there, retreating in a leisurely fashion that made it certain that the alarm had been false. He was plastered with dirt, and he said that the road was in a deplorable condition, and all the surrounding country deep in mud. As far as he had been able to ascertain from the various conflicting stories he had listened to, the army was retiring to a position in front of the village of Mont St Jean, a little to the south of Waterloo, on the Charleroi chaussée. It seemed to be true enough that the Prussians had suffered a heavy defeat at Ligny, on the previous day, and had fallen back on Wavre, eighteen miles to the rear; but everyone he had spoken to was agreed that the action at Quatre-Bras had ended in the Duke's favour.

'Ha!' said Lambert. 'That's not the real thing. We shall see a major engagement tomorrow.'

'If the weather's anything to go by, we shall,' agreed Harry. 'We're in for a true Wellington-night.'

6

The rain continued all night, and a ceaseless rumble of baggage-waggons passing through the village towards Brussels made sleep almost impossible. In the small hours, orders came for the brigade to move up to Mont St Jean. The troops assembled at the alarm-posts at dawn, and were about to move on when Sir George Scovell, A.Q.M.G. at headquarters, came up, saying that he had been sent by the Duke to see that the rear was clear.

'Clear, my God!' he exclaimed. 'It's choked all the way to the front, and here's his lordship expecting to be attacked immediately! Your brigade must clear the road before you move on, Smith.'

'The devil it must! Well, I can tell you this, Scovell, our fellows are so on fire to get up to the front they'll clear the road quicker than any magican could! But how is it going?'

'Oh, we licked Ney, and Boney licked Blücher, and the result is that the Duke has drawn the army up where he always meant to. If the Prussians come up, there'll be an end to Boney; if they don't, may the Lord help us! Picton's holding the left wing, but he's devilish weak. His losses at Quatre-Bras were shocking, you know. I fancy you'll be ordered up to support him, if Blücher can't get there in time.'

Harry went off to report the order to clear the road to Lambert. He found Juana just finishing a very early breakfast, and said abruptly: 'I'm sending you back to Brussels with West.'

Her face fell ludicrously. 'Oh, Enrique, no!'

'Yes, don't argue! I've just seen Scovell, and it's as plain as a pikestaff that we're in for a stiff fight. You must stay with the baggage: God knows what the end is going to be!'

'The Duke has *never* lost a battle, Enrique!'

'No, and by Jupiter he won't to-day! But you'll stay with the baggage, for all that. It's an order, *querida!*'

She swallowed a lump in her throat. '*Muy bien.* But I think you do not know the agony of waiting in the rear, out of reach, not knowing what may have become of you!'

'Yes, my darling, I do know, but I dare not let you stay here. If we were forced to fall back suddenly, you might even be taken prisoner. Come! you are too good a soldier to question your orders!'

She nodded. 'It is true. I will go.'

'Kiss me then – *un beso de despedida*!'

She clung to him, passionately embracing him. 'Enrique, *mi querido, mi esposo!*'

'Till we meet again!' he said, holding her tightly.

'Enrique, if – if we do not meet again, I want to tell you how happy I have been, how *very* happy!'

'And I, my soul! But what is this nonsense? *Viva Enrique!*'

'I am afraid, more afraid than ever before! This time it is Napoleon *himself*! Oh, if I could only go with you, stay beside you, share it all with you!'

'Very much in the way you'd be, *hija*, I assure you! One last kiss!'

'Don't say that!' she cried sharply. 'It is a bad omen!'

But he only laughed, and told her not to be a goose.

West soon had the Brass Mare saddled; he put Juana into the saddle, and handed Vitty up to her; and in a few minutes they had started on their ride back to Brussels. It took them some time to reach the town, and when they got there they found Juana's own groom standing guard over her baggage in the market-place, while Matty sat upon her bundle, from time to time wiping her eyes with the corner of her shawl. She had been bewailing her lot to Jenkins, and regretting that she had ever been fool enough to leave dear, safe Whittlesey, but she quite cheered up when she saw Juana and began to think that now, surely, she would be able to go into a house, instead of sitting in the open. But just as Juana rode into Brussels, an order came for the whole baggage-train to evacuate the town, and move on the road towards Antwerp. Since Harry had ordered her to remain with the baggage-train, she felt obliged to accompany it, but it was with a very heavy heart that she left Brussels.

The movement of the train of carts and sumpters was necessarily slow; it was a long time before it had all passed out of the northern gate, and when the Canal, some miles beyond Brussels, was at last crossed, it was going on for four o'clock in the afternoon. No firing was heard in the rear, a circumstance which made Juana feel lighter-hearted, until she overheard one of the mule-drivers remarking that the wind was in the wrong quarter to carry any sound from the front to Brussels.

The train halted at a village on the other side of the Canal; Juana and Matty went into a small inn, while West, leaving Jenkins to mind the horses, tried to induce the innkeeper, who seemed quite distracted, to prepare some kind of a meal for his mistress. He had just seen a pan of bacon and eggs put on the stove, when the alarm was sounded. He ran out, to be met by the intelligence that the French had carried the day, and were upon them. How much truth there was in the story he had no opportunity of ascertaining, for the whole village was instantly plunged into confusion. His master's orders had been definite; he shouted to Juana to come downstairs quickly, and ran to bring the Brass Mare to the door of the inn.

'But what has happened?' Juana cried.

'I don't know, missus, but they do say as the French are coming. There's no time to be lost: you must go to Antwerp at once. Ah, stand, will you?'

The last sentence was addressed to the Brass Mare, who had taken fright at all the commotion round her, and was plunging and rearing in some alarm. It was as much as West could do to toss Juana into the saddle. She managed to reach it at last, and to settle herself securely. 'Vitty, West! Give me Vitty!' she commanded patting the mare's neck soothingly.

Still retaining his grasp on the bridle, above the bit, West bent, lifted Vitty by the scruff of her fat little neck, and put her into Juana's lap. Thinking that he was holding the mare, Juana let the rein fall for a moment, while she disposed the pug more safely. At the same instant, West let go of the bridle. The Brass Mare, finding herself held only on a light snaffle, leaped forward, nearly unseating Juana, and bolted down the road at full stretch.

The snaffle was almost useless, for no amount of pulling on it had any effect on the mare. So headlong was the pace, and so hampered was Juana by having poor, frightened Vitty in her lap, that for the first mile or two she had the greatest difficulty in retaining her seat. The heavy rain-storm of the previous day had turned the road into a slough of black mud, with water lying in all the pits and ruts, and it was not long before she was plastered with dirt. Every effort to recover the loose curb-rein failed; the mare bore straight on without the least check, galloping through the small town of Malines with such fury that Juana's heart was in her mouth; and rapidly overhauling on the road every horse-man, or carriage bound for Antwerp. There were plenty of these, the stream of fugitives from Brussels having continued to leave the capital ever since the first sounds of firing had been heard two days before, but Juana had no leisure to observe them with any particularity. She was quite out of breath, but not too much alarmed to reflect that the Brass Mare was exhibiting a staying-power and a turn of speed which made her invaluable as a campaigner.

She had galloped quite a mile beyond Malines before Juana was able to check her. A waggon, lying upset across the road, loomed ahead; Juana tried with all the strength remaining to her to turn the mare, but she would not answer to the snaffle, and bore straight on, charging down upon the waggon. It was far too large an obstacle for any horse to clear, and for a few rather horrible moments it seemed certain to Juana that she was going to be dashed to pieces. The Brass Mare gathered herself for the leap, but as she did so the loose curb-rein caught, and she came to a sudden stop, which threw Juana, still clutching Vitty, forward on to her neck.

Fortunately, the mare was as out of breath as her mistress. Juana managed to get back into the saddle before she could career off again, and to possess herself of the curb-rein. The mare still seemed very much excited, but with the curb held firmly between her fingers Juana felt herself safe. She straightened her habit, tucked away the strands of hair which had been blown from under her hat, and, hearing the sound of horses coming up behind her, looked round. To her dismay, she saw some five or six men, whom she took to be French Dragoons, bearing down upon her. She was so exhausted that she made no attempt to escape, but told Vitty in a despairing way that if she was to be taken prisoner she might as well surrender at once.

However, the first of the horsemen to reach her was her own groom. With remarkable presence of mind, he had seized the second of the horses Harry had bought at Newmarket as soon as he saw the Brass Mare bolting with his mistress, and had made off after her as fast as he could, and without so much as listening to West's commands to him on no account to go off with Master's charger.

'Oh, thank heaven it is you, Jenkins!' said Juana. 'I was afraid those men were French Dragoons!'

'Not they, mum. Deserters, that's what they are!' exclaimed Jenkins scornfully. 'Fair scared out of their wits, the way you'd think they'd be ashamed for anyone to see them! Still, two of 'em's Germans, and one's a Commissary.'

'Oh, a Commissary!' said Juana, with a great deal of contempt. 'If *that* is all – !'

But it was not quite all. Upon the horsemen's drawing abreast of her, she discovered that one of them was an English Hussar officer. She was very much shocked to see him escaping in such a way, but as this was no time for indulging in quite useless demonstrations of disdain, she ranged along beside him, asking in her broken English if there were any danger.

'Danger!' he exclaimed. 'When I left Brussels, the French were in pursuit down the hill!'

'Oh, sir, what shall I do?' Juana cried, appalled by this news.

'Come on to Antwerp with me! I'll take care of you.'

She was too much shocked to reflect that an officer who deserted his regiment in a moment of danger would hardly be likely to prove a very trustworthy escort. He did not show any disposition to pull up; he had not, in fact, drawn rein at all; so, as the Brass Mare seemed to have plenty of life left in her, Juana galloped on beside her new-found acquaintance.

She naturally wanted to know all he could tell her about the battle, but although he seemed willing enough to talk it was evident that he had left the field too early in the day to be able to tell her much. He said that the French were opposed to them in great numbers, and with an overwhelming force of cavalry. The action had begun at eleven o'clock, with such a cannonade as he had never in his life experienced. One of the semi-fortified country houses of the district, called the Château de Hougoumont, which was being held by a detachment of Coldstream Guards, under Colonel MacDonnell, in advance of the extreme right of the line, had immediately been assailed by Reille's division; it must by this time, the Hussar thought, have fallen into the enemy's hands, for it had been set on fire by bursting shells before he had left the field, and it must have been impossible for a single brigade of Guards to have held it in the teeth of the whole of Reille's division. The rest of his narrative was too disjointed to be readily understood. He spoke in a hurried way of huge columns of Frenchmen advancing down the hill like a mighty tide upon the attenuated British line on the reverse slope; he said that a whole brigade of Belgians had broken before them, and had fled to the shelter of the forest; that there was no sign of any Prussian troops coming up in support; that there could be no standing up against the weight of men and of artillery opposed to them. He knew nothing of Lambert's brigade, nor could he tell where the 95th Rifles were placed. He had the impression that he had left all in the most dreadful confusion. She gave a moan of dismay, which reached the ears of the other Englishman in the party, the Commissary, a narrow-faced man, who said roughly: 'You deserve no pity! You may well be fatigued, carrying that dog! Throw it down!'

Juana was not accustomed to being addressed in such a tone by Commissaries, and without the smallest hesitation she rounded on the man, demanding to know how he dared to speak to her with such rudeness. 'Let me tell you that I am not such a coward as to run away, leaving my poor little dog to be lost or killed! If I did that I should indeed deserve no pity! And also I must tell you that to receive the pity of such a person as you would make me sick! It is plain to me that you are not one of the old army, but, on the contrary, nothing but a Johnny Raw, and if the Duke has many such persons with him to-day, I am extremely sorry for him, yes, and for all the veterans who will certainly be betrayed by them!'

The Commissary looked very much taken aback by this outburst, and muttered that he had meant no harm, only it was folly to think of saving a lap-dog when they would very likely all of them be killed before nightfall.

'Oh, do not disturb yourself!' said Juana swiftly. 'There are plenty of real soldiers with the Duke, after all!'

At this, the Commissary flushed darkly, and fell a little behind. Juana, her spirits momentarily restored by this brush, remarked confidentially to the Hussar that she disliked all Commissaries, and thought this one a particularly poor specimen. 'We used to suffer from them a great deal in Spain,' she said. 'They *never* brought up the supplies when they should, and once they even took them by the wrong road, so that we were obliged to eat acorns.'

The Hussar looked round at her wonderingly. 'Were you with the army in Spain, then?'

'Oh, yes! I am Spanish, you know, though married to an Englishman. I made the war with the Light division, from Badajos to Toulouse.'

'A little delicate creature like you!' he said. 'Is it possible?'

'I am not at all delicate, and as for being small, there is nothing in that. My husband is not large, not at all, and everyone says he is the toughest man in the whole division, besides being one of the biggest dare-devils!' The thought of Harry, of what might even now be happening to him, suddenly overcame her. She burst into tears, exclaiming: 'Oh, what shall I do? Perhaps he is dead, or wounded, and I not there!'

'Pray do not distress yourself, ma'am! pray do not! Very likely he will have escaped, and you will see him presently.'

This suggestion had the effect of stopping Juana's tears at once. She said indignantly: 'Escaped! That he will never do, I assure you! My husband is Major of Brigade, and if you were at all acquainted with him, you would know that while a man of ours is not accounted for my husband will not be found out of the saddle!'

He coloured, and turned away his head. After a moment's pause, he said awkwardly: 'I daresay you despise me for having left the field.'

She replied candidly: 'Well, it certainly seems very odd to me.'

'I am aware of how my conduct must appear to you. But there are circumstances – there are those who are dependent on me – but it does not signify talking, after all! There is Antwerp ahead of us.'

In a few more minutes they had entered the town. The Hussar very kindly offered to find a room for Juana in one of the hotels. She gladly accepted his help, but soon found that there was no accommodation to be had anywhere, the town being already full to overflowing with refugees from Brussels. There was nothing for it but to repair to the Hôtel de Ville, and to try to get a billet. The Hussar went in on this errand, leaving Juana outside with Jenkins and the horses. She was splashed from head to foot with mud; her habit was soaked; and she felt pretty certain from the curious glances cast at her by the many passers-by that she must look a perfect figure of fun. She was past caring for that; all her thoughts were fixed on Harry, and because she was quite worn-out and suffering the most torturing anxiety, large tears chased one another down her cheeks.

Suddenly an officer came out of the Hôtel de Ville, and stepped up to her where she sat drooping on the Brass Mare's back. 'Mrs Smith?'

She looked down at him. 'Yes, I am Mrs Smith,' she said brushing her hand across her eyes.

'My name is Peters. You don't know me, but I'm on garrison-duty here. Your servant told me your name. You are in such a terrible plight, and there's no getting you in to any of the hotels: will you let me take you to Colonel Craufurd, the Commandant? His wife and daughters are the kindest people, and would do anything for you, I know!'

It seemed likely that if she refused this offer she would be obliged to bivouac in the street, so Juana thanked Mr Peters, and said she would go with him if she might first take leave of her helpful Hussar-acquaintance. This was soon done, and Mr Peters, bringing up his own horse, led her through several crowded streets to a respectable house not far from the citadel. They were admitted at once by an astonished butler, and received in the salon by a very tall woman, who no sooner set eyes on her muddied, tear-stained visitor than she exclaimed: 'Oh, you poor little thing!' and came quickly forward to take Juana's hand.

'Mrs Smith's husband is Brigade-Major to Sir John Lambert, ma'am,' explained Mr Peters. 'She has ridden all the way from the battlefield, as I understand. I took the liberty of bringing her to you, for there is nowhere –'

'I should think so indeed!' interrupted Mrs Craufurd. 'Never mind talking! Ring the bell, man! My poor child, we must get you out of those wet clothes at once, or you will catch your death of cold!'

'Oh, how kind you are!' Juana stammered: 'I am so ashamed to come into your house in *such* a state! Please forgive! I did not know what else to do.'

'Why, you're a foreigner!' said Mrs Craufurd. 'As for forgiveness – what nonsense, child! But what is all this talk about a husband? You are a baby!'

'Oh, no, no! I am seventeen years old, and I have been married for three years already! Also I am Spanish.'

'Spanish or English, married or single, into a hot bath you go!' said her hostess briskly. 'Yes, I rang, Johnson. Be so good as to take hot water up to my bedchamber. Don't stand staring, man! Bustle about!'

Within half an hour, Juana, stripped of her mud-plastered garments, washed, and enveloped in one of Mrs Craufurd's dresses, which was quite three sizes too large for her, was seated before the fire in the salon, partaking of a comforting bowl of broth, and telling her story in her pretty, hesitant English to an audience composed of Mrs Craufurd and her two tall daughters. They could hardly believe that such a scrap of a girl could have gone through such a series of adventures; the Misses Craufurd plied her with questions, until their mother intervened, saying that it was not fair to plague their guest so.

No news came from the front that evening, and at about ten o'clock, Mrs Craufurd persuaded Juana to go to bed. She was so tired that although she had been sure she would not be able to sleep, she dropped off within ten minutes of her head's being laid on the pillow.

7

While the family was seated at breakfast next morning, Mr Peters called to inform Juana that quantities of baggage were arriving in Antwerp, and that he would be very happy to look for hers if she would give him a description of it. An hour later, he came back, bringing West, and Matty, the spare horses, and all the baggage except Juana's mattress, and the precious new dressing-case, which, in the sudden uproar, had been left behind at the village where the Brass Mare had bolted.

As the morning wore on, without any certain news being received from the front, Juana's anxiety increased so much that she was unable to sit still, but walked about the room looking so distraught that Mrs Craufurd was half-inclined to persuade her to drink a few drops of laudanum to calm her nerves.

But in the afternoon, Colonel Craufurd came in with tidings that a great battle had been fought and won before the village of Waterloo. The French army was said to be utterly put to rout, and Napoleon himself flying towards Paris. There was no news of Harry, and after waiting all day for a message, Juana, to the dismay of her hostess, ordered West to have the Brass Mare brought round to the house at daybreak next morning.

'But, my dear, you cannot venture alone!' protested Mrs Craufurd. 'At such an hour, too!'

'I must rejoin my husband,' Juana said resolutely. 'I am accustomed to marching at dawn. Please do not try to dissuade me!'

'I fear it would be impossible. Dearest child, how shall I say it? I don't wish to frighten you, but have you considered – they say our casualties have been the heaviest ever known!'

'Yes, I have considered,' Juana replied, quite calmly, but with a constricted throat. 'If my husband has been killed, I must find his body.'

There was no moving her; she seemed all at once to be older than Mrs Craufurd had thought her; and nothing could have been more assured than the orders she gave for her servant's following her with the baggage. She was plainly an experienced campaigner, and after trying for a little while to persuade her to await news of her husband in Antwerp, Mrs Craufurd gave it up, and busied herself instead with superintending the drying and cleaning of her soiled habit.

Taking an affectionate and grateful leave of her kind hosts, Juana rode out of Antwerp at three o'clock next morning, accompanied only by West. They reached the village by the Canal in time for breakfast, and were fortunate enough to discover the lost dressing-case hidden away in the hayloft. By seven o'clock, they had reached Brussels, and almost the first sight encountered was that of a party of Riflemen, all of them wounded, and making their way through the streets to one of the tent-hospitals which had been hurriedly set up in the town. Juana spurred up to them, and was instantly recognized. They saluted her, but when she asked eagerly if they could tell her what had become of her husband, their replies were rather evasive, and they exchanged glances which at once aroused her suspicion. Finally, one of them said with a roughness which concealed his pity: 'Missus, it ain't no manner of use riding to the battlefield! There's sights there not fit for a female. You go and bide quietly within doors!'

'*Loco!* I was at Tarbes!' she cried, striking her fist against the pummel of her saddle. 'Tell me, *instanteamente*, is my husband alive? Is he well?'

'You'd best know the truth, missus,' he said bluntly. 'Brigade-Major Smith of ours was killed yesterday, quite early on in the day.'

She reeled in the saddle, growing so deathly pale that West put out a hand to catch her arm, fearing that she would faint. She did not, however. She looked at him in a blind fashion that quite unmanned him, and said: 'We must hurry. We must make haste, for I must find his body.'

'Missus, missus, don't ask me to take you there!' he begged. 'Master wouldn't have it so.'

'Master is dead,' she said tonelessly. 'I shall be dead, too, very soon, but I must see him once again before I kill myself. You need not come with me. I want no one now.'

He saw that it would be useless to try to stop her; he could only hope that on the battlefield she would meet some friend who would have more power to persuade her than he possessed.

They rode in silence, mostly at a gallop. The sights encountered on the chaussée leading through the Forest of Soignies were so terrible that West was not surprised to see Juana's eyes dilated, with a look of horror bordering on madness in them. The endless procession of wounded soldiers, and horses, of carts with corpses in them, of dead men lying by the road, too shattered to have been able to crawl the weary miles to Brussels, was a nightmarish phantasmagoria comparable to nothing seen in all the years of the campaigning in the Peninsula. The village of Waterloo was full of wounded officers; farther on, at Mont St Jean, a horrible, creeping aroma of corruption set the horses jibbing, and squealing, and made West break the long silence to beg his mistress to go no farther.

'On!' was all she said, forcing the Brass Mare through the village-street.

He followed, now seriously alarmed for her sanity, but unable to think of any way of stopping her. In a few minutes, the battlefield was reached, a stretch of rolling country covered with fields of wheat and rye which had been trampled down by countless hooves. A cross-road, a deep, sunken lane, leading to Wavre, marked the line of the Allied front. Where it bisected the chaussée, in the angle between the two roads, Juana saw mound upon mound of dead men, with soldiers nearby, digging pits to throw the bodies into.

'Oh, my God, missus, don't look, don't look!' West begged. 'Poor devils, they must have been killed in square! Oh, come away!'

She paid no heed to him, but addressed one of the men who were digging. 'What regiment?'

'The 27th, mum.'

Her eyes started; she said hoarsely: 'Ours! one of ours! *This* was where he stood!'

The man stared at her. 'Lambert's brigade, mum. Was you looking for someone?'

'Major Smith!' she managed to utter.

He shook his head. 'I dunno, mum, I'm sure. The officers has mostly been buried.' She became aware of graves, many graves, some with rough boards set up, others no more than mounds of freshly-turned sods. Suddenly it became of immense importance to look upon Harry's face for the last time. She cried out in an anguished voice: 'No, no, not buried! not buried! I must see him once more! I must, I must!'

Distracted, she began to ride from one grave to another, wildly reading the names scratched upon the rough crosses at their heads. She saw the body of a man lying a little way off, and spurred up to it, convinced it was Harry's. The distorted face was strange to her; she passed on, searching frantically amongst the dead. Some Flemish peasants were dragging the stripped corpses to the pits, with hooks stuck callously through their heels; in the sunken road, and beyond it, French cuirassiers lay in tangled heaps of men, and breastplates; a little farther, a sand-pit yawned beside the chaussée, opposite a white farmstead whose walls were blackened and riddled by shot. Some green-jackets lay there, stiff and still under the hot sun. Juana began to moan, but softly, repeating over and over again: 'Dear God, let me find him! Dear God, let me not be mad!'

She was unaware of West, dumbly following her; a wounded Frenchman groaned to her from the ground at her feet. He wanted water; she had none, and shook her head.

Suddenly a voice penetrated to her brain. She heard her name called, and looked round in a blank way.

'Juana, Juana, what are you doing here? My dear, it is not fit for you!'

A man on horseback rode up to her; she saw that it was Charlie Gore, and cried out: 'Oh, where is he? Where is my Enrique?'

His voice, the one sane thing in a mad world, sounded reassuringly in her ears. 'Why, near Bavay by this time, as well as ever he was in his life! Not wounded even, nor either of his brothers!'

'Oh, dear Charlie Gore, why do you deceive me?' she said in bitter reproach. 'The soldiers told me Brigade-Major Smith was killed!'

'Dearest Juana, believe me!' Gore said, trying to take her hand. 'It was poor Charles Smyth who was killed – Pack's Brigade-Major. I swear to you on my honour I left Harry riding Lochinvar, in perfect health, but very anxious about you!'

Her strained eyes searched his face. She said: 'Oh, if I could believe you, Charlie, my heart must burst!'

'Why should you doubt me?' he said quietly. 'You know I would not lie to you, and upon *such* a subject!'

She broke into a storm of weeping, bowed over the Brass Mare's withers, and so shaken by sobs of sheer relief that West was afraid that the shock of hearing that Harry was safe had really turned her brain. But presently she managed to stop crying, and to straighten herself. Charlie Gore wiped her tears away with his handkerchief, murmuring a few soothing phrases.

'I prayed to God for help, and He sent you, like a guardian angel!' she said huskily. 'How foolish you must think me, to cry so! Indeed, I am sorry, for crying women are *the devil*!'

He laughed to hear such an expression on her lips. 'Ah, you had that from Harry, I know! But listen, *amiga*, I am on my way to Mons: can you muster strength to ride with me there?'

'Strength!' she exclaimed. 'Yes, for anything *now*!'

He was anxious to get her away from the battlefield, and urged her to push on at once. She was very willing, and they rode together down the chaussée, past the sand-pit, and the riddled farmhouse. He told her, when she asked, that it was called La Haye Sainte, and had been held by four hundred soldiers of the King's German Legion. 'They cut their way out at the end, forty left out of all their number! They had no ammunition. The French took the place towards the end of the day.'

'And that other place? An officer of Hussars told me of a château that was burning, and could not be held.'

'He was wrong,' replied Gore. 'You mean Hougoumont. Can you see that blackened ruin over to your right? That is it. The Guards held it to the very end.'

She looked timidly up into his face. 'Was it as bad as Badajos, Charlie, this battle?'

He shuddered. 'Juana, none of us have ever known a worse, not even those who were at Albuera! It was a horrible business! a *slogging* match! There was no manoeuvring, scarcely any Light troop work. We stood there to be pounded for eight solid hours, till those damned Prussians came up! At the end, the smoke was so dense where my brigade was placed that we could only see where the French were by the flashes of their pieces. Man after man went down; we were shot to pieces at Quatre-Bras: we could do nothing here but hold the line. But we did hold it! by God, how we held it, even though the Belgians in our front broke through, and ran for their lives! Picton extended my brigade and Pack's in line two deep to fill the gap: a mass of infantry was advancing upon us. Picton fell, but we stood fast, till the cavalry came up from our rear, and smashed the French columns. Oh, I never saw anything to equal that charge!'

'Is Picton dead?' Juana demanded.

'Oh, yes! He was killed as he gave the word to charge. At the last, there was hardly a senior officer left standing on the field.'

'Not the Duke!'

'No, he came through untouched. By Jove, it was as well he did so! We could not have done the thing without him. You know his way! Wherever the line was weakest, there he was, cool as if upon a field-day. While we could see his hook-nose amongst us, there could be no thought of retreating! Ney tried everything: artillery, infantry, cavalry! I was talking to a fellow in Halkett's brigade: he told me that on the other side of the chaussée they were formed in squares for over an hour, while the French cavalry rode round and round, trying to break through! Then, just before eight o'clock, they attacked all along our front. The Middle Guard was sent against our right, in five huge columns. We could see nothing from where we stood, but they say Maitland's Guards threw the leading column back first. And then Colborne right-shouldered the 52nd forward, and swept clean across the plain, driving the French before him like so many sheep! It was after that that we heard the cheering swelling along the front from our right, and knew that old Douro had given the signal for a general advance at last.'

'And Napoleon is rompéd, really rompéd?' she cried.

'Oh, there were only three French squares still standing when Blücher took up the pursuit! There never was such a rout: Salamanca was nothing to it! But oh, Juanita, the losses we have suffered! our dearest friends! It doesn't bear thinking of!'

'Tell me!' she said, in a low voice. 'I must know. You said that Tom and Charles were safe?'

'Oh yes! And Kincaid hasn't a scratch on him either. But poor Charlie Eeles, and Smyth, young Lister, Elliot Johnston – do you remember Johnston, who shared that château at Toulouse with you, and Harry, and Jack Molloy.'

'Yes, yes, indeed! Not *dead*?' she cried.

'Killed instantly. Eeles too. I had been searching for his grave when I came upon you just now.'

Her tears fell fast. 'He came to see us in Ghent, with Johnny! Johnny was teasing him, and he laughed, and was so gay! Oh, Charlie, who else? Let me know quickly!'

'I can't tell for certain yet. I've just seen Beckwith, and poor George. Beckwith has had his leg off, and George is so bad I don't know whether he will live. He has been shot through the liver, and is in the greatest agony. Barnard was wounded, and carried off; then Cameron. The command of the battalion fell upon Jonathan Leach, but I know he was carried off, for I saw him. Jack Molloy was hit, but not badly, I think. I don't know what their losses were in the 2nd and 3rd battalions, though I heard someone say John Ross had had to leave the field. Juana, do you recall how we used to say after our Peninsular battles: "Well, who's been killed?" This time, we said: "Who's alive?" It – do you know, after the hell we had gone through, it did not seem possible that anyone could still be alive, and unhurt?'

She could not speak. They rode on in silence for some time, and when next Gore opened his lips, it was to ask her, in a more cheerful tone, what had become of her during the battle.

They did not reach Mons until midnight. Juana had been in the saddle ever since three o'clock, and had ridden a distance from point to point of sixty miles. She was so exhausted that she fell asleep over the supper she ate in the bivouac. She did not so much as stir when Gore wrapped a blanket round her, but lay as though dead, until the daylight woke her.

As soon as she had eaten a hurried breakfast, she was in the saddle again. It was not far to Bavay from Mons; she and West reached it a few hours later. She saw Sir John Lambert almost at once. He exclaimed at her, horrified to think of her having come all the way from Ghent, attended only by her groom. She said only one word: 'Enrique?'

'Yes, yes, my dear, he's here, safe enough!' Lambert said. 'I'll take you to him at once.'

She tried to smile. 'I know he is well. I *know* he is, for Charlie Gore told me so, upon his honour, but still I cannot believe in my heart that I shall find him. Isn't – isn't it silly?'

He patted her hand. 'Poor little soul! There, never fear! Whom do you suppose that is, standing over there with his back to us?'

She looked eagerly to where he pointed. He called out: 'Hi, Smith! See what I have here for you!'

Harry turned, as Juana slid down from the Brass Mare's back. 'Juana!' he exclaimed, and hurried to meet her.

She fell into his outstretched arms, the wild flurry of her heart almost suffocating her. She could not speak; she could only cling to him as though she would never let him go again. He held her tightly in his arms, his cheek against her hair. 'Oh, my soul! my treasure!'

She found enough voice to say: 'You are safe! Never part from me again! Never, mi Enrique, never! Oh, promise me!'

'Never again!' he said. 'No matter what comes to us! How could I bear to send you from me again? We'll stay together from now till we die of ripe old age, my little varmint, my little love!'

'It is a promise?' she said urgently.

'It is a promise,' he answered. He took her face between his hands. They were shaking a little, as once before, in his tent outside the walls of Badajos. 'When I was first troubled with you,' he said, with a twisted smile, 'we had so many actions to live through! My poor darling, you suffered so much anxiety, and you have been so good all through! Well, it's over now: do you understand? We've rompéd Boney at last, and there's nothing for you to be afraid of any more. Now smile at me, faithful, loving, bad-tempered little devil that you are! Or box my ears, if you will! Only don't look at me with those scared eyes!'

'Kiss me!' Juana commanded. '*Espadachín! Mi tirano odioso!*'

Also Available

Georgette Heyer trade paperbacks available from Sourcebooks

An Infamous Army

Cotillion

Royal Escape

Friday's Child

False Colours

Lady of Quality

Black Sheep

About the Author

AUTHOR OF OVER FIFTY BOOKS, GEORGETTE HEYER IS ONE OF the best-known and best-loved of all historical novelists, making the Regency period her own. Her first novel, *The Black Moth*, published in 1921, was written at the age of fifteen to amuse her convalescent brother; her last was *My Lord John*. Although most famous for her historical novels, she also wrote twelve detective stories. Georgette Heyer died in 1974 at the age of seventy-one.